LIES AND WEDDINGS

LIES AND WEDDINGS

A NOVEL

KEVIN KWAN

DOUBLEDAY   NEW YORK

Book design by Anna B. Knighton
Jacket illustrations: couple © Malte Mueller/Getty Images;
volcano © MuchMania/Getty Images; dress © Nataliia Reshetova/Getty Images;
palm trees © arvitalya/Getty Images; frame © amtitus/Getty Images
Jacket design by Grace Han
Interior illustrations © Adobe Stock

Library of Congress Cataloging-in-Publication Data
Names: Kwan, Kevin, author.
Title: Lies and weddings : a novel / Kevin Kwan.
Description: First edition. | New York : Doubleday, 2024.
Identifiers: LCCN 2023051698 | ISBN 9780385546294 (hardcover) |
ISBN 9780385546300 (ebook) | ISBN 9780385546379 (open market)
Subjects: LCGFT: Novels.
Classification: LCC PS3611.W36 L54 2024 | DDC 813/.6—dc23/eng/20231103
LC record available at https://lccn.loc.gov/2023051698

MANUFACTURED IN THE UNITED STATES OF AMERICA
1 3 5 7 9 10 8 6 4 2
First Edition

For

Tūtū Pele,

*who told me to have
trust and patience*

LIES AND WEDDINGS

Hong Kong, 1995

SOUTH CHINA SEA

"If I had a flower for every time I thought of you, I could walk in my garden forever." Henry kept chanting the line out loud over the roar of the helicopter's engine. He had just seen it in an ad at the jewelry shop, and he did not want to forget it tonight. Against the ink blue of the evening sky, the jagged ridges of the mountain pass reminded him of a great slumbering beast. The Dragon's Back, as it was known to locals. Looking out over the twinkling lights that came into view as the chopper crested Shek O Peak, Henry remembered what his mother always said: The feng shui was especially good on Hong Kong Island because the city was situated with the mountain at its back and the ocean at its feet. This was why so many great fortunes were made here.

And no one felt more fortunate tonight than Henry Tong. He was flying home from a weekend on the nearby island of Macau, where, after winning $7.4 million at the high-stakes poker table of the Casino Lisboa, he had directed the pilot to take him straight to his favorite watering hole at the best hotel in Hong Kong, where his closest chums had been commanded to meet him. What none of his friends knew was that before jumping aboard the helicopter, Henry had made a pit stop at the jeweler on the mezzanine level of the casino and hastily snapped up a twelve-carat canary diamond ring.*

---

* *To be precise, an 11.68-carat fancy yellow VVS2 Asscher-cut diamond ring accented by two large kite-shaped diamond side stones.*

This night called for a grand celebration—he was going to make Gabriella Soong his fiancée.

The helicopter descended atop the Peninsula Hotel on Kowloon's waterfront, and Henry impatiently jumped out before the rotor blades came to a stop. Rakishly handsome with his hair slicked back and his Armani jacket flapping against the wind, the twenty-six-year-old strode across the landing pad feeling as if he owned the whole joint. A uniformed attendant in the hotel's signature Brewster Green livery bowed deferentially as he held open the door. One level down—on the twenty-eighth floor of the hotel—was the city's most exclusive nightspot: Felix.

At that moment in time, no place on the planet could compete with Felix in terms of sheer wow factor. As one entered the main dining room through a darkened hallway, the space suddenly opened up to soaring floor-to-ceiling windows that framed the stunning view of the Hong Kong skyline across Victoria Harbour. Only here, the view had to compete with the jaw-dropping design:* a massive shimmering steel focal wall etched with undulating waves and a glowing, long white alabaster communal table that appeared to float across the entire north end of the dining room. On the opposite side, a pair of conical towers with spiral stairways wound their way up to twin VIP champagne bars overlooking the bustling scene below.

The Aussie bouncer standing guard recognized Henry immediately and unclipped the purple velvet rope at the foot of the stairway. "Mr. Tong, your party's waiting," he said with an affable nod.

"But the party doesn't start till I get here!" Henry shot back as he fastened the top button of his blazer and bounded up the steps three at a time. Even in a VIP lounge packed with the city's bright young things, Henry's friends stood out as the brightest as they clustered along the pale pink leather banquette that wrapped around the low

---

* Designed by Philippe Starck, the original enfant terrible starchitect responsible for such stellar spaces as the original Royalton Hotel in New York, Kong in Paris, and the Delano in South Beach, where I highly recommend the delicious Sunday brunch buffet—especially if somebody else is paying.

balcony overlooking the cacophonous scene below. Everyone had been waiting impatiently for his arrival, and it was clear they had already enjoyed a few bottles too many.

"Henry! Over here!" Rosina Ko-Tung squealed as she waved her bare arms wildly.

"Finally! We've been waiting for hours," Brendan Lam slurred.

"*Yau mou gau cho, ah!* Can't believe you're still standing!" Edwin Chan clapped Henry on the back.

"Filthy crook! How many mainlanders did you fuck over this time?" Roger Gao chimed in, his face flushed bright red from doing vodka shots with the guys.

"They were *gweilos*. Mainlanders are getting way too good at poker," Henry said, grinning, as he slumped down beside Roger's sister, Mary, a former Miss Hong Kong. "I'm so knackered," Henry sighed. He was finally feeling the effects of his marathon gambling binge.

Mary gave him an assessing look and raised an eyebrow. "How long have you been drinking?"

"Only for the past thirty or forty hours."

"Rumor has it you almost bankrupted Stanley Ho this time."

"I wish! My winnings are a day's pocket money to him," Henry chuckled, looking around the lounge. "Where's Gabby?"

"Waiting to make her entrance, of course," Rosina quipped.

No sooner had she uttered the words than a ravishingly pretty girl in a metallic gray Barney Cheng minidress appeared at the top of the steps.

"Princess Gabriella has arrived!" Brendan cheered. "All hail the princess!"

Gabriella Soong rolled her eyes and gave Brendan a playful slap on his arm.

"Champagne for everyone!" Henry declared, making eye contact with the bartender he knew so well. "Hey, Jason! We need your best champagne tonight! What do you have?"

"How about some Louis Roederer Cristal 1988?" Jason replied merrily, mentally calculating his gratuity as he reached under the bar for the private reserve bottles. Maybe he'd even take a taxi home tonight.

"Wait, wait, before you pop the bottle open . . . ," Henry yelled at the bartender as he stood on the banquette. "My friends, I summoned all of you here today under false pretenses. You're not actually here to witness my historic win at the gaming tables of Macau. You're here to witness Henry Tong a changed man tonight."

"Have you finally accepted Jesus as your lord and savior?" Roger cackled.

"No, I've found the most precious flower in all the world." Henry suddenly leapt off the banquette and landed on his knees right before Gabriella. The room went silent as everyone stared at him.

"Gabby, if I . . . if I had a flower for every time I think of you, I could walk in my garden forever . . ."

"Stop it, Henry, you're drunk," Gabriella said, shaking her head.

"I'm drunk on love. I'm intoxicated by you." Fumbling into his jacket pocket, he took out a midnight-blue velvet box and presented it to the stunned girl. "Gabriella Soong, I realized tonight that all the money in the world would never make me a happy man unless I can enjoy it with you. I will present your father with every last cent of my winnings tomorrow to show him how serious I am. Will you please make me the happiest man on earth by saying yes?"

Edwin, Brendan, and Roger froze in disbelief at the whole scene. Rosina, her mouth wide open in shock, looked across the room at Mary.

Henry opened the box and Gabriella stared down at the sparkling rock. She held her hands up to her face and her body started to tremble. "Oh, Henry . . . ," she sighed as her eyes brimmed with tears.

"Is that a yes?" Henry looked up at her pleadingly.

"Yes! Yes!" Gabriella cried as Henry stood up and embraced her tightly.

Jason popped the champagne cork, and everyone in the lounge began clapping and cheering. Standing behind the bar, Jason had the perfect vantage point to witness everything unfolding, and for the rest of his life he would remember it like it happened in slow motion:

George Michael's "Fastlove" blasting on the sound system.

Henry whirling Gabby around the tight space.

Rosina and Roger whispering tensely over the music.

Mary sitting alone gazing at the tiny bubbles in her champagne glass.

Edwin and Brendan doing sloppy tequila shots with a famous Muay Thai star.

Roger walking over to his sister, Mary, and grabbing her by the shoulders.

Mary shaking her head, sobbing.

Henry and Gabby dancing as Roger rushed over yelling, "Fucking pig!"

Henry jumping onto the banquette as Roger lunged at him in a blind rage.

Henry scrambling backward and toppling over the low glass railing.

Rosina not believing her own eyes as Henry tumbled through space like an Olympic diver in slow motion and landed on a dinner table twenty feet below.

Edwin grabbing Roger as he shouted, "What the hell? What the hell?"

Brendan staring in horror at Henry impaled onto a crystal candelabra.

Gabby screaming as blood pooled around Henry's body on the immaculate white tablecloth.

THE MAIN PLAYERS

THE EARL
Francis Gresham

FORMAL TITLE: The Right Honorable the Earl of Greshamsbury
VERBAL ADDRESS: my lord (formal), Lord Greshamsbury (social)
ASTROLOGICAL SIGN: Cancer

HIS WIFE
Arabella Leung Gresham

FORMAL TITLE: The Right Honorable the Countess of Greshamsbury
VERBAL ADDRESS: madam (formal), Lady Greshamsbury (social)
ASTROLOGICAL SIGN: Scorpio

THEIR SON
Rufus Leung Gresham

FORMAL TITLE: The Right Honorable the Viscount St. Ives
VERBAL ADDRESS: my lord (formal), Lord St. Ives (social)
KNOWN WITHIN THE FAMILY AS "Rufus"
ASTROLOGICAL SIGN: Sagittarius

THEIR ELDER DAUGHTER
Augusta Leung Gresham

FORMAL TITLE: Lady Augusta Gresham
VERBAL ADDRESS: Lady Augusta (formal), Lady Augusta (social)
KNOWN WITHIN THE FAMILY AS "Augie"
ASTROLOGICAL SIGN: Aries

Beatrice Leung Gresham

FORMAL TITLE: Lady Beatrice Gresham
VERBAL ADDRESS: Lady Beatrice (formal), Lady Beatrice (social)
KNOWN WITHIN THE FAMILY AS "Bea"
ASTROLOGICAL SIGN: Pisces

THE NEIGHBOR

Thomas Tong

FORMAL TITLE: Dr. Thomas Tong
VERBAL ADDRESS: Dr. Tong (formal), Thomas (social)
ASTROLOGICAL SIGN: Gemini

HIS DAUGHTER

Eden Tong

FORMAL TITLE: Dr. Eden Tong
VERBAL ADDRESS: Dr. Tong (formal), Eden (social)
ASTROLOGICAL SIGN: Capricorn

Greshamsbury

*Anyone who lives within their means
suffers from a lack of imagination.*

—LIONEL STANDER

ANNOUNCEMENT IN THE
"FORTHCOMING MARRIAGES"
SECTION OF *THE TIMES:*

HSH PRINCE M. ZU LIECHTENBURG
AND LADY A. GRESHAM

The engagement is announced between Maximillian, first son of Their Serene Highnesses Prince and Princess Julius zu Liechtenburg, and Augusta, elder daughter of the Earl and Countess of Greshamsbury. A spring wedding is planned.

Dr. Eden Tong and Rufus, Viscount St. Ives

GRESHAMSBURY, ENGLAND • *PRESENT DAY*

Eden Tong and Rufus Gresham, who grew up as neighbors and had been the closest of friends since they were very young, used to leave each other secret notes in the hollow of a majestic holm oak that grew on the pathway between their houses. Nowadays, since they were quite often on opposite ends of the world—with Eden in England and Rufus constantly on the go—they would text every morning without fail. Eden (Greshamsbury Nursery School/Mount House/ Downe House/Cambridge) would be awakened by her phone alarm playing the first few notes of Radiohead's "High and Dry," and after swiping snooze a couple of times, she'd eventually grab her phone and peer at the text message on Signal that was invariably waiting from Rufus (Mount House/Radley/Exeter/Central Saint Martins). Today's text:

> **RUFUS GRESHAM:** What do you think of my nails?

Eden lazily texted back:

> **EDEN TONG:** I don't.
> **RG:** Do I need a manicure?
> **ET:** Because you chew them to the quick?
> **RG:** That noticeable huh?
> **ET:** Not really. Doubt anyone but your mum would care.
> **RG:** Haha, she's insisting I get a manicure before the wedding.

ET: Up to you. You might find it addictive.

RG: Hmmm. Seems decadent. Speaking of which, I had Shanghai Fried Buns last night. Like soup dumplings except bigger and pan fried so the bottom's all toasty.

ET: Yummmmm. Same place as the hand-pulled noodles?

RG: No, new place in Chinatown. Can't wait to take you there.

ET: Our list keeps growing.

RG: When do you arrive in Hawaii?

ET: Not going to Hawaii.

RG: You wish.

ET: I'm serious. Won't be there.

RG: What?!?! Those NHS tyrants won't give you time off?

ET: Um . . . not exactly.

RG: No excuses then.

ET: I didn't make the cut. I'm not a royal or a trillionaire.

RG: Wait. SERIOUSLY? Why am I only finding out now?

ET: Thought you knew.

RG: This is bollocks. I'm calling Mum now.

ET: Please don't. It's fine.

RG: No it's not!!! How can YOU of all people not be at my sister's wedding?!?

ET: I was at the blessing at Greshamsbury Rectory.

RG: Not the same and you know it. I'll call Augie.

ET: Please don't. The last thing she needs now is more drama with your mum.

RG: She's used to it. With Mum there's drama 24/7. How often did you speak to your dad when you were away at uni?

ET: Maybe every couple of weeks.

RG: Mum calls me 5 times a day. If I miss 2 calls in a row she freaks out and thinks I'm dead.

ET: All mothers worry.

RG: 5 times a day is not normal when your son is 28.

ET: You know you don't have to pick up every time she calls.

RG: I know. But I have Asian son guilt.

ET: You're half Asian, so you should only have half the guilt.

RG: ;-) If only. I CAN'T BELIEVE YOU WON'T BE HERE! I was planning our itinerary. Swimming with dolphins. Flat whites at Arvo. Roadside rotisserie chicken in Waimea. Gill's Lanai for the BEST fish tacos. Hiking to the waterfalls in Waipi'o Valley.

ET: I'll come this summer.

RG: You say that, but you never have time. Who am I going to talk to at the wedding now? :-(

ET: All the pretty posh girls strategically positioned by your mum.

RG: She's up to something . . . she's fussing over me as if it were my own wedding.

ET: Maybe it is. You'll get there and it'll be: "Surprise! Here's your bride, just stand on this mark and shove this ring onto her finger."

RG: Wouldn't put it past Mum. You know she's been obsessing over who I should marry since the day I was born. She drives me CRAZY with it. You're so lucky.

ET: Because my mum's dead?

RG: Oof. Sorry! Didn't mean it that way.

ET: It's fine. I had the dream again.

RG: The one where your mother appears in random places?

ET: This time it was in the ice cream section at Waitrose.

RG: That's not too weird.

ET: She was INSIDE one of those refrigerators dressed like Glinda the Good Witch.

RG: Isn't she always in something sparkly when you see her?

ET: Yup. She was trying to tell me something, but when she spoke, there was no sound, just vapors coming out of her mouth.

RG: What do you think she was trying to say?

ET: Wish I knew . . .

RG: I know this amazing tarot card reader, Viv, who can help decipher your dreams. She's up in Hawi. Dammit, you NEED to be here.

ET: I'll come this summer, I promise.

RG: I'll hold you to it.

ET: Gotta run.

RG: Bye.

Moments after their text conversation had ended, Rufus sent off another text to his sister Augusta.

RG: Why am I the last one to find out that Eden isn't coming to Hawaii? I find it hard to believe that you wouldn't want her beside you on your special day. Shall I talk to Mum? Happy to take the heat on this.

II

Lady Augusta Gresham

SOUTH KONA, THE ISLAND OF HAWAII · *MOMENTS LATER*

Augusta saw the text come in from her brother, but she chose to ignore it. She had other problems to deal with that were of far more importance to her, and at present she and Gopal Das were strolling through the exquisite grounds of the Bellaloha Resort, where every blade of grass had been perfectly positioned as if god had intended it, although it was really the work of Augusta's mother, Lady Arabella, and her very expensive team of Belgian landscape designers. Augusta (Willcocks/Cheltenham/UWC Atlantic/Bard) headed toward the cliffside promontory where an elaborate Balinese pavilion had been erected and gestured halfheartedly to her spiritual advisor. "This is where we're supposed to do the vows."

"It's beautiful," Gopal Das said, smiling serenely at his beautiful British-Chinese acolyte.

"You think so?"

"Absolutely. Just look at these beams, and the love that was put into carving them."

They approached the altar positioned at the edge of the cliff and gazed out at the dramatic view of the Kona coastline just as the sun was dipping into the ocean. Gopal Das (Brimmer and May/Groton/Williams/UC Berkeley/Four Winds Shaman School), a tall, lanky Caucasian man in his midforties with shoulder-length strawberry-blond hair and a matching beard stretched out his densely freckled arms in a godlike manner. "Let us welcome this blessed sunset.

I've never seen a painting that captures the beauty of the ocean at a moment like this."

Augusta cocked her head. "That sounds so familiar. Is that Pema Chödrön?"

"Er . . . no."

"Oh, I know, it's a quote from Ram Dass."

"Could've been him," Gopal Das said vaguely.* "Tell me, Augie, how do you feel, standing here in this sacred space, where in just four days you and Maxxie will be exchanging your vows?"

A cloud came over Augie's face. "It doesn't feel sacred to me at all."

"It doesn't?"

"Mummy designed every square meter of this resort. It's the new jewel in her hotel empire that she's waiting to show off to the world, and she's turning my soul union with Maxxie into a coronation for herself. This entire resort makes me feel very . . . ungrounded."

"Well then, let's ground you." The guru led his acolyte down the steps of the pavilion onto the dewy grass, and they sat facing each other in lotus position.

Gopal Das tucked the tight white tee that showed off his sinewy pecs into his camo-green cargo shorts and said, "Close your eyes. Now breathe in deeply. . . . Let your first chakra connect with the ground, rooting in the earth, connecting with Gaia, connecting with spirit. Now, what do you feel?"

"Sadness," Augie admitted.

"Good. Sadness cannot hurt you. Let us not judge this sadness, but rather, think of it as a ball, a white ball floating just in front of you. Tell me what you see in the ball."

"I see my mother. She's such a controlling bitch. She's forcing me to get married here in this fake Balinese temple and not actually in Bali where I've dreamed of having my wedding ever since I saw *Eat Pray Love*. I can't believe she's forcing me to wear Valentino."

---

* *It was actually Gordon Gekko in* Wall Street.

"Valentino cannot hurt you. You are a grown woman and your mother cannot force you to do anything. She has no control over your body."

Augie let out a sharp sob.

"Shall we go deeper into that? What is hiding behind that sob?"

"Avocados," Augie muttered as she began to cry softly.

"Good. Avocados cannot hurt you. Why do avocados make you feel this way?"

"Mummy forced me to eat half an avocado every morning as a child. That's all I was ever allowed for breakfast, while Rufus and Bea got to have all the scrambled eggs and Cumberland sausages and Nutella crepes they wanted. Rufus was 'a growing boy,' my little sister Bea was always 'the perfect angel,' but I was the *jyu pa.*' That's 'pork chop' in Cantonese. Mummy would make me strip naked, pinch my tummy hard, and measure my body fat with these freezing-cold calipers. She said no handsome prince would ever want to marry a pork chop."

"But look at you today. You are not a pork chop and you have found your handsome prince."

Augie cracked a smile for the first time that evening. "I have, haven't I?"

"A prince who treasures you for your beautiful heart and your beautiful soul, not your body, which, I might add, is beautiful too."

"He does, doesn't he?"

"Yes, and *you* manifested him into your life."

"Actually, my mother manifested him, with the help of Nicolai Chalamet-Chaude, that fucking social clim—"

"Augie, every word you say carries its own energy. There is no need to drop the F-bomb at this moment."

"Sorry. I am just so angry, Gopal Das."

"Your anger cannot hurt you."

"I can feel myself burning up. I feel so much rage."

"Your rage cannot hurt you. Just visualize that rage as a little red ball, a red ball that is spinning from your crown chakra, through your heart chakra, through your solar plexus, and out your base chakra. Exhale fully and just let the ball flow through you from top to bottom, top to bottom . . ."

Augie exhaled forcefully, deflating like a balloon.

"Is it flowing?"

"Ye-ess," Augie exhaled, her body trembling.

"Now, take a deep breath, and using all the goddess energy you possess within you, just expel the ball to the center of the earth, where it can no longer hurt you."

Augie breathed in, and she breathed out. She clenched her eyes tight and imagined a hot ball of rage tunneling through all the layers of the earth till it reached the inner core.

"Can you feel it leaving your body?"

"Yes! Yes! I can feel it moving through my body. I can feel the heat."

"Good. I can feel it too." Gopal Das took a deep breath and felt a sulfuric burning in his nostrils. He opened his eyes and saw that the ground behind Augie was literally cracking open with smoke.

"Motherfucker! Augie, run! FUCKING RUN!" Gopal Das screamed.

III

Dr. Thomas Tong

The route of Eden's morning run never wavered. She would jog up the field behind the cottage where she lived with her father, skirting the grounds of Greshamsbury Hall for 1.5 miles before she made a quick descent down the hilly path leading to the village. After popping into Nero's to grab her usual latte, she would take the long way around the village square before ending up back at the cottage.

It was early enough when Eden returned from her run that mist still shrouded the lilac hedges in the garden. Entering through the kitchen door, she was surprised to find her father seated at the table, spooning marmalade onto his toast. Dr. Thomas Tong (Diocesan Boys'/Radley/Cambridge/MD Anderson UT Health) usually slept in on Saturdays, as he spent all of Friday up in London doing surgeries and would return quite late in the evening.

"Everything okay?" Eden kissed the back of her father's head as she passed behind him.

"Hemsworth woke me. Needs me to make a house call."

"Oh, I was going to pop over too. Got an urgent text from Bea."

"She sick as well?"

"Fashion emergency."

"Toast?" Thomas handed Eden the slice he had just prepared and they sat in their usual cozy silence, Thomas taking slow sips of malty Lapsang from his favorite blue enamel mug as he flipped through the

morning paper* and Eden dipping her marmalade toast in her latte
while scanning the news† on her phone. After both of them felt suf-
ficiently caffeinated, Thomas grabbed his black leather medical bag
and they left through the kitchen door and took the shortcut through
the boxwood maze onto the grounds of "the Big House," as both of
them referred to it.

It was a short stroll up to Greshamsbury Hall—five minutes if you
walked quickly—and the route was so well traveled by Thomas and
Eden that they could have done it blindfolded. The Big House was
originally built as the hunting lodge of a much grander estate, Boxall
Park, as it was situated on the very edge of the estate's vast lands by
the ancient Dartmoor Forest. The sixteenth earl had been forced to
implement austerity measures after a particularly disastrous series
of margin calls during the crash of 1929 and was obliged to lease out
Boxall Park and move his family seat to Greshamsbury Hall. These
reduced circumstances proved to be a rather fortuitous change for
his wife, the countess, who sighed in relief at no longer having to run
a two-hundred-room stately. Instead, she reveled in making do with
a mere forty-three rooms set on a hundred and eight acres.

The other advantage of Greshamsbury Hall was its splendid situation. Majestically set on a hilltop along the upper reaches of the
river Feign, it afforded every room with sweeping views of the glorious Devonshire countryside. To arrive at the house, visitors were
given a unique set of directions: "When you arrive at the village
of Greshamsbury, turn down the narrow country lane between the
wooden fenceposts directly facing the HSBC bank and follow it for
1.5 miles." That particular country lane gently rambled past a field of
lavender and a postcard-perfect paddock where a pair of long-haired
white horses grazed, and curved up a sloping allée of towering
oaks, where beyond an old wooden bridge over the bubbling river
the gracious mock-Tudor house dramatically came into view. With
the sunlight against the elegant black and white timbered façade and

* The Guardian.

† *Dailymail.co.uk.*

the sparkling river cascading down the hill, the effect was mesmerizing. Elsie de Wolfe, who paid a visit in 1938, purportedly proclaimed it "the most romantic house in all of England."

This idyllic setting had been the Tongs' refuge ever since Eden's mother passed away when she was only five. Thomas had been granted a grace-and-favor lease to the handsome Grade II–listed Jacobean cottage* neighboring Greshamsbury Hall by Francis Gresham—the current earl and his best friend since their Radley days. After Thomas completed his fellowship training in Houston, Francis had lured him into opening his clinic in the little town instead of returning to Hong Kong, where he had been offered a partnership at a prestigious private clinic. "It will give our corner of the world more cachet to have an oncologist of your standing here, and besides, who else would I watch Pink Floyd's *The Wall* with twice a year?" Francis reasoned.

Thomas was actually glad to be making a fresh start away from Hong Kong and Houston, and truth be told he felt more comfortable in England, having more or less spent the majority of his formative years there since being sent away to boarding school at the age of thirteen. But what compelled him most to set up home in Greshamsbury were the three ready-made playmates for Eden. She and Rufus were the same age, while Augie was two years older and Bea had just been born.

"She'll grow up with my kids, and our nannies will take care of her while you're at the clinic. Rufus will be like a brother to her, and Augusta and Bea will be like sisters," Francis declared. The earl's prediction had exceeded his own expectations, and in the ensuing years Eden and the Gresham children became so inseparable that after finishing her medical foundation-year program in London, Eden decided to return home to Greshamsbury. Though she was doing her core medical training at a hospital in Plymouth, she was

---

* *Although "cottage" could be rather misleading for the spacious four-bedroom house with a thatched roof that was decomposing so perfectly, Thomas was constantly finding DIY influencers taking selfies by the garden gate.*

happy to commute every day and live at the cottage so that she could be with her adored father and next door to her dear friends.

As Thomas and Eden walked past the impeccably pruned lime trees that lined the gravel driveway to Greshamsbury Hall, the side door was quietly opened by a strapping sandy-haired butler dressed in the bespoke uniform of squid-ink-dyed Japanese denim shirt and jeans that Lady Arabella had designed for her staff.

"Morning, Hemsworth," Thomas and Eden greeted him in unison.

"Good morning, Doctors," the butler said warmly. Hemsworth (Ringwood/Heathmont/Screenwise/International Butler Academy) gestured to the back stairs but did not bother to escort Thomas and Eden up, being accustomed to the doctor's frequent morning visits. The two of them bounded up the stairs quickly, and at the second-floor landing where three delicate Ruth Asawa woven mesh sculptures hung, Eden split off and wandered down the Long Gallery toward Bea's rooms while Thomas approached the hallway leading to Arabella's suite. Gracie, the countess's lady's maid, who was hovering outside the suite, greeted Thomas with a look of relief and immediately turned to knock on the door.

"Dr. Tong, ma'am," Gracie announced as she pushed the door open without waiting for acknowledgment. Thomas entered the countess's morning room, where he found her arranged dramatically on her Carlo Bugatti chaise longue, swathed in an apricot silk robe, propped up by a dozen velvet pillows in assorted crimson hues with a cashmere eye pillow over her face and the blood pressure monitor conveniently tied around her left arm. Even in her discomfort, not a single strand of her signature chin-length bob appeared out of place, and the countess in her sixth decade retained the strikingly photogenic features that had once upon a time made her a sought-after fashion model.

"Lady Greshamsbury," Thomas greeted her formally, observing the protocol he knew she expected even though he was her husband's closest friend and had been her neighbor and family doctor for decades.

The countess removed her eye pillow almost in slow motion but kept her eyes closed. "*Hiyah,* what took you so long?" Arabella (Maryknoll Convent School/City University of Hong Kong/King's College) said in the tone she reserved for Thomas Tong and other Asians she deemed inferior to her.* "I can't open my eyes. The room keeps spinning. Gracie just checked my blood pressure two minutes ago. One ninety over one forty."

"Not likely. You'd be quite dead if that were the case," Thomas said,† looking down at the machine. "You know your arm needs to be level with your heart when you take a reading."

"Did I have a transient ischemic stroke? I'm absolutely convinced I did. You have no idea what happened in the middle of the night!"

"Tell me," Thomas said calmly, taking out his own blood pressure monitor and strapping it on her upper arm.

"Where's my phone?" Arabella felt around the cushions weakly with her right hand.

"Your diction is impeccable as ever; you're certainly not slurring. Any numbness or loss of vision?"

"I'm numb everywhere. My fingers and toes feel like they are on fire."

"That's not numbness," Thomas said patiently.

Arabella waved a hand in the air helplessly. "Gracie, where the hell is my phone?"

"It's in your other hand, ma'am."

Arabella held it up to Thomas. "Look! Look!"

"Now, you need to be completely still while I take the reading. No talking. That's a very nice picture of you on the cover of *¡Hola!*"

"*Hiyah,* not that one. Gracie, show him the video!"

---

* *Though Arabella was raised speaking the Queen's English in what was then the British Crown Colony of Hong Kong and spoke with the poshest of accents, whenever she came into contact with other Asians—particularly family members and service people—her accent would take on the inflections and sentence structuring that were peculiar to upper-crust Hong Kongers. Linguistic experts call this phenomenon code-switching, while others might call it snobby* tai tai *syndrome.*

† *Dr. Tong's British accent did not code-switch and always remained the same. He always sounded a bit like Benedict Cumberbatch in* Sherlock.

Gracie swiped past the screensaver and held up the video that had been sent to Arabella in the middle of the night.

"Spectacular," Thomas said, marveling at the high-res video of lava shooting out of the cliffside like a geyser.

Arabella bolted up from the chaise, her cashmere eye pillow falling to the floor. "Spectacular? Seeing that almost killed me! That lava you see is a volcanic fissure that opened up earlier today—right in the middle of the garden where Augusta's wedding ceremony is supposed to be!"

"Looks like it will be a spectacular ceremony . . ."

"You don't get it. A volcano basically erupted at the wedding site! The Balinese pavilion, the replica of the bar at Loulou's, the ballroom mimicking the checkerboard floors at Château d'Anet, it's all ruined! *Everything* has been ruined!"

"I'm sorry to hear that. But the good news is, you'll be safe from the molten lava and your blood pressure is only slightly elevated, which is to be expected considering the circumstances."

"I think the circumstances are going to be the end of me. Ooi! Ooi! See? Still spinning. I can't even sit up," Arabella moaned, sinking against her pillows again.

"What medications did you take last night?"

"Only Ambien, melatonin, Cipralex, and Zoloft. And I added two baby aspirin when I was feeling symptoms of the stroke."*

* *Let's be clear, the signs of an actual stroke may include these sudden symptoms: facial drooping on one side of the face, arm weakness, and speech difficulty. Unless there is a kindly doctor next door whom your butler can quickly summon, please call your emergency medical service immediately if you experience these symptoms.*

IV

Lady Beatrice Gresham

GRESHAMSBURY HALL • *THE SAME MORNING*

Eden lounged on the Jorge Zalszupin daybed in Bea's suite, trying to find a comfortable position on the emaciated cushion. The problem with Brazilian modernist furniture, Eden felt, was that it looked great in photo shoots but really killed your back. Bea's bedroom used to be a cozy haven decorated with Oka hand-me-downs and mountains of throw pillows, but when *Elle Decor* came calling a year ago to do a feature, Bea and her mother had transformed her rooms into a painfully chic showcase of museum-quality torture devices all upholstered in the drabbest Belgian linen.

Bea (Greshamsbury Nursery School/Mount House/Cheltenham/Aiglon/Georgetown) emerged from her dressing room and twirled around in a ruffled confection by Giambattista Valli. With her five-foot-nine-inch frame and her startlingly auburn hair cascading down to her waist, she looked good in almost everything she put on.* "Be honest. It reads as white, doesn't it?"

"It does look rather white," Eden admitted.

"Giamba promised it'd be the most ravishing shade of celadon, so what the bloody hell is this? And it will look even whiter outdoors against the Pacific Ocean, won't it? What do I do now? I can't wear this, I can't wear the pink Valentino anymore, because—you are sworn to secrecy—that's who Augie's wearing, and I can't do

---

* *There was that pair of ruffled culottes that made her legs look like they were being attacked by vicious doilies.*

the black Gaultier or Mummy will have a fit. God, I wish I'd asked Viktor & Rolf to design me something. I had a feeling I would need more backups for the wedding-day look."

"Augie's wearing Valentino?" Eden remarked, thinking it was rather out of character for Bea's elder sister, who usually eschewed designer brands and had talked for years about getting married in a dress that was "a replica of Carolyn Bessette Kennedy's but made out of organic hemp."

"You don't know the half of it—Augie and Mummy have been at each other's throats for months now. First there was the row over the engagement ring that Mummy detested."

"What? I love Augie's moonstone ring! Didn't her friend Bliss Lau design it specially for her?" Eden asked.

"She did, but Mummy felt that Maxxie was being a cheapskate and Augie needed a proper diamond from Harry Collins.* Then Augie wanted to ask another friend from Hawaii to design a wedding dress in keeping with local traditions, but Mummy threatened to cut her off if she did that. She said, 'You are marrying into the noble house of Liechtenburg, so you will be compared to all royal brides. You can't wear some tropical muumuu! Whether you like it or not, you *must* wear Valentino like Rosario, Marie-Chantal, Máxima, Sibilla, and Madeleine† did or we will be absolutely disgraced.' "

Eden sighed sympathetically. "Poor Augie! Imagine not being allowed to wear what she wants to her own wedding. All she ever wanted was a dreamy beach wedding where she could be barefoot on the sand."

There was a brief knock on the door, and Hemsworth entered with a covered breakfast tray and placed it on the bed next to Eden.

---

* *Harry Collins MVO, with his family-run G. Collins & Sons in Royal Tunbridge Wells, was appointed the personal jeweler to Queen Elizabeth II in 2005.*

† *Princess Rosario of Bulgaria, Crown Princess Marie-Chantal of Greece, Queen Máxima of the Netherlands, Princess Sibilla of Luxembourg, and Princess Madeleine of Sweden, all Valentino brides.*

He removed the silver dome to reveal a plate piled high with chocolate croissants. "Margaret heard you were here, so she wanted to send this up."

Eden gasped in delight. "Oh, I've been craving Margaret's *pain au chocolat*. Please thank her for me."

"Margaret loves you more than me," Bea said as she eyed the pastries enviously.

"That's because I'm the only one around here who eats carbs," Eden said as she took a bite of her chocolate croissant, still warm from the oven. "You really ought to try one."

"Not possible. I'm already on an all-water diet in preparation for next week. Now, what can I wear besides the Giamba?"

"How about that peach gown you decided not to wear for Augie's blessing at the rectory?"

"The Dolce? But it's not even Alta Moda."

"You look so pretty in it. Who's going to care if it's Alta Moda or *alte kaker*?"

"I wish it were that simple. You don't understand the crowd that's coming. Every crowned, uncrowned, and deposed head in Europe will be there. It's going to be next-level, the who's who of the International Best-Dressed List. You know every fashion magazine is covering the wedding—I have four shoots scheduled and I'm not even the bride! All eyes are going to be on us, and I'll be torn to shreds for wearing off-the-rack Dolce on the big day. Mummy thinks that I'm so close to getting a major endorsement deal with one of the Big Three."*

Eden nodded supportively. Privately, she was quite relieved not to be attending the wedding, just like she was perfectly happy being spared from engaging in all the society madness that the Gresham girls were so caught up in. It was a world she got to peek into occasionally, helping the sisters get ready for their soirées and hearing the stories afterward, but she was perfectly happy to be a spectator from a

---

* *In Beatrice's mind, the Big Three were Chanel, Dior, and Valentino.*

distance. There was a knock on the door as Anya, one of the younger maids, peeked her head in. "The countess needs you immediately."

Bea groaned. "I've been hiding from her all morning. On a scale of one to ten, how mad does she seem?"

Anya thought about it for a moment. "Eight point five?"

"Fuck." Bea turned to Eden pleadingly. "Come with me?"

"You realize my presence is not going to be the shield you think it is."

"True, but it will help distract her a bit. Here, put this on." Bea fastened a diamond-and-ruby necklace around Eden's neck. Her short gamine hairstyle, cropped to the nape of her neck, showed off the elaborate jewels to their full advantage, and Bea thought for the millionth time how lucky Eden was to have those naturally pouty lips and perfect cheekbones—if only she would wear a little more makeup to enhance her assets and not dress like she was an underpaid NHS first-year doctor (even though she was).

"There! The necklace looks better on you than it does on me! Really, you must wear more rubies on a regular basis."

Eden began protesting. "Bea, are you sure I should be—"

"Shush, it's perfect. It was my great-grandmother's. The San Francisco one who replenished all the coffers with her railroad money. Now Mummy will scold me for letting you wear it and forget what she really wants to scold me about."

Eden was led off reluctantly, and they entered the countess's bedroom to find a rather strange scene: Thomas seated in a chair, observing with the detachment of a Jungian therapist, and Lord Francis (Harrodian/Radley/Exeter) standing helplessly in the corner, while Arabella was flinging things into her Globe-Trotter trunks as three maids rushed around in terror. To Bea, she seemed to be hovering at more of a 9.5 on the scale of maternal insanity.

"What's going on?" Bea asked gingerly.

Arabella looked up. "BEATRICE!* Jackie the wedding planner

---

* *Arabella pronounces her daughter's name in the Italian way,* Be-ah-TREE-chey, *not because she's Italian but because she's pretentious.*

says we can buy out all the other resorts on the island for our guests, especially since so many cowards have canceled and there are plenty of other spots on the island where we can restage the wedding! I'm going to need your help! I need you to pack your bags now and come with me! My dear brother, god bless his soul, is sending one of his planes to Farnborough for us! Wheels up at nine a.m. tomorrow! I need all hands on deck! We need to divide and conquer! Where is Rufus? Have you heard from your brother? He's not responding to my texts and—"

Bea cut in boldly. "MUMMY! I have the most brilliant idea. Now that we're putting the guests at different resorts and so many cowards are canceling, won't we have room for Eden?"

Eden shook her head, trying to make eye contact with Bea. Not a brilliant idea, especially when the countess was clearly in a hypomanic state.

Arabella froze for a moment, looking up from her packing but not saying anything. Suddenly, her eyes caught on Eden. "Why are you wearing Granny's Burmese-ruby Boucheron necklace?"

"I was just using Eden's neck as my mannequin. Hasn't she got the most gorgeous long Audrey Hepburn neck? See how useful she can be? Like you said, we need all hands on deck. And, Papa, remember how we felt so bad that Mummy couldn't find enough room for the Tongs on the guest list, try as she might? We can have both Eden AND Uncle Thomas at the wedding now!"

Eden and Thomas exchanged wide-eyed looks, like mice trapped in the midst of stampeding elephants.

"Good thinking, Bea, but I do think the Tongs are too busy to get away on such short notice," Francis said haltingly. He was all too aware that the last thing his friend wanted was to be anywhere near the cursed event.

"Yes, terribly busy week. Lots of patients," Thomas chimed in.

Bea wouldn't give up. "Dr. Tong, there will be lots of patients for you at the wedding! Think of the hundreds of guests and the life-threatening things they'll be doing—whale watching, volcano trampling, all-you-can-eat-buffet eating. What if one of those decrepit ex-royals keels over from too much Spam Loco Moco?* It'll be good to have a doctor around. Two doctors, actually. I keep forgetting Eden's a doctor. And, Mummy, don't you see, Eden will be especially helpful . . . with *OS*."

Suddenly Arabella's eyes lit up and she seemed to recover slightly. "Yes, she will be good for *OS,* won't she? Eden, you'll offer your assistance, won't you, in our time of need?"

Eden couldn't fathom what the countess was referring to, but she knew the only appropriate response at this moment was to nod. She had been aware since a very young age that the countess didn't consider the Tongs as equals to the Greshams—as the family doctor, Thomas Tong was barely a notch above the butler, and Eden merely a playmate for her children when it suited them. The countess, in her infinite self-absorption, hadn't a clue how beloved Eden had become to her own children.

Bea, of course, did not make the same distinctions as her mother, and she cheered jubilantly. "Yay! It's settled then. The Tongs are coming to Hawaii!" She grabbed Eden by the hand and pulled her out of the room before her mother could change her mind.

"My god, Bea. What have you done?"

"I can't believe my plan actually worked! You have no idea, I've been scheming *for months* to get you invited!"

"Bea, I can't just take off work for a whole week at the last minute, and I know nothing about organizing weddings," Eden grumbled at this sudden turn of events. As much as she wanted to visit Hawaii, she didn't fancy going as a glorified member of the Gresham staff.

"You can Zoom with your patients, and don't worry, my mother has an army of wedding planners working around the clock as it is.

* *A local Hawaiian delicacy consisting of white rice topped with slices of fried Spam, brown gravy, and a sunny-side-up egg, it was said to have been created in the 1940s when Hawaiian diners requested a dish they could afford. Spam is beloved comfort food throughout the Pacific, ever since the luncheon meat was served to GIs during World War II and adopted into local cuisines from Singapore to Saipan. My favorite Spam Loco Moco is at Tex Drive-In in Honokaa, and be sure to try their freshly made malasadas, a Portuguese fried donut that, similar to Spam, also found its way to Hawaii somehow.*

We won't have to do much except order them around and work on our tans."

"So what's this OS you keep talking about?"

"Plenty of time to tell you about OS later. Go pack your bags!"

"That's the other thing—I have nothing to wear!" Eden sighed in exasperation.

"Sure you do. You can borrow my clothes. I'll lend you the peach Dolce. Oh my god I'm so excited I need to have a wee! WHEELS UP AT NINE A.M.!!!"

LADY ARABELLA'S REVENGE

That roar you hear in the sky is the swoosh of all the private jets that will be landing at Kona airport this week for the nuptials of Lady Augusta Gresham and Prince Maximillian zu Liechtenburg. Despite an unfortunately timed volcanic eruption at the wedding site, the show must go on for this season's most superb dynastic match. It's a rule the Greshams have always followed, a rule that's made them one of the most chronicled clans in these pages.

First there was Countess Arabella Gresham's iconic portrait dressed in a gothic Alexander McQueen gown astride a zebra in the drawing room of Greshamsbury Hall. Then there was Lady Augusta and Lady Beatrice commanding the cover in vintage Shanghainese cheongsams to mark their twenty-first and sixteenth birthdays, respectively. And who could forget the photo that became the home screen of every girl in SW3—the bare-chested Viscount Rufus ironing his shirt before Radley's Charity Fashion Show.

"My children were fortunate enough to be born at the right time—when being half Asian is seen as an asset rather than a curse," the countess declares in the matter-of-fact manner that has endeared her to so many. But there's a story from Arabella's early years in London that she likes to tell. The young mother was playing with her infant daughter in the gardens by her Thurloe Square house (the big one on the corner) when she was approached by two ladies—a middle-aged mother and her thirtysomething daughter.

"The older woman said, 'Excuse me, do you speak English?' I was used to this question, so I simply nodded. The younger woman said, 'We see you here every day. You're so good with the baby. She clearly adores you.' 'Thank you,' I replied. And then the older woman leaned over and whispered, 'Whatever they're paying you, we'll double it.' I was so confused, and then it hit me: *These women think I'm the nanny! Because I'm Chinese, and my half-British daughter doesn't look like me!*" Lady Arabella recalls with a laugh.

It's easy for Lady Arabella to dismiss the casual racism that she encountered back then, because no one would ever mistake her for the help nowadays. The couture-clad countess is regarded as one of the world's best-dressed women and the visionary behind some of the most drop-dead chic hotels on the planet. It all began three decades ago when Arabella first caught the fashion world's attention—and, more important, the eye of Francis, 18th Earl of Greshamsbury—as she walked the runway of Azzedine Alaïa's show in Paris.

A whirlwind romance followed by a glorious wedding ensued, though Arabella soon discovered that life at Greshamsbury Hall wasn't exactly a fairy tale. The local gentry, it seemed, weren't prepared to put out their welcome mats for the Hong Kong girl who had snagged the dashing viscount who could trace his lineage back to Edward the Confessor (and perhaps more crucially was heir to one of the few earldoms still in possession of its vast lands and even vaster trusts).

"Oh, they were downright mean at first. Every move I made was criticized—from the stiletto boots I wore to the village fête to how badly I curtseyed to Princess Alexandra when she came to visit. Nowadays, everyone pretends that it never happened, but they know who they are," the preternaturally youthful countess says with a wink. While Lord Francis "could not have cared less what anyone thought," Arabella decided to rethink her game.

"Look, I was never under the illusion it would be easy. I knew my family was never going to be accepted as truly English. At first I tried to follow my mother-in-law, who was a stickler for tradition, but everything I did only made me stand out. Then I realized, I'll never *not* stand out, so why fight it? I knew then I had to create my own style and do things my way."

The first thing she did was give Greshamsbury Hall a sorely needed restoration—its first in more than a century. Out went the ancient Aga and the decomposing Tassinari et Chatel damask, and in came a bold, futurist East meets West look that designers now dub "Arabella Chic." "I was the first to do forty-eight layers of tobacco lacquer on the floors of a manor house. I was the first to mix brutalist furniture with wicker."

Arabella credits her own mother for her confidence to upend centuries of tradition. "My mother grew up in Shanghai, which was the Paris of the East, so for her, Asian Fusion wasn't a fad, it was a way of life." Arabella's barrister father hailed from one of Hong Kong's most respected legal families. "People are constantly surprised to learn that I didn't grow up in a rice paddy. My grandfather and father both went to Oxford, and we had a house in Kowloon Tong with five servants."

After every shelter magazine raved over the transformation of Greshamsbury Hall, everyone jockeyed to be invited. By this time, the Greshams had no need for the neighbors—they were already playing in a different social stratum, one that mixed Hollywood royalty, design pashas, and global plutocrats. "We host truly diverse, inclusive weekends. We invite Malay sultans, Nigerian oil barons, Indian oligarchs. Everyone is welcome!" Arabella proudly declares.

The countess never imagined that her modern spin on Marco Polo would spawn her own design and hospitality empire, but after a famously finicky Qatari prince spent the weekend and was wowed by the countess's hospitality, he commanded her to design a hotel in London "for people who can only bear to stay in palaces when they travel," promising to book out the entire place every year for the London Season. Arabella quickly conceived of Bella's, the gemlike London oasis that has set the standard for boutique establishments everywhere. Then came the Bella outposts in Hong Kong, Antwerp, and the Maldives, all of which possess the perfect alchemy of understated glamour, exquisite service, and discretion that have made them de rigueur destinations for the cognoscenti.

Now Arabella is poised to unveil her biggest creation—a super-luxe eco-resort on the Big Island of Hawaii that, if early whispers are to be believed, should make the Aman folks *very* nervous. (Three of the villas come with their own private waterfalls.) One might think all this was part of Arabella's master plan all along. "Never my intention—I just needed a home that wasn't so drafty my babies would die of pneumonia."

Speaking of which, Arabella's babies are all grown up and have clearly inherited their parents' unaffected charm and effortless style. Lady Augusta, whose ethereal beauty and gravity-defying Ashtanga yoga poses on the beaches of Bali log millions of views, is merging her own wellness brand with that of Prince Max, the social entrepreneur and microdosing coach who grew up between his father Prince Julius of Liechtenburg's Ibizan villa and his Norwegian mother's Malibu ranch (Princess Hanne Marit hails from the von Melke av Sjokolade clan, who have so many gallons of Norwegian North Sea Brent crude gushing through their veins you can't light a match anywhere near them). Younger sister Lady Beatrice made her sensational runway debut at the Iris van Herpen show in Paris last year. With her Titianesque hair and Swintonesque cheekbones, this year's hottest It Girl is poised to nab any prince she sets her pretty eyes on.

And then there's the prodigal heir—Rufus, Viscount St. Ives, or "Viscount St. Abs" as he was nicknamed after that famous ironing photo went viral, a pro surfer turned travel photographer currently based in Hawaii who's broken a string of hearts on both sides of the Atlantic. Now that his big sis has made such a splendid match, the pressure's been turned up for Rufus to deliver another royal match made in heaven. The Gresham siblings seem to effortlessly embody everything that modern aristocrats are supposed to be—stylish, conscious, global. It would not be surprising at all if Arabella's kids ended up siring the next generation of Europe's royals, and what fitting revenge that would be for the countess who was mistaken for the nanny.

II

Hawaii

Hawaii is a paradise—and I can never cease proclaiming it. But I must append one word of qualification: Hawaii is a paradise for the well-to-do.

—JACK LONDON

Dr. Thomas Tong was in the midst of enjoying a cup of tea in the break room when his flatmate peeked his head through the open door.

"Dominic! What are you doing here?"

"There was an urgent call for you at home from Hong Kong. I didn't know what to do, so I came to look for you."

"Hong Kong?"

Dominic looked at him uncomfortably. "It was the police calling. It's about your brother . . ."

At that moment he knew, he just knew. Nothing more needed to be said by Dominic for him to know that his brother, Henry, was dead. It was as though he had been preparing for this call his entire life.

Thomas, who was in the second year of his residency at the Royal Marsden Hospital, quickly requested emergency leave and took the next available Cathay flight back to Hong Kong. Upon landing he went straight to the police morgue to identify the body, sparing his elderly parents the distress of having to do it. He steeled himself as he entered the building, thinking it would be a piece of cake. How many bodies had he dissected? How many patients had he lost? And then he saw Rosina sitting there. Of all his brother's friends who had been with him at Felix the previous night when it happened, Rosina Ko-Tung was the only one who came.

"It was an accident. A freak accident. If only Henry hadn't jumped onto the pink banquette he wouldn't have fallen so far down . . ."

"I still don't understand why it happened. Weren't you all the best of friends?"

"*We were all drunk. Roger got very upset when your brother sprung his proposal. You see, Mary is his sister, and Mary is pregnant with your brother's baby.*"

"*I don't understand. Why was Roger upset that Henry wanted to marry his sister?*"

"*No, Henry proposed to Gabriella Soong. We were all shocked.*"

Thomas sighed, understanding at last.

"*He didn't feel a thing, I promise. He didn't feel anything,*" *Rosina said, her entire body trembling with sobs as she hugged him.*

That was always the problem, Thomas thought. Henry never felt anything.

I

Puako Beach

BIG ISLAND, HAWAII • *LATER THAT WEEK*

Eden awoke to the sound of unfamiliar chirps. The chorus of birds outside sounded more spirited than anything she'd heard before, and they had been at it all night. Having arrived very late the previous evening to a house at the end of a pitch-black road, she had no inkling of what lay outside. She rose from the bed lazily, flung open the louvered plantation doors, and almost gasped in disbelief.

Before her was an emerald-green lawn that sloped down to swaying palm trees and a blinding blue ocean. She padded barefoot across the grass down to the narrow strip of silver-gray sand where the waves lapped gently into shallow tide pools formed by lava rocks. It was her first time seeing the Pacific, and she scampered joyously over the rocks, looking for the perfect place to dip her feet into the crystalline waters.

"Watch your step!" came a shout behind her. Eden looked down and saw the large gray rock she was about to step on suddenly move. It was a sea turtle basking in the sun.

"Oh my god!" Eden exclaimed, backing off. She turned around to see a woman in her late twenties sitting on a sun-bleached tree trunk.

"This beach is a resting ground for endangered sea turtles. We're supposed to stay at least twenty-five feet away," the woman said as she took a sip from her coffee mug.

"Sorry, I had no idea. It's my first time here."

"I don't need an apology, but maybe the turtle might appreciate one?"

"Oh, of course." Eden crouched down and looked directly into the turtle's heavily lidded eyes. "Sorry I almost stepped on you. I'll be more careful from now on." Turning around, she gave the woman a friendly smile. "Hi, I'm Eden."

"Kiana" (Punahou School/UC Berkeley/Central St. Martins). "Which team are you on?"

"Team?"

"Allison's or Kirsten's team?"

"I'm sorry, I'm not on any team. Or maybe I am . . . I'm on Arabella's team."

"Is she the pastry chef?"

"Er, no. What do you do?"

"I'm doing the ice sculptures. Sorry, I thought everyone staying here was on the F & B team."

Eden finally understood. With Arabella's new eco-resort forced to shut down suddenly, there had been a scramble to house all the wedding staff in addition to the arriving guests. Bea and her father had been shuttled off someplace down the road, while Eden had ended up at this house on Puako Beach Drive. She couldn't help but chuckle to herself—*of course* Arabella would stick her with the catering staff. Not that she minded one bit—this sprawling Hawaiian clapboard house on the beach was fabulous by any standard, and her room was comfortably furnished in vintage rattan and charmingly kitschy hula-girl lamps.

"So you're an ice sculptor?" Eden asked.

"I usually work in stone, but this is my side gig. My buddy Francisco hooked me up. In fact, speak of the devil . . ." Kiana pointed out to the sea. Eden could make out a figure backlit against the sun, snorkeling in a shallow reef down the beach.

"Francisco!" Kiana shouted. "See anything good?"

The man surfaced, looked in their direction, and removed his snorkeling mask. Much to Eden's surprise, it was Rufus.

"Eden!!" Rufus shouted excitedly as he emerged from the waves, stretching his arms out in welcome as water dripped from his shoulder-length hair down his bare chest in rivulets. "You're about to get very wet," he warned as he went in for a big bear hug. "I've missed you!" Rufus said, squeezing Eden tight.

"I'm soaked," Eden giggled. "What are you doing over here?"

"Been waiting all morning for you to wake up, sleepyhead!"

"You're lucky I got up this early. It's . . . what? Eight p.m. in England."

"Excuses, excuses!" Rufus teased.

Kiana observed their familiar banter with interest. "So *you're* the Eden Francisco keeps talking about! I might have guessed from your accent. You both sound exactly alike!"

"We do?" Eden said.

"Yes, Francisco sounds like Harry Styles, while you're more Kate Middleton."*

"That's a bit alarming," Eden laughed.

"To Hawaiians, we all sound like we're on *Downton Abbey,*" Rufus teased, before explaining to Eden, "Kiana and I met at school in London, but she's actually from right here."

"Really?"

"Yep. My family's in Waimea. This gig was a free ticket to see them."

"Kiana's a much better artist than I'll ever be."

Kiana smiled. "Don't believe a word Francisco says. His work is going to be in museums before long and I'll still be chain-sawing ice at bougie weddings."

"Rubbish!" Rufus exclaimed.

"Speaking of ice, I gotta run to a meeting with the snotty wedding decorators. They're stressing out about my sculptures 'ruining their sightlines,' " Kiana said.

"Tell them all to shove it. Eden, coffee at my place?" Rufus asked.

"I should put on some proper clothes first," Eden said, realizing she was still in her sleeping clothes—an old pair of cotton jersey shorts and a skinny tee.

* *The Princess of Wales has made it known that she prefers to be called Catherine, so for God's sake please stop calling her Kate Middleton.*

"Why? Are you going to the Wolseley? Look how I'm dressed." Rufus gestured to his tattered board shorts and bare feet as they cut through a wooded path that led from the beach to a road that to Eden seemed straight out of a dream. Tall coconut palms, fragrant hibiscus bushes, and mango trees lined the winding lane of relaxed old bungalows and wooden beach cottages next door to the occasional sprawling mansion. Rufus reached up into one of the low-hanging branches as they walked past and plucked two ripe mangoes. "For breakfast." He grinned.

"This is paradise! How in the world did I end up here?"

"Me, of course. I conspired to get you that room in the bungalow!"

"So, I'm missing out on a five-star resort because of you?" Eden scolded.

"Puako Beach Road is one of the only places left on the entire island that still has these original cottages from the sixties right on the beach," Rufus explained. "It's a real neighborhood, as opposed to some poncy resort. You love hunting down the local hangouts whenever you travel, so I thought you'd prefer it over here."

"I love it! But hey, Tom Ripley, why on earth does Kiana call you 'Francisco'?"

"It's my alias, my artist name—Francisco Ives."

"Clever."

"I'm trying not to use 'Viscount St. Ives' in London—my name walks into every room before I can."

Eden nodded, knowing how conflicted Rufus was about the title that had been assigned to him at birth.

"Here we are," Rufus announced as they approached a simple white A-frame house with a bleached wooden deck.

"At long last, the infamous surf cabin!" Eden said.

"I built it entirely of salvaged wood," Rufus said proudly. Arriving at the front door, they saw a garment bag along with several other bags hanging on the handle with a note attached. Rufus glanced at the note and handed it to Eden. "This one's a keeper."

Eden peered at the note, which was hastily scrawled on COUNTESS OF GRESHAMSBURY stationery:

The countess would like you to wear this beige linen Margaret Howell suit tonight. She says to please tuck the shirt in and wear the outfit with the Duret belt and the George Cleverley loafers provided. PLEASE DO NOT SUBSTITUTE WITH YOUR OWN SHOES. And please use the mouthwash provided. And please shave. And please clean under your fingernails and trim your nose hairs. PEOPLE WILL NOTICE!

"It's as if I'm not housebroken," Rufus scoffed.

"Your mum's just a perfectionist."

"More like extreme OCD. I feel sorry for the lackey that had to write this," Rufus groused as he crumpled up the note. He unlocked the front door and waved his arm with a flourish, inviting Eden inside. Eden entered to find an airy loftlike space cleverly divided into different areas by bamboo screens. A battered leather couch[*] took up the front area, while a platform bed in the back corner faced a wall of sliding glass pocket doors. On the adjacent corner, next to a small galley kitchen, was a round metal bistro table flanked by a pair of classic Eames chairs. A line of surfboards against the main wall was the only decoration.

"I turned the loo into my darkroom," Rufus said, opening the narrow door so Eden could peer into the tiny space where a photo enlarger had been propped up on a plank of plywood under the shower.

"So where do you bathe?"

Rufus gestured outside. On one end of the back deck was an outdoor shower nestled between thick tropical bushes and a wall of stacked volcanic rocks. Rufus pointed to a galvanized steel cistern on the roof. "That tank collects rainwater for the shower."

"So cool! I've never taken an outdoor shower," Eden said.

"Then you must take one while you're here. It's absolutely glori-

---

[*] *Actually, they were a pair of Togo love seats by Michel Ducaroy pushed together, but Eden wouldn't have recognized a $20,000 vintage leather sofa and would have been appalled at the cost.*

ous, you'll love it. Sometimes I turn out all the lights and sit in the shower late at night just to gaze at the stars."

"Sounds amazing," Eden said.

They went back into the house and Eden noticed Rufus's worktable by the back corner across from the bed. Tacked to the wall all the way up to the ceiling was a collage of dried palm fronds, magazine clippings, and his own photographs. Along with pictures of the ocean, tide pools, and bright green geckos were snapshots of Bea, Augie, and an old black-and-white print of Eden, looking directly at the camera and laughing as a long clump of hair blew across her face. She remembered the exact moment he took the photo, when they went hiking along the cliffs of Tintagel many summers back.

"Why do you have that picture up?" Eden asked.

"It's my favorite picture of you."

"Not my best look."

He was about to protest but decided instead to change tracks. "So . . . I guess you're not impressed?"

"What do you mean? You know I always enjoy looking at your work."

"I'm talking about the cabin."

"Oh, I *adore* it! It suits you perfectly and I can see why you love spending so much time here."

Rufus smiled in relief. "Mum came here once and called it a rat's nest. She stayed less than ten minutes."

"I wouldn't expect her to appreciate any of this. There's nothing for her to lacquer in here."

"Haha, no there isn't! But I do take credit for this little cabin being the inspiration for her new resort."

"She'd never have visited Hawaii if you hadn't been spending so much time here."

"Not only that, but I think she saw what was special about the cabin, even though this isn't her aesthetic. It's no coincidence she put twelve surf cabins on the hills above her resort. Of course, hers are built of trendy blackened wood and are tricked out with cashmere throw pillows, soaking tubs, and movie screens that retract from the ceiling. She knows her crowd and she's got the perfect plan to lure them here."

Eden glanced around Rufus's unassuming cabin, thinking how much the space embodied his free-spirited ethos. The way he had fashioned a beautiful worktable out of an old glass door and a pair of tree stumps; the seashells and ocean pebbles arranged in an intricate mandala along the window ledge. This was what she loved about Rufus, his raw creativity and how much of a nature boy he was, so much happier in his surf shack than in a grand manor. For the first time since arriving on the island, she felt a pang of guilt over what had happened the night before. How in the world had she allowed herself to be roped into the countess's maniacal scheme?

II

The Countess's Bedroom

GRESHAMSBURY HALL • 24 HOURS EARLIER

The evening before her flight to Hawaii, Eden had been summoned back to the Big House, where she found the countess propped up against a dozen plush Luigi Bevilacqua silk-velvet pillows[*] while Bea lounged at the foot of the bed, petting Noel and Liam.

Arabella glanced up at Eden as she entered. "Shut the door. It's time to tell you about OS. You are sworn to secrecy, do you hear me?"

Eden nodded dutifully.

"Now, you and I both know that Rufus is wasting his life away in Hawaii. It's high time Rufus settled down and did something with his life . . ."

"Is it? He's one of the hardest-working people I know," Eden insisted.

"Doing what, pray tell? Cleaning surfboards?"

"He's an artist."

"A failed artist. Five years out of art school and he hasn't even managed to get into a decent group show. And he refuses to let me help—one phone call to my friend Jessica and he'd have a solo exhibition at her gallery in San Francisco, but the boy is so stubborn. Anyway, that's beside the point, Rufus doesn't need to be a famous

---

[*] *Founded in 1875 in Venice, Tessitura Luigi Bevilacqua was also the official supplier of precious fabrics to the Vatican until Pope Paul VI decided to tighten the belt on luxury goods. (This would explain the pillows from Target I saw in the waiting room during my last audience with the Pope.)*

artist—he's going to be the Earl of Greshamsbury. He's had enough fun fooling around with his cameras and bumming around the world in those stinky flip-flops. It's high time he came back to England and stepped up to his real duty—he must get married and give me lots of grandsons."

"Don't you mean *grandchildren*, Mummy?" Bea interjected.

"Grandsons FIRST," Arabella said sternly. "Eden, you've met the parade of undesirables that Rufus has brought home over the years: The one who didn't shave her armpits. The one with the pet lizard. The one that lied about her age. The Australian one. And the worst one of all was the folksinger."

"Savannah's a *pop* star! And a billionaire now, Mum," Bea cut in.

"Who cares? She was a vegan!"

"She sold her line of vegan lip balms for eight hundred million dollars!" Bea continued.

"Precisely my point—she was a money-grubbing vegan. Now, I've spent the past two years vetting hundreds of candidates from all over the world, cross-referencing each of them with Debrett's, Burke's, the *Almanach de Gotha*, and the *Social Register*, and consulting with my secret panel of experts.* After an exhaustive search, I've found the ideal candidate to matchmake with Rufus."

"With all due respect, Lady Arabella, I'm not sure trying to matchmake Rufus is the best idea," Eden said.

"Nonsense! Matchmaking is still the custom in half the world—think of the billions of Indians that are matchmade every year. And especially in great families like ours, unions have always been entered into with great intention and great strategy. You know Rufus cannot just marry any girl he wants—he *must* marry someone that fits all the necessary criteria. And I've found the girl that checks every single box. Actually, Bea is to be partly thanked."

---

* *Arabella's secret panel of experts included the* première vendeuse *at* Christian Dior, *the president of the* Bal des Débutantes, *the admissions director at* Institut Villa Pierrefeu, *the* maître d'hôtel *at* Le Voltaire, *the executive vice president of private banking at Roths-child & Co, and, of course, Sima from Mumbai.*

Eden looked curiously to Bea, who breathlessly announced, " 'OS' stands for 'Operation Solène,' as in Solène de Courcy. Remember her—my flatmate in Paris? We did that shoot together for *L'Officiel*?"

"Oh yes, I remember now. She's gorgeous! Isn't she an artist as well?" Eden remembered Bea stressing out over what to wear to Solène's opening at Timothy Taylor.

Arabella nodded. "She is one of the hottest emerging artists around. She already has important galleries in London, Paris, and LA, and everyone's flipping her work, so she can satisfy all of Rufus's artistic pretensions."

"I'm not sure it works quite like that . . . ," Eden demurred.

"*Hiyah,* you're missing the point! She is the daughter of Gaspard and Olimpia de Courcy. She was born in the right hospital, grew up in the right arrondissement, went to the right schools, speaks the right languages, and understands innately what it means to be to the manor born."

"Not only is she to the manor born, she is to the hotel born too!" Bea jumped in. "The de Courcys own a fabulous crop of hotels all over France and the French Caribbean. That's why it's a match made in heaven—she already knows what it feels like to be constantly harassed by friends angling for room upgrades!"

Arabella nodded. "Yes, I can already picture her as the future chatelaine of our lifestyle empire. She has the right look and her style is impeccable. When you meet her, you'll see right away that she's a dead ringer for a young Betty Catroux."[*]

Eden hadn't a clue who that was, but she nodded politely anyway.

"Now, Bea managed to get me a snippet of her hair, so I was able to run some tests." Arabella registered Eden's look. "Why so shocked? We needed to make sure she doesn't have any of those terrible genes that so many of those European royals have, you know, like the ones

---

[*] *The iconic muse to Yves Saint Laurent, she wore his safari jackets and* Le Smoking *suits better than anyone else.*

who can't stop bleeding from a papercut or who commit double sui-
cide in hunting lodges with their lovers. Anyway, she has decent
genes—not as fine as Gresham genes, mind you, but good enough
to ensure that my grandchildren won't have any major deformities.
More importantly, her lineage is magnificent—she is a *princesse du
sang royal,* a direct descendant of Marie Antoinette* on her father's
side and Lucrezia Borgia on her mother's side."

"Er . . . didn't Lucrezia Borgia poison a few of her husbands?"
Eden asked.

"Don't believe those nasty rumors!† She was a very fine Renais-
sance noblewoman and we will be very lucky to welcome her descendant into our family. So, I'm arranging for you and Bea to go on
special excursions around the island with Rufus and Solène over the
next few days."

"You'll be my co-conspirator!" Bea giggled.

Arabella cut in impatiently. "Now, Eden, here is the brilliant part
of the plan: *Rufus is going to think he's being set up with someone else.*"

"Oh really? Who?"

"The princess of Thailand. She's beautiful and royal and totally
off-limits. But I will make a big show of introducing them and Rufus
will think she's the one and of course he will go out of his way to
resist her. But meanwhile, Solène will conveniently be right there,

---

* *Arabella is either incorrect or has been given wrong information. Marie Antoinette's
last descendant was her daughter Princesse Marie-Thérèse-Charlotte, who had no children and died in Vienna in 1851. The de Courcys are* princes du sang—*princes of royal
blood—through a Bourbon great-grandmother, but they generally use the honorific only in
select circumstances—for instance, whenever they wish to book tables at Michelin-starred
restaurants.*

† *Among the nasty rumors surrounding Lucrezia Borgia: that she wore a ring with a secret
compartment filled with poison; that she attended "the Banquet of the Chestnuts," an infamous orgy; that she had an incestuous relationship with her father, Pope Alexander VI;
that she also had an incestuous relationship with her brother Cesare, who was planning to
murder her first husband, Giovanni; that she was having an affair with her father's valet,
Pedro Calderon, who later turned up dead on the banks of the Tiber. If ever anyone was in
need of a better publicist, Lucrezia was it.*

and your job is to covertly talk her up to Rufus. The minute you meet Solène you will see how much sense she makes as my future daughter-in-law. You want what's best for my family, don't you?"

"Of course I do," Eden replied, wondering if Arabella cared about what might actually be best for her son. She had met almost all of Rufus's girlfriends over the years, and the problem wasn't really the women. It was just that Rufus was never in love with any of them. As eligible as Rufus might have been made to look by the glossy magazines, in reality he was the opposite of a Casanova. He was slightly awkward around women he didn't know well, and he truly had no game. He was never the pursuer, always the pursued. After he had exploded onto the social radar, legions of girls had become fixated on becoming the next Countess Greshamsbury, and being the amenable sort, Rufus ended up being dragged into relationships that were far more intense than he ever intended.

Would the same thing happen with Solène de Courcy? Eden was willing to suspend judgment and give this candidate a chance. After all, Rufus's future happiness was at stake here, and she wanted nothing more than for him to find his true soul mate. If his mother was convinced this girl was *the one*, she was grateful to be playing a part in vetting Solène herself. After all, they'd all be seeing a lot of each other. And Rufus was going to trust her opinion more than that of his own mother or sister. But she did pose a last question to Lady Arabella: "How can you be so absolutely certain Rufus will fall for Solène?"

Arabella glared at Eden as if she had said something ridiculous. "It's natural selection. Beautiful people always fall for beautiful people. Look at me and my husband. I took one look at him and I immediately felt myself begin to ovulate."

"We also have a secret weapon on the way . . . ," Bea whispered conspiratorially.

"A secret weapon?"

"You'll see," Bea said with a gleam in her eye.

·

Eden was wondering what "secret weapon" Arabella and Bea could possibly have when she was jolted out of her daydream by Rufus's tapping her on the shoulder and handing her a ceramic mug. "You still like your coffee with a spot of half-and-half?"

"I do."

"Can I add one more thing to your coffee? It's something I picked up here."

"Sure."

They went outside to the wooden deck and sat down on a pair of canvas butterfly chairs. Eden inhaled the steam from her coffee mug, which was infused with a sweet scent. "Did you add vanilla?"

"It's actually Big Island lehua honey blended with vanilla beans."

"Mmm. Love it." Eden smiled as she took a long, slow sip, closed her eyes, and eased into her chair. The sun on her face felt so lovely, she could hardly believe that it was the middle of winter back in Britain. "Now I feel like I'm truly on holiday."

"I think this is our last moment of peace before guests start flooding the island. Ready for the craziest wedding weekend ever?" Rufus asked.

"I'm just a spectator. How about you? Are you ready?"

"I'm as much a spectator as you."

No you're not, Eden thought to herself as she sipped on her coffee, taking in the sounds of the waves pounding onto the lava rocks and the ecstatic screech of birds. "I've never heard birds quite like this before," she said.

Rufus laughed. "Because they aren't birds. That's the sound of the coqui frog. They're everywhere on the island. That's their mating call."

Eden gave him a curious look. "No wonder."

The Earl & Countess of Greshamsbury
invite you to a Sunset Feast celebrating

LADY AUGUSTA GRESHAM

and

PRINCE MAXIMILLIAN
ZU LIECHTENBURG

TIME: 6:00 p.m.

LOCATION: Bellaloha Resort

DRESS: Festive

* Shuttle buses will depart from designated hotels at 5:30 p.m. sharp

** Please dress lightly for extreme temperatures

III

Bellaloha Resort

SOUTH KONA, HAWAII • *SUNSET FEAST*

Bea was just fastening the labradorite-bead* necklace around her sister Augusta's neck when there was a series of quick raps on the door.

"Come in!" Bea said.

A blond woman in a stylishly unobtrusive black Nili Lotan jumpsuit and Roger Vivier ankle boots opened the door to the suite slightly and poked her headset-clad head in. "How are we doing in there?"

"Almost ready. What do you think, Jackie?" Augusta said, turning to present herself to the event producer, Jackie Zivenchy (Hillcrest Elementary/Kakiat Junior High/Ramapo High/Hobart and William Smith/Brooklyn Law). She had on an off-the-shoulder silk print dress with delicate flared sleeves that draped beautifully around her like butterfly wings. Even though she was five years older than Bea, with her more petite frame, dusting of freckles across her cheeks, and long chestnut hair blown into bouncy loose curls, Augie looked more like the younger sister.

"You look stunning," Jackie said.

"This was the compromise. It's not couture, exactly, but the style pays homage to Queen Emma of Hawaii," Augusta explained.

"Doesn't look like a compromise to me. It's an original look that's totally *you*, and I love that necklace!"

---

* *It is said the northern lights are trapped in the iridescent, changing colors of labradorite. The mineral supposedly protects against negativity, which is precisely why Augie chose to wear it when she knew she'd be spending an ungodly amount of time with her mother.*

"Thank you. Will you please say that in front of Mummy? She's morally opposed to semiprecious stones."

"I'd be happy to say it in front of anyone," Jackie replied, careful to remain diplomatically neutral in the ongoing tug-of-war between bride and mother. "Now, let's get you downstairs. We can't hold back the crowd much longer."

As the three of them walked down the hotel corridor, Jackie turned to Bea. "You look gorgeous as well. I love the flowers on your dress. Is it Oscar de la Renta?"

"Yes! I had nothing to wear for this evening and they came to my rescue. This just arrived an hour ago from New York," Bea replied of her strapless gown with its dramatic purple bodice bow sash and painted anemones on the skirt. Unlike her sister, she had no issues with looking like she had just stepped off a fashion catwalk.

"I have the bride and sister. ETA two minutes," Jackie barked into her headset.

Augie grabbed Jackie's arm lightly. "One more thing. Maxxie has asked Gopal Das to say a welcome blessing. He is such a dear friend; can we possibly allow him a few minutes somewhere? Maybe before my father's toast?"

"Of course. Don't worry about a thing."

"My only worry is—"

"—to not have any worries. Lady Augusta, my job is to make sure that any heat falls on *me*. Your only job is to have a wonderful time with all your friends tonight. Okay, ladies, camera faces ready? Because *Tattle* and *Vogue* are going to start snapping the moment we go outside." Jackie parted the glass double doors, and sure enough, two photographers immediately trained their lenses on Augusta and scrambled backward like intrepid crabs to get their optimal shots. Augusta ignored them, her eyes searching for her mother's reaction.

Lady Arabella, resplendent in a black vintage couture Givenchy dress with a gigantic white satin bow tied at her hip and dazzling Wallace Chan pink sapphire earrings, looked both her daughters up and down before remarking, "Bea, the Oscar looks *perfect* on you."

"You both look too lovely for words," Francis said as he kissed his daughters.

A few moments later, Rufus came rushing up with Prince Maximillian (Bygdøy/Le Rosey/Crossroads/Bard) in tow, and both gave quick hugs to Augusta and Bea.

"Okay, we're all here at last! Time to let the guests in?" Jackie asked.

"One minute," Arabella said as she rushed over to Rufus and brushed his shoulders even though there was nothing there that needed brushing off. "Get your hair out of your face. Now, there is someone special arriving tonight. The princess of Thailand. When she arrives, I want you to be the one to escort her into dinner."

Rufus rolled his eyes but nodded.

"Okay, we're ready," Arabella said to Jackie.

"Gotcha. Doesn't Augusta look stunning? I love that her dress was hand-painted by a local designer," Jackie gushed.

"It looks like she found it on the clearance rack at Mango," Arabella replied curtly as the first guests appeared at the top of the steps, and Augusta burst into tears.

•

After enduring a shuttle bus ride that shook violently as it wound down a vertiginous path, Thomas and Eden found themselves entering the lush rain forest gardens of Arabella's new resort as greeters dressed in sharply tailored shocking-pink suits handed out tall flutes bubbling with cocktails. "Would you like an M & A? This cocktail was created to honor the fusion of Prince Max and Lady Augusta's heritage. It's Norwegian aquavit, Chinese plum wine, Devonshire elderflower syrup, and sparkling water made from a secret spring in Topanga Canyon," a young man who looked like he had just been flown in by an LA modeling agency carefully recited.

"Yes please!" Eden said merrily, grabbing a glass for her father and one for herself.

"Looks like you're in full holiday mode," Thomas remarked.

"You know, I didn't realize how badly I needed a break until now."

"I'm glad you realize that. I've been watching you work yourself to the bone!"

"It's not work when you love what you do."

"True, but I do think the hours your hospital forces you to put in are downright criminal. It was never like that in my day."

"The NHS was very different in your day, Dad."

"Bloody hell, it was. But let's enjoy these beautiful cocktails and not talk shop while we're in paradise, okay? Doctor's orders!" Taking their drinks, Thomas and Eden wandered down a stone pathway that led to an otherworldly sight. They were perched at the entrance to a clifftop garden with panoramic views of the ocean at sunset. Except today, there was something far more spectacular than the legendary Hawaiian sunset to marvel at—a glowing river of lava that bisected the lawn and flowed dramatically down the cliff into the clear blue sea. And before them was a magnificent series of ingeniously canti-levered platforms that formed a hexagonal walkway high above the lava. As they climbed up the walkway, Eden stared in fascination at the crimson channel of 2,200-degree lava moving in slow motion across the charred lawn and down the cliff, producing great plumes of smoke as it hit the water. "I feel like I'm dreaming, don't you?"

Thomas nodded slowly. "I've got to hand it to Arabella—she does know how to throw one heck of a welcome party." They soon arrived at the receiving line, where Francis, Arabella, and Rufus stood with Prince Max greeting the intimidatingly glamorous guests. As Eden caught sight of the family, she couldn't help but well up with pride at the sight of Rufus and Lord Francis looking so dapper in their crisp linen suits. Prince Max, on the other hand, had gone in a decidedly casual direction in his Hawaiian shirt, linen slacks, and woven leather sandals.

"*Hei!* It's the doctors Tong and Tong! So good of you both to come all this way!" he said in his peculiar Nordic-meets-SoCal accent, his ice-blond hair flopping over his eyes as he bowed for-mally before shaking Thomas's hand and giving Eden a kiss on the cheek. "Your presence here is so very heart opening for me."

"I'm so happy we could be here, Maxxie," Eden said, beaming.

"Eden—*hiyah*! Please address Prince Maximillian as 'Your Serene Highness'!" Arabella scolded.

Maxxie rolled his eyes. "Lady Arabella, Eden has been calling me Maxxie for eons."

"Has she?" Arabella looked surprised. "I thought you scarcely knew her."

"How can you say such a thing, Countess? I have known Eden since my very first visit to Greshamsbury Hall three years ago, and the girls and I even went camping in the Outer Hebrides last year. When someone has seen you empty your bowels into a hole you have just dug in the sand with your bare hands, I don't think they have to call you 'Serene Highness' anymore."

"Speaking of the girls, where's Augie and Bea?" Eden asked, deftly changing the subject.

"Ah, they will be right back. There was a little issue with Augie's mascara and Bea went to help her fix it."

"This walkway is marvelous. I can't believe we're standing so close to the lava and not getting singed!" Eden remarked.

"Can you believe this was all built just two hours ago? My brah Rufus deserves all the credit for this genius idea," Max said, rubbing Rufus's shoulders affectionately.

Rufus gave a bashful grin. "I thought, why not turn bad luck into good? It's not every day that an eruption occurs at a wedding site, so let's have everyone enjoy the experience!"

"Spectacular idea," Thomas complimented him.

"Yes, I wonder what the spectacular bill is going to be," Francis muttered under his breath to Thomas.

Just then, a phalanx of guests arrived, each one of them blonder than the next. Max grabbed Eden's hand eagerly. "Here comes my family. Eden, you must meet my father. He's also a big *Ozark* fan and I'm sure he will want to talk to you about it."

Eden dutifully went to meet Prince Julius and was in the midst of debating whether Wendy Byrde could possibly have borderline personality disorder when Arabella swooped in to monopolize his royal attention. She waded through the crowd, recognizing almost no one except for someone she thought looked like a famous supermodel. Based on the caliber of jewelry and incredible fashion parade before her, Eden was rather glad that she had chosen to "go glam," as Bea had advised, wearing a cream off-the-shoulder taffeta faille dress with green roses by Emilia Wickstead and borrowing a pair of pearl drop earrings from Bea.

Augusta and Bea finally returned to the receiving line, but before Eden could properly greet the girls, Max gleefully announced, "Okay, we are all here now. Everyone, we have a very special treat. My guru Gopal Das—the man I credit with saving my life by introducing me to the wonders of psilocybin—has agreed to honor us with a welcome blessing!"

"What? Who?" Arabella turned around, recoiling at the sight of the man with a bushy red beard braided down the middle. Who was this ridiculous pirate creature in a sapphire-blue turban and matching Nehru jacket over silk patchwork pants that looked suspiciously like pajama bottoms?

Gopal Das took command of the mic and began to speak in a deep, booming voice:

"Beautiful souls, I bid you aloha! Now, I realize there are many honored guests and great dignitaries among us tonight—counts and countesses, princes and princesses, Miss Kate Moss, kings and queens. But here on this island, we are all mere mortals who must all bow down before the real queen—Pele, the one true goddess. It is said that Pele resides at the summit of Kilauea and exerts her power over everything on these islands. We are all standing on the vagina of our planet, as it births fresh new land right before our very eyes in the form of this beautiful molten lava flowing below us. This island is literally growing in size every day, like a teenager in puberty watching her titties swell . . ."

Arabella craned her neck trying to make eye contact with Jackie the wedding planner but could find her nowhere. Who was this long-winded fool? She took out her phone and began texting frantically:

AG: WHO IS THIS MADMAN? MAKE HIM STOP NOW.

JZ: Sorry, can't.

AG: TURN OFF HIS MIC!!!!

JZ: He never turned it on.

Gopal Das continued: "Everything here is fresh and fecund. The flora and the fauna, the guavas and the macadamias, the lizards and the mongeese.* Now, I invite you to join me in a moment's meditation. Close your eyes and take a deep, slow breath. Breathe innnnnnnnnn . . . and out, allowing the oxygen to flow through you all the way to the tips of your toes. Do you smell that? What you smell is the freshest air on earth, the freshest air on this virgin land. Let us give thanks to Pele and to the people of Hawaii for allowing us to be here today in this special place. Now, a warning to you all. The sea here must be respected. It is fierce, it is fickle, it can change within moments. Before you step into the ocean, open your eyes and look around you. If you don't see anybody swimming or surfing or frolicking in the water, *there is a reason*. I've seen Olympic swimmers get sucked out to sea and then battered against the rocks by giant waves until their bodies shattered like lightbulbs. There are no lifeguards on most beaches—Pamela Anderson is not going to come running out in a red bikini and rescue you if you get caught in a riptide."

Arabella decided she'd heard enough. She marched up to Gopal Das and was about to grab the microphone out of his hands when he suddenly enveloped her in a powerful embrace, rendering her speechless. "Now, let us all give thanks to Mama Bear here, who I'm told moved mountains to make this magical evening possible."

The crowd began clapping, and Arabella, still trapped in the arms of Gopal Das, smiled uncomfortably. The guru looked her in the eyes and said softly, "You are a beautiful woman. Why don't you let your inner beauty shine? There is nothing to fear. Have trust and patience, and all will be good."

---

* *Who knew that the mongoose has overrun the Hawaiian Islands?*

Arabella glared at him as he released her. "Now, as we celebrate the love of Maxxie and Augusta, I leave you with two simple thoughts: Love this Earth. Love one another. Namaste."

"Namaste," the guests chanted back.

Augusta turned to her mother with tears in her eyes. "Wasn't that just beautiful?"

Arabella stared at her blankly, still too incensed to speak. As the guests began to disperse, Francis turned to Arabella, knowing all too well how she was truly feeling. "You all right?"

"Where were you when I needed you?"

"Standing right behind you," Francis replied calmly.

"I want that odious man arrested right now!"

"You want him arrested for what?"

"For hugging me!"

"Well, he's hugging Princess Hanne Marit of Liechtenburg right now. Do you think she'll want him arrested too?"

Arabella was about to answer when she noticed something in the distance. "Wait a minute. That's Olimpia de Courcy! When did she get here? I've been on the lookout for the de Courcys all evening."

"The de Courcys got here in the middle of the blessing," Jackie said as she arrived breathlessly at Arabella's side.

"And the princess of Thailand?"

"Her Royal Highness's jet got diverted to Maui. Oprah invited her to a luau."

"Oprah stole my princess! If Olimpia is over there, then where's Solène?" Arabella murmured anxiously. "Bea! Bea!"

Bea, who had been chatting with a strapping young man, came rushing over to her mother. "What's wrong? Are you okay?"

"What happened to Solène de Courcy? Did she not make it?"

"Relax, Mum, she's right over there!"

Arabella turned to where Bea was pointing and saw Solène standing on the beach in a wispy golden chiffon dress, chatting with Rufus as the wind blew her honey-blond tresses like a modern-day Bardot. Her heart soared. "Don't they look marvelous together?"

"They do. I made Rufus bring her champagne," Bea noted.

"Well done. Are sparks flying?"

"Like Guy Fawkes Day."

"Thank god!" Arabella sighed in satisfaction.

A rumble echoed through the cliffs, and the most eye-catching boat suddenly roared around the cove. Everyone gaped as the 118 WallyPower boat pulled up at the jetty by the beach, its sharp metallic prow and black-tinted windows resembling an invading spacecraft. An extremely ripped and tan young man with a baby face offset by an incongruously chiseled jawline emerged from the cabin and jumped onto the dock in his bare feet, holding a pair of blue suede Corthay loafers in his hands. The photographers snapped away as he slipped on his shoes and strode down the jetty in his double-breasted navy jacket, skinny white jeans, and blue-tinted sunglasses.

"Who is *that*?" Eden asked.

"Freddy Farman-Farmihian," Bea replied, giving Eden a little nudge. "Our secret weapon!"

IV

Kohala Coast

Bea sped along Queen Kaʻahumanu Highway in a BMW 4 Series convertible as Eden tried to read the text on Bea's phone for her.

"It's from your mother," Eden reported.

Bea groaned. "Twentieth text this morning. Go on."

" 'British *Vogue* has added another photo shoot before the ceremony. This means you will need to switch to another designer for the beach shoot, and I am insisting to Edward that they fly in more options for you. We've already reserved the Chanel for *Vogue* Hong Kong, the Oscar for American *Vogue,* and the Schiaparelli for *Bazaar.* You CANNOT'—she put that in all caps—'wear the Giamba in photos, as it makes you look too fat. Please also stop eating and keep liquids to a minimum until after the wedding.' Bea, this is absurd."

"Which part?" Bea snorted as Eden continued reading aloud.

" 'You are also getting too much sun and people will think you are a peasant. Please do not expose yourself to any sunlight today—' "

"How am I supposed to do that? We're going out on a boat!" Bea protested.

"Mind if I stop? The text goes on and on and I'm feeling a bit sick reading off your phone." Eden closed her eyes, trying to enjoy the feel of the sun on her face and the cool breeze in her hair, but it wasn't working. She felt miserably hungover from the previous evening. After sunset cocktails at the lava-viewing platform, the party had moved into a magnificent inner courtyard with four reflecting pools where an eight-course banquet commenced, and Eden had fallen victim to the exquisite wine pairings.

"I can't believe you got plastered last night! I didn't think you drank that much," Bea remarked.

"It crept up on me—I don't have your hollow leg."

"Well, I had too much myself, but I couldn't resist. Every wine was paired perfectly with Heston's menu, didn't you think? Mummy was fretting about the wines meeting the standards of our royal guests, especially the de Courcys."

"Hopefully my hangover will be worth it if it impressed the de Courcys. But why wasn't Rufus seated next to Solène?"

"Not on the first night, darling. We've got to make him work for it! We made sure Rufus was seated at the table directly facing her. Did you notice we placed Solène right under those enormous lanterns, so the glowing light would glint perfectly off her hair?"

"She looked like an angel. Even I couldn't stop staring at her all night!"

"Hopefully Rufus couldn't stop staring either. Today he'll finally get to spend a bit of time with her, but we're going to complicate things for him by adding Freddy to the mix."

"I still don't understand exactly how this Freddy fellow's the secret weapon."

"Freddy Farman-Farmihian has been head-over-heels in love with Solène ever since he spent a semester abroad in Paris. Absolutely obsessed. Back then he was too shy to even whisper in her direction. He was a bit on the pudgy side, but as you can see he's completely transformed himself. That's a very expensive new face he's got there."

"Really? I did think there was something a bit off about the way he looked. I just assumed it was the Joey Essex eyebrows."

"No, everything's new—the nose, the cheekbones, and the jawline. It's apparently what every guy does in LA, along with bottom bleaching and Mounjaro injections. It's all a bit too perfect for me, but I will admit he has gained a great deal of confidence along with all that muscle mass."

"So why is he here if he's after Solène?"

"Tell me, what makes a woman absolutely irresistible to a man?"

"I can't begin to fathom . . ."

"Competition."

"So you think giving Rufus some competition will egg him on?"

"Eden, you know my brother. He's a lovely lad but he's not a very complicated soul."

Eden was about to protest, but Bea continued expounding: "Rufus is like a well-bred hound. He's a regal, silky borzoi. Put a fox in front of him, and he might sniff it out of curiosity and play with it for a moment. Now, put him with another hound, say, an eager beagle like Freddy, and they will chase the fox to their deaths."

"But what if your plan backfires and the eager beagle wins the chase?"

"Solène doesn't like beagles. She wants a borzoi. Trust me, I shared a flat with her in Paris for a year. I know what kinds of dogs she's into."

They pulled up at the driveway entrance of the Mauna Lani hotel, expecting to find Solène waiting.

"That girl is always late," Bea groaned. "Can you please go get her?"

Eden jumped out of the car and wandered into the sleek lobby, a huge open-air atrium dominated by a dark reflecting pool and a vintage wood outrigger canoe. She saw Solène strolling down a breezeway, the very picture of St. Tropez chic in a long white sarong skirt and a navy and white striped bandeau top that exposed her splendidly toned and bronzed midriff. She wore a huge straw hat and held a matching oversized straw tote bag that even from thirty feet away looked hideously expensive.

Eden waved at her. "Solène! Hi, I'm Eden. Bea's waiting in the car."

Solène (Marymount Neuilly/Ecole Jeannine Manuel/Sorbonne/ AUP) gave her a startled look. "What?"

"I'm here to collect you. For Lady Beatrice Gresham?" Eden said, realizing that they had not met the previous night.

"Ah, *Béatrissssssse*," Solène said in a deep, gravelly voice, over-emphasizing Bea's name in the French manner as she nonchalantly shoved her expensive tote into Eden's hands. Eden smiled at her, a bit confused, but accepted the heavy straw bag stuffed with several pairs of shoes, three big bottles of San Pellegrino, and what seemed like half a closet's worth of outfits.

"How's the hotel?" Eden asked as they headed toward the entrance.

Solène frowned, giving her a curious look. "It's okay. I need more towels."

They reached the car and Solène jumped eagerly into the front passenger seat as Eden handed her the tote.

"Put it in the back," Solène said.

"Solène!" Bea greeted her friend with a quick peck on the cheek. "Wait, you have to get out for a minute so Eden can get in."

"Ah, she's coming with us?" Solène frowned again.

"Of course. We're going to need her help," Bea said.

Solène got out of her seat, allowing Eden to jump into the backseat of the convertible. As they drove out of the resort and down a road that circled a golf course, Solène turned to Bea with a mischievous grin. "So . . . who was that guy you were chatting up all night?"

"Which guy?"

"Don't play dumb with me. The *comment dit-on* . . . fit bloke."

"Oh, Josh. He's the water sports director at the resort. He's not just some fit bloke, you know, he's a Rhodes scholar that used to play for a professional football team. I recruited him for my swimwear photo shoot with British *Vogue*. He's going to be rowing me in one of those antique outrigger canoes."

"And rowing right into your bedroom after that!"

"Oh stop, Solène! Now, did you have a good time last night?"

"I would have had a better time if I had been seated next to your brother. I know what you're doing, Béatrice—you're trying to drive me crazy!"

"Nonsense! We had to seat everyone by order of precedence. Rufus is only a viscount, so he cannot be seated at a table with a *princesse*," Bea said, lying through her teeth.

"So why was I seated next to Nicolai Chalamet-Chaude? He's only a baron.* I had to endure all his relentless name-dropping while your brother stared at me all night."

Bea cackled, glancing in the rearview mirror at Eden. "Eden, do you remember what you said the first time you met Nicolai at Glorious Twelfth?"

"I said I couldn't stop thinking of peaches every time I heard his name," Eden deadpanned.

A look of alarm suddenly flashed on Solène's face. "Wait a minute. You two are *friends*?"

"Of course! Did you two not meet last night? Solène, this is Eden. Remember I told you about her?"

Solène put a hand to her mouth as she stared at Eden. "Oh fuck! I thought you worked at the hotel. I thought you were the maid!"

Bea stared at Eden, not sure whether to laugh or to be appalled. She supposed that in her simple white piqué shirt and khaki shorts, Eden could be mistaken for being on the housekeeping staff at a tropical resort.

Solène continued to apologize. "I'm so sorry! You must think I'm some crazy bitch, making you carry my tote!"

Eden laughed it off lightly. "Don't even think about it for another second. I was happy to help."

They soon arrived at the marina, where Rufus could be seen at the far end of the small parking lot leaning against his Jeep. Bea pulled up right next to Rufus. "Where's Freddy? I thought you were giving him a ride."

"Change of plans. When Freddy realized we were going whale watching on a fishing boat, he insisted that we take his Walrus or whatever that thing is called."

"But what about our whale guide?"

---

* In the British peerage, the order of rank goes: monarch > prince/princess > duke/ duchess > marquess/marchioness > earl/countess > viscount/viscountess > baron/ baroness. Where do you rank and what sort of feelings does this bring up?

"He's picking the whale guide up from Honokohau Marina and they should be here any minute now."

No sooner had Rufus said this than a now-familiar roar filled the air and Freddy's fantastical boat pulled up to the dock. As everyone climbed on board, a pair of dark-tinted glass doors automatically opened, revealing a sleek, Zenlike interior cabin where Freddy (CEE/Crossroads/NYU/Pepperdine), dressed in a pale beige cashmere sweater over a white linen shirt and pleated linen trousers, lounged like a pasha on plush white cashmere cushions. Beside him sat a brunette with a mass of pretty curls in a chic vintage floral-print maxi dress, and arrayed before them on the Ipe wood floor was a massive clamshell piled high with tropical fruits, champagne, oysters, and caviar.

"Welcome aboard *Babyshark*!" Freddy said with a huge toothy grin. He jumped up from his cushioned seat and extended his arms in a clumsy attempt to give Solène a hug and a double-cheeked kiss at the same time. He gestured to the open seat next to him, but Solène hovered about for a moment and then chose to sit next to Rufus.

Freddy grinned through his disappointment. "Everyone, make yourselves comfortable. *Mi barco es su barco.* And meet Laurel, world-famous author and cetologist. A cetologist is a whale biologist, I've just learned."

Bea gushed, "Freddy, this boat is incredible. It's so much bigger up close!"

"That's what she said. Heh heh. *Babyshark* has all the comforts of a luxury superyacht, but really, it's a high-performance sporting boat. Wait till you see her go." Freddy shouted toward the cockpit, where the captain stood ready. "Hey, Captain Lee,* are we ready to go hunt Moby-Dick?"

Laurel (Balboa/Thacher/Cornell/MIT) winced. "We're not hunt-

---

* *Yes, it's that Captain Lee, taking a little break from the Caribbean, incompetent deckhands, psychotic chefs, and chief stews who will never be as good as Kate Chastain.*

ing whales, Mr. Farman-Farmihian. Not today or any other day. We're going to observe these magnificent creatures that have traveled three thousand miles from Alaska to spend the winter in our tropical waters."

"Of course, of course. No one's gonna hurt Shamu while he's on vacay. Captain Lee, let's get the show on the road. *Ándale, ándale!* Everyone, grab a seat and hold on tight. This beast takes off like the *Millennium Falcon*," Freddy warned. The boat taxied out of the dock slowly, gliding on the water smoothly, and then without warning took off at what seemed like warp speed, the G-force sending the caviar dish flying right into Solène's lap.

Solène reflexively brushed the tiny black eggs off with her hand but immediately smeared them all over her linen skirt. *"Merde!"* she cursed.

"Captain Lee, slow down! We have a caviar incident!" Freddy shouted, not wanting anything to upset Solène. He rushed over and began wiping her skirt frantically with his napkin while eyeing her beautifully bronzed legs.

"You're making it worse," Solène said.

"Oh, sorry. Where's the damn deckhand? Bruno! Go grab some towels in the can downstairs."

"I'll get one," Rufus offered, getting up as a uniformed deckhand came rushing in.

"No, please stay. I can go myself," Solène said as she pulled away from Freddy and quickly ducked downstairs.

"It's a good thing we slowed down. We're coming to the whales' winter feeding grounds, and we don't want to cause too much of a disturbance around them," Laurel said.

"No, of course not. We don't want *Babyshark* to scare them," Freddy said earnestly.

"I don't think we're going to scare any whales today. I think a young calf could probably capsize this boat with a flick of its tail," Rufus laughed.

Bea clutched her cushion as she looked at Laurel with huge eyes. "Is that really possible?"

"Whales have been known to capsize boats, but you know, they are incredibly intelligent creatures. They use their own biosonar system to locate prey, so they can recognize other objects around them. Any incidents with boats are extremely rare," Laurel explained.

"Good, because if we're going to be capsized I've brought the wrong handbag," Bea said as she cradled her Maison Halaby Hydra bag like a baby.

Eden was beginning to feel intensely queasy from the boat rocking against the choppy waves. She was wondering whether she might need to dash to the loo herself when Solène returned to the main deck looking pristine again.

"Are you okay? How's the dress?" Freddy asked solicitously.

"Everything's fine," Solène said with a smile. "I love your Richter."

"Actually this is a WallyPower 118," Freddy replied.

"No, I meant the painting in the toilet—isn't that a Gerhard Richter?"

"Uh, probably. My art consultant put it there."

"Ah, so you are collecting these days?"

"I am! Love being a collector, love going to all the parties—Frieze, Felix, TEFAF, FIAC, Art Basel Basel, but of course my favorite is Art Basel Miami."

Bea glanced at Solène. "Didn't you just have a big show in Miami?"

"She sure did! I bought one of her paintings," Freddy proudly declared.

Solène looked surprised. "Did you really? Which one?"

"Just Shut Up and Blow Me."

"That's a bit rude, Freddy!" Bea scolded.

"No, no, that's the name of her painting," Freddy explained.

Solène nodded. "Yes, it is part of my latest series. It's my examination of toxic masculinity, based on actual words my exes would say to me."

"I almost bought *It's Your Fault I Came Too Fast*," Freddy added.

"I think some museum in Texas acquired *It's Your Fault I Came Too Fast* for their permanent collection," Solène noted.

"Congratulations. It's a super painting," Freddy said as Solène ignored his compliment and addressed Rufus.

"Rufus, your sister tells me you went to art school. What is your art like?"

"I utilize nineteenth-century photo techniques to document climate change in this century. Right now I'm working on a series of platinum prints that explore tidal patterns and beach erosion."

"I'd love to see your work. Who are your galleries?"

"I don't have one," Rufus replied.

"Oh. Are you between galleries?"

"No. I . . . uh . . . I've been in a few group shows but I've never had representation from a gallery."

Solène looked incredulous. "You must let me introduce you to my dealers! Emmanuel, maybe, I'm sure he'd love to give the Vicomte St. Ives a show."

Eden could sense Rufus's discomfort and attempted to change the subject. She noticed a distinctive spray shoot out from the water in the near distance and blurted out, "Look! Isn't that a whale?" Everyone turned to stare where she was pointing.

"Yes! It's a humpback! Do you see the blowhole?" Laurel said. "Let's go outside to get a better look."

As everyone emerged from the cabin, an immense whale could be seen gliding past them barely under the surface of the water.

"That thing is gigantic!" Bea exclaimed.

"That's what she said," Freddy said, giggling again at his tired joke while the others rolled their eyes.

"It's just a calf, isn't it, Laurel? I'd reckon it's about fifteen feet?" Rufus asked.

"Yeah, that's still a calf. If we're lucky maybe we'll spot the mother."

"It's so silent. How can they be so gigantic and yet so quiet?" Eden observed.

"It's quiet for now. You should listen to their beautiful, haunting songs sometime," Laurel said. A moment later, another, much larger whale burst out of the water and breached twenty feet into the air, splashing everyone on the boat. "It's the mother!" Laurel shouted ecstatically.

The waves from the whale's breaching rocked the boat violently, and Eden could feel herself turning green. She sat down in a corner, taking deep breaths as she tried to hold it all in.

"You guys have no idea how lucky you are today to see a breaching up close! And a mother with her calf! You know, to the native Hawaiians, the whale is the natural incarnation of the Hawaiian god Kanaloa, the god of all ocean life," Laurel breathlessly explained.

Suddenly, Eden began to retch uncontrollably. Knowing she wouldn't be able to make it downstairs in time, she leaned off the side of the boat and proceeded to be sick. Rufus darted to her side and held her steady.

Freddy sprang into action as though he was in competition with Rufus. He hadn't exchanged a single word with Eden the entire morning, but now he knelt down beside her and began patting her back rapidly.

"I don't think that's really helping . . . ," Rufus interjected.

"Are you going to be okay? You want some ginger ale? Dramamine, maybe?" Freddy asked anxiously.

Eden glanced up for a moment, and before she could help herself, another wave of nausea overcame her and she spewed a torrent of vomit all over Freddy.

"Bloody hell!" Bea burst into uncontrollable giggles. Freddy froze, too stunned to react.

"Sorry . . . so sorry," Eden cried as she coughed.

"It's okay, it's okay. This is last season's Cucinelli," Freddy said as he ripped off his sweater and flung it into the ocean.

"Great move. Now some turtle's going to choke on ten-ply cashmere," Laurel grumbled under her breath.

Rufus stood up and shouted toward the captain. "Captain Lee, we need to head back to shore immediately."

"Sure. The nearest marina is by the Four Seasons Hualalai," the captain answered.

"Perfect. Let's get to the resort so Eden can convalesce," Freddy said. "Eden, you must convalesce."

Solène had watched the entire scene unfold with increasing irritation. She couldn't fathom why Rufus and Freddy were paying so much attention to a girl who dressed like a deckhand. "I need some champagne," she declared. "Who wants some champagne?"

V

Hale I'a Da Fish House

WAIMEA, HAWAII • *LUNCHTIME*

Dr. Tong arrived at a modest wooden building painted bright blue with white trim and walked up a little slope toward the queue of customers standing in the blazing sun by the outdoor counter.

"Tom! Over here!" Thomas turned to see Francis waving at him from across the parking lot. He smiled at the sight of the Earl of Greshamsbury incongruously dressed in perfectly pressed ruby-red corduroy trousers and a pale blue Ede & Ravenscroft Sea Island cotton shirt rolled up to the elbows, sitting at a table under a plastic tarp that had been strung up between makeshift poles. He knew there was nothing Francis liked more than finding little out-of-the-way places like this.

Francis gestured to the sweating bottles of beer and takeaway plastic bento boxes on the table. "I went ahead and ordered us the catch of the day. They have the freshest fish in the world here."

Thomas removed the lid of his bento box to reveal delicious-looking grilled mahi mahi along with a heaping portion of wasabi pistachio poke and crab salad over rice.

"Hurrah! I was craving rice today!" Thomas happily remarked. "But what's this—a brown and white rice mix?"

"Yes, they call it hapa rice here. Isn't that funny?" Francis remarked as he took his first mouthful. "I should take a picture of the menu board for my hapa kids."

"How in the world did you find this spot?" Thomas said as he dug into the deliciously spicy poke while looking out at the view of the ocean in the distance.

"Stumbled on it a few years ago when I was hunting for a quiet beach. Now it's become my go-to hideaway—it's the last place on earth Arabella would ever look for me."

"Can't picture her here," Thomas chuckled as an inquisitive hen wandered under the table and began pecking at something by his feet. "Especially after the remarkable feat she pulled off last night at the welcome party."

Francis grimaced, taking a swig of his beer. "That's the problem. I'm afraid to know what she's spending to restage this entire wedding. Might you, ah, see if your old friend might throw me a line?"

Thomas stared at Francis in surprise. Any mention of the "old friend" always jarred him at first. "Another one? On top of what you've already borrowed this year?"

Francis nodded cautiously.

"I don't know . . . how much would you need?"

"Oh, I don't know. Ten or twenty, maybe? It's pennies for him."

"What happened to the twenty million you got three months ago?"

"Half of it went toward paying off capital calls. The other half went toward this bloody wedding. I have no idea how we're going to pay the next bill," Francis said wearily.

"Francis, you've got to rein her in," Thomas pleaded, even though he knew it was rather pointless to say it.

"I know, I know. Perhaps there's something he might want from me . . . ?"

"On top of what he already has? I don't think he would take kindly to providing another infusion so soon. It sends a bad signal. Besides, he already owns too much of your assets. I've purposely structured the deal so that you can maintain some autonomy."

Francis gave his friend a weary smile. "Yes, I'm very grateful for the terms you were able to negotiate for me. Truly."

Thomas smiled back, even though his eyes couldn't hide his dismay. He was the only person in the world who had the full picture of the earl's finances, and he wished he'd never been made aware of them. No one had any inkling that behind all the magazine features and Instagram stories of the glamorous Greshams—luxuriating in couture at their swoon-worthy manor, glistening with golden tans aboard their antique black-sailed yacht in the Ionian Sea—rose a gargantuan mountain of debt.

Decades of profligate spending by previous earls had all but depleted the ancient Gresham trusts by the time Francis had succeeded to the earldom, and Arabella's extravagant ambitions to expand her empire only made things worse. With the hotels mortgaged to the hilt and every line of credit from his various bankers nearly exhausted, Francis had several years back confessed everything to Thomas in a moment of desperation, hoping his friend might know of someone, anyone, who could throw him a lifeline. And Thomas had actually succeeded against all odds in convincing Rene Tan—the exceedingly wealthy and obsessively private billionaire from the Philippines—to loan Francis the staggering amounts that would stave off the banks. But that had meant mortgaging more and more parcels of land on the once-great Greshamsbury estate, and now there was precious little to offer as collateral aside from the Big House itself.

The two friends sat in silence, Francis scooping out the last bits of rice. Thomas looked up for a moment and saw a jet streak across the cloudless blue sky. He thought of the dozens of aristocratic and glamorous names that were about to descend on the island for the wedding of the year.

"Isn't there someone on the guest list you could approach for a loan? Hasn't Arabella invited a dozen billionaires?"

"You know I've never been comfortable talking about money with anyone, and none of those people are really the sort I'd ever hit up."

"So naturally you are spending millions of pounds to entertain them all week."

"Naturally," Francis said with a wry smile.

"Is Arabella's brother out of the question? Peter was rather nice to lend us his plane for the ride over."

"Peter loves to lend his fleet—I'm told it actually saves him money
to keep all his planes constantly moving. But Arabella would rip her
own tongue out and feed it to herself before ever asking her brother
for a cent."

"How about your Norwegian soon-to-be relatives? Don't they
own all the oil in the North Sea?"

"That's an idea! The Norwegians are a generous bunch, aren't
they? Perhaps Max's parents will take pity on me now that we're
going to be kin."

"Let's drink to that." Thomas raised his bottle of beer hopefully.

Francis clinked his bottle against his old chum's. *"Skål!"*

After the friends parted, Thomas's Uber was ferrying him back
to his hotel when he noticed something on the hilltop overlooking
the ocean.

"Is that an old fort over there?" Thomas asked the driver.

"That's Pu'ukohola Heiau, the temple built by King Kamehameha. It's a very sacred place for Hawaiians," the driver replied.

"Can one get close to it?"

"You can walk right up to it. There's also a smaller temple that's
now submerged in Pelekane Bay where Kamehameha used to sit and
watch the sharks, so the legend goes."

"Really? A submerged temple?"

"Yes. It used to sit at the water's edge, but thanks to rising water
levels, it hasn't been seen since the 1950s. You wanna take a look-see?"

"Sure."

"You know, in all my years driving, you're the first person that's
ever wanted to go there."

"I suppose most people who visit the Big Island just want to enjoy
the beach."

"They don't ever leave their resorts, or if they do they just want to
go to the Tommy Bahama restaurant."

The car turned off Kawaihae Road onto a narrow road that led to
a newish-looking visitor's center. "Take your time, and don't go into
the water in the bay unless you want to be shark food," the driver
quipped.

"I'll try my best not to." Thomas headed into the visitor's center to get a quick lay of the land before walking up the hill to the temple. He strolled around the perimeter, marveling at the meticulously arranged stones used to create the structure. There was something about the place that reminded him of the ancient stone circles that could be found throughout the countryside in Devon.

Following the winding path through a meadow of beach grass that shimmered gold in the sunlight, he came to a point overlooking the small bay. Although nothing could be seen in the water and gentle waves lapped invitingly onto the picturesque little beach, a sign read:

WARNING: Although sharks usually avoid shallow water in bright sunlight, their frequent presence in this bay has been observed for centuries. Their dorsal fins (primarily of black-tipped reef sharks) are often seen from here. Please don't wade or swim in these waters.

Thomas tried to imagine what it had been like in the early 1800s for King Kamehameha to sit atop his thronelike temple at the water's edge, surveying the island and all the islands beyond that he had conquered. Something flashed in the ocean, and for a moment Thomas thought he saw the fin of a shark glinting in the water. He knew it was a myth that sharks were naturally violent, just like it was a myth that sharks never got cancer. Because of this, so many cancer patients around the world believed that taking shark cartilage supplements would cure them, and Thomas had to constantly tell patients that they were wasting their money.

His mind suddenly wandered back to Rene Tan, the man who had battled his own demons and conquered the global construction industry, but who was now in the battle of his life, quite literally.

For the past four years, Rene had been fighting pancreatic cancer—a disease with one of the lowest survival rates—and it was a miracle he was even still alive. Last autumn, with cancer metastasizing throughout Rene's body, Thomas had made a last-ditch effort on behalf of his old friend. He'd had Rene secretly flown on a medical transport jet to Houston.

Thomas had done his oncology fellowship at MD Anderson Cancer Center and knew of the pioneering treatments that were done there—it was consistently rated the top cancer center in the world, the place that celebrities, royals, heads of state, and the most desperately ill patients would flock to hoping for miraculous cures. Five months later, Rene remained in Houston undergoing an experimental clinical trial. It was the real reason why Thomas didn't want to approach him for another loan on behalf of the Greshams. In the best of times, Rene was a mercurial and unpredictable soul, but now he was downright dangerous. Just like one shouldn't disturb the sharks in the water, Thomas didn't wish to rattle a man who was staring his mortality squarely in the face, desperately chasing his own myths.

VI

Four Seasons Resort Hualalai

BIG ISLAND, HAWAII • LATER THAT AFTERNOON

The dream was always the same. She was six, maybe seven years old. Her mother, dressed in a white Lacoste piqué polo and a flared tennis skirt, would come into the room and ask her, "I'm going to the supermarket. Do you want to come on a walk with me?" Eden would shake her head. Minutes after her mother had left the house, Eden would miss her terribly and decide to run after her. She would run out the door of the redbrick house and down a long hill, chasing the figure in white at the end of the road. But for some reason she could never catch up with her mother. She would run and run, her heart pounding so fast she could barely breathe, but the figure in white only got smaller and smaller.

Eden suddenly awoke, out of breath and drenched in sweat. She was someplace unfamiliar, and the bed felt like a big puffy cloud. Was this still a dream? As her vision came into focus, she noticed a very stylish midcentury modern lamp next to an equally stylish armchair accented with a marble and brushed bronze side table. She realized where she was—a luxuriously appointed suite at the Four Seasons resort, where she had been rushed to in the moment of her distress. She vaguely remembered someone carrying her into the room and drawing the curtains . . . was it Rufus? She rose from the bed reluctantly and went into the huge marble bathroom to splash some water on her face. Feeling a bit more refreshed, she entered the suite's living room to find her father sitting on a leather club chair flipping through a magazine.

"How's the patient?" he asked.

"Much better, oddly enough," Eden said, sinking into the curved sofa across from him. "How long was I out?"

"Three or four hours, I'd imagine. I only got here half an hour ago. I was having lunch with Francis."

"You really needn't have come . . ."

Thomas ignored her, leaning over to examine her pupils. "Any headache or nausea?"

"Not anymore. I'm fine, Dad, I got seasick, that's all. And being hungover and jet-lagged didn't help."

Thomas placed a hand on her cheek to feel her temperature. "You could have had heatstroke. Most people don't realize they have heatstroke until it's too late."

"Dr. Tong, in case you forgot, I am a qualified doctor too."

"Doctors make the worst patients—you especially," Thomas chided as he walked over to the bar, opened the minifridge behind the wenge wood cabinet, and took out a bottle of water. He retrieved a small packet of electrolytes from his pocket and mixed it with water in a tall glass. He handed the foaming elixir to Eden. "Here, drink. You need to replenish your system."

"Thanks," Eden said, gulping down the drink. "Dad, did Mum ever play tennis?"

"Tennis? I don't think so . . . why?"

"I keep seeing her in my dreams, and she's wearing either a sparkly silver ball gown or a white tennis outfit."

"Hmm. I don't recall her having either, but she could have played tennis in her younger days. Or maybe badminton, which was quite popular in Hong Kong in the early nineties," Thomas mused as he slid open the wooden slatted doors to reveal a large balcony.

"So this is how the other half live. Whose room are we in?" Eden asked as she wandered onto the balcony and took in the view of the infinity pool surrounded by white tented cabanas and the pristine beach beyond.

"I assumed it's Bea's. She was the one who let me in. By the way, speaking of sparkly dresses, wait till you see the dress Bea dropped off for tonight's festivities. Only if you're feeling up to it, of course."

"What's happening tonight? I can't keep track of all the events."

"Rosina is hosting a fancy-dress party in honor of Prince Max's parents."

Eden raised an eyebrow. "The great and glorious *Rosina Leung* actually deigned to host a party that's not in honor of herself?"

Thomas grinned. "We mustn't miss out on this historic event."

"Indeed. Where's my costume?"

"It's hanging in the coat closet by the foyer."

Eden fetched the bulky garment bag and unzipped it, staring at its contents in confusion. There was a shimmering ice-blue evening gown complemented by a turquoise faux-fur coat. "A fur coat? Bea's out of her mind . . ."

"From what I understand, you're going to need that tonight," Thomas said. "We're about to go from sea level to an altitude of fourteen thousand feet!"*

---

* *The Big Island of Hawaii is the only island on Earth to possess ten of the world's fourteen climate zones. This means you can sunbathe in the morning on a sizzling-hot beach in Kona, head to the Waimea Valley for a fog-bound lunch reminiscent of the Scottish Highlands, go hiking through the humid Puna rain forest in an afternoon downpour, and freeze your ass off on the summit of Mauna Kea at sunset.*

MR. & MRS. PETER LEUNG

REQUEST THE PRESENCE OF YOUR COMPANY AT

The Winter Ball

IN HONOR OF THEIR SERENE HIGHNESSES

Prince Julius &
Princess Hanne Marit
Zu Liechtenburg

TIME: 6:00PM

LOCATION: THE WINTER LODGE ON MAUNA KEA

DRESS: IMPERIAL NORWEGIAN COURT, TIARAS OPTIONAL

Shuttle buses will depart promptly from designated hotels at 5:00pm

**Please dress warmly for subarctic temperatures*

VII

Mauna Kea Volcano

BIG ISLAND, HAWAII • *THE WINTER BALL*

All of the titled tons and international who's whos knew that Rosina Leung's wedding-eve ball was not to be missed, the social event that perhaps superseded the wedding itself. Augie's aunt—the formidable wife of the eye-wateringly wealthy Peter Leung—was famous for her legendary parties, and the luxury shuttle bus that transported Drs. Thomas Tong and Eden Tong to the summit of Mauna Kea, the dormant volcanic mountain that loomed over the Big Island, included three lords, two dukes, one polo-playing maharaja, one hereditary grand duchess, one Malaysian tin-mining heiress, a former head of the International Monetary Fund, a Nobel laureate, a couple that owned most of Uttar Pradesh, and a Pritzker-prize-winning architect, all of whom were rendered speechless when they disembarked from the bus and found themselves in a freezing lunar landscape of undulating bare red hills high above the cloud line.

But it wasn't just the otherworldly majesty of being on top of a volcano that stunned them—it was the sight of the enormous sparkling palace carved entirely out of ice that loomed before them, its dramatic triple naves and carved dragon heads a replica of the Borgund Stave Church* in Norway.

---

* *This iconic Norwegian stave church was also the inspiration for much of the architecture in Disney's* Frozen. *(Unbeknownst to even her children, Arabella would watch Disney musicals late at night during her bouts of insomnia. Rufus liked to think that his surf cabin had inspired his mother to open the resort in Hawaii, but actually, it was because of her secret love for* Moana.*)*

"My god, it's as if Vikings landed on the moon!" the famed architect decreed.

"Only Rosina could have thought of this!" the Malaysian heiress commented, her neck festooned with such humongous diamonds that Eden was seriously concerned the lady might throw her back out.

"Arabella must be furious to be outdone!" said the grand duchess, the dangling pearls on her tiara shaking back and forth as she giggled.

Arabella was anything but furious. The idea to create a majestic Nordic wonderland as a tribute to the groom's Norwegian and Liechtenburger relations had been all hers, and she was only too happy to let her sister-in-law write the check for the gargantuan expense. (The way Arabella saw it, Rosina was spending her brother's money—family money.) Now Arabella proudly held court at the majestic entrance arch of the ice palace in a deep-crimson velvet Schiaparelli couture gown with a dramatic Elizabethan collar of ostrich feathers.

Rosina (Maryknoll/Miss Porter's/Wellesley) stood alongside Arabella welcoming her guests, but unlike her sister-in-law, she was a study in subtlety, swathed in a white mink cape and an astonishing opera-length necklace composed of flawless matched twenty-millimeter pearls. Only the dozen or so women in the world privileged enough to own pearls of a comparable size would have any clue how near impossible it was to possess a necklace like this.*

A few steps away, looking at her aunt's gigantic mound of mink in great dismay, was Augusta, who wore an alpine-green winter coatdress made from recycled vintage Victorian brocades by Gary Graham, while Max sported a dashing dark navy nineteenth-century

---

* For reference, mere mortals can only dream of creating a strand of graduated sixteen-to-eighteen-millimeter pearls. To assemble an opera-length necklace (thirty-six inches) composed entirely of twenty-millimeter pearls would take decades and cost more than a beachfront pad in Malibu.

Norwegian naval uniform. As Thomas and Eden approached the receiving line, Augie, Bea, and Rufus immediately clustered around Eden in concern.

"Feeling better?" Rufus asked, hugging her gently as he stared at her face.

"I'm fine, it was just a little bout of seasickness," Eden said, not enjoying being fussed over.

Bea, who was resplendent in a vintage Lacroix mandarin-collared yellow silk dress and faux-fur-edged robe embroidered with blue dragons, hugged Eden in relief, while Augie gushed over Eden's ice-blue gown. "You've stolen the show, Eden! The color's absolutely perfect for tonight's setting! Bea, isn't this the dress Karl designed for you for the Venetian Heritage Ball a few years ago?"

"I think so," Bea said, slightly annoyed that her sister would so publicly call attention to the fact that Eden had borrowed her outfit.

Eden was too distracted anyway by Rufus's dramatically gothic costume of black mohair and leather to mind Augie's comment. "Is that some sort of Viking costume?" she asked.

Rufus flashed a naughty grin. "Not sure—I found it on Etsy."[*]

"Mother approved?"

"Definitely not. I've already been scolded."

Rosina nodded at Eden in a formal manner, as though she were meeting her for the first time, but then a spark of recognition ignited when she noticed Thomas coming up behind Eden. "Thomas! *Hou noi mou gin!*[†] My goodness, is this your Eden? I didn't recognize you at first! What a beauty you've become! She looks a bit like Maggie Cheung, don't you think, Thomas?"

"Does she?" Thomas said distractedly.

"Yes, she does. Exactly like Maggie in *Days of Being Wild*. How I remember the premiere like it was yesterday. Weren't you with us? The whole gang was there—Gabby, Edwin, Henry—" Rosina

---

[*] *It was a Jon Snow Halloween costume.*

[†] *"Long time no see!" in Cantonese.*

stopped midsentence, as if she realized she'd just said something inappropriate.

"I wasn't there. I was still in England then," Thomas replied flatly.

"Yes, of course you were," Rosina said, a strange look suddenly crossing her face as she stared intently at Eden. Eden wasn't sure what to make of Rosina's strange behavior, but she smiled graciously anyway as Thomas prodded her to keep moving down the receiving line.

"What was that all about?" Eden asked her father as soon as they were out of earshot.

"Rosina's just being Rosina," Thomas said. "She's always . . . how would you put it . . . a bit out to lunch?"

"I always forget that you were friends back in your Hong Kong days."

"She wasn't really my friend . . . she hung around with people I knew."

Father and daughter proceeded up the steps of the ice palace and came upon a banquet hall with three immensely long tables carved entirely out of ice, the frozen blocks filled with flowers and hauntingly lit so that the petals seemed suspended in space. Above the tables hovered six enormous crystal chandeliers lit with hundreds of candles, and the open archways at the far end of the palace perfectly framed the stupendous views. The sun had just dipped below the clouds, rendering the sky a deep violet that shimmered through the crystalline walls of the palace.

"We're so high up that you can see the curve of the horizon!" Eden exclaimed, glancing at her father and noticing that he suddenly appeared a bit pale. "Dad! Are you all right?" she said in alarm.

"Fine, fine. I think it's the sudden change in altitude, that's all," Thomas replied.

"Well, let's go find you your seat," Eden said, quickly leading him to his table. The seating was comprised of long ice benches, thankfully covered with faux-fur throws, and Thomas sat down gratefully. The centerpiece on his table was a replica of Brancusi's *Sleeping Muse* sculpture carved out of ice.

"Oh look! This sculpture must have been carved by Rufus's friend Kiana," Eden remarked.

"Marvelous," Thomas said. "Now, don't you worry one minute about me. I feel much better already."

"Are you sure?" Eden looked at him worriedly.

"Absolutely. Go find your seat and enjoy your dinner."

"I'll come check on you in a bit," Eden said.

Thomas breathed a sigh of relief as soon as Eden had left. Truth be told, it was not the altitude that had gotten to him, but the encounter with Rosina. Seeing her always jogged painful memories in his head that he tried so hard to keep buried. An elderly British lady took the seat next to him and peered at his place card dismissively. "Dr. Thomas Tong. What kind of doctor are you?"

"I'm an oncologist," Thomas answered, steeling himself all over again.

"Ah. My husband is the gynecologist to the queen," the lady sniffed.

·

As Eden sat admiring the ice-sculpture centerpiece of Louise Bourgeois's *Maman*, someone slipped into the chair next to her. She turned to see Freddy Farman-Farmihian grinning at her.

"You again! Do I need to go find a face shield?" Freddy joked.

"Depending on what's for dinner, it might be wise," Eden replied, thinking it was going to be a very long night with Freddy as her dinner partner. "I'm sorry again for what happened on your boat."

"Don't even think about it. I hope you were comfortable in your room at the Four Seasons."

"It's not my room."

"Of course it is! I booked it for you—thought you'd like to have the suite adjoining Bea's."

"*You* got me the room?" Eden said in surprise. "You really needn't have—"

"It was my pleasure."

"That's much too generous of you. I already have a place to stay in Puako."

"No, no, no. You getting sick was all my fault. Not everyone can handle being on *Babyshark*."

"No, your boat was fine. Incredible, actually. I'm just a bad sailor."

"Well, the room is paid for through the week whether you choose to stay there or not."

Just as Eden was about to continue protesting, the sound of heraldic trumpets echoed through the great hall. A dozen trumpeters dressed in full regalia entered, and then from both ends of the hall, hundreds of Nordic men in traditional folk costumes and ice skates glided around an ice track along the outer perimeter of the space, each bearing silver trays laden with glasses. The crowd clapped merrily in approval.

"You think they hired every model in Scandinavia for this gig?" Freddy quipped.

"Sure looks like it," Eden said as one of the floppy-haired waiters skated up and placed a tall fluted glass filled with a frothy dark liquid in front of her. She took a sip of the warm, rich broth and realized it was the first course—wild foraged mushroom cappuccino with white truffle froth.

"What do you think of all this? I heard this ice palace alone cost five million dollars to build."

"Five million dollars? For a building made out of *ice*?" Eden was incredulous.

"They flew in the ice blocks from New Zealand. Think of the manpower it took to build everything up here—it's basically a giant set of ice Legos. Pretty cool, yeah?"

"Actually, it's rather appalling."

"Really?" Freddy couldn't tell if she was being serious.

"Think of what that money could do to help people in need, people on this very island. We're sitting here watching five million dollars literally melt away before our eyes, just to amuse the most privileged people on the planet. People who, by the way, already live in their own palaces!"

"Uh-oh . . . I'm guessing you're not a fan of royalty."

"I don't spend much time thinking about them, to be honest. Most Brits my age aren't all that interested in the royal family in the way that Americans seem to be."

"But you're good friends with the Greshams. Aren't they sorta royal?"

"The Greshams are part of the landed aristocracy—it's different from the royal family, who are figureheads with little actual power. Lord Greshamsbury's family has owned the land around the estate for centuries, and they have been the stewards of the land for generations. The earl is devoted to his village and improving the lives of everyone in the community. Everyone in the whole county, really."

"That's pretty cool. I had no idea. I don't really follow this royalty stuff much either. My mom was obsessed with Princess Diana and the Iranian royals, but the way I see it, it's just dumb luck that all these people were born into the right families."

Eden was surprised to hear him say that. "Wouldn't you consider yourself a recipient of dumb luck too?"

"Hell yeah, I'm pretty friggin' lucky! My dad, he left Iran with the shoes on his feet and a backpack with one rolled-up rug. He traded the rug in Paris for a plane ticket to Los Angeles and some cash, where he built a fortune with his own ingenuity and hard work. And now he's passed down that same work ethic to me."

"So you work for your dad?"

"No, actually I compete with him."

"Really?"

"Yeah. My goal is to make more money than he has by the time I'm forty."

"How are you doing on that score?"

"Not bad, actually. My dad wanted me to go to med school, but I dropped out after my first semester and got my real estate license instead. Last year I sold over three hundred fifty million dollars' worth of properties, residential and commercial, and I've expanded into private jet and yacht brokering. I know where my passions lie, and I didn't want to spend my life treating people with conjunctivitis."

Eden studied him with interest. She had presumed Freddy was just another boring rich kid, but there was clearly more to him than met the eye.

"So what do you do?" Freddy asked.

"I treat people with conjunctivitis."

"Ha! You're a doctor? You look way too young to be a doctor!"

Before Eden could respond, Bea came up behind Freddy and tapped him on the shoulder. "Freddy, I don't recall you being assigned to this table."

"Um—I think the place cards might have magically been switched."

Bea glowered at Freddy. "Why would such a thing happen?"

"Because our sick friend here needs some special attention."

"The last thing Eden needs is more attention from you."

"It's actually worked out great, Bea. Freddy and I are having a fabulous time," Eden interjected.

Bea bent down and whispered furiously in Eden's ear. "Freddy was supposed to be next to Solène tonight! You were supposed to be chaperoning Rufus so he could spend the whole night staring at Freddy flirting with Solène! Remember, the hounds need to give chase . . ."

Eden gazed across at the neighboring table, where Rufus and Solène were huddled side by side, deep in conversation. "I think it's fine. The fox and the hound are well beyond the point of chasing."

•

At the central banquet table, Solène, in a puffy silver quilted Moncler ball gown that unfortunately made her look a bit like the Michelin man, was trying to lift her dinner partner's foul mood. "Cheer up, Rufus! This soufflé is wonderful, the Sancerre even better, and this palace is magical. I feel like I am in the middle of a Hans Christian Andersen fairy tale."

Rufus sighed. "A fairy tale? Everything about this is wrong. This ice palace was supposed to be half the size and built at the resort, not up here. Its presence here is an insult to Hawaiians and to all the activists who have been fighting so hard to block the construction of a new telescope on the mountain."

"Won't this palace melt in a few days' time? It's not permanent."

"That's beside the point. We're being very disrespectful, and we shouldn't be up here at all."

"But Jacqueline, the event director, told me that they made a big donation to the Hawaii Land Trust," Solène offered.

Rufus scoffed. "That's just like my mum. She thinks any problem can be solved by throwing money at it."

Solène laughed lightly. "Viscount St. Ives, don't tell me you are a *socialiste*?"

"Do not mock a man when he speaks his truth," Gopal Das, who'd overheard their exchange from across the table, suddenly interrupted. "Do you know where you are, young lady?"

"What do you mean? Aren't we on top of Mauna Kea?"

"The Native Hawaiians call this mountain Mauna a Wakea, the place where Wakea, the sky god, communed with Papa Hanau Moku, the earth goddess, leading to the creation of these islands. This is one of the most sacred places to all Hawaiians, and only the highest-ranking chiefs were ever allowed to set foot here. We have no right to be here, least of all throwing a party—it is a grave offense to the gods. We have made Pele angry, and mark my words, there will be a price to pay."

At the far end of the ice palace, the orchestra began to play the first notes of a grand waltz, as Prince Max ceremoniously led his mother onto the dance floor while Augusta took her father's arm. "Well, if the gods are angry, we might as well dance for them!" Solène declared, dragging a reluctant Rufus onto the dance floor. As more of the guests got up from their tables, Freddy turned to Eden and said, "My lady, may I have this dance?"

"Of course," Eden said. They made a beeline onto the dance floor, where Eden discovered Freddy to be a more expert and enthusiastic dance partner than she had been expecting. Freddy had some serious moves, twirling her around the dance floor with great flair, and as the waltz reached its crescendo, he suddenly dipped her dangerously low to the ground.

Eden burst out laughing. "You're trying to kill me, aren't you? Where did you learn your moves?"

"I was a finalist on *Dancing with the Stars.* Just kidding. My mom enrolled me in the Arthur Murray studio in Beverly Hills when I was twelve. Other Persian moms sent all their kids to Mohammad Khordadian to learn Persian dance, but my mom insisted that I needed to learn how to ballroom dance if I ever hoped to marry a beautiful princess."

"Do you think your mom was right?"

"Well, I'm dancing with you, aren't I?"

Gazing upon Rufus and Solène on the dance floor waltzing graciously, Arabella turned to Solène's mother with a triumphant look. "What did I tell you? Don't they make a dazzling pair?"

Olimpia de Courcy gave an almost imperceptible nod.

Arabella continued eagerly, "I can't help picturing how our grandchildren will look. They will be so stunning, and of course they will speak fluent French, English, and Chinese."

"Does Rufus speak Chinese?" Olimpia inquired.

"Sadly, no. Back when I was first living in London, I had the notion that I needed to raise my children to be more British than the British. I didn't want them to have even a hint of a Hong Kong accent like I had."

"But you don't have any accent. You sound as English as Claire Foy."

"Precisely."

"Who is that Asian girl over there?" Olimpia said, noticing Eden with Freddy looking as though they were reenacting a sequence from *La La Land.*

Arabella peered onto the now-crowded dance floor. "Which girl?"

"The one wearing the ice-blue Chanel. Is she the Thai princess everyone keeps talking about?"

"No, the Thai princess isn't arriving until tomorrow. That girl is nobody."

"She dances quite beautifully," Olimpia commented as she wondered why Rufus couldn't seem to take his eyes off the nobody.

VIII

Puako Beach Road

Eden stood under the shower on Rufus's back deck, feeling the spray of hot water stream down her neck and shoulders and letting the warmth soak through her entire body. The shower was separated from the rest of the deck by a stacked wall of volcanic rocks and a thicket of tall bamboo, and the smooth ocean pebbles on the ground only added to the tranquility of the space. Staring up through the steam at the stars in the night sky, Eden felt completely blissful.

"You still alive?" Rufus called out from the other side of the wall.

"Ummmm, I'm in heaven."

"There is nothing quite like an outdoor shower at night, is there?"

"Especially when you're trying to defrost your bum! It was positively arctic up there!"

"I saw you laughing nonstop on the dance floor, so it mustn't have been that bad."

"Freddy was doing his best Patrick Swayze impersonation, just to see if anyone noticed."

"When I first saw you seated next to Freddy at dinner, I was worried. Now I'm *very* worried."

"You needn't be. Underneath all that stubble Freddy's quite tolerable. How were things on your end?"

"All right."

"Looked more than all right to me. Solène's a gorgeous dancer."

"She's been doing ballet since she was three."

"Of course she has. There's no other way to get a body like that."

"I hadn't really noticed," Rufus replied, as he found his mind drifting to the body just inches away behind the rock wall.

"Okay, where's the shampoo?"

"It should be right in front of you—the blue one on the right labeled 'shampoo.' "

Eden giggled as she felt around for the bottle. "It's pitch-black in here! You could be showering next to me and I wouldn't even see you."

For a moment, he almost felt like saying, *So you won't mind if I join you in the shower?*, but he stopped himself. Instead, he said, "That's the whole point of how I designed the shower. You don't want to see anything except the stars."

Rufus was about to leave and allow her to enjoy her shower in peace when Eden suddenly called out, "So what do you think of her?"

"Who?"

"Solène!"

"She's okay. What do *you* think of her?"

"She seems smart, ambitious, and very self-assured."

"Translation: you think she's a total bitch."

"I never said that! I like her, but she has that French veneer of formality that takes time to penetrate."

Rufus lay back onto the bench, staring up at the stars himself. "You don't think she seems a bit . . . self-involved?"

"Show me someone that beautiful who isn't."

"You're not."

Eden snorted. "Next to Solène I am a little squirrel. A very wet one."

"Rubbish! You can hold your own next to Solène any day."

"You're being much too charitable. Freddy certainly thinks she's a goddess. Didn't you feel his longing stares from across the dance floor?"

"Not really. But you know who I could feel? Mum. She was fixating on me and Solène like the Eye of Sauron. It ruined the whole dinner for me. I swear I could feel every wave of her anxiety—it's as if it's connected directly to my gut."

"I'm sorry. Why do you think she's so anxious?"

"She's obviously fretting that the princess of Thailand still hasn't shown up, and worried that Solène might try to steal me away in the meantime."

Eden smiled in the shower. Was Rufus really that clueless about his mother's true intentions? "So where *is* the fabled princess?"

"Apparently at a jam session with Willie Nelson in Maui."

"Can you blame her? I'd rather be jamming with Willie Nelson!" Eden turned off the shower reluctantly and began toweling off.

"I'm dreading her arrival. I'm glad Solène's been hanging out with us, but I just can't get a proper read on her . . ."

"Then stop trying. Just relax and have fun and you'll probably get to know her much better that way."

"Well, I'm taking you all to one of the most amazing surf spots on the planet tomorrow."

Eden came out onto the deck with a towel wrapped around her. "If we're going surfing tomorrow, I really need to get some sleep. I'm absolutely knackered!"

"It's only twenty minutes to your hotel," Rufus said, getting up from the bench and jangling the keys to his Jeep. He opened the sliding glass door and Eden stepped inside the house.

"That bed looks awfully comfy."

"Why don't you spend the night? I'm picking you up in about six hours anyway, it'd be silly to go back to your hotel now."

"You know what, that hot shower turned me into an absolute puddle. I'm ready to crawl right into bed! Are you sure you don't mind?"

"I wouldn't have said it if I didn't mean it."

"But wait—I have no clothes except this ball gown!" Eden laughed.

Rufus opened a nearby cupboard and gestured to the neat stacks of pouches inside. "Voilà! My stash of airline pajamas. Take your pick, we've got Hawaiian Airlines, Cathay Pacific, Etihad, these fun kangaroo ones from Qantas. Oh, these ones are from Emirates—they actually hydrate you while you sleep."*

"Sold," Eden said, grabbing the packet and disappearing into the bathroom to change. She emerged a few moments later and jumped straight into the bed.

Rufus bustled around the house for a few moments, locking up and turning off lights, before getting into bed.

"Good night," he said as he slipped under the sheets next to her.

"Night," Eden murmured, already half-asleep. Rufus thought back fondly to all the times they'd shared a bed over the years, from the treehouse they had built together on the grounds of Greshamsbury Hall to the tents and campers and odd little B & Bs up and down the Cornish coast. The moon came out from behind the clouds, casting a gossamer light onto Eden's face as she slept. Rufus gazed at her for a few minutes, listening to her soft breathing. He turned to face the other side and fell into a deep, contented sleep.

---

* *Matrix designed the world's first moisturizing pajamas exclusively for Emirates first-class passengers. The futuristic sleepwear actually releases tiny amounts of sea kelp into your skin to prevent dehydration while you sleep.*

IX

Pololu Valley Lookout

KOHALA COAST, HAWAII • *NEXT MORNING*

"Just when you thought it couldn't possibly get more beautiful." Eden shook her head in awe as she stood with Rufus, Solène, and Freddy gazing at the view of the magnificent Pololu Valley. Unlike the Kona side of the island, the Kohala Coast consisted of five-hundred-foot-tall sea cliffs stretching down the coastline as far as the eye could see.

"It does not feel like Hawaii here," Solène remarked, staring at the moody cumulus clouds framing the cliffs. "It does not feel like we are anywhere on this Earth."

Freddy nodded in agreement. "It's Middle Earth! I feel like any minute, a dragon could come flying out from behind one of those cliffs."

"This is my favorite view on the whole island," Rufus said. "We're looking down at the first of seven valleys that were carved into the coastline when the Kohala volcano erupted eons ago. Look, the waves are really starting to kick up. Ready to head down?" Rufus clutched his surfboard and led the others on a hike along the steep path that zigzagged its way down the cliff to the valley floor. As the group descended, hopping over boulders and rocks, the view became more and more breathtaking as the thick foliage along the trail opened up to reveal a spectacular black-sand beach backed by a lush tropical forest. Looking at the surf pounding against the towering cliffs took Eden back to the rugged landscape at Tintagel, the

windswept village on the north coast of Cornwall, and the time she
went camping with Rufus and his sisters when she was thirteen . . .

*While Augie and Bea opted for tan maintenance on the pebbled beach,
Eden and Rufus decided to climb up the hill to explore the medieval
castle dramatically perched on the clifftop. As they wandered around
the grounds, Rufus snapped away at crumbling medieval ruins with his
Leica while Eden offered her commentary.* "Richard, the First Earl of
Cornwall, built most of the structure that remains today, but apparently
it's been some sort of royal residence since the early sixth century.* King
Arthur was born here, if you believe the legend."

"I believe it," Rufus said as he brushed his fingers over a mossy stone
wall. *"Whoa! Eden, put your hand right here."*

Eden placed her palm onto the ancient stone.

"Can you feel it?" Rufus asked excitedly.

"I think so. What am I supposed to feel?"

*"The vibration. The energy. Don't you feel like there's a portal into
another dimension right here?"*

*Eden closed her eyes as the wind whistled through the castle ramparts.
Suddenly the lines of Tennyson's poem came rushing through her head . . .*

> Four gray walls, and four gray towers
> Overlook a space of flowers,
> And the silent isle imbowers
> The Lady of Shalott.

"Stop! Don't move an inch," Rufus said as he adjusted the focus and
took her picture. *"That's perfect!"*

"My hair's in my face," Eden said, trying to swipe away her windswept hair.

"Stop fussing. Now open your eyes." He clicked again. *"You look
beautiful."*

Eden made a face.

---

* *Tintagel Castle in modern times is part of the land holdings of the Duke of Cornwall,
a.k.a. the Prince of Wales, a.k.a. Prince William, a.k.a. Willy the Wombat.*

"I wish you could see what I see," Rufus said. "You look like the fair maiden of the castle. Don't you wish you could go back in time and see how life was back then?"

"Sure. I'd love to be a druid and learn how to make magic healing potions. Like Getafix."

"Wouldn't you rather be Queen Guinevere, and I could be Lancelot?"

"No thanks. Things didn't end up going so well for them."

"That's because they were having a secret affair. They should have done things the right way and gotten married," Rufus said, putting his camera down and ceremoniously getting down onto one knee. He gazed up at Eden earnestly. "Eden Tong, will you marry me?"

Eden rolled her eyes. "Ew."

"I'm not talking about now. Twenty years from now."

"Trust me, by the time you're that old you'll already be married to some girl named Pippa or Poppy, the type who goes to Marlborough."

"Not a chance, I'll be loyal to you forever. There's no one in the entire world I'd ever marry except you. You're going to be my countess."

"Don't be daft," Eden scoffed, walking ahead dismissively. She stretched her arms out and raced down the emerald-green hill, the salty mist on her face making her feel as if she were flying.

"WOO HOO! THIS IS FUCKING AMAZING!" Freddy shouted, his arms outstretched as he ran along the black-sand beach joyously like a little kid. Stopping right in front of Eden, he said breathlessly, "Isn't this one of the most incredible beaches you've ever seen? It's right up there with the Amalfi Coast. You ever been?"

"I've only been to Florence and Rome—I'm dying to visit the Amalfi Coast."

"Well, allow me to invite you to come yachting with me this summer. I'm on the Amalfi every August."

"You take *Babyshark* around the Mediterranean?" Rufus asked, a bit surprised.

"Hell no. I take the papa boat—*Beluga*—and we cruise around the Italian coast from Portofino to Sardinia to Capri."

"Capri is so passé. Everyone I know is going to Greece these days," Solène sniffed.

"Well, let everyone else go to Greece and get wasted on ouzo—I'll take Capri any day. You've got the most amazing food, nature, and shopping all on one island. Where else on the planet can you at midnight be enjoying homemade gelato in a warm waffle cone while shopping for loafers at Tod's?"

"My friend George moved to Capri with his girlfriend—he's been trying to get me to visit," Rufus said.

"If you have friends there, you have no excuse not to go. You'll get invited to all the best parties at all the private villas!" Freddy said.

Solène was annoyed that Rufus did not come to her defense about Greece. She knew from all her exhaustive googling that he'd once enjoyed sailing through the Aegean with his family. British *Vogue* had done a feature on his trip, and Rufus had looked particularly alluring in one of the photos—bronzed and glistening with sweat as he hoisted a sail in just a pair of cream Orlebar Brown terry cloth shorts and stared broodingly into the camera. Now, what exactly was Rufus staring at so intently?

Rufus stood on the beach, assessing the biblical, churning waves in anticipation.

"This beach is incredible! Bea's going to regret missing this," Eden said.

"I don't think so. She's doing a photo shoot with Augusta for *Town & Country*, and you know she's always happiest in front of the camera," Solène remarked.

"I hear the photo shoot is on some nude beach that Ram Dass dude took them to," Freddy added.

"Oh, Gopal Das took them to Kehena Beach?" Rufus said. "That's another magical spot where I was thinking of taking you all, but then I thought some of you might not want to parade around in your birthday suit in front of everyone."

"Yeah, that'd be weird. The water's a bit too cold to be letting it all hang out, if you catch my drift," Freddy said, winking at Rufus.

"I think being naked on a beach is the most natural thing in the world. I wish you would have taken me there," Solène said, giving Rufus a flirty look.

"Remember how we used to go skinny-dipping in that hidden cove near Combe Martin?" Eden said to Rufus.

Freddy looked a bit shocked. "You and Eden went skinny-dipping . . . together?"

"Yah, with my sisters," Rufus recalled with a laugh.

"You Brits are crazy. The last time anyone in my family saw me naked was at my bris," Freddy quipped.

Eden gazed at the grassy dunes and tall ironwood trees behind the beach, beyond which was a wide stream that flowed into the romantic-looking valley. "I think I'm going to take a walk by that stream."

"Great idea. Just don't wander off the trail. There are ancient burial sites deeper in the valley that are very sacred to the locals, so it's best to keep a respectful distance," Rufus answered.

"Of course," Eden said.

"You gonna surf?" Freddy asked Rufus.

"It's double overhead today and there's no way I'm missing it."

"You know what? I'll take my walk later—I haven't watched you surf in ages!" Eden said excitedly.

"Better yet, come in with me!" Rufus prodded.

"Why not?" Eden said.

Rufus stripped off his T-shirt and tightened the drawstring of his swimming trunks while Eden took off her sweater and stepped out of her shorts, revealing a one-piece bathing suit underneath. Freddy gawked appreciatively, while Solène was stunned at the body Eden had been hiding. Who knew the girl had the boobs and butt of a goddess? Those cheap Bon Marché clothes and short haircut did her no favors, that's for sure. But then she noticed even Rufus giving a sideways glance in Eden's direction. Men were all the same. Just a flash of skin and they all became animals. That boy had been oblivious to her hints all morning; maybe she should strip naked and walk into the ocean. *Really* give him a show. No, no, she had a better idea. Noticing a gap in the boulder she was standing on, she shoved her foot into the crack, deliberately tripping herself.

"*Putain de merde!*" Solène groaned in agony.

Everyone turned to see Solène crumpled on the ground. Rufus and Freddy rushed to her side. "You okay?" Rufus saw the blood gushing out from the large gash in her knee.

"You're bleeding!" Freddy gasped.

"I think I broke my foot," Solène cried.

Eden approached Solène and crouched down beside her. "Just stay still. Don't try to get up. Let me just take a look."

"Why?" Solène said, slightly disoriented.

"Because she's a doctor," Rufus said.

"For real?" Solène stared at Eden in disbelief.

Eden took her time palpating Solène's ankle slowly, ignoring the blood. "Does this hurt?"

"Ow! Ow! *Oui! Oui!*"

Rufus leaned in. "Is it broken?"

"I don't think so, I think it's just badly sprained. You're probably going to need crutches for a few weeks," Eden assessed.

"I'm bleeding to death!"

Eden nodded. "Looks like it could use a few stitches."

Solène cursed herself. She had only meant to fall slightly and pretend to twist something, but she had done too good a job. Now she was in real pain, and the Jacquemus dress she had planned to wear tonight would not go well with crutches. Freddy returned with a towel soaked in water, and he began pressing it against the open gash in her knee.

"Oooh. *Merci*, Freddy. That feels good," Solène said as Freddy continued to squeeze water onto her wound.

"Wait a minute . . . where did you get that water?" Rufus asked.

"From the stream over there," Freddy replied.

Rufus gave Eden a slightly ominous look. "Uh . . . that stream is teeming with leptospirosis."

"Brilliant," Eden said flatly.

"What's that?" Solène asked.

"It's a flesh-eating bacteria," Rufus blurted out before he could stop himself.

"Shit on my dick!" Freddy cursed.

Solène began to whimper. "Am I to lose my whole leg?"

"Not necessarily," Rufus replied.

"It's all my fault!" Freddy cried, throwing up his hands in despair.

"She'll be fine, Freddy," Eden said calmly. "Solène, your exposure to the water has been minimal, and we don't know if it's actually contaminated. My main concern is to get the swelling down on your ankle. Let's get your foot on ice, and we'll also get you some antibiotics for the *Leptospira,* just to be on the safe side."

"Put your arms around my shoulders. Let's get you back to the car," Rufus said to Solène, who looked up eagerly. That was the best thing she'd heard all day. Rufus was going to take her in his arms and carry her up the cliff as though they were reenacting a scene from *Poldark*.

"Wait, wait, I have a better idea. We can get a chopper evac. I have an emergency evac service that can land right here on this beach," Freddy said, springing into action as he began jabbing his phone.

X

Mauna Lani Resort

"That was some impressive stitching there, Dr. Tong," Rufus remarked.

"Yes, I still cannot believe you did it so quickly!" Solène said as she lay comfortably ensconced on the bed in her suite at the Mauna Lani resort, her ankle elevated on a pile of pillows and cocooned in ice packs after Eden had properly disinfected and stitched up her wound.

"You're lucky you only needed a few stitches," Eden said as she handed Solène a bottle of pills. "Take two of these every four hours."

"Will there be any side effects?" Solène asked as she readjusted her silk robe to display just a little too much thigh.

"It's only azithromycin, so any adverse effects are unlikely. Perhaps some abdominal cramping, loose stools—"

"Okay, enough! Stop!" Solène sputtered in embarrassment, stopping Eden from going any further. She couldn't deal with such frank medical talk when she was lying in bed trying to look seductive. "I'm not sure how I can ever thank you properly. Tell me, do you prefer the Kelly or the Birkin?"

"Birkin?" Eden was confused.

"Maybe you want a little black Kelly?"

"I'm sorry, I'm not following you."

"My family has a special relationship with Hermès. I could get you on the VIP list for a Kelly handbag. You would only have to wait two or three years, maximum."

"Oh. That's so kind of you, but it's really not necessary," Eden said, not bothering to mention that she had a trunk full of Kellys and Birkins and Gabrielle Hobos that had belonged to her mother that she couldn't bear to use. "Now, get some rest before the wedding and be sure to take two more pills at four p.m."

"Ah, yes! I would not want this thing to devour my flesh."

Freddy grimaced at the thought. "Yikes! Definitely not. Again, I'm so sorry, Solène! I know it's not even noon yet, but I could really use a drink. Can I buy everyone a round, especially our heroine here?"

"Our heroine definitely deserves a drink!" Rufus concurred.

"Oh, I don't think I should drink since I am taking this medication," Solène said, not realizing that Rufus and Freddy were not referring to her.

There was an awkward pause, until Eden said, "Yes, you might want to stay off the hard stuff today. Now, do get some rest!" The three of them started to move toward the door.

"Wait! Rufus, could you maybe stay a little while? Just to make sure I have no reactions to the *antibiotique*?" Solène said in a babyish voice.

"Uh . . . sure . . . of course," Rufus replied.

"We'll be at the bar by the pool," Freddy told Rufus as he and Eden left the room. They soon found a table by the bar overlooking the resort's huge swimming pool, which was flanked by a sleek row of square white umbrellas and deck chairs under which guests lounged contentedly.

A waitress appeared at their table moments later. "Beautiful day, isn't it? What can I get for you two?"

"What's your favorite cocktail here? Something fun and beachy?" Freddy asked.

"The ube colada, definitely."

"What's an ube?"

"It's a purple yam, grown right here on the island. It's sweet like vanilla. Trust me, you'll love it."

"Let's go for it! Two ube coladas, please. Also, do you have any chips and guac?"

"I can definitely make that happen."

As soon as the waitress left, Eden looked at Freddy with a smile. "Your mood's totally changed. You seemed a bit distressed a little earlier."

"I have a hard time seeing anyone in pain. It was so amazing to see you spring into action like that, despite all that blood and the flesh-eating bacteria. How do you do it?"

"Training, mostly. I go right into problem-solving mode."

"When did you know you wanted to be a doctor?"

"Probably when I was around seven or eight—it was just something that came to me naturally. I was always taking in injured birds, abandoned baby field mice. At first I thought I wanted to be a vet. Of course, my father's a doctor, so seeing him go about his work every day had its effect, but I also have this distinct memory of being with my mother when she was in and out of hospitals, and the extremely kind people who treated her. That also had a huge effect on me."

"How's your mother now?"

"She passed away when I was five."

"You were five years old and you remember being at the hospital with your mom?"

"Believe it or not, yes. I have flashes of it, of the rooms."

"Wow. I can barely remember what happened last week."

"Well, it's often much easier to remember things from long ago."

Freddy stared at the kids playing in the pool for a moment. A teenage boy was shouting "Marco!" while wandering around the shallow end with his eyes tightly shut, as a few younger kids encircled him, squealing "Polo! Polo!" He looked back at Eden, his voice getting a little choked up. "My mom died when I was twelve. Ovarian cancer. They hid it from me and my sister and never allowed us to visit her in the hospital. One day she just left . . . and never came home."

"I'm sorry," Eden said, placing her hand over his and giving it a comforting squeeze. She wondered what was worse, not getting a chance to say goodbye to your mother, or having the distinct memory of seeing your mother in a hospital bed, surrounded by loud machines and writhing in pain.

The waitress returned with two tall tumblers decorated with large pineapple wedges and filled with a creamy frosty drink accented by a deep-purple syrup. Seeing the cocktails made Freddy snap out of his funk.

"*Bé salamati!*" Freddy toasted. He took his first sip and looked at Eden in amazement. "Wow, she was right. This stuff is better than crack!"

Eden took a sip, immediately breaking into a smile. "The ube has a sort of nutty sweetness," Eden assessed. "Rufus is going to love it."

"Ha! We'll be lucky if we see Rufus for the rest of the weekend!"

"What do you mean?"

"You didn't pick up on all that chemistry back in the room?"

"Not really. I was more focused on treating Solène's injury."

"I think she's recovering pretty well! I bet you a thousand bucks there's some adult-only content happening in that room right now. The sick patient needs a hunky surfer to make her pain go away."

Eden laughed lightly, although she found it oddly unsettling to think of Rufus in that way. Besides, she'd known within five seconds of meeting Solène that she just wasn't going to be right for Rufus. She might have had all the pedigree and the poise in the world, but she would never make Rufus happy in the long run. He might enjoy the diversion for the moment, but he'd soon lose interest. Oddly enough, she felt that Freddy and Solène together made a lot more sense. She looked across the table at Freddy thoughtfully. "What about you? Don't tell me you've thrown in the towel with Solène so quickly?"

Freddy sighed. "You know, for the past five years I've nursed this fantasy about Solène de Courcy, ever since the day I first saw her sitting across from me at a banquette at Alcazar. I thought once I perfected my six-pack she'd show some interest in me. I spent the past three years being tortured by my sadistic trainer six times a week and eating boiled chicken with steamed broccoli florets—I fucking hate broccoli florets—just to get rid of my man boobs. I was totally focused on what Solène would think of the new me."

"And have you learned what Solène thinks . . . ?" Eden asked.

Freddy grinned for a moment, and then his expression changed as he peered deep into Eden's eyes. "You know, until this week, I would never have imagined that the new me might not give a rat's ass what Solène thinks anymore."

"Really?"

"Yup. I think seeing her again has really put things in perspective for me. I don't actually want someone who only likes me depending on the way I look. And Solène doesn't even see me, she sees right through me. She only sees Rufus."

"I don't think that's true . . ."

"It is, and it's fine. I needed to have this revelation myself before I could come to my senses. The only thing that bothers me is that my sister's right, yet again."

"What is your sister right about?"

"She's been telling me to forget about Solène since the beginning. She said: 'That girl clearly does not eat, and any girl who doesn't eat is going to be a bitch because she's hungry. You need to meet a nice Persian girl who enjoys good food as much as you do.' "

"I hate to say this, but I think your sister's right."

"About which part? Solène being a bitch or me marrying a nice Persian girl?"

"Both," Eden replied as they both laughed heartily.

Fifty yards away in Solène's suite, Rufus was having his own revelation as he sat in the club chair beside Solène's bed, where he had the perfect bird's-eye view of Freddy and Eden at their table by the pool. Solène lay in her bed talking animatedly, but Rufus had long ceased to listen to her. He kept looking out the window, where he could see Freddy clinking cocktail glasses with Eden. He could see Freddy and Eden laughing together at something. He could see Freddy lean across the table and take Eden's hand. He could see them get up from the table and leave together. If he was being honest with himself, he didn't like what he was seeing, or what he imagined might happen next.

XI

The Milo Suite

Freddy drove Eden back to her hotel, and she returned to her suite to discover that some American fashion magazine had commandeered it for a live-stream video shoot of Bea and Augie getting ready for the wedding. The door adjoining their suites had been unlocked, and an entire battalion of stylists, photo assistants, and various technicians were camped out in the living room and on the verandah.

Eden peeked into Bea's room, where she sat in her makeup chair while two hairstylists were wrestling with her updo. "Eden, I'm soooo knackered. I just got back from my beach shoot, and now I have to do this Instagram Live and another shoot before the ceremony. I'm so jealous you got to go to the beach! How's Solène? Did she really break her foot?"

"It's just a sprain. She's convalescing in her room very happily . . . with Rufus."

"Shit, she works fast," Bea said excitedly.

"She's a force of nature indeed."

There was a knock on the door as Josh the water sports director entered with a fresh chilled coconut with a straw sticking out the top. "Thought you could use a good refresher after that last shoot in the hot sun."

"Thanks, luv. So thoughtful of you," Bea said gratefully as she chugged the coconut water. Josh (Immaculate Conception/Mount Vernon High/Whitman/Middlebury) lingered in the room, eyeing Eden as though he wished she weren't there.

Eden protectively looked at Bea in the mirror. "Do you need help with anything?"

"No, I'm fine. You should go get ready."

Eden got the hint. "Okay. Have fun on your live stream."

She left Bea with her fanboy and entered her bedroom to find a thirtysomething woman sprawled out on the bed barking into her phone: "The shoes never arrived, and neither did the tiaras, so we switched the concept and Matthias was going to shoot Lady Beatrice jumping on the bed barefoot in the Balenciaga. But then the little bitch said, 'I don't wear Balenciaga.' This means we're going to put her in the Chanel that the bride was supposed to wear. My life is fucked. How am I going to explain to Anna that—"

"Oh, hello," Eden said.

The woman looked up. "Still no sign of coffee?"

"I'm sorry?"

"My iced latte with oat milk? Where is it?"

"I think you're mistaking me for—"

"I don't fucking care, I just want my latte. How many times do I have to ask?"

Eden's eyes widened and she put on her calming doctor's voice, the one she used on fussy children. "Let's see . . . why don't we call room service and see if they can get this sorted for you?"

The woman suddenly looked confused. "Who are you?"

Just then, a Hawaiian woman distinctly outfitted in the hotel's signature uniform entered the room with iced coffee on a tray. "Here you go, ma'am. Iced latte with oat milk."

The woman turned beet red, realizing the enormity of her faux pas. "I'm so sorry, I'm the fashion editor for this shoot, and I thought this was Lady Beatrice's room."

"It's fine. Lady Beatrice is next door; I'm Dr. Eden Tong, her best friend, and I need to get changed for the wedding myself."

"Of course you do," the fashion editor said, taking her coffee and leaving the bedroom without another word.

The hotel staffer winked at Eden. "Can I get you anything?"

"I'm fine, thanks," Eden replied as something began to dawn on her. Since arriving on the Big Island, she had on two separate occasions now been mistaken for being, to put it bluntly, a hotel maid. Was it a coincidence that in each instance, it had been a particular type of woman who had made the assumption about her? Until this trip, she had never spent much time in a place where most of the staff at every resort consisted of people with a similar skin tone to hers. She could pass for Hawaiian, or Chinese, or Filipino, and to some of these privileged, oblivious tourists, she was just another interchangeable Asian staffer who would bring them their drinks.

For most of her life, she had lived in a village in England where she and her father were treated as beloved members of the community. Everyone knew she had been raised alongside Viscount Rufus and the Ladies Augusta and Beatrice, the British-Chinese children who made up the noblest family in the county. She had always attended schools where there was plenty of diversity and moved in circles where her race seemed to be invisible or irrelevant to her peers. Eden realized she had been exceedingly fortunate to have grown up in this protected way, to have lived in England as a Chinese woman but to have never truly suffered the real stings of prejudice in her daily life. Until now. For the very first time, she was experiencing what other people like her living in the West must feel every single day.

Eden contemplated all this as she slipped on the peach organdy and lace Dolce & Gabbana halter-neck gown that Bea had lent her, a gown that she knew from the price tag still affixed to the label cost £4,700 but had been deemed not special enough for her best friend to consider wearing to this august occasion. Something came over her, and instead of fastening the hooks, she unzipped it, stepped out of the dress, and threw on a pair of jeans and a tank top. She rushed out of her room and down to the resort's boutique, where she remembered seeing a dress she loved. It was a black floor-length dress printed with a gold fan pattern on a voluminous skirt created by the Hawaiian designer Manaola. Eden quickly bought the dress and rushed back to her room. Entering the suite, she saw the friendly hotel staffer again, this time laden with another trayful of drinks for the magazine stylists.

"Are you sure I can't get you anything, Dr. Tong? Afternoon tea? Vodka martini?"

"You know my name?"

"Of course. You're the *actual* guest in this suite, but you're the only one who doesn't seem to need anything."

Eden smiled. "What's your name?"

"Nicole."

"Nicole, thank you. I really don't need anything." Eden laughed. "Actually . . . do you know where I could find some fresh flowers?"

"Like for a lei?"

"No, bigger, like hibiscus blossoms?"

"Oh, I know just where to get some of those! Give me a few minutes!"

Eden went into her bathroom, where she saw a mess of makeup bags arrayed on the floor for Bea's shoot. She rummaged around till she found what she was looking for. Then she looked in the mirror, took a deep breath, and did something she had never done before: she put on red lipstick.

XII

Kukio Beach

FOUR SEASONS RESORT HUALALAI • SUNSET

Under an open-air pavilion created from an intricate latticework of bamboo, palm fronds, and selenite shards, the wedding guests sat in rows of white-slipcovered chairs overlooking the crescent-shaped beach, scrutinizing each other and tittering sotto voce. Some of the European royals were being cattier than usual . . .

"Arabella's like the von Trapps, climbing every mountain. Now that one daughter's snatched her prince, I expect she will want to be made an archduchess."

"Did you see Mrs. Mittambani's gigantic sapphire choker? Bought from the heirs of the nizam of Hyderabad for a song, so I'm told."

"Now, who in the world is that stunning creature with the hibiscus in her hair? Is that the princess of Thailand?"

At the appointed moment, Jackie the event director gave the green light, and the orchestra began playing Vivaldi's "Spring 1" recomposed by Max Richter as the wedding party began their procession into the pavilion. Leading the charge was the younger brother of the groom, His Serene Highness Prince Tassilo zu Liechtenburg (Crossroads/Aiglon/Santa Monica College), in a seersucker suit that looked two sizes too small,* accompanying the Honorable Lady Beatrice in a scene-stealing rose-pink Giambattista Valli gown that frothed over with so many layers of ruffles she could barely sit down.

---

* *Everyone who was anyone knew Prince Tassilo's weight gain was a result of his recent stay at Paracelsus, the world's most exclusive rehab.*

Next came the parents of the groom, His Serene Highness Prince Julius (privately tutored/Le Rosey/Heidelberg University) in a periwinkle-blue suit and natty white fedora, arm-in-arm with his wife, Her Serene Highness Princess Hanne Marit (Oslo International School/Parsons), who wore a beaded Giorgio Armani bolero jacket and matching cream sheath dress that she had purchased at the Armani outlet at Bicester Village and had already worn to the wedding of Prince Manuel of Bavaria and Princess Anna of Sayn-Wittgenstein-Berleburg in 2005. Bea gawked at her outfit in shock, wondering why she had bothered with rushing a new Giamba to Hawaii when the mother of the groom obviously gave zero fucks about wedding protocol and had chosen to wear an outfit that was as white as any bridal gown.[*]

At this point, the triumphant chords of Rupert Gregson-Williams's "Duck Shoot"[†] filled the air as Rufus, the Viscount St. Ives, looking particularly dashing in a bespoke pearl-gray linen suit from Sartoria Ripense and loafers from Bocache & Salvucci, entered with Lady Arabella, who wore a gold cape dress with a plunging neckline, architectural shoulders, and a flowing train of overlapping gold disks designed by Jean Paul Gaultier, whom she lured out of retirement for this special couture commission. As Rufus escorted his mother up the aisle, he beamed charmingly at the few guests he recognized and the many he did not. He smiled at the marchioness who used to force him to sit in her lap as a little boy while she guzzled martini after martini and pinched his nipples; he smiled at Auntie Rosina and Uncle Peter (Diocesan Boys'/Andover/Harvard/Wharton), who had just jetted in for the ceremony, along with their sons Alexander (Diocesan Boys'/Andover/Harvard/Wharton), Adam (Diocesan Boys'/Andover/Harvard/Harvard Law), and

---

* *The Princess Hanne Marit, who came from a long line of very aristocratic yet very practical Norwegians, had no awareness of bourgeois wedding traditions and spent most of her life in Johnny Was tunic tops and Alo Yoga leggings on her alpaca ranch in Ojai.*

† *Sharp ears might recognize this song as the main theme to* The Crown. *Of course Arabella would select this particular tune to make her entrance.*

Aurelius (Diocesan Boys'/American School Hong Kong/Mill-brook/Colorado College), who had also arrived at the last possible moment in their own separate planes, all bearing the surly expression of men who were much too important to attend family weddings but had decided to honor everyone with their presence anyway; he smiled at Dr. Tong and the strikingly gorgeous girl beside him that he did not recognize but figured must be the Thai princess every-one was talking about. The princess winked at him, startling him into the realization that it was *Eden*. But this was an Eden utterly transformed—she was breathtaking in a starkly simple off-the-shoulder black linen dress, her exquisite features somehow even lovelier with her short hair dramatically slicked back and pinned with three beautiful hibiscus blossoms.

At the front of the pavilion, a tall archway composed of gigan-tic pieces of driftwood framed the spectacular view of the beach for every wedding guest. The Reverend Caleb Oriel, the rector at Greshamsbury, stood alongside Gopal Das as each prepared to deliver his homily. As the sun began to set over the cloudless sky, bathing everything in golden light, Josh the water sports director suddenly appeared on the beach, wearing nothing but a crown of leaves on his head and a traditional grass skirt, his buff torso glisten-ing with oil. He stood perfectly centered in the archway, held up a large white conch shell to the sky, and then blew into it slowly, creat-ing a deep, haunting peal.

As the primeval sound echoed over the sand dunes, a dozen simi-larly dressed Hawaiian men marched along the beach holding up a Qing dynasty *huanghuali* palanquin, on which sat Lady Augusta. The men set the palanquin down just as a cluster of young flower girls in white slip dresses approached from the other side. The Earl of Greshamsbury, in a pale blue tropical linen suit from Davies and Son, strutted proudly up to the palanquin, took his daughter by the arm, and walked her up the beach path as the flower girls led the way, scattering rose petals in the sand as they sang "Somewhere over the Rainbow" a cappella.

The crowd stood up and murmured in approval when the bride

walked up the aisle toward the archway, allowing the full glory of her exquisite Maison Valentino couture gown to be admired by all. Her sleeveless, high-neckline gown of Chantilly lace attached to a balloon skirt featuring a ten-foot-long train embellished with crystals and golden pearls was a feat that had taken a team of seamstresses three months to sew, and it was fittingly crowned by the heirloom diamond-and-pearl Greshamsbury Tiara, made by Asprey in 1818.

Arabella beamed proudly, savoring her victory. Seeing her beautiful daughter walk down the aisle clutching her crescent-shaped bouquet of white native flowers,* looking like the dignified princess she was meant to be, was worth all the screaming rows they'd had over the dress. If only all those snotty classmates of hers at Maryknoll could see her now. As soon as the rector consecrated them as husband and wife, Augie would automatically become the Princess Maximillian zu Liechtenburg, signifying the first in a trifecta of royal marriages that Arabella would orchestrate. Next, Rufus would take Princess Solène de Courcy as his bride, linking the Greshams with not one but two of the noblest houses of Europe. Then Bea would surely follow in her siblings' footsteps and snag her own prince—not fat Tassilo but maybe one of the dashing Greek or Danish ones—and it would be a fait accompli. Her legacy as the matriarch of her own royal dynasty would at last be secure.

Josh blew on the conch shell again, and this time a band of drummers appeared on the sand and formed a drum circle. As they began drumming energetically, an ancient wa'a—a wooden outrigger canoe—could be seen coming around the bay. Six men rowed the canoe through the waves, their oars perfectly synchronized, and perched at the prow was Prince Maximillian, dressed in a white and sky-blue paisley Etro robe. As the men rowed closer to shore, Max suddenly threw off the robe, stood up to reveal white boxer briefs embellished with gold fleur-de-lis, and dove off the canoe into the ocean. The wedding guests gasped.

---

* An homage to the bouquet Babe Cushing Paley carried at her wedding to Stanley Mortimer. Arabella, of course, idolized Mrs. Paley, while Augie didn't have a clue who she was.

"My crazy son," Prince Julius guffawed as the crowd began to cheer him on. Max swam just a few yards before the water became too shallow, and he stood up in the waves and ran toward the beach. A trio of attendants appeared, quickly toweling him off and helping him into a white linen jacket and pants. He remained shirtless underneath the jacket, his only adornment an ornate puka shell necklace.

Max marched up to the archway and immediately embraced Augie, bending her over in a dramatic kiss. "Sorry, I couldn't wait," he said as everyone roared with laughter.

"Dear god, I'm completely soaked!" Augie announced through her giggles. "Maxxie, my gown is ruined!" Then, to the absolute horror of her mother, Max began to unzip her from behind, allowing her to step graciously out of the encrusted gown to reveal a lusciously beachy white slip dress woven from the finest organic unbleached hemp. Like a butterfly finally free from the confines of its cocoon, Augie turned to the crowd, grinning from ear to ear. The bride was going to get her way after all.

XIII

The Wai'olu Suite

Jackie Zivenchy was one of the world's foremost event planners. She had once shut down the East River in New York for a private party on Randall's Island. She had masterminded political conventions and multimillion-dollar product-launch events held at stadiums involving thousands of guests. She knew how to handle the most demanding clients on the planet, people who were too famous and too rich to ever hear the word "no." But she had never imagined that an intimate wedding for three hundred on the Big Island of Hawaii would mark the nadir of her illustrious career, and that things could ever go so, so wrong.

Her first inkling that this evening was not going as planned came as soon as the wedding ceremony ended, when the Countess of Greshamsbury requested that Lady Augusta meet her *immediately* at the secure location closest to the wedding pavilion. Jackie suggested Lady Beatrice's suite at the Four Seasons, which was just a short walk around the cove and safely out of earshot from the wedding guests. As soon as Augie arrived, still giddy from the six-minute-long affirmation chant that Gopal Das had led at the close of the ceremony, the event director was oh-so-politely asked to leave the room by Arabella.

Jackie made a hasty exit through the door adjoining Bea's suite, and she did not even need to huddle close by to overhear the conversation or feel the countess's rage vibrating through the walls.

"Why do you hate me so much?" Arabella glared icily at her daughter.

"I don't hate you. Why would you—"

"*How dare you?* How dare you disgrace me, disgrace your father, disgrace all your Gresham and Leung ancestors, and more importantly, disgrace *yourself* like this?"

"I don't understand what you mean."

"You performed a striptease at your own wedding!"

"Everyone loved it, Mother. Everyone was laughing!"

"They were not laughing with you, they were laughing *at* you."

"It was Maxxie's idea. He thought it would be wicked fun if we both—"

Arabella massaged her temples like she was having a migraine attack. "Don't you see? Don't you see that Maxxie can flash his pale white buttocks at the whole world and everyone will laugh? Maxxie can get away with anything because he is *Prince Maximillian zu Liechtenburg*. You, on the other hand, are nothing more than an earl's daughter, but you have succeeded, with my help, I might add, in accomplishing the impossible. Despite all your inadequacies, you have managed to marry into his illustrious clan, and every single member of that clan—which as you know includes most of the crowned and uncrowned heads of Europe—now thinks that their darling Prince Maxxie has married a harlot."

"I am not a harlot."

"After that stunt you pulled, you're nothing more than a low-class stripper! You're no better than one of those Wan Chai *gai!*"*

Augie's nostrils flared; she had reached the last straw with her mother. "I'm so tired of you projecting all your issues onto me!"

"Issues? What issues?"

"Whenever you talk about trashy people, why must they always

---

* *Literally "chicken" in Cantonese, but it also means "whore" or "prostitute." Wan Chai is the red-light district of Hong Kong that was made famous in the film* The World of Suzie Wong.

be Chinese? Why are they never European or royal? Have you seen how tacky some of Maxxie's Norwegian cousins are? You know what you are? You're a . . . a self-loathing Asian!"

Arabella laughed dramatically. "How is it self-loathing for a mother to want to instill some dignity and common sense into her daughter? It is *precisely* because you are half Asian that you must always present yourself in the best manner. You must be the prettiest, smartest, most charming woman in every room you enter, and you must always behave impeccably—that is what I have been trying to impress into your numb little skull all your life, but you have fought me every step of the way. All I ever wanted was for you to have an intimate, elegant, history-making wedding that *Point de Vue* and *¡Hola!* would chronicle for posterity and everyone would remember for the rest of their lives. I'm just trying to help you to be looked upon favorably as you begin your new life in a family that will not be as kind to you as your blood family."

"Maxxie's family loves me. Sometimes I feel like they love me and accept me more than my own family," Augie said, her voice quavering with emotion.

"Just wait, you'll see. Now that you're actually married to him the knives will come out. And I will not be there to protect you anymore, to shield you from the millions of things you will do wrong in the eyes of the zu Liechtenburgs and the von Melke av Sjokolades."

"You're totally deluded, Mother. The zu Liechtenburgs are by no means the perfect family you think they are. Prince Julius lives most of the year with his mistress in Ibiza, and Maxxie's mother spends her whole life shoveling alpaca shit and sucking on her bong."

"You keep missing the point. All I ever want is the best for my children, and all they ever do is disappoint me. All they ever do is break my heart!" Tears began flowing down Arabella's cheeks, shocking Augusta, who had never before seen her mother cry. Arabella fled the room, almost colliding into Jackie, who let out a little gasp as the door nearly hit her in the face.

"Where's the bathroom?" Arabella asked through her tears.

"Just to your left down this hallway," Jackie said quickly, deliberately looking away.

Arabella locked herself into the bathroom and stared at herself in the mirror. *Thank god for waterproof mascara,* she thought as she carefully dabbed away the dampness from her eyes with a sheet of tissue. When she was finished, she wadded up the tissue and looked around for someplace to dispose of it. Why wasn't the dustbin under the sink, as it should be? Arabella scanned the space until she saw the dustbin next to the toilet. She threw the tissue ball toward the bin, missing it by a few inches. *Bloody hell,* she thought as she marched over and picked it up. Chucking the tissue properly into the bin, she noticed something peeking out among the other random bits of refuse. Something unmistakable. It was a home pregnancy test. She fished out the plastic test stick and saw that both of the two vertical pink strips had darkened. *Pregnant.*

Arabella could feel her heart palpitations coming on. "Jackie!" she shouted from the bathroom. "Jaaaaackie!"

"Yes, ma'am." Jackie rushed to the door just as Arabella opened it.

"Is this Bea's bathroom?"

"No, Lady Beatrice's bathroom is next door, in the suite you were just in with Lady Augusta."

"Oh thank god thank god thank god," Arabella sighed, clutching her chest with relief. "It's so confusing, I'm not sure where one suite ends and the other begins. Whose suite are we in?"

"This is Dr. Eden Tong's suite."

"Eden Tong! How in the world did she end up here?"

"I believe Mr. Farman-Farmihian booked the room for her."

"Freddy Farman-Farmihian! How *interesting* . . ." Arabella's mind began to race. Did Eden accidentally get preggers with the rich Persian's baby? If only the self-righteous Dr. Tong realized what that precious daughter of his got up to!

Augie entered the suite, dressed again in the Valentino gown. "Forgive me, Mother?"

Arabella paused for a moment, and then she beamed. "My princess! How beautiful you look!"

XIV

Bellaloha Resort

SOUTH KONA, BIG ISLAND • *COCKTAIL HOUR*

Jackie had just successfully transported three hundred VVIP guests—many with their own security details—from a pavilion overlooking the beach at the Four Seasons Hualalai to another pavilion overlooking another beach at the Bellaloha Resort ten miles south. Here, these pampered pashas would be plied with Chilean wine bearing fake French labels till the chef informed her that dinner was ready. Since Arabella could not be convinced to stage the wedding banquet anywhere but in the rain forest of her beloved resort, the chef was forced to cook in a makeshift tent with generators, since the latest eruption had rendered the state-of-the-art kitchen kaput, and it could take a while before three hundred Dover sole fillets could be poached, deboned, and plated. Jackie would also never understand why Arabella had insisted on Dover sole being flown in when they were on an island surrounded by some of the freshest fish in the world. Just as she was trying to make sure her team had lit all eight hundred of the paper lanterns hanging from the aerial roots of the great banyan tree in the center of the banquet site, the earl tapped her on the shoulder.

No sooner had Francis done this than he realized that his mind had gone blank. *What was this lady's bloody name?* "Ah . . . Lee, isn't it?"

"Excuse me?" Jackie replied politely. *What now?*

"Isn't your name Lee?"

"It's Jackie actually, but you can call me whatever you want, Lord Greshamsbury."

"Jackie! My apologies. Ah, would you be able to do me a tiny little favor?"

"Yes?" *He means a big favor.*

"I need to find a place where I can, you know, *be* with Prince Julius."

"Where you can *be*?" *Does he want to shtup the prince?*

"You know, two fathers having a celebratory toast. Someplace where we won't be disturbed. Perhaps the wine cellar at the resort . . ."

"I'd love to get you the wine cellar but the fire department has chained the doors to every building on the property. No one has access until they've stabilized things."

"How unfortunate. Can you perhaps set up a tent, like one of those fabulous tents that the Maasai Mara do, with zebra skins and oil lamps and campaign tables and whatnot?"

Yougottabefuckingkiddingme. "Lord Greshamsbury, I don't have a single spare Maasai Mara tent at the moment, but you know, there's a bunch of surf cabins overlooking the beach where we could set you up with a bartender with some drinks."

"Oh, no, no, no. No bartender necessary. I know how short-staffed you must be as it is. But the surf cabin is a great idea."

"So you'd like this cabin prepared for you after the wedding banquet?"

"Well, no . . . I'd like to do this right now."

Of course he would. "I'll see what I can do. It might take a little time to get things set up at the cabin."

"Fabulous. Can you make it a little clubby, like the card room at White's, perhaps, where I could offer the prince something to smoke and a good scotch?"

Fuck my life. "We'll make it feel just like the card room at White's. You'd never know the difference." *Google "card room at White's."*

"You're an angel, Lee, you really are."

Twenty minutes later, Francis found himself in a hipster surf cabin that looked like one of those sickeningly perfect Zen wabi-sabi spaces featured in *Kinfolk* magazine. The only nod to White's was the tattered old Oushak rug Jackie had miraculously found, on which she placed a folding games table with a box of Cohibas, two whiskey tumblers, and a bottle of Gordon & MacPhail scotch.[*] The scotch that Prince Julius now swirled through his teeth in great satisfaction.

"I have to hand it to you, Francis. You and Arabella have really outdone yourselves. I haven't been to an affair like this since the Earl of Palliser married that Colette girl and her rich Chinese father paid for everything. Even my dear cousin Margrethe told me she's never been to a wedding this special, and you must know she gets invited to everything. I'm very relieved that I didn't have to foot the bill, ho ho ho."

"Well, funny you mention that. I'm sure you realize . . . ah . . . that the expenses have been adding up, especially since we were forced to change *all* the venues for the wedding at the very last minute."

"For sure, for sure. Rather unlucky timing, that little jism of lava. But glorious to look at. Mother Nature at her best."

Francis took a deep breath, deciding it was best to rip off the bandage quickly. "Might there be any chance . . . you could float me a little loan?"

"A loan? What could I possibly loan to you that would actually make a difference? What I have is a drop in the hat compared to you people. You know Hanne and I are so grateful, so grateful . . ." Prince Julius selected a cigar from the box and began unwrapping the plastic noisily.

"Yes, thank you. All the same, Arabella and I would be dead chuffed if you might express some of that gratitude in the form of a little loan. Don't ever tell her I asked, of course."

"Of course, of course. Say I *was* able to help out, how much would you need?"

Francis rubbed his chin nervously. "Oh, nothing much. Say, fifteen to eighteen."

---

[*] Forbes *calls this seventy-five-year-old Generations Mortlach single-malt scotch a "bargain" at $30,000 a bottle.*

"Fifteen to eighteen . . . million?"

"Yes. Or twenty to twenty-five. You know, whatever is easiest. Perhaps a round number like thirty is easier to remember."

"Thirty million . . . American?"

"Or pounds sterling if that's easier."

Prince Julius stared Francis in the eye for a second. "Ho ho ho, you're pulling my leg, aren't you?" Francis laughed politely as the prince smacked him on the back. "Bastard! You had me going for a second there."

"I did, didn't I?"

"That was a good one! *Skål!* You know, we have been so worried about Maxxie. First he got kicked out of that hippie college for selling illegal mushrooms, and ever since then he's been totally adrift. He has been nothing but a drain on me, a huge drain, and all his so-called social entrepreneur schemes have done nothing but hemorrhage money. Of course, he is a good boy, with the best of intentions. He hasn't gotten himself in the sort of trouble that his little brother has."

"Your son is in trouble?"

The prince took a puff of his cigar. "Don't you know? My little Tassilo is a junkie."

"Oh dear . . ."

"Yes, it's all those new party drugs . . . NDA, YMCA, whatever they're called. Much too addictive, I tell you. I should never have let him spend his summer DJ'ing at all the clubs in Ibiza when he was thirteen. He just came out of rehab in Switzerland—you know the rehab that's nicer than the Hotel du Cap? Cost me three hundred fifty thousand euros a month. And he stayed for THREE months! My god, can you imagine if he was actually hooked on something truly addictive? I'd be flat broke."

"You don't say."

"I say! And you know, I have not so much left in the kitty these days. I maybe have enough to see myself and Natalia through another ten, fifteen years, and then I'll have to start selling off shit. I have a pretty decent Diebenkorn and one good Bacon left; the rest are nasty old Rembrandts and Flemish landscapes that no one wants anymore.* Natalia wants to have a baby, and I said over my dead body. What are we going to live on if we have to feed a baby? Sell the Bacon? I can barely afford to pay my crew on the yacht. You know those Aussie yachties are so spoiled. You have to pay them top dollar. I might have to start hiring South Afrikaners."

Francis stared at him in disbelief. "You're really running out of money?"

"Of course. Why would I lie to you about such things? We are family now; we have no secrets. I might have to ask *you* for a loan someday."

"But what about your wife?"

"My wife? Hahaha! What makes you think Hanne's got any money? She has a flat in Oslo, one disturbing Munch she inherited from her great-aunt, and a ranch in Ojai, that's about it. I'm footing all the bills for my whole clan."

"I thought her family controlled all the oil reserves in the North Sea? For years every magazine has called her 'the Norwegian oil heiress.' "

"You of all people should know those magazines are full of ca-ca. Her von Melke av Sjokolade cousins are rolling in billions, those little piggies, they hoarded all the Class A shares starting in the seventies. But Hanne Marit's father, who ran the oil company for three decades and made his whole family so rich, was too decent to take a single Class A share. Didn't want to seem greedy. The old fool only had about eight hundred million kroners left when he kicked the bucket, and you know there were four kids to fight over the crumbs. Hanne has barely enough to feed her alpacas. And you know, those alpacas can really eat. They're worse than locusts, and when they spit, those bastards can blind you in the eye."

"Can they really?" Francis said, feeling sick to his stomach. All

---

* *At Christie's Post-War and Contemporary Art auction in 2013, Francis Bacon's* Three Studies of Lucien Freud *sold for $142.4 million.*

this time, he'd thought Augie was finally safe, that she had finally married money.

Prince Julius poured himself another glass of scotch. "This is why we are so relieved that Augusta accepted Maxxie. My boy is just so goddamn lucky to marry into the Gresham family! That's one big worry off my mind. He's your problem now, ho ho ho."

•

The wedding banquet was the pièce de résistance of the nuptial weekend. Upon arriving at Bellaloha, the dinner guests followed the torch-lit path into the rain forest, where they came upon one long curving banquet table for three hundred that snaked playfully between towering trees and verdant bushes. Not content with the natural beauty of the flora, Arabella had demanded that each tree be festooned with flowers, and hovering over the middle of the table was a floral sculpture canopy composed of thousands of orchids, dahlias, and Icelandic poppies. At the very center of the banquet was a gigantic banyan tree with thousands of ancient roots descending from the branches, and hundreds of flickering lanterns were entwined in the roots, casting a magical glow onto everyone. As the guests supped on Dover sole à la Augusta on the eighteenth-century Greshams-bury Sèvres that had not been used since Edward VII had come to stay when he was still the Prince of Wales,* Jackie was by the side of the stage, in the midst of fitting a remote microphone onto Rufus's jacket collar, when Arabella came rushing up.

"Rufus, are you giving the first toast?" Arabella excitedly inquired.

"That's the plan."

"Very good. Now, will you be saying nice things about a certain somebody?"

---

* *The request for a royal stay from Edward VII was considered both an honor and a curse by many of the English aristocracy, who would go to such elaborate lengths to make sure their great estates were up to the royal standard (knowing the king's legendary appetite and penchant for luxury) that they would sometimes go into debt renovating, redecorating, and hiring new chefs before the royal visit. Pity there wasn't a Best Western in those days.*

"I plan to say very nice things about Augie and Maxxie, yes, after I humiliate them for a few rounds, of course."

"That's not what I'm talking about. Will you have *something special* to announce in your speech?"

"Something special?" Rufus looked confused.

"About a certain entente cordiale, perhaps?"

"Mother, English please. I haven't a clue what you're talking about."

"Oh come on, no need to be coy with me," Arabella giggled. "I'm talking about your *petit plaisir de l'après-midi?* A little bird told me that you spent the better part of the day holed up in Solène de Courcy's suite at the Mauna Lani."

Rufus rolled his eyes. "Solène sprained her ankle and exposed her bleeding knee to water contaminated with flesh-eating bacteria. Eden had her on so many antibiotics I had to make sure she didn't have a bad reaction."

"Is that what you were doing? Making sure she had no bad reaction?" Arabella sniggered gleefully.

"Precisely. And she spent an hour giving me advice on how to improve my art career—unsolicited, I might add."

"How kind of her. She's such a sensible girl. Now, you must repay the favor by saying something nice about Solène and her mother during your toast."

"You want me to mention Solène and her mother *during my toast to the bride and groom?*"

"Why not? Haven't the de Courcys been the highlight of your weekend?"

Rufus gaped at his mother. "Wait a minute. Have you been trying to set me up with Solène all this time?"

"I know it might be a little premature, but it would be so fun to give our audience a little preview of what's coming next season."

"Next season? Do you think we're living in a television series? Let me make this very simple for you: Solène de Courcy is a very nice girl, but it's never going to happen in a million years. She's not my type."

Arabella looked at her son in exasperation. "Not your type? What's wrong with you? She's one of the most beautiful women on the planet! She has an exclusive modeling contract with Chanel!"

"Mum, when will you realize that I don't give a damn about any of that?"

"I don't understand . . . Bea told me things were going perfectly!"

"How would Bea know what's going on? I haven't seen her for days."

"I'm going to murder those silly girls! Bea's too distracted by her photo shoots, and Eden has been an utter failure."

"What does Eden have to do with any of this?"

"Bea and Eden are rooting for you to fall in love with Solène! They both adore her. Everyone adores her. Why can't you?"

"*Eden's* been part of your maniacal plans?"

"She was supposed to earn her keep, but it looks like she's been far too distracted herself, sleeping with that Freddy guy."

"Wait—what? Eden and Freddy are *not* sleeping together!"

"Of course they are. They're having a torrid fling. Eden's desperately been trying to catch Freddy since the moment he arrived on that ridiculous shark boat. And you don't even know the half of it, that stupid girl has been so careless that she's gotten herself—"

Rufus rushed off before she could finish.

•

At the other end of the banquet table, Nicolai Chalamet-Chaude (Wetherby/Dragon/Eton/Balliol) was in the midst of explaining to Eden how Hawaii had become quite the haven for billionaires ("You've got Larry in Lanai, Mark and Priscilla kicking it in Kauai, and Pierre over in Oahu")* when Rufus came rushing up with an unmistakably urgent look. "Eden, may I have a word?"

"Of course. Baron, if you'll excuse me for a moment," Eden said politely.

Rufus grabbed her by the hand and led her down a pathway, cut-

---

* *Ellison, Zuckerberg, Omidyar.*

ting through a thicket of bushes until they found a quiet clearing in the forest. A warm crimson glow filtered through the trees, making everything seem otherworldly.

"Everything okay?" Eden asked.

"Yes. Are *you* okay?"

"I am, now that you've rescued me from that man."

"Good, good. I just need to know something . . ."

"Yes?"

"Are you sleeping with Freddy Farman-Farmihian?"

"What in the world would make you think that?"

"Er . . . I just . . . you've spent all afternoon with him."

"And you spent all afternoon in Solène's room, not that I'd ever ask what happened in there."

"Nothing happened with Solène! Well, nothing I initiated anyway. She did lunge at me several times, but when I rebuffed her, she started ranting that I couldn't get it up and was too intimidated by her success."

"Solène *lunged at you?*"

"Like a raccoon on meth, but you know I'd never touch her even with a ten-foot pole."

"What made you think I was sleeping with Freddy?"

"My mother told me."

"Your *mother?*" Eden grimaced in disbelief, not comprehending how the countess could have come to that conclusion. "Either your mother's deranged from all the stress or someone's been spreading vicious gossip."

"No, you're right, Mummy's deranged. But I was watching the two of you all weekend . . . dancing at the ball, laughing like old friends during our excursions . . . I'm not sure . . . I got worried."

"Worried? Rufus, I'm perfectly capable of taking care of myself. I told you, Freddy's a sweet soul underneath all that swagger."

"So you *do* like him. Today when I saw how intimate you were with him down by the pool, I just—"

"Intimate?"

"You were caressing his hand . . ."

"I was comforting him. He was telling me about his mother, she died when he was twelve."

Rufus suddenly felt very foolish. "Oh god, I'm sorry. I've gotten everything all wrong, haven't I? I was sure he fancied you, and I thought that you were trying to make me jealous."

"Why on earth would I do that?"

"Because . . . bloody hell, I'm so confused . . ." Rufus found himself fumbling his words. He took a deep breath and gazed deep into Eden's eyes. "It's just that I'm in love with you."

"Whaaat?" Eden stared at him in utter shock.

"I'm utterly, crazily in love with you, Eden. This entire week has made me realize how special you are to me, how special you've always been. Remember how I told you in Tintagel that you were the only girl I'd ever want to marry?"

"We were so young then—"

"I meant every word of it. And after you spent the night in Puako, after that shower under the moonlight, I haven't been able to stop thinking about you. I can still smell you on my sheets, and seeing you tonight, looking so unbelievably beautiful, I just needed to—"

"Stop. Please stop before you say something you'll regret," Eden pleaded.

"I'm not going to regret this." Without any warning, Rufus pulled Eden into an embrace and kissed her.

Eden could hardly process what was happening, but she found herself yielding to his passionate kiss. She found that she could not stop kissing him, she found that her lips were on fire and the ground beneath her feet was spinning out of control but she couldn't make it stop even though she wanted it to stop. "STOP! STOP!" It took Rufus a second to realize that it wasn't Eden speaking.

They parted and looked up to see Jackie rushing toward them through the bushes. "DON'T SAY ANOTHER WORD!" Jackie shouted breathlessly as she reached behind his waist for the microphone remote pack that was clipped to his belt and turned it off. "You've got a hot mic! You must have brushed up against something—the mic was on the whole time. Everybody at the banquet could hear you! Even the queen of Denmark!"

Rufus and Eden looked at her in horror.

"Actually, Rufus, they could only hear *you*," Jackie clarified.

"I'm not sure if that's better or worse,"* Rufus said, grimacing. "My god—Solène!"

Jackie nodded slowly. "Yeah, Solène heard you loud and very clear. I've never seen anyone on crutches run off so fast."

Eden stared wide-eyed at Rufus, too shocked by everything that had just happened to say anything. A beam of light suddenly hit her face, and then more lights began to shine on all their faces as five firemen wielding bright flashlights emerged from the thicket.

"Everybody out! We need to clear this entire site now."

"Clear? What do you mean 'clear'?" Arabella cried.

"We're evacuating everybody. Party's over."

Jackie shook her head vehemently. "That's not possible, sir. We are in the middle of a wedding banquet, and Bonnae Gokson's wedding cake hasn't even been served yet. Do you know who our guests are? The governor is here, Senator Mazie Hirono is here. The Weeknd is about to perform."

The lead fireman snorted. "The Weeknd's going to have to find another weekend to perform. Don't you people see the orange glow over there? A big new fissure vent has opened up and the lava's moving downhill fast. Your lives are in danger! We need to get everyone out NOW!"

---

* *Go back and read just Rufus's lines again if you wish. It was far worse if you could only hear one side of the conversation.*

LONDON

The best thing about London is Paris.

—DIANA VREELAND

Hong Kong, 1995

"If they hadn't all been drinking so much, Roger Gao might not have reacted so recklessly. And if the victim hadn't jumped up onto the banquette, the trajectory of his fall would not have sent him over the railing. And if those new Philippe Starck candelabras made of Czechoslovakian crystal had not just been placed on the dining tables that evening, the victim would in all likelihood have survived the fall. Maybe he would have broken his back, at worst," the chief inspector reported.

"It was a chain of very unfortunate events," the police commissioner said, shaking his head.

"How many years will Roger Gao get?" Dr. George Tong asked.

"Voluntary manslaughter. Given his age, clean record, and the circumstances . . . ten-year sentence, at minimum."

"Depends on the judge," the chief inspector chimed in.

As they left the police headquarters and walked along Lockhart Road, the old doctor turned to his son Thomas Tong with a weary look. *"Henry is dead. Nothing we do will bring him back. And now the Gaos will be ruined. The poor girl who loved Henry, and her brother in prison for decades."*

"It's all very sad," Thomas said.

"My only consolation is that your mother didn't live to see this day. It would have broken her heart."

Thomas thought about his mother and the way she'd worshipped his younger brother. He could never do wrong in her eyes.

"I feel we should use a portion of Henry's windfall to help the Gaos

obtain the best solicitor possible. Perhaps they can help get him a reduced sentence. It does no one any good for this boy to rot away in prison during the most productive years of his life."

"Not many people would think the way you do, Dad, after losing a son."

"The Gaos have lost a son too. I feel that I bear some responsibility in all this tragedy. Because I was never able to say no to my son."

"None of us could."

The old doctor nodded. "Now, what do we do for the sister?"

I

THE NAGS HEAD

BELGRAVIA, LONDON • *FIVE DAYS LATER*

Thomas walked nearly to the end of Kinnerton Street and entered the tiny pub that had been a watering hole since Victorian times. The quaintly misshapen room was plastered with over a century's worth of paraphernalia, the walls and ceiling so thick with picture frames, news clippings, and armed service patches that you felt as if you'd stepped into a giant, teeming collage. Passing the crowded bar festooned with naval hats, Thomas gave the bartender a friendly nod as he ducked into the back room, where he knew he'd find Francis.

Sure enough, the earl was there nursing a whiskey at his usual corner table, and in his rumpled cords and Pringle jumper, Francis would have appeared to Thomas almost as he had back when they were cramming for their GCSEs, if only his slumped posture didn't betray the decades that had passed. Thomas sat down on the rickety leather chair across from him. Francis looked up, his expression almost one of surprise. "Isn't it strange? Lava can erupt on an island in the middle of the Pacific Ocean, but the Nags Head never seems to change."

"Thank god for that!" Thomas said.

"I'm surprised you could meet up on such short notice."

"My last patient canceled, so it worked out perfectly."

"Ah, that's right. You're always up in London on Fridays, aren't you?"

"I've been here since yesterday, catching up on the backlog. Did you just get back this morning?"

"We landed at noon. Been trying to stay awake ever since."

The bartender came around the corner and plonked a frothy pint of beer in front of Thomas, who immediately reached into the breast pocket of his houndstooth blazer for his wallet.

"Put that away! Your money's no good here, Dr. Tong!" the barman said gruffly before retreating.

"What's that about?" Francis inquired.

"His sister's a patient of mine," Thomas replied simply.

"Ah, of course. You're always saving lives, while I just seem to ruin them . . ."

Thomas knew that Francis was likely to keep sinking into his own pity party, so he cut to the chase: "So, how was the survey?"

"Terrible! They flew us around in a chopper over the resort. Only way to see it as they've closed all the roads leading down."

"How'd it look?" Thomas asked as he took a swig from his mug.

"Even worse than we expected. A third vent has opened on top of the hill, and the main buildings are now in the direct line of the lava flow."

"I don't suppose there's any way to divert it?"

"Pointless—the lava just obliterates everything in its path. Only a matter of days till the entire resort is destroyed. Thank god no houses or towns are in danger. The Hawaii County Civil Defense Agency wants to declare all of Bellaloha a disaster zone."

"Jesus," Thomas muttered, shaking his head. "I'm very sorry."

Francis shrugged. "Do you remember the first time I brought you to Greshamsbury Hall at half term? When we were fourteen?"

"Of course," Thomas said with a grin.

"I'll never forget what you said when I took you through the house, when you saw the Long Gallery. You said, 'All this is yours? I'm very sorry.' You were taking the piss, but I knew right then we'd be friends for life. You understood precisely how I felt about the place. Funny, from the day it dawned on me that I would one day inherit Greshamsbury Hall, I always suspected it would end with me. I'm the eighteenth generation in a long line of poor sods trying to keep the old pile afloat. Just never thought Mother Nature would be the one to finally do the trick."

"It's not going to end with you . . ."

"Ah, but it will. Bellaloha going up in flames—or disintegrating into volcanic ash—is the final nail in the coffin."

"Surely Lloyd's will help offset whatever damage there is?"

Francis let out a mordant laugh. "Lloyd's? It's never been possible to insure commercial property on the Big Island because of the volcanic activity."

Thomas almost choked on his lager. "You mean to say you let Arabella spend—how many hundreds of millions—building the resort of her dreams, and *none of it is insured*?"

Francis nodded slowly.

"My god," Thomas whispered as he sank into his chair, suddenly feeling the true weight of their conversation. He began doing some calculations in his head. "If you liquidated everything and allowed the creditors to take over the hotels . . . London and Hong Kong, particularly . . ."

"Even if we sold off all the hotels, there's still a huge shortfall because of Bellaloha. We'd still be about two fifty to three hundred million in the hole."

Thomas shook his head in disbelief, but of course he knew the stark truth about the Gresham finances. It was all a precarious house of cards, and it was finally about to come toppling down.

Francis gave Thomas a pleading look. "I know we've been through this before, but is there any way you could make an appeal to . . . Rene?"

Thomas sighed. "If you weren't already so indebted to Rene, I'd say it would be worth trying, but it's too risky at this point. He's too unpredictable, and last thing we want him to do is call in all his chips now. I don't suppose you had a chance to talk to Prince Julius?"

"I did. Turns out the prince has been keeping up appearances as well. He made it quite clear he was never going to be in a position to help me—or his son, for that matter. In fact, his precise words regarding Max were, 'He's your problem now.' "

"He really said that?"

"Yes. I'm afraid it's going to be quite a disappointing honeymoon for Augie and Maxxie, as it sinks in that neither has quite the fortune they assumed the other has," Francis laughed wearily.

"They'll be fine."

"I'm not worried about those two. I'm more concerned about everyone in Greshamsbury that depends on us—the workers, the tenants, the families who've lived there for generations. And of course, I'm worried sick about that patient of yours that canceled at the last minute today."

"Arabella." Thomas nodded. "Any idea why she canceled?"

"Heaven knows. I tried to talk to her on the flight back, but she locked herself in the bedroom of the plane and refused to come out."

"She's still in shock," Thomas said, shaking his head as he recalled the chaos that ensued as everyone scrambled to evacuate the resort in the midst of the wedding banquet. Most of the guests who had come on their own jets fled the island the same evening, while the remaining few left after the farewell brunch at the Nanea Golf Club the next morning, which better resembled a wake. Eden and Thomas had been fortunate enough to be offered a ride on Freddy Farman-Farmihian's plane that afternoon, while Bea flew off with one of her Leung cousins and the bridal couple departed for their honeymoon.[*] Only Rufus remained on the island.

"The wedding was supposed to be Arabella's crowning glory, but now it's turned out to be the royal fiasco of the century. She acts like she's above it all, but you know how she is about such things. Face is so bloody important to her. She thinks Bellaloha is only a temporary loss—I can't imagine how she'll react when she finds out the truth," Francis said numbly.

---

[*] *Augie and Maxxie's honeymoon consisted of a shaman training retreat in Peru, led by Gopal Das, of course.*

"How much does she know?" Thomas asked warily.

"She's known things have been a bit dicey here and there, but she hasn't a clue how bad it is. It's all my fault, Tom. I've shielded her all these years from the reality of the situation, I can't really explain why. Maybe I've always felt guilty . . ."

"Guilty of what?"

Francis stared into his whiskey and let out a deep sigh. "Call me crazy—I adore my wife, but when we first got married everyone was just rotten to her. The women, especially. Oh, they were always polite to a fault, but I could see how they closed ranks and froze her out. And of course I pretended nothing was happening but I was so damn ashamed—ashamed of my family, of my friends . . . people I had known all my life behaving so ignorantly, so cruelly, toward Arabella and the children. If I hadn't been the earl, I can't imagine how much worse the kids might have had it."

"Francis, I had no idea . . . ," Thomas said.

"No, by the time you arrived in Greshamsbury things were all good. Arabella had turned things around remarkably. She transformed Greshamsbury, and after Min Hogg blessed the house and Derry Moore took his photos, many of those who'd snubbed us were clamoring to be let back in. I was in awe of what Arabella had achieved, and I began to believe in her vision to take things to the next level and go global. If Rocco Forte could bloody do it, why couldn't we? I have no one to blame but myself—I was the one who decided to double down and indulge her every whim. It was our revenge against the establishment. I thought I was being bold and visionary, unlike my father, who did fuck all. So many old families like mine just let their fortunes wither away; I wanted to set things up right for future generations. I thought I was being brilliant, but I've really shat the bed, haven't I? For Arabella and the girls and especially for Rufus. I'm not sure how I'll ever be able to look him in the face."

Thomas leaned back in his chair and gazed into the flickering flames for a few moments. He realized that he had misjudged his friend. He had always assumed that Francis was born into a charmed life and took it for granted that everything would always work out for him. He'd thought that all this time, Francis was like a well-bred ostrich with his head in the sand, ignoring the circling lions that were waiting to kill.* But it turned out Francis was not as oblivious as he had seemed, that he was a desperate man trying to do all he could for the family he loved.

Thomas took a deep breath. "Bloody hell, I'll talk to Rene. I can't promise much, but I will try. It wouldn't be in his interest for you to become insolvent."

A glimmer of hope flashed through Francis's eyes. "You'll call him?"

"No . . . I think I'll need to put in a personal appearance for this."

Francis could hear the hesitancy in his friend's voice. "Look, I know how hard it must be for you . . . to . . . to do this. You've done more for me than I deserve. Whatever happens, I'm enormously grateful."

Thomas simply nodded.

---

* *In reality, it would be difficult for a lion to kill a grown ostrich. Lions are terrific sprinters with a top speed of over eighty kmh, but they can only maintain this speed for very short periods. Ostriches may only manage seventy kmh, but they have much greater stamina and could outrun a lazy lion. BUT . . . lions are skilled predators and could ambush the ostrich in a sneak attack. However, the ostrich has two extremely sharp claws on each foot, allowing it to, hypothetically, disembowel a lion with a single well-placed kick. All this is rather moot, because lions don't particularly enjoy the taste of ostrich. They much prefer antelope or zebra, served very rare.*

II

GRESHAMSBURY HALL

GRESHAMSBURY, ENGLAND • *THE NEXT MORNING*

The email from the Countess of Greshamsbury's secretary stated:

Arrive at 10:00 a.m. sharp. Take the upper driveway and park in any of the spaces to the left of the mews. You will be met at the front door and given a tour of the public rooms, approx. forty-five minutes.

The countess will meet with you at 10:45 a.m., and you will have approx. fifteen minutes for the interview.

After the interview, you may tour the grounds at your leisure for approx. sixty mins. Mud boots are advisable.

The countess will not be talking about the wedding.

Cosima Money-Coutts (Broomwood Hall/Stowe/St. Andrews), who was writing a feature on Greshamsbury Hall for *Cabana* magazine, did precisely as she was instructed and pulled her Saab into the first parking spot next to the mews. She walked across the driveway, noting the immaculately raked gravel, and as she was about to approach the front door, which was flanked by a pair of bronze wolves by Harumi Klossowska de Rola, a set of French doors along the side of the house suddenly opened up.

"Miss Money-Coutts?" an imposing blond man who looked as if

he had stepped off the cover of a paranormal romance novel inquired with an easy grin.

"Ye-yes," Cosima stuttered, disarmed by his piercing green eyes.

"Good morning. I'm Hemsworth. I'll be giving you the tour today."

"Thank you," Cosima said. *An Aussie. I'm in trouble.*

"Come in through here," Hemsworth said. Cosima entered a room that was bathed in soft morning light and furnished in a stunningly simple manner, with low-slung sofas slipcovered in white linen and matching tufted ottomans scattered about the space, billowing curtains of gray shot silk, and Venetian plaster walls that glowed the loveliest shade of rose. A pair of Irish setters lazed on one of the ottomans, barely deigning to notice her. She was not expecting such an intimate, inviting space to be her first impression of Greshamsbury Hall.

"The countess has a way with color," Cosima remarked, quietly marveling at how the massive chartreuse and rose art deco–patterned carpet perfectly echoed the radiating hues of the Judy Chicago lithograph *Mary Queen of Scots* over the mantel. "Is the rug an heirloom?"

"It's from Shanghai, from the thirties. The countess rescued it from a private club that was about to be refurbished," Hemsworth noted.

"Marvelous. This is the drawing room, I presume?"

"Yes, it's where the family usually gather."

"Is the family home at the moment?"

"Lady Beatrice is out of the country, Princess Augusta[*] is on her honeymoon with Prince Maxxie, and his lordship just returned from London."

"And Rufus?"

"The viscount is out of the country as well."

---

[*] *Hemsworth is incorrect to refer to Augie as "Princess Augusta." Since she was not born a princess, her new name upon marriage is actually Augusta, the Princess Maximillian zu Liechtenburg.*

"My brother went to Radley with him."

"Ah, you're friends with the viscount?"

"God no, he wouldn't know me. I was two years younger, but many girls I knew had mad crushes on Rufus."

"So I've heard." Hemsworth grinned, and as he turned to lead the way through the doorway, she couldn't help but stare appreciatively at his tight black jeans. *Blimey, you could stack a row of pottery on that arse.*

"This is the Great Hall, where you'd normally enter from," Hemsworth explained. Cosima's eyes adjusted to the dimness of the double-height-ceilinged room, where medieval tapestries hung on the paneled walls alongside portraits of various Greshams through the centuries. She turned and stopped dead in her tracks. Before her, commanding the center of the room in front of the wide timbered staircase, was a massive bronze sculpture of what could only be described as a goddesslike alien riding a dragon. "Is that a—"

"Yes, Wangechi Mutu. The countess was her very first collector in England."

"Of course she was! Astonishing! It makes me feel like I'm in a Kubrick film," Cosima said as she circled the otherworldly sculpture.

"Which one?" Hemsworth inquired.

"*2001: A Space Odyssey.*"

"With a bit of *Barry Lyndon* thrown in, perhaps?"

"Of course," Cosima said. *Aussie, blond, AND a cinephile. I think I'm in love.*

Hemsworth added, "I've always felt that *Eyes Wide Shut* didn't quite get its due."

"I couldn't agree more." *I'd like you to rail me with my eyes wide shut.*

Just then, Arabella descended the stairs, looking pristine in a Roland Mouret emerald silk shirtdress. On each wrist flashed matching Hemmerle Harmony bangles of amber, peroba wood, and bronze.

"Lady Greshamsbury," Cosima greeted her, slightly awed that the famously youthful countess displayed no visible sign of fillers up close.

"Good morning," Arabella replied. "Thank you, Hemsworth. I can take it from here. Could we have tea in the orangerie?"

"Of course, ma'am," Hemsworth said as he left the room.

"Now, you've seen the Great Room and my Mutu. What can I show you next?"

"Let's see . . . if we only have fifteen minutes to spare, what do you think is most important for me to see?" Cosima inquired.

"*Hiyah,* don't worry about that fifteen-minute nonsense. You are my guest for the day. Now, why don't I show you the library?"

Cosima smiled appreciatively as she followed the countess eagerly into the next room. She was expecting a traditional library with dark oak shelves and tufted leather, but instead she was met by a jewel box of a room lined with floor-to-ceiling steel bookcases set against a wall that seemed to shimmer with the faintest whisper of gold.

Standing on the rolling library ladder at the far end of the room was Lord Francis.

"Ah, here's the earl. Whatever are you doing, Francis?" Arabella chirped.

"Hallelujah! She's speaking to me again!" Francis said from atop the ladder.

Arabella laughed merrily. "Hahaha! My husband the jokester! Francis, this is the writer from *Cabana* magazine. You remember she's doing a BIG FEATURE ON GRESHAMSBURY HALL for their next issue?"

"Oh, ah, yes," Francis replied, clueing in at last. He climbed down the ladder with a copy of Benjamin Graham's *The Intelligent Investor* in his hand.* "I know no one ever really uses this library, but I actually do read a book from time to time."

Arabella glared at Francis as he scurried out of the room. "He's joking again. We all read. We are a reading family."

---

* *One of the most popular and influential investing books ever written, the said volume was purchased by the current earl's father back in the 1970s, but sadly, no one seems to have ever opened it. No less a sage than Warren Buffett proclaimed, "Picking up that book was one of the luckiest moments of my life."*

"I'm sure you are. What's the last book you enjoyed?" Cosima inquired.

"Let me see . . . yes . . . I'm so bad at remembering names . . . you know what I recently read? *Lace,* by Shirley Conran," Arabella said, noticing the book jutting out on the shelf right behind Cosima's shoulder.

"WHICH ONE OF YOU BITCHES IS MY MOTHER?" Cosima said with a sneer.

Arabella looked at her in shock. "I'm sorry?"

"I said, 'Which one of you bitches is my mother?' It's the most memorable line from the book, don't you think?"

"Yes! Yes, of course," Arabella replied, still a bit confused.

"These steel structures are stunning. They almost seem to float off the wall. I'm reminded of Richard Serra's metalworks."

Arabella nodded. "The original bookcases dated back to the eighteenth century and were infested with termites, so we were forced to tear them all down. And then I thought, why not do something different in here? Fabricate the shelves out of steel and really reinvent the library but also ensure that all these precious books remain preserved for generations to come. I mean, *Lace,* it's such a classic. I want my grandchildren to be able to read it."

"Er, I suppose. Now, I must ask . . . what in the world is that wall finish made of?" Cosima asked, peering at the gloriously patinated surface behind the leatherbound volumes.

"Those are the original walls. We took it right down to the timber and this was what we found. Apparently the walls were originally all covered with gilt, and these are the remnants of it."

Cosima moaned in ecstasy. "It's glorious! Like warm treacle! You've succeeded in preserving a great manor house while propelling it decidedly into the future. In fact, I see the title of my piece: 'A Stately Future!'"

"Thank you." Arabella smiled Buddha-like, basking in the praise.

"Lady Greshamsbury, I have to confess that before coming, I'd heard so many stories, I had certain preconceptions in my mind. I was prepared to be . . . unmoved. But Greshamsbury Hall is a revelation. It's been quite a while since I've seen a stately that seamlessly integrates the avant-garde with the historical in such a timeless, unaffected way. I thought I'd be visiting someplace dripping with, to quote the Baron Alexis de Redé, 'the kind of luxury of which Americans are so fond,' but I feel as though I'm at Villa Necchi Campiglio in Milan or Dominique de Menil's house in River Oaks."

"My god, Dominique! I'm not worthy of the comparison," Arabella said mock bashfully.

"Why not? The relationship you've created between your art collection and a living, breathing family manor house is rather inspired."

"Well, for me, it begins with the art. The art sets the tone and the structure in every room."

"But your choices are so original, so sui generis. In most of the houses we visit, I glance at the walls and everything looks like it came straight out of a Christie's catalog. Everyone collects the same ten artists, the same furniture—it bores me to death. Here, I find myself confounded and surprised by the choices you've made every time I turn the corner."

"Well, anyone can have a James Turrell swimming pool or a flock of Lalanne sheep. I wanted to do something unexpected here. I wanted to celebrate the artists who challenge me."

"Now, hasn't your son, Rufus, become an artist as well? No doubt he's been inspired by what's on the walls of his home."

Arabella flinched almost imperceptibly. "Rufus does dabble in art, but he is involved in many exciting projects preparing him to be the future earl."

"Well, whatever he may be doing, you're clearly one of our leading lifestyle oracles, and everyone's dying to see your new resort in Hawai—" Cosima stopped mid-syllable, realizing her faux pas as she saw Arabella's face freeze up. "I'm sorry, er . . . I mean, everyone's dying to . . . know which designers have inspired you."

Arabella visibly relaxed. "Ah, well, Rory Cameron, Geoffrey Bennison, and Edward Tuttle have always inspired me."

"Superb, but are there any designers you love who are perhaps alive?"

"Oh yes. Let's see . . . I love Cathy Vedovi, the Misczynskis, and Rose Uniacke, of course. François-Joseph Graf, Serdar Gülgün, and Lorenzo Castillo never fail to astonish me, and I think Remy Renzullo, Child Studio, and Fabrizio Casiraghi are doing some very exciting things these days."

"Quite."

The sound of tires crunching on the gravel could suddenly be heard as the Irish setters rushed out the front door barking excitedly. Arabella glanced out the window and saw Bea emerging from an Ardennes green Range Rover. Hemsworth scurried around with other footmen unloading vast amounts of luggage. Bea entered through the front door and walked into the drawing room as the dogs jumped up on her excitedly. "Noel, Liam, I've missed you so much," Bea cried as she kissed them both.

Arabella smiled tightly at Cosima. "Would you give me a moment?" She crossed the Great Hall into the drawing room and found Bea sitting on a sofa struggling to remove her Gianvito Rossi boots.

"Where the hell have you been?" Arabella demanded.

"What do you mean?" Bea looked up in surprise.

"You were supposed to fly straight back to England from Hawaii!"

"Oh. Was I? We stopped off in Penang for lunch. You know, Penang truly has the yummiest food—the *char kuey teow* is second to none."

"And your *char kuey teow* took five days to eat?"

"May I remind you that I was on Cousin Aurelius's plane? And you know what the etiquette is when you're a guest on someone else's jet—you have to go wherever they want to go, and Aurelius suddenly had a hankering for some Penang street food, so we diverted the plane. Then after lunch in Penang, Aurelius wanted to drop by Dubai for a party. So we stopped over and that's where we met this marvelous fellow, Turki, who invited us to an art exposition in the middle of the Arabian desert, in AlUla. Mummy, you would have loved it. The art installations were set among these fabulous tombs from the Nabataean civilization, and there was an incredible resort there that Turki insisted we stay at for a couple of nights. I think Turki's family built it."

"Stop this Turki nonsense! How dare you!" Arabella shouted.

"I'm sorry?" Bea looked taken aback.

"How dare you abandon ship and leave the scene of the crime! You let your eyes off the prize!"

"So many mixed metaphors. What crime are you referring to precisely?"

"You ruined the wedding!"

"How did *I* ruin the wedding? I don't seem to recall being able to control magma."

"You were supposed to make Rufus and Freddy fight over Solène! You were supposed to make sure Rufus fell for her!"

"Look, as far as I knew, Freddy and Rufus were both pursuing Solène like cheetahs in heat—I don't understand what went wrong."

"Well, I do. You were far too preoccupied with all those damn photographers to realize that the cheetahs were after the wrong gazelle—"

"Wait a minute—*you* set up most of those shoots, Mummy! I was just doing what you wanted! I ran around nonstop trying to do a million things and missed out on the best parts of—"

"Ahem!" Arabella and Bea turned to see Hemsworth standing at the open door. "Lady Gresham, shall we show Miss Money-Coutts into the orangerie, where tea is being served? *The sound does travel in these parts . . .*"

Arabella took a deep breath, collecting herself. "Yes, of course. Thank you for reminding me, Hemsworth. I will return to Miss Money-Coutts now." Arabella turned to Bea with an icy glare. "Don't even *think* I'm done with you!" She stalked off, returning to the library, where Cosima was peering at the Oswald Birley portrait and pretending not to have heard anything.

"So sorry! My daughter has been away and I wanted to welcome her home properly. Now, where were we? Shall we have some tea?"

Arabella took Cosima across the Great Lawn, explaining how she had painstakingly restored the upper gardens originally laid out by Capability Brown, and led her into the Victorian wrought iron and glass orangerie, where an unexpected suite of furniture hid among the thickets of citrus plants. In the center of the room, a delectable array of teatime treats had been set out on an ancient, moss-covered stone table. Cosima sat down on a surprisingly comfortable stool and stared up at the huge golden disks hovering above them like a flying saucer.

"Are the disks from Blackman Cruz?" Cosima asked.

"It's an installation by Anish Kapoor, actually," Arabella replied.

"Of course it is! And these decomposing stools . . . let me guess . . . Rick Owens and Michèle Lamy?"

Arabella shook her head. "I found these at a flea market in Antwerp many years ago. I think they were twenty euros each."

"How inspired! I love how you mix high and low, periods and styles, especially here—there's such an interesting tension between the delicate and the robust, such a charming decay."

"Thank you. I'm sure you know how hard it is to do charming decay. Now, try one of these *ling yung bao*," Arabella said as she placed one of the treats onto Cosima's plate.

"What is this?" Cosima looked at the steamed white bun with the pink dot in the center a little dubiously.

"It's a bun filled with lotus seed paste—it's sweet and aromatic. My afternoon teas always include the classic treats like scones and sandwiches along with Cantonese delicacies, just like our cook did in Hong Kong when I was growing up. If you fancy something on the savory side, try these coronation chicken curry puffs."

"Curry puffs, how novel! And what are these little yellow tarts?"

"*Daan taat.* Egg custard tarts. Try one."

Cosima nibbled gingerly on her tart, before her eyes widened in delight. "Oh my," she said, gobbling the entire tart. "What perfect treats to complement these precious Lucie Rie plates! Now, tell me, where is the famous tobacco-lacquered room I've heard so much about?"

"Ah, the tobacco-lacquered room. Everyone always wants to know about the tob—" Arabella stopped midsentence as she noticed Eden strolling across the lawn toward the main house with a pile of garment bags. She bolted up from the table and stormed out of the orangerie like a demon possessed.

III

THE GREAT LAWN

"What are you doing here?" Arabella called out as she came marching out into the middle of the upper garden.

Eden stopped dead in her tracks. "Good morning, Lady Arabella. Bea texted that she was home—I'm returning the dresses she lent."

"You made very good use of those dresses, didn't you?" *And even better use taking them off!*

"I did. I'm so grateful, Lady Arabella."

Grateful you got to seduce my son with a moonlit shower. Suddenly, a horrifying thought occurred to Arabella. *Could Eden be pregnant with Rufus's baby?* She scrutinized Eden hard. "How are you feeling?"

"Fine."

"How's your nausea?"

Eden looked at her in confusion. "Er . . . I haven't been nauseous since that morning on Freddy's boat."

"That's right, you were on Freddy's boat too, weren't you? Looks like you've been everywhere with everyone." *I'm not as deranged as you think, girl. I know everything that's going on.*

"Um . . . I'm not sure what you mean."

Like hell you don't. You were in my son's bed. He can still smell you in his sheets. "Give me the dresses."

"I can take them in to Bea."

"No, no, hand them over. Hurry up, I'm in the midst of a very important interview with *Cabana* magazine at the moment."

"Sorry, I didn't realize. I'll get out of the way," Eden replied, handing over the clothes and making a hasty exit.

Arabella stood holding the heavy stack of garment bags. Suddenly she called out, "Bea . . ." And then much louder: "BEEEEEA!"

Bea came rushing out onto the lawn. "What's the matter? Are you okay?"

"Take these," Arabella said, shoving the stack of garment bags into Bea's arms.

"Oh, was Eden here? Why didn't she come up?"

"Because I didn't allow her to. Now, please burn those dresses."

"What?"

"You heard me. Burn them!"

"Even the ice-blue Chanel couture gown?"

"It's tainted. I don't want any of those dresses in my house. Just like I never want that *sor hai*[*] to set foot in my house ever again!"

"Mummy, Eden's really not the one to be blamed . . . ," Bea said cautiously, knowing her mother was rapidly losing it—the Cantonese swearing was always a dead giveaway.

"Like hell she's not! She was supposed to help Rufus fall for Solène . . ."

"And she tried . . ."

"She sure did. She swanned around in these couture gowns— paid for with *my* money—in order to entrap your poor brother and Freddy Farman-Farmihian!"

"What do you mean *entrap*?"

"Beatrice Gresham, are you really *that* slow? Can't you see how she's been toying with both of them? First of all, she seduced Freddy on his boat—"

"Mummy, I was with Eden on Freddy's boat. We all were. Trust me, she was too busy projectile vomiting to seduce anyone."

"Then she seduced your brother at his beach shack! That gold-digging tramp forced him into that slimy outdoor shower and had her

---

[*] *A quaint Cantonese expression that translates to "dumb cunt."*

way with him! I know things about Eden Tong that you don't . . . ," Arabella said ominously.

Francis, who had heard all the commotion, wandered into the garden. "Hellooo. Is anything the matter?"

Bea said in a low voice, "Mummy has officially lost her mind."

"I have not! Francis, that little slut slept with Rufus!"

Francis looked horrified. "God in heaven! What could ever possess you to think that Bea would sleep with her own brother?"

"Not Bea, you nincompoop! EDEN!!" Arabella screeched.

"Eden Tong?"

"What other Eden do we know? Don't pretend you didn't hear Rufus on the sound system. We all did. She was shagging our son in the rain forest, right under our very noses!"

Bea spied Cosima peeking out the window of the orangerie and nudged her father urgently. "Let's get Mummy to her bedroom. I think she's feeling out of sorts—"

"I am not out of sorts!" Arabella protested.

"Darling, do come inside," Francis said, grasping Arabella's hand gently.

Arabella swatted him away. "Stop ordering me around!"

Francis steeled himself to remain calm. "Darling, please come inside with me. I need to tell you something rather important—"

"Tell me right here!"

"Trust me, you really won't want me to do that."

"I'm not going anywhere with you! Spit it out now!"

"All right then, have it your way. We're broke, Arabella. Completely, utterly, flat broke. We've been mortgaged to the hilt for years, but now that Bellaloha's destroyed we owe the banks hundreds of millions that we have no way of paying back. We're going to have to give up all the hotels, all the houses, the art, your jewelry, even the clothes on your back—"

"Eek! Eek! Shut up, you fool! Come inside for god's sake!" Arabella shrieked as she disappeared into the house.

Francis sighed as he reluctantly followed after his wife, leaving Bea standing in the garden holding on to the garment bags, utterly stupefied.

IV

THE ORANGERIE

GRESHAMSBURY HALL · *MOMENTS LATER*

Cosima Money-Coutts could hardly believe what was happening in the garden. Did that Chinese girl really shag Rufus in the rain forest? Were the Greshams really flat broke? She had a front-row seat to the scoop of the century. Maybe she ought to call Graydon and offer up this morsel for *Air Mail*. She took her phone out of her purse and began fumbling away, trying to find the video function to record more of the hysterical scene.

"I'd put that away if I were you." Cosima looked up and saw Hemsworth standing at the back door of the orangerie.

"I . . . er . . . I was just trying to take some photos of these glorious orchids," Cosima stuttered, jabbing at the screen frantically to turn off the video. "Vandas, aren't they?"

"Yes. They're all special hybrids that were cultivated by the earl's mother, the late dowager countess. I'm afraid your interview is over for today."

"Oh. Lady Greshamsbury was just about to tell me about the tobacco-lacquered room."

"The tobacco-lacquered room no longer exists—the countess had it repainted the day she discovered Yves Klein. Let me show you to your car . . ."

"That won't be necessary."

"It'll be my pleasure." Hemsworth flashed his killer smile as he led Cosima out the back door of the orangerie. As he escorted her through the kitchen garden toward the mews, Hemsworth added, "I hope you've enjoyed your time here. You'll be hearing from Sir Peter Nicholls very shortly."

"Sir Peter Nicholls?"

"He's the Greshams' solicitor at Mishcon de Reya. He'll be needing you to sign an NDA."

"A nondisclosure agreement?"

"This was by no means a regular day at Greshamsbury Hall. I'm sure you understand that the countess is suffering from horrendous jet lag. It's given her temporary bouts of anxiety and delusion."

"Of course it has," Cosima replied.

·

Bea strolled up to the cottage just as Thomas was placing his luggage into a waiting taxi. Eden stood at the doorway, waving him off.

"Off again so soon, Uncle Thomas?" Bea inquired.

"No rest for the wicked, I'm afraid. I have to go see a patient overseas."

"Safe travels. I'll try to keep Eden out of trouble while you're gone," Bea said, giving him a quick peck on the cheek.

"Isn't it the other way around?" Thomas teased.

Bea winked as she walked down the front pathway toward Eden.

"I came round a little while ago," Eden said as she showed her friend in.

"I know." Bea could feel the muscles in her shoulders relax the moment the front door of the cottage closed behind her. Plopping down onto the plush velvet Knole sofa, she pulled her hair back from her face and groaned, "Let's get shit-faced."

"What can I fix you?"

"Vodka tonic, please."

"*That* bad, eh?" Eden popped over to the bar to mix Bea her drink. She could tell from her brief encounter with Arabella that she was in the foulest mood, and she had an inkling that what the countess had overheard on the hot mic was partly to blame.

"Mummy's been a ticking time bomb ever since Hawaii. Today the bomb finally went off."

"Sounds like that needed to happen. Is she all better now?" Eden asked lightly.

"Definitely not. She's in her bedroom with my father and they're both screaming their heads off. Correction, *she's* screaming her head off. Poor bugger."

Eden handed Bea her cocktail, which she chugged in one go. Seeing Eden's raised eyebrow, Bea burst out laughing. "Sorry, I'm not sure why I'm laughing. I think I'm in shock. You won't believe what happened!"

"Tell me," Eden said, sitting down on the ottoman in front of Bea. "Here, put your feet up."

"A foot rub! God I love you!" Bea sighed as she stretched her feet onto a cushion on Eden's lap. "So . . . apparently we're going broke."

"Broke? The Greshams of Greshamsbury?"

"Ridiculous, isn't it? I think Pa's just fretting as usual whenever Mummy overspends. I mean, Augie's wedding wasn't cheap."

Eden laughed at Bea's understatement. "No, it wasn't. Still, it must be upsetting to your mum to think she'll have to tighten her belt."

"If you ask me, she's more upset about Rufus and Solène fizzling out."

"Of course she is."

"Fair warning . . . she's putting the blame squarely on us."

"I had a feeling she would. Didn't she notice herself that Rufus and Solène had about as much chemistry as a box of wet matches?"

"Well . . . she thinks you were the one who wet the matches."

"You know very well I didn't."

"Yes, but she has somehow convinced herself that you . . . erm . . . shagged Rufus during the wedding banquet."

Eden burst out laughing. "She's out of her mind."

"Precisely what I told her! I think Mummy was just shocked when Rufus's voice came booming out of nowhere in the jungle, declaring his undying love for you. We were all shocked. And then the mic cutting out didn't help things. Mummy's imagination ran wild in the silence."

"Obviously," Eden said, more troubled by Arabella's imagination running rampant than she let on. She felt her cheeks flush, and she looked away from Bea for a few moments.

"OWWW!" Bea suddenly yelled out.

Eden startled and let go of Bea's foot, realizing she had been kneading it too vigorously. "Sorry! Um . . . that's your kidney point. The kidneys hold fear when your chi is out of balance," Eden hurriedly explained.

Bea gave Eden a curious look. "So . . . nothing happened between you and my brother? Not even during your midnight shower?"

"I was in Rufus's shower *alone*. I was trying to thaw my limbs after that damned ice ball!" Eden sputtered in frustration. "Bea, you were there, you know what insanity the whole week was. I promise you nothing happened."

Bea believed her friend. "I suppose you were shocked by Rufus's declaration?"

"Of course I was! But I also know your brother much better than he knows himself. He's such a romantic, and we were in the midst of the most wildly magical week. Between the sunset beach ceremony and the rain forest dinner, Rufus got swept up in the moment and . . . you know . . . confused about his own feelings."

Bea let out a sigh. "Poor Rufus. He's always been a rather confused boy, hasn't he? I mean, how could he possibly fall for you of all people? You're practically a sister to him. And doesn't he text you a million times a day? It's completely absurd."

"Completely absurd," Eden agreed, trying to convince herself as she nodded.

"Well, I'm glad we cleared things up. I can defend you to the death now!"

"I wish you needn't."

Bea got up from the sofa reluctantly. "Look, Mummy will come to her senses eventually, but in the meantime, it might be best to . . . um . . . lie low till things have calmed down a bit."

"Don't worry, I will," Eden said, giving Bea a tight hug as she left the cottage.

A short while later, Eden's phone dinged with a text message from Rufus, the first one she'd received from him since that night on the Big Island . . .

RUFUS GRESHAM: Aloha.

EDEN TONG: Aloha.

RG: Sorry for the silence.

ET: No need to apologize. I know you're dealing with a lot.

RG: Yeah, been helping my father settle everything. Between the fire department and Hawaii Civil Defense, it's been a rotten mess at the resort.

ET: I'm so sorry. At least no one was hurt.

RG: Thank god for that. Isn't it strange . . . when the lava is done doing its thing, it will be like Mum's resort was never there. It's sort of poetic in a way.

ET: You seem okay with that.

RG: I'm managing. I've been surfing, thinking, talking to the turtles.

ET: How are the turtles?

RG: Never better. There was a HUGE one on the beach this morning. Must have been a meter and a half long, just napping in the sun.

ET: Wish I could have spent more time in Puako. I miss the turtles.

RG: And they miss you. And I miss you. I'm sorry for how I acted that night at the wedding.

ET: It's fine.

RG: I behaved very inappropriately.

ET: Really okay.

RG: No it's not! It really wasn't fair to you and I feel terrible about everything.

ET: Don't. Everything's fine.

RG: You are the last person I ever want to hurt.

ET: I'm not hurt.

RG: Whew. So relieved.

ET: Good. I'm relieved too.

RG: I'm coming home on Friday.

ET: Great.

RG: Dinner maybe?

ET: Sure.

RG: Or maybe a drive somewhere on Sat?

ET: Might have to work in the morning, but I'll be free by one.

RG: Ok. See you soon.

ET: Safe travels.

RG: Thanks.

Eden felt a wave of relief wash over her. She'd thought things were going to be weird between them after his confession, but thankfully this exchange didn't feel too uncomfortable. In fact, it felt pretty close to normal. She was so glad Rufus seemed to be coming back to his senses. She desperately wanted everything to go back to normal between them again. She missed their morning texts so much. She wanted her best friend back. She couldn't stop replaying that scene at the wedding banquet over and over again. She felt her stomach tighten as she was suddenly transported back to the moment Rufus embraced her without warning, back to the sensation of his soft, sweet mouth against hers, the dewy tropical ferns grazing her bare shoulders as she dug her fingers into the sculpted muscles on his back, the seismic spark shooting from her lips right into the pit of her belly, burning so hot she didn't even notice the forest catching fire all around them. No, no, no, no, no. She needed to stop all this nonsense. She needed to forget everything that had happened in that rain forest.

V

SIR JOHN SOANE'S HOUSE

13 LINCOLN'S INN FIELDS, LONDON • *A FEW DAYS LATER*

"The Canalettos are marvelous, aren't they? I could look at them all day, and imagine I'm standing in the Piazza San Marco surrounded by pigeons," the friendly silver-haired docent said to Arabella as he gestured to a painting hung salon-style with other masterpieces from floor to ceiling in the room.

"Could you open this panel, please?" Arabella asked.

"Ah, you've been here before, then," the docent said, looking pleased that this lady knew about the remarkable feature of the Picture Room. Sir John Soane, the architect and collector who had built this house for himself in 1808, designed special "picture planes"—ingenious wall panels that moved and flipped open—allowing him to double his hanging space and fill the small thirteen-by-twelve-foot room with over a hundred of his favorite paintings. The docent released a catch, opening the wall like a secret cupboard door to reveal an interior panel chock-full of art.

"Is there a particular work you're looking for? A Turner, perhaps?" the docent asked.

"Not really. I just like the overall effect," Arabella said as she took a step back to get the full view of the paintings.

"It's all about the effect, isn't it?" the docent remarked, studying his visitor with renewed interest. When this lady had first entered, he assumed she was going to be no different from most of the tourists who visited. People trampled through the museum house all day long taking selfies and seeing nothing unless it was through the screen of their phones. This lady, though, was different. She'd headed purposefully into the Picture Room, knew about the hidden picture planes, and stood scrutinizing every painting. Who was she? She looked much too posh to be an academic, in her Garboesque tweed car coat, chocolate-brown slacks, and suede ankle boots.

"Thank you," Arabella murmured quietly before heading down the corridor toward the mezzanine. She had been in London for three days now, having left Greshamsbury Hall shortly after Francis had delivered his shocking confession. She had gone someplace where she knew no one would ever look for her—the Shangri-La at the Shard, checking into a suite under the name "Han Suyin" and requesting not to be disturbed under any circumstances.

This morning, she'd emerged for the first time and headed straight to Sir John Soane's house, one of London's—if not the world's— most remarkable architectural treasures.* Behind the neoclassical façade of a small, unassuming town house was a space so brilliantly designed, so full of confounding construction feats and trompe l'oeil trickery, it stood as a testament to Soane's astounding talent. Walking through these rooms as they revealed themselves like a giant cabinet of wonders always inspired her and transported her to another place. Or at least it used to.

Arabella stood on the mezzanine and stared down into the lower level, where the immense sarcophagus of Seti I lay in the center of a room crowded with Egyptian antiquities. She peered into the pearlescent abyss of the alabaster tomb, trying to imagine the royal personage who once lay within. Arabella thought of her own life and how the curious twists of fate had led her to this moment. Less than two weeks ago, as the sun set over the beach and her daughter walked down an aisle littered with thousands of rose petals on the way to marry her prince, Arabella had felt like Nefertiti—like a true

---

* *The house was designated a museum by a private act of Parliament in 1833. The act required that the house be maintained "as nearly as possible" as it was left at the time of Soane's death, and was specifically created by Soane to disinherit his son George, whom he loathed because he disapproved of his debts, his "refusal to engage in a trade," and his choice of a wife. Hmm . . . sound familiar?*

queen surveying her vast empire. But now she was the laughing-stock of society, having orchestrated the royal wedding disaster of the decade. Once the news got out that she was also bankrupt, the laughter would turn to outright pity, and there was nothing on earth Arabella abhorred more than pity.

By the time she was twelve years old, Arabella was already a gangly five feet five. She towered above all the other girls at Maryknoll Convent School in Hong Kong, and to make matters worse her unconventional features—eyes set too far apart and dramatically high cheekbones—earned her the moniker *yeung neui:* Goat Girl. While all the pretty girls began attracting the kind of boys who grew up on the Peak, Goat Girl was never asked out on a date, and Goat Girl was pitied by all her classmates as she kept growing taller and taller.

But Arabella pretended to pay no attention. She knew if she studied hard enough, she would gain entry to a good university in Australia or Canada, and she could leave the mediocrity of upper-middle-class Hong Kong behind. No more boring Methodist Youth Fellowship meetings that her mother would force her to attend every Saturday, no more interminable family lunches at the Jockey Club or the Chinese Recreation Club. Arabella surprised even herself, graduating with three A-level distinctions and a scholarship to King's College in London. She leapt at the opportunity to leave Hong Kong, and in her second year of uni, while standing at a CD listening booth at the HMV on Oxford Street, a woman with a French accent tapped her on the shoulder and asked her if she had ever heard of Anh Duong.

"Anne who?" Arabella asked.

"Anh Duong, the supermodel. I can make you the next Anh Duong," the woman replied.

One test shoot later, Arabella found herself being flown to Milan and walking the runway at the Byblos show. She dropped out of King's, moved to Paris, and three years sped by like a blur as she not only found success as a model but, more importantly, found a new life as the girl who wasn't pitied, but, rather, worshipped. The Goat Girl had morphed into a mesmerizing beauty. While she never truly attained supermodel status, it did lead her to Francis, not at the Azzedine Alaïa fashion show in Paris, as had been widely reported, but actually at a late-night curry house on Brick Lane.*

It was a fortuitous meeting, not only because sparks flew and they ended up falling in love, but because they found themselves anointed the "It Couple" at the precise moment when London was just becoming the mecca for a whole new generation of international rich who were arriving in droves, snapping up properties and making the city their preferred playground. And Arabella knew full well that while the Gresham fortune lacked the necessary number of zeros to compare to the astounding billions that all these people seemed to have, she possessed something that was of greater value to them: an old British title, an old manor house, and her own je ne sais quoi—that inimitable combination of style, taste, and chutzpah that all the billions in the world couldn't buy.

Arabella understood early on that no matter how wealthy these new people were, most of them suffered from imposter syndrome. They were status obsessed, and even though they pretended not to give a damn, they craved relevance and being seen as *originals*, even though all they actually did was ape the true originals who came before them. All the women longed to be latter-day C. Z.s or Bunnys or Marellas, a new flock of Capote-esque swans who would be celebrated for their iconic style, while the men all fancied themselves as Aris or Giannis or Rubirosas—swinging-dicked lotharios who wore Pateks over their shirt cuffs. Arabella understood how to create a mystique around herself and quickly became the supreme arbiter of taste. She knew how to parlay her style into creating the chicest house in the country and a mini-empire of ultra-insidery resorts these people would be clamoring to stay at.

But all her dreams had come crashing down on the night of the wedding banquet. It was as if the gods were trying to spite her. She

---

* *He was pissed and vomited chicken korma all over her new Alaïa boots. He was charmingly apologetic and showed up the next morning on her doorstep with a clutch of daisies and an invitation to lunch at Le Caprice; the rest is history.*

knew she was ambitious, and that she was a risk-taker, but she was never reckless. Contrary to what others might have thought, Arabella was not clueless about the vagaries of the Gresham finances. She knew that loans had been taken out, but she had assumed that the family trusts—while never as gargantuan as the Grosvenors' or the Cadogans'—were formidable enough to secure all the lines of credit they would ever need. Arabella subscribed to a philosophy that had been ingrained in her since childhood: *Fake it till you make it*. She thought that if they could just sustain the Gresham fantasy a little longer, that if she succeeded in marrying off her children to A-list aristocrats, then everyone who was anyone would continue to flock to the hotels, and her dreams of creating a global lifestyle luxury brand that she could sell off to some private equity group for billions would at last be realized.

But Francis never told her how depleted the Gresham trusts actually were. He never told her about the bridge loans to keep the hotels afloat. He never told her he used the Gresham land and the hotels and the art as collateral. He never told her Bellaloha was uninsured. He never told her anything until three days ago. She was so mad at Francis she didn't realize that she had wandered back into the Picture Room once more, and the chatty silver-haired docent was still there. This time he had the picture planes on the north wall open, and he was in the midst of showing two tall young men *A Rake's Progress,* a series of paintings Arabella didn't think much of because they were rendered in that eighteenth-century English realist style she found particularly dreary.

"Hogarth illustrated the cautionary tale of Tom Rakewell, a young man who inherits a fortune but squanders it with his gambling and reckless spending. The first painting shows the young heir being fitted for new clothes by his tailor, but the seventh painting over here is my favorite, *The Prison,*" the docent said, pointing up at it. "Tom's in debtor's prison with his wife, and he's trying to repay his debts by writing a play that he hopes to sell for a great deal of money. Look at Hogarth's incredible eye for detail . . . do you see the letter next to his elbow . . . can you make out the words?"

The young man squinted at the tiny inscription on the darkened canvas and read aloud in a Dutch accent, " 'I have read your . . . play and find it will . . . not do.' Oh—haha, it's a rejection letter!"

"Awfully wicked, wasn't he?" the docent said, laughing along with the two Dutchmen.

"Look at his wife now, how ugly and haggard she's become with her dirty hair and her . . . are those teeth blackened or broken?" the other young man asked.

"Broken, I think," his friend said.

"Yes. But what gets me is her clenched fist and that look of rage in her face," the docent remarked. "Marvelous, isn't it? She clearly can't fathom how she went from a rich woman to ending up in such a squalid, pathetic state."

Arabella studied the painting, her pulse beginning to race. This was an omen. This was going to be Francis and her in a few months. How could she survive in prison without seeing her cosmetic dentist three times a year? Arabella rushed out of the Picture Room and down the steps of the town house. She crossed the street and sat on a park bench, hyperventilating.

I refuse to be broke. I refuse to be broken, she thought. She realized that there was only one person on earth who could possibly help her now. The one person who understood Francis, who understood the children, who understood everything she had been trying to achieve from day one. She knew she would be judged. She knew she would be shamed. But she knew it was time to admit defeat and beg for mercy. As much as she hated to do it, she forced herself to open her Moynat Gabrielle clutch, fish out her telephone, and press the number that she had programmed into her speed dial: *Rosina.*

VI

31 RUE CAMBON

The phone rang eight times before it was picked up. *"Wei?"* a youthful voice answered in Cantonese.

Arabella did not recognize the voice. "Er . . . *nei go bin go ah?*"*

The voice switched immediately to perfect English. "Mrs. Leung cannot come to the phone at the moment, but she asked me to pick up because she saw it was you. This is Kit, her personal assistant."

"Hello, Kit. When might Rosina be available?"

"Please hold . . ." Kit could be heard mumbling offline in Cantonese. "I'm putting you on speaker . . ."

"Arabella! Are you okay?" Rosina said, her voice sounding slightly echoey.

"I'm fine."

"*Hiyah,* I'm so relieved! We were worried sick about you! Francis must have called us about a dozen times. He's beside himself."

"Good. He needs to suffer."

Rosina laughed. "It's good to make the hubby sweat once in a while, but you should have at least called me. We thought you might have been kidnapped! Madame, don't you think the beading should go around the back too?"

Arabella realized Rosina was talking to someone else in the room. A voice could be heard. "Madame Leung, there are already

---

* *"Who is this?"* in Cantonese.

eighty-two thousand five hundred sequins and stones hand-sewn onto the jacket. If we embroider the back, you will not be able to sit down."

"Sitting is overrated. Will you ask the nice ladies at Lesage to do the back for me?"

Arabella cut in. "*Lesage?* Are you in Paris?"

"I'm at Chanel, in the couture salon. I'm having a fitting."

"How long will you be there? Can you come to London?" Arabella asked excitedly.

"I have a better idea. Meet me here. I'll get Kit to send a chopper. How soon can you get to Battersea?"

"Thirty minutes."

•

Barely two hours later, Arabella found herself at a table on the glorious outdoor terrace of Rosina's rooftop garden suite at the Peninsula Paris, alternately sipping champagne and chrysanthemum tea and enjoying a simple lunch of flamed blue lobster with caviar, Sichuan-style *mapo* tofu with minced Ibérico pork, lacquered abalone with ginger butter and lime, lotus roots with seasonal vegetables and golden garlic, braised boneless beef ribs flambéed with Shaoxing wine, goji berries and radish in a stone pot, and wok-fried rice noodles with Wagyu beef and bok choy in silky egg gravy.

"There's nothing better than *chau ho fan,* is there?" Arabella moaned in pleasure as she devoured some of the wok-fried noodles. "Do you know that after all these years Francis still can't eat his noodles with chopsticks?"

"Of course he can't. He's a typical *gweilo.*"

"Can you believe that *gweilo* put up all my contemporary art as collateral for the loans? It would have been one thing if he offered them his heirlooms at Greshamsbury Hall, but he specifically gave them my favorite artworks."

"Of course he had to. All that dusty old British art is worthless. I mean, how much can you get for a Turner these days compared to a good Hockney?"* Rosina sniffed as she chewed on a tender piece of lotus root.

"He lied to me. At any point over the last decade he could have said, 'Arabella, if you want to dig four stories underground at the Hong Kong hotel to build an authentic Turkish *hammam* with hot and cold plunge pools, I'll have to leverage the Agnes Martins.' But he never said anything! Now, tell me what I'm supposed to do without my Martins? My powder room will never look the same!"

"Just get three sheets of A4 graph paper, frame them in white birch, and no one will ever know the difference," Rosina suggested.

"You know, that's not such a bad idea . . ."

"It's like my pearl necklace, no one knows it's fake."

"Which pearl necklace?" Arabella asked, reaching across the table for a slice of abalone.

"The big ones I wore at the Winter Ball in Hawaii. Who would ever suspect they're fake when it's *me* wearing them?"

"Those gorgeous grape pearls? I assumed they were Van Cleef."

"You see!" Rosina smiled triumphantly. "You know where I found them? Accessorize."

Arabella snorted. "In all my years living in England, I've never once set foot in an Accessorize!"

"That's because you're a snob. There's a very nice one on High Street Ken."

"Don't you own most of the buildings on High Street Ken?"

"Shhh!! No one is supposed to know that!" Rosina admonished her as the two women giggled conspiratorially.

"Now, what happened to all the money? Doesn't the legendary Gresham Trust own swaths of land in Marylebone?" Rosina asked.

Arabella shook her head pitifully. "Sold to the Portmans in the

* *J. M. W. Turner's auction high is $47.6 million, achieved at Sotheby's London in December 2014 for* Rome, from Mount Aventine, *painted in 1835, while David Hockney's 1972* Portrait of an Artist (Pool with Two Figures) *sold at Christie's New York for $90.3 million. The lesson here, all you young artists, is to be British and to auction your work in New York. The accent always helps raise the prices, as does including a parenthesis in the title of your work.*

nineteenth century. *Sam tung, ah!*[*] The legendary Gresham Trust was exactly that—a legend. When I think of all the prime real estate my husband's ancestors used to own, and the mistakes they made generation after generation, I think, *Why have I bothered to spend all these years trying to restore the fortunes of this godforsaken family?*"

"You're the best thing that's ever happened to them! I've seen the ancestral portraits hanging in that house—each person in that family was uglier than the last. Not a single chin among any of them! And then you came along and now look, gorgeous Greshams everywhere! You've infused a strain of beauty into the lineage that will last ten generations!"

Arabella sighed. "What is the point of beauty when we are going to be penniless?"

"You're looking at things the wrong way, Arabella. Beauty attracts fortune. Your greatest asset now is your beautiful son."

"My stupid son has been nothing but a liability! Let's face it, he's never been the academic type, he couldn't even get into Oxford. And now he's ruined things with Solène de Courcy by letting himself be seduced by Eden Tong, of all people. Who knew that little mouse could turn out to be such a hussy? I blame her for everything!"

"It takes two to tango, and Eden's actually quite pretty."

Arabella looked at Rosina in surprise. "How can you say that? That common little face, she looks like she should be running a stall in Mong Kok selling fake Gucci bags."

"Who was the girl's mother again?"

"I have no idea. Some Chinese nobody from Vancouver. Thomas met her in America and was too ashamed to ever show her off back home, from what I heard."

"He never brought her back home to Hong Kong, did he?"

"No, she died before he could do that. He moved to Greshamsbury with Eden to escape his grief."

"And now Rufus is in love with Eden."

---

[*] *"My heart aches!" in Cantonese.*

"There's no way he's really in love with her! It's just a momentary infatuation, and you can be sure I will put a stop to anything going further."

"You must. I personally have nothing against the girl, but it's out of the question for Rufus to be involved with her. It would be such a waste of those bedroom eyes."

"Shush! My son does not have bedroom eyes."

"Arabella, come on. Let's be honest here. Rufus is . . . how to put it politely . . . sex on a stick."

"Shut your mouth!" Arabella looked scandalized for a second, before collapsing into giggles.

"Don't try to deny it. Now, what you need to do is exploit Rufus properly, and all your problems will be solved. Rufus must marry money!"

"If only he would! But who? I had dossiers done on so many candidates, and we narrowed it down to Solène."

"Tell me, did you ever consider an Asian family?"

Arabella winced a little. "I didn't."

"That, in a nutshell, is your problem. You've been so focused on marrying off your children to the debilitated descendants of Victoria and Albert that you've forgotten where all the action really is nowadays: Asia. You need to put aside your snobbery and consider how many desperate Asian mothers there are who would gladly pay billions to have Rufus's genes populating future generations of their family."

"You really think so?"

"His brow ridges alone could command half a billion.* Leave it to me, I'm going to find the perfect someone for Rufus. I just need to flip through my little black book. Kit! Kit!"

Rosina's assistant came rushing out onto the terrace.

"Where's my little black book?"

---

* Helen Fisher, an anthropologist at Rutgers who studies love and attraction, when discussing rocker Adam Levine in a Live Science interview: "His brow ridges are such that he could probably stand in the shower and keep his eyes open."

"Right here," Kit said, ceremoniously handing Rosina a black leather desk planner diary.[*] Rosina began flipping through the pages and muttering to herself:

"Too young . . . too old . . . too fat . . . this one just got engaged . . . this one is a they now . . . oh, wait a minute—" Rosina looked up from her book with a gleam in her eye. "I think I know *just* the girl. Why didn't I think of her before? Vicky's daughter, Martha!"

Arabella eyed Rosina suspiciously. "How old is this Martha?"

"She's young enough."

"She's older than him, isn't she? No one under the age of sixty is named Martha."

"Her mother was a dancer. She was obsessed with Martha Graham."

"Is she pretty?"

Rosina paused for a moment. She knew she mustn't mention the tattoos. "Does it matter? I realize you may have been a model, but there are more important things in life than looks, you know."

"You just told me I brought beauty back to the Gresham family. I know my son. Rufus didn't even fall for Solène, and she looks like a goddess. What makes you think he'll have any interest in an older not-so-pretty woman named Martha?"

"Because it's Martha Dung."

"Her name is *Martha Dung*? Never in a million years will Ru—"

"Arabella, if you want me to help you, you need to promise me two things . . ."

"What?"

"First of all, you need to shut up and trust me."

"Of course I will, but—"

"Second, you will not interfere. I'm doing things my way, do you understand?"

"*Hiyah*, okay," Arabella said reluctantly.

"Tell me, where is the boy now?"

---

[*] *One of the complimentary diaries in fake leather that UBS sends to their clients as a holiday gift every year along with their insulated mugs.*

"He's on his way home to Greshamsbury on one of your planes," Arabella answered.

"Kit! Kit! Find out which plane Rufus is on," Rosina called out.

Kit stood at the doorway, peering at her iPad. "He's on Adam's Citation. It's scheduled to land at Exeter in two hours."

"Call the pilot and have the plane diverted to Paris."

Arabella looked alarmed. "Don't do that! He'll be furious when he sees us."

"What makes you think you'll be involved? Kit, please cancel my plans going forward."

"Even your dinner with Madame Deneuve?"

"Catherine will forgive me. We have a family emergency!"

VII

LE BOURGET AIRPORT

PARIS, FRANCE • *LATER THAT AFTERNOON*

Seeing the runway lights flickering in the distance as the plane made its final approach to land, Rufus could feel the anticipation build. Only forty more minutes. From Exeter Airport, Greshamsbury was a thirty-five-minute car ride, so give or take a few added minutes for traffic, he'd be on the front steps of the cottage and seeing Eden again. He wondered whether he should book a table at the Shy Frog, their local gastropub, or he should take her someplace more special tonight? Was it too last-minute to get a table at Gidleigh Park? He wanted a quiet, beautiful place with spectacular food where they could talk with no interruptions this time.

As soon as the jet door opened, Rufus bounded down the steps and took his seat in the Range Rover waiting on the tarmac. The car drove a hundred yards around the corner and came to an abrupt stop.

"*Monsieur St. Ives, nous sommes arrivés.*"

"I'm sorry?" Rufus peered at the driver through his reflection in the rearview mirror, confused that he was speaking French.

"We 'ave arrived," the driver said in English.

"Arrived where?"

"Deez eez your plane!"

Rufus looked out the tinted windows and saw a black and silver Bombardier Global 7500 outside a private hangar. A flight attendant in a chic navy suit stood by the steps smiling at him. He suddenly realized that the signs on the buildings all around were in French. "*Où suis-je?*" he asked urgently.

"Le Bourget Aéroport."

"Fucking hell." Rufus got out of the car and stormed toward the plane. He climbed aboard the jet, expecting to find his mother waiting. Instead, he found a pretty raven-haired flight attendant standing by the front galley holding a gleaming Puiforcat platter with a rolled-up towel on which was placed a single cymbidium orchid.

"Welcome aboard, sir. May I offer you a warm towel?"

"Thank you." Rufus's anger subsided as he sat down on the curved velvet sofa, flung open the towel, and enveloped his face in the soft fragrant steam. Just then, the toilet door opened and Rosina came out as the scent of Frederic Malle's Portrait of a Lady wafted into the main cabin.

"Auntie Rosina!" Rufus said in astonishment.

"There you are! Good, good, we can go now."

The flight attendant immediately shut the main cabin door as Rufus looked at his aunt in alarm. "Where are we going? Are my parents okay?"

"Everyone's fine, don't worry. We're going to take a little trip together."

"Where? Who else is coming?"

"Just the two of us."

Rufus eyed her suspiciously. "Mum put you up to this, didn't she?"

"Your mother had nothing to do with this, I promise. This was all my idea. Have a seat and I'll explain," Rosina said as she reposed elegantly in an art deco–style club chair* while the flight attendant brought over two glasses of champagne and chilled bowls filled with strawberries and freshly whipped cream.

"Try this champagne. It's an ancient vintage that's existed since the time of Louis XV. I just bought the winery, the last one I'll ever buy, actually," Rosina said.

Rufus took a glass of the bubbly and sat down across from her. "I

---

* Art deco aficionados would recognize that the entire cabin had been designed as an homage to the entrance hall at Eltham Palace.

was supposed to land at Exeter, but somehow I'm in Paris. You realize this is kidnapping."

Rosina laughed merrily. "Only little children get kidnapped. You're too big to be kidnapped."

"But you diverted my plane!"

"It's *my* plane, dear, or did you forget that?"

Rufus glanced out the window with a sense of dread as the jet began taxiing down the runway and taking off.

"Look at me, Rufus. I've known you since you were in diapers, and I've always been very up-front with you, haven't I? Remember the time you smashed my priceless Qianlong vase with a soccer ball but I didn't get mad because you owned up to it immediately?"

"I do. And again, I'm sorry. Aurelius was betting me I couldn't bend it like Beckham."

"You've always been an honest boy. It's unfortunate that your father has not been honest with you. It's not his fault entirely—he comes from a world where he's been taught never to express himself directly. I come from that world too, in a roundabout way. My great-grandfather was Eurasian like you and he was educated in England, you know."

"I don't think I ever knew that."

"Sir Alistair Ko-Tung. He adopted the English ways so well that he became one of those impenetrable Englishmen and remained one even when he returned to Hong Kong, and it filtered down through the generations. But you are different; even as a little boy you always spoke exactly what was on your mind. You have your mother to thank for that. She's not afraid to express herself."

"Mum expresses herself too much."

"Perhaps, but we are not talking about her right now. We are talking about your father, and the lies he has told you."

"Listen, Dad never lied to me. I know all about the money situation. Dad called me two days ago and told me everything."

"*Money situation.* How quaint to call it that. Rufus, the fact that you only found out two days ago that your family is nearing total financial ruin is an absolute travesty. You're the future Earl of Greshamsbury, but you're in danger of becoming the Earl of Nothing. What are you going to do about it?"

"That's why I was on my way home. I figured I needed to talk with my parents."

Rosina sat back in her seat and chuckled at how nonchalant her nephew seemed about everything. Classic Rufus, his head always in the clouds. "You know, I look at you. You have been so lucky all your life. My sons aren't so lucky." Rufus couldn't help but roll his eyes, while Rosina caught his look and smiled. "I know what you're thinking. You think your cousins are more fortunate than you."

"It's not that I think they're more fortunate. But the fact is, they do live in a completely different way than I do, and they have trust funds worth hundreds of millions . . ."

"I don't know how that rumor ever got started. What trust funds? My boys have no trust funds. Sure, they have the use of houses and cars and planes and they can send their bills to the family office, but you must realize that their father controls every last penny. He has ruled over each of them since the day they were born, and they have no choice but to follow his precise wishes. Peter molded Alexander into a clone of himself and made him go to Harvard. He saw that Adam was a bit of a scoundrel, so he sent him to Harvard Law. And Aurelius, you know what happened on that damn safari* and that's why Peter always chose a different track for him. My point is, my sons did not have the luxury of pursuing their own passions in the way you and your sisters have been allowed to all your lives."

"They seem to be doing just fine."

"They are, because they are obedient. As long as they fulfill their duties to the family, they can enjoy their hobbies. So, Alex wants to build time-share condos on Mars, go right ahead. Adam wants to keep Fl drivers fed and watered, so be it. Aurelius likes to finance paramilitary groups, more power to him. So let me ask you: How are you fulfilling your duty to your family? You got to go to that terribly

* Kicked in the head by a baby giraffe when he was seven years old.

expensive art school.* You got to spend all your summers chasing waves around the world. You got to convince your mother to build a resort on an island that's got a live volcano."

"I never did that! When I took her to see that property, I was hoping she'd buy the land to preserve it, not develop a resort there!"

"Have you ever asked yourself *why* your mother wanted to develop a resort on the Big Island in the first place? You started spending all your free time in Hawaii. She wanted to be closer to you. She wanted to find a way for you to become more involved in the family business."

"Are you trying to guilt-trip me? Because I already feel guilty enough . . ."

"Rufus, I am not interested in guilt. I am only interested in solutions. I want to help you gain access to the funds you'll need to rescue your family from financial catastrophe."

"And how are we going to do that?"

"You mean how are *you* going to do that? I'm going to introduce you to a few key people this weekend, and the rest is up to you. The problem is, you're far too sheltered; your parents have unfortunately raised you among the children of all these fashionable, grand, and utterly irrelevant aristocrats—the Duke of Upper Colon, the Baroness of Shiba Inu . . ."

"Wait a minute—aren't they your friends too? They were all at your Winter Ball on Mauna Kea."

"Those are your *mother's* friends. I might be acquainted with some of them, but to be honest I wouldn't consider them my friends. If you are the absolute monarch of a country with a hundred billion barrels of proven oil reserves like my darling friend the emir, that's one thing, but how many of those titled twits came to your mother's rescue? Exactly zero. They clutched their tiaras and ran straight for their borrowed planes the minute the soufflés started collapsing. *My*

---

* *Don't you love rich aunties who judge the expenditures of their relatives when they themselves spend exponentially more on their own children who want to restore crumbling castles in Scotland or fund their own dolphin research institutes? No, not personal.*

friends are people who invent entire industries, people who influence policy, people who move economies."

"Oligarchs and despots, how fun," Rufus muttered through gritted teeth.

"Look, if you're not going to have an open mind, you're wasting my time . . ."

"Okay, okay. You still haven't told me where we're going. Let me guess . . . we're off to the Davos conference?"

"My god, how boring would that be. I like to have fun, you know? We are going to a wedding in Morocco. So sit back and relax, enjoy some dinner."

No sooner had Rosina uttered those words than the pretty attendant returned, bearing a square block of granite and placing it on the macassar ebony table that folded out in front of Rufus. Four sashimi-like strips of marbled beef sizzled on the granite. "For the first course, may I offer a hot-stone Miyazaki Prefecture Wagyu with a whiskey-butter foam?"

"I suppose," Rufus replied.

MARRAKECH

Marrakech taught me color.
Before Marrakech, everything was black.

—YVES SAINT LAURENT

Hong Kong, 1995

Mary Gao stared into her bowl of wonton noodles, the faint hint of pink in a curled prawn wrapped in delicate wonton skin reminding her of the tiny baby growing within her.

"I want to keep it," Mary said weakly.

Rosina Ko-Tung stared at her friend in dismay from across the tiny Formica table. "Why do you want to ruin your life?"

"It's what Henry would have wanted."

"You are deluded. He would have made you get rid of it."

"No, he wouldn't have. He loved me. He would have loved our baby."

Rosina sighed, shaking her head. The only person Henry had loved was himself, but it was pointless to try to convince Mary in her current state. "Mary, I'm going to give it to you straight, since no one else seems to have the heart to do it. Henry is dead. Your family is already facing disgrace, with your brother's trial coming up. Now, there is still a great deal of sympathy for you at the moment. You were an innocent bystander at a drunken brawl. But if the public catches wind of what really happened that night, the sentiment will change."

"I lost my brother and my lover in one night. Will people be so heartless?"

"You will be seen as the woman who caused it all to happen. You will be tainted forever. You will go down in history as the only disgraced Miss Hong Kong and be forced to give up your crown."

"I couldn't care less about my fucking crown. I want to be a mother. I'm ready."

"*Are you sure? I don't think you're thinking clearly at the moment. You really want to be a single mother, here? You want your baby to grow up being called a bastard? You will be shunned by society. Every door will be closed to you, Mary. Every opportunity, every sponsorship deal, will evaporate. You will become a nobody. How are you going to support your baby if you're a nobody? Look, as it stands I'm the only one in our circle still talking to you. Where's Gabby? Where are Edwin and Brendan? I couldn't even meet you at a proper restaurant for* yum cha. *We had to come here and hide like thieves. Don't sacrifice your life like this. It's still so early, you're barely pregnant. Turn the page, and start over. When the court case is settled and the news dies down, you can still find a husband. Maybe one of those mainlanders who are getting so rich these days, or a Brit in finance. You could have many other children then. A whole new family. You could have a beautiful life. Isn't that what you want?*"

Yes, *Mary thought*. I want a beautiful life.

It all began with a fight over a golf cart at Sun Valley. Amanda Joy Finch was trying to secure a golf cart for a legendary nonagenarian investor at the annual conference nicknamed the "Billionaires' Summer Camp," but the golf cart was stolen "right under our very noses by someone I will not name . . . let's just say he's a tech mogul infamous for his adolescent behavior," Ms. Finch recalls. "We were late to the morning session, but a knight in shining armor sped up and offered us a ride in his cart." The young man turned out to be Christian Lewis Radford, who was still healing from a diving injury. "Mandy and I were two of the few people under thirty at the conference who weren't billionaires at the time, so we bonded over our lowly status," Mr. Radford laughs. This weekend, the bride will marry her knight in shining golf cart in Marrakech, Morocco. The bride, 30, a summa cum laude graduate of Tulane University and Harvard Business School, previously worked for Berkshire Hathaway before founding her own socially responsible venture capital firm, Scout Finch Capital, named by *Fast Company* as one of the "most visionary venture capital firms." She is the daughter of Alan Finch, a breeder of exotic chickens in Pensacola, Florida, and Debbie Craig, a guitar instructor in Sedona, Arizona. The groom, 32, who grew up in Sydney, Australia, attended the University of Sydney and Stanford Graduate School of Business, and previously worked for Y Combinator. He is the founder of Lizard Island Ventures, which specializes in AI start-ups. He is the son of Marc Radford, chairman and CEO of the diversified minerals conglomerate Radford International, and Carolyne Radford, chairwoman of the Radford Foundation and a former trustee of the Aspen Institute. The couple plan to split their time between Berkeley, California, and Byron Bay, Australia.

YOU ARE CORDIALLY INVITED TO

Rock the Casbah

AT OUR WELCOME PARTY
CELEBRATING THE NUPTIALS OF

*Amanda & Christian
Dar Yacout*

8 P.M.*

ROCK OUT IN YOUR BEST
TALITHA & JEAN PAUL LOOKS

*Shuttles will depart from Amanjena, Royal Mansour,
La Mamounia, El Fenn, Jnane Tamsna, and L'Hotel at 7:45 p.m.*

DAR YACOUT

The outer walls of the ancient medina glowed pink against the sapphire-blue night as the call to prayer echoed in the distance. Rufus gazed out the window of their speeding car in anticipation as the old city came into view. "The colors are amazing! No wonder Matisse came here."

"Marrakech is known as the red city. Every city in Morocco is painted a different color—Casablanca is white, Chefchaouen is blue. I can't believe you've never been here!" Rosina said as she tightened the knot on her black and gold silk headscarf.

"I have no idea why it's taken me this long. I've wanted to come here since reading *The Sheltering Sky*," Rufus mused.

"Well, there's no better way to experience Morocco than with Carolyne organizing things—she always goes all out."

"Carolyne's the bride?"

"No, the groom's mother. Christian is her son—you'll like him, he surfs too—and the bride is Alison . . . Amy? I can't remember her name now. She's American, medium-size blond, Harvard, the usual."

"How do you know these people again?"

"I told you, our families do a lot of business together."

"So why didn't Uncle Peter come?"

"*Hiyah*, you know your uncle has so little time to spare these days—you're lucky he even managed to show his face at Augie's wedding!"

"It's a bit weird going to a wedding where I don't know the couple at all."

"What's so weird about that? I go to so many weddings where I don't even know the bride and groom's *names*! You know, weddings aren't about the couple. They're for the families to impress their guests. I mean, look at your own sister's wedding."

"That's not how my wedding is going to be."

Rosina gave him a pitying look, as if to say, *Like you have a choice.* "Well, this wedding is going to be totally different from Augusta's. You'll see. The Radfords have no need to impress anyone, so they are making it a very intimate affair—only a hundred and fifty of their closest friends."

"Then it's even weirder that I'm here," Rufus groaned.

"Nonsense! I am an honored guest, and you're my plus-one."

Rufus simply chuckled at the absurdity of it all as the forest-green Audi came to a stop by the side of a busy roadway and the chauffeur pointed to an archway leading into the medina. "You wait there."

"Are you sure?" Rufus said, peering dubiously at the seemingly random spot.

"Yes, they come," the chauffeur said.

Rufus helped his aunt out of the car, and as soon as he shut the door it quickly sped off, leaving them standing alone by the walls of the souk. Aside from two cats that came skulking along, the street suddenly became deserted and a bit foreboding. Rufus glanced at his aunt's magnificent string of pearls glistening in the darkness and whispered, "Auntie, you should cover your pearls with your scarf."

Rosina scoffed, "*Hiyah, moh daam sam!*[*] This necklace cost less than twenty pounds."

Rufus stared at the pearls in surprise. Even though they were fake, he still wondered why his aunt didn't bring any bodyguards on this trip when he recalled the Leungs were constantly trailed by a retinue of men in dark suits wherever they went. "Where's your security this time?" he asked.

---

[*] *"Stop worrying!"* in Cantonese.

Rosina scoffed. "When I'm traveling by myself, I never bring security. Calls too much attention. Besides, who wants to come after me? It's Peter they want."

"But you're his wife . . ."

"Your uncle already said a long time ago, 'Rosina, if you ever get kidnapped, don't expect me to pay the ransom.' Now, if one of the boys ever got kidnapped, that's a different story. He would run and deliver the bags of cash himself."

"Why would he do that?"

"Typical Hong Kong man—his sons are more precious than his wife. Peter and my sons are *Leungs,* I am not. He can always get another wife, *hai ma?* A younger, tighter model."

Rufus laughed. "Auntie Rosina, you can never be replaced and everyone knows that!"

"You are too sweet. Of course I can be replaced, but your uncle knows that I will cut off his balls if he ever tries. Now, where is this person that's supposed to meet us?" As she uttered those words, an elderly man in a hooded brown djellaba emerged from the alleyway holding a dim brass lantern that swayed precariously on a long wooden stick.

"Dar Yacout?" he asked them.

"Yes, Yacout, that's where we're going, isn't it?" Rufus replied, a little relieved.

Without another word, the man turned and started walking much more briskly than either of them expected, darting down the labyrinthine alleyways with surprising agility. The walls of the old souk seemed to transform at every turn, changing in color and texture. Rosina gasped as they passed by the spice quarter of the souk, where spice traders sat beside hundreds of bins bursting with mountainous piles of saffron, cumin, rose petals, nuts, and dried fruit lit with bright overhead lamps. "Oh my goodness, look at those giant medjool dates! I need to come back to get some tomorrow! Doesn't it feel like we've stepped back in time? What I love about the souk is that the people here are living exactly like their ancestors did in medieval times."

Rufus looked up at the roofs crowded with satellite dishes. "I wish I had brought my Leica along. I could spend days here just taking pictures!"

"Where the hell is he taking us?" Rosina whispered in Cantonese to her nephew as they went deeper into the old city. Just as Rufus was beginning to wonder the same, the old man abruptly stopped at a corner by the unmarked rusted iron door of a nondescript *riad*. He banged twice, and the heavy door was opened by a tall man in a pristine white djellaba with a red fez on his head. The tall man bowed graciously and said, "Madame Leung, Vicomte St. Ives? *As-salaam alaykum!*" He stepped aside and waved his hand with a flourish to reveal a tiny foyer lined with flickering lanterns. They followed him down a narrow hallway through another doorway, which opened abruptly into one of the most exquisite spaces either of them had ever seen—a palatial courtyard that shimmered in jewel tones, from the emerald pool in the center of the *zellige* mosaic tiled floors to the antique bronze and crimson glass lanterns that cast kaleidoscopic shadows along the sparkling *tadelakt* plaster walls. Along each side of the courtyard were intimate dining alcoves caressed by the lush foliage of tall palms and cooled by burbling marble fountains.

"A secret palace!" Rufus exclaimed in awe.

"In Marrakech, there are secret palaces everywhere, but this is the one that started it all. This is the masterpiece of Monsieur Bill Willis,"* the host explained as he ushered them down the steps into the courtyard, where wedding guests dressed in posh-hippie cos-tumes sat at tables around the pool watching a troupe of Gnawa musicians perform.

"Why didn't you tell me it was a fancy-dress party?" Rufus said to his aunt, suddenly feeling out of place in his white linen suit.

---

* *The legendary designer who pretty much invented "Moroccan style," Bill designed the Morocco residences of such icons as Yves Saint Laurent and Pierre Bergé, J. Paul Getty Jr., Marella Agnelli, and Marie-Hélène de Rothschild. You may not know it, but he's the reason you bought that Moroccan shag rug with the curled corner you keep tripping over from CB2.*

"We *are* in costume. I'm channeling Loulou de la Falaise, and you're my Yves."

Before Rufus could ask his aunt who Yves was, a grande dame in a turquoise and gold caftan with iridescent eye shadow matching her huge aquamarines pounced on them.

"Rosiiiiiii! I was about to send a search party for ya!" the woman said in her distinctive Queenslander accent.

"Carolyne, I'm sorry we're so late. We came straight from the airport," Rosina apologized.

"I don't believe a damn word you say! Did you have a glam team on your jet? That jumpsuit looks fantabulous! Vintage Saint Laurent, *ness pah?* And those pearls, fuckin' hell, what monstrous clams did you rob?"

"Haha, no clams were robbed."

"Where did you steal this one from? Thunder from Down Under?" Carolyne (C&K Townsville/St. Hilda's/University of Queensland) said, scanning Rufus up and down.

"This is my nephew Rufus."

"Uh-huh. I wish we all had *nephews* who could accompany us for a long weekend in Morocco."

Rosina slapped her friend's arm playfully. "Stop it, he really *is* my nephew."

"Whatever you say, darl. Nephew, you're at table thirteen. Rosina, you're with us, of course," Carolyne said, steering her to the table of honor by the center of the courtyard. Rufus was escorted to an alcove where other guests were already tucking into the lavish banquet. He was delighted to see John Grey, a fellow Old Radleian, seated at his table. At least there was one person he knew. Rufus took his seat and proceeded to sample the mouthwatering array of meze and flatbreads in front of him.

Taking in the conversations around the table, Rufus quickly realized that he was among a crowd unlike any he had ever encountered. Though he had grown up cosseted in extreme privilege, his friends by and large came from families that had already been in possession of their country houses or companies or countries for many generations and were for the most part a decidedly low-key and unambitious lot. Here before him was the next generation of tech savants, financial gurus, thought leaders, and visionary entrepreneurs, and in between bites of seafood *bastilla,* chicken roasted with preserved lemons and olives, lamb tagine, and couscous, they were humblebragging about how each of them came to be invited to this ultra-exclusive wedding:

"Christian joined the latest funding round of my new pubic-grooming AI start-up. We've been BFFs ever since."*

"I'm the CFO of a family office in New York, and we have a wonderful relationship with the Radford family office in Sydney."

"I'm ex-Meta, ex-McKinsey, ex-Tesla, ex-Twitter, and I was on a panel with Amanda at the Milken conference."

Only a Chinese man in dark gold-rimmed glasses sitting directly opposite Rufus remained inscrutably silent, while next to Rufus, a hyper-chatty fellow was demonstrating his latest app to Rufus's old schoolmate John. Meanwhile, the American girl to his right who said she was "a socially responsible angel" huddled with her dinner partner whispering about some problematic colleague.

"I'm telling you, that proxy-battle bullshit he tried to pull was textbook borderline," the girl insisted.

The man beside her seemed doubtful. "Is he actually borderline, or does he just have narcissistic personality disorder like his father did?"

"It's probably both."

"They're all so fucked up, none of them deserved control of the company!"

---

* *Speaking of AI, this is how ChatGPT rewrote this line in the style of a certain author to make it funnier: "You won't believe how Christian and I became BFFs. He invested in my start-up! But not just any start-up. Oh no, this one's a game-changer. It's a pubic-grooming AI, and let me tell you, it's got more blades than a Gillette Fusion ProGlide. With our cutting-edge technology, you'll never have to worry about nicking your nether regions again. Plus, we've got a new feature in development that'll make your downstairs look like Michelangelo's David. I mean, who needs friends when you've got a start-up that keeps you trimmed, primed, and ready for action?"*

"The only one I like is whatshisname."

"Cousin Greg?"

"No, no, Shiv's husband."

"Oh, Tom! I love Tom. How brilliant is his performance? He runs laps around Cameron Frye and that junior Culkin."

"Can you believe Tom was Darcy in *Pride & Prejudice*?"

"What?! No fucking way!"

Rufus was trying to figure out how Jane Austen suddenly factored into the conversation when the chap to his left turned to him with a big grin.

"Hey! Ryan Chandani" (EtonHouse/St. Andrews/ACS/UWC/SAS/Yale). "Huuuuge fan of your work, dude!"

"Really? You know my work?" Rufus replied, rather surprised that this fellow had seen his artwork.

"Sure do."

"Which series did you like?" Rufus probed.

"All of them, dude! Speaking of which, I want you to be part of *my* latest series offering. We just got a $1.5 billion valuation, we're cash-flowing $9.2 mil per month, with NPS at 4.8/5, and we're currently not raising but I'll do you a massive favor and let you into our Series B at last year's valuation."

"Er . . . let me in?" Rufus asked, a bit mystified.

"Yes. Max is normally twenty, but for you I can do twenty-five."

"Twenty-five works?"

"Sure. In my opinion, it's an easy four X in six months, and twenty to thirty X if we IPO in the next year. Did I mention that Vinod Khosla is on our board?"

"Is Vinod the curator?" Rufus asked, noticing the Chinese man staring at him from across the table.

"Dude, you're funny. Vinod's more than the curator, he's our GOD. Are you in?"

"Let me just clarify . . . you're asking me to be in your group show?"

Now it was Ryan's turn to be confused. "Group show? You wanna bring in your group of VCs?"

Just then, Rufus's old schoolmate John Grey (Thomas's Battersea/
Radley/Brasenose/Saïd) came from behind and clapped Rufus on
the back. "Been ages, mate! You're the last person I expected to see
at this table!"

Rufus beamed at his friend. "Likewise. How's life?"

"Can't complain. Moved to London, work for the family bank,
got married."

"I heard you married Alice Vavasor!"

"She *finally* said yes, can you believe it?"

"So I take it you could finally forgive her?"

"I sure did. She's eight months pregnant, which is why I'm flying
solo. And you, still doing the art thing?"

"Still doing the art thing."

"Art thing? You funding NFTs or something?" Ryan interrupted.

Rufus had had enough. "I'm sorry, Ryan, but I haven't the faintest clue what you're talking about. I create unique platinum prints
using an archival nineteenth-century process that is the antithesis of
NFTs."

Ryan reached over and snatched up the gold engraved place card
in front of Rufus's plate. "Aren't you Rufus St. Ives of the St. Ives
Fund?"

"That place card's wrong. My surname isn't actually St. Ives. It's
Gresham," Rufus replied.

"So you don't run a venture capital firm with thirty-eight billion
dollars under management?"

"Nope."

"Ryan, I think you're mistaking Rufus here for *Russell* St. Ives?"
John interjected.

"Fuck, dude. Rufus, Russell, whatever. You still want to invest
twenty-five million dollars in my start-up?"

Rufus chuckled. "Twenty-five million *dollars*? I thought you
wanted twenty-five artworks from me."

Ryan rolled his eyes, suddenly deflated.

"Hey, switch seats with me for a minute," John offered.

Ryan's face lit up like a kid's. "And sit beside Feng? Duuuude, thank you!"

"Godspeed," John said as Ryan bolted from his seat.

Rufus stared after him, somewhat mystified by the entire exchange. "I didn't realize I was such an intolerable dinner partner until now."

"Oh, don't mind him," John said, lowering his voice. "I don't think he was too worried that you're not investing in his start-up. He was just trying to get Phineas's attention. Now he can really get his rocks off sitting next to him." John gestured covertly toward the Chinese man in the dark glasses.

"Who is he?" Rufus asked quietly.

"You don't know? Phineas Feng, the gatekeeper for MD Capital. Largest privately held venture capital fund in Asia."

"I'm beginning to get the picture . . ."

"Yes. Everyone here is putting on a big show for Phineas. If he fancies their idea, they might make it to the next level."

"The next level?"

"They get to pitch the big boss directly," John said, tilting his head toward the table of honor by the pool. "Sitting next to the bride."

Rufus turned to see a Chinese woman in a black caftan with coral-pink piping. "Really, that woman is the big boss?"

"Yes. The 'MD' in MD Capital herself, Martha Dung. What do you have to pitch today?"

"Nothing."

"Come on, you don't have some buzzy new venture that needs seed money? Why were you seated here then?"

"I have no idea. Thought I was attending a wedding, not a taping of *Shark Tank*."

"Pity, because Martha regularly drops millions on start-ups like she's handing out lollipops," John said.

"Good for her," Rufus remarked right as the sound of a knife clinking against a wineglass could be heard coming from the table of honor.

Rufus saw a man around the same age as him get up from his

chair and look expectantly at the gathered crowd. With his long hair pulled up into a man bun, scraggly stubble, and tattooed arms, he looked very much like one of the guys at the Saturday drum circle that Rufus would frequent at Kehena Beach. The man tapped a microphone to get the crowd's attention before he began his speech:

"Hiya everyone! For those of you that don't know me, I'm Christian"—(Queenwood/Geelong Grammar/University of Sydney/Stanford GSB)—"the lucky fella getting hitched. I just wanna say a few words before things get crazy tomorrow. First off, thank you for being here tonight. There's a reason we're all packed into this place like sardines: because this is where I proposed to Mandy a little over a year ago. Actually, I got down on my hands and knees in that alcove right over there"—he pointed straight at where Rufus was sitting—"and I've dreamed of sharing the magic of that night all over again with the people I love. I know so many of you have busy, important schedules, so I appreciate your taking the time to come to the ends of the earth with me. I wanna thank my parents, who have put up with all my shit over the years. Da, Mum, I know you never thought you'd see the day I'd finally bring home a woman that was worthy of you two, a woman who's smarter than me, a better surfer than me, and much better looking than me, the one woman who can . . . who can . . . "

At this point, Christian's voice cracked and he put down the mic as he choked back a sob, before catching his breath and continuing, "The one woman who can put up with all my shit too. Mandy, never in my wildest dreams did I imagine I'd ever meet anyone like you. You are so kind, so generous, and you bring so much joy to everyone who knows you. I feel like the luckiest man on the planet, and I cannot believe I get to spend the rest of my life with you." Christian glanced down at his bride, whose face was wet with tears as well, before continuing, "And last but not least, I need to thank someone amazing that's here with us tonight. As many of you may know, two years ago I went surfing in the Great Barrier Reef and a friendly shark decided to give my leg a little kiss. This crazy girl over here"—he looked across the long banquet table at Martha Dung—

"who, as many of you know, has more bodyguards than the Mossad, dove right into the water from her yacht and scooped me out herself, not thinking of her own safety for one second. And within minutes she had me in her chopper and I was being flown to Cairns Private Hospital, where they were able to save my leg. Because of you, Martha, I am quite literally able to *stand* here today and get ready to walk down the aisle and marry the love of my life." Christian began to clap, and the entire crowd rose to their feet and began clapping as Martha cracked a quick smile before casting her eyes downward, clearly embarrassed by the attention.

Rufus stared at Martha and felt as though he was having a premonition. He had a sense that this woman—who had saved Christian's life and made it possible for him to marry the woman of his dreams—was somehow going to change his life as well.

KSAR CHAR-BAGH

LA PALMERAIE, MARRAKECH • *EARLY THE NEXT MORNING*

With its intricately carved Moorish arches evoking the Alhambra, perfectly sculpted topiaries in hidden cloisters, and elegantly curated antiques mingling with chic minimalist furnishings, everything about Ksar Char-Bagh—a fourteenth-century-style palace set among ancient palm groves—exuded a serene, regal glamour. Rufus and Rosina arrived on a shuttle with other wedding guests at the crack of dawn, and they took their seats on cushioned stone benches placed along one side of the majestic central courtyard facing a tranquil reflecting pool.

"You know, I have to hand it to Christian and Amanda—they've managed to keep their wedding so personal and unpretentious. Just a nice dinner last night and now a simple ceremony in a courtyard, bright and early, no fuss," Rufus said approvingly.

"You must be a morning person," Rosina remarked.

"I'm usually up at dawn to catch the morning waves. That's when the surf's best."

"I've never in my life had to wake up so early for a wedding!" Rosina grumbled as she adjusted the angle of her saffron-colored hat, which had a brim so wide it kept poking Rufus in the cheek every time he turned to talk to her. "Thank goodness my butler could help me with my updo. I wonder how the other guests found hairdressers to come and service them at five in the morning."

Rufus peered at the arriving guests and saw Martha Dung flanked by two bodyguards who looked like they were ex-Mossad. As Martha took her seat next to Phineas, the Chinese man who never took his dark glasses off, a low drumbeat could be heard emanating from someplace deep within the palace. The rhythmic drumbeat continued to build, closer and closer, until a line of Berber drummers appeared through a doorway and marched through the courtyard. Their drumming was joined by the sound of violins as everyone discovered that there was an orchestra playing on the terrace right above them.

The massive chiseled-and-hammered-copper double doors on the east side of the courtyard opened slowly as four men cloaked in hooded white and gold djellabas astride four white horses were silhouetted in the doorway. The horses cantered into the courtyard and came to a standstill by the central fountain, and the riders jumped off their horses and flung off their hoods, revealing themselves to be the two groomsmen, the best man, and the groom. The assembled guests applauded at the audacious entrance.

Then, as the iconic overture from Maurice Jarre's "Theme from *Lawrence of Arabia*" filled the air, the massive matching doors on the opposite end of the courtyard opened to a procession of three brides-maids entering on foot, each holding a hammered-bronze platter of rose petals, which they scattered along the pathway as they walked. They were followed by the bride, making her entrance atop a camel festooned with jewels and rose garlands while her father walked by its side leading them in. Amanda dismounted gracefully from the camel via a set of mother-of-pearl steps with a gallant assist from her father, allowing everyone to admire her ivory silk tulle gown by Giorgio Armani Privé with its pleated silk tulle cape fastened at the shoulders by two art deco diamond-and-emerald brooches. She took the hand of her husband-to-be, and without a word to the assembled guests, they proceeded out the north doors followed by their entou-rage, still scattering rose petals.

The guests stared after them in confusion, before a man dressed in a priest's robes announced in a booming voice, "Ladies and gentle-men, please follow the rose petal trail to the sacred ceremony." As Rufus and Rosina joined the procession heading outside, gasps could be heard from the guests walking ahead of them.

"Ohmygod!"

"No waaaaay!"

"Unbe-fucking-lievable!"

"What's happening?" Rufus wondered as he tried to peer over the crowd. There was a bottleneck at the doorway as the guests made their way into the garden, but they finally crossed the threshold and stood gawking at the sight before them. Fifty hot-air balloons, positioned in a perfect circle in the vast palm grove, were all fired up and ready to take off.

"Here's your very simple wedding," Rosina said, nudging Rufus with her elbow.

A team of concierges stood by with iPads, directing each guest to their assigned balloon. "Mrs. Leung, you're in balloon number two, with the Radfords," the attendant said to Rosina.

"Wonderful." Rosina nodded as she and Rufus began walking toward their balloon.

"Sir, wait a minute, sir, you're in a different balloon," the concierge called after them.

"No, he's with me. He's my plus-one," Rosina insisted.

"I'm sorry, but there's only room for *you* on the Radford balloon. It says here 'Leung Guest—balloon number eighteen,' " the concierge confirmed.

"See you up there," Rufus said amiably as he parted ways with his aunt and headed toward his assigned balloon. Arriving at a striped silver and blue balloon, he was helped aboard the wicker gondola by the pilot, who introduced himself as Mehmet. As Rufus observed the other balloons quickly filling up with three or four guests per gondola, he was just beginning to wonder who else was going to be riding with him when he spotted John Grey heading over with Martha Dung.

As Mehmet helped Martha aboard, Rufus was able to study her up close for the first time. For some reason, whenever he met Asian women in particular, he would always hear his mother's voice invading his head. It was something he found annoying but unavoidable. He knew that Arabella would consider Martha's face "common" and disapprove of her tan, but Rufus could clearly see that her complexion came from a life lived outdoors. She looked to be in her midthirties, and had the physique of an athlete and a cool bohemian style that reminded him of some of the female surfers he knew in Hawaii—she was dressed in an indigo-dyed sleeveless linen shirtdress that revealed a serpentine tattoo going up her right arm (another thing his mother would have abhorred), a broad leather belt with hammered silver studs, and a straw fedora over shoulder-length black hair that had been pulled into a ponytail.

Rufus greeted them cheerily. "Hello! I wasn't expecting you two as my ballooning companions today."

"We might have gotten to choose our balloon," John said with a wink.

"Really? And I passed the security clearance?"

"With flying colors! I have a confession, mate. I was vetting you a bit last night, just to be sure you hadn't become some kind of crypto-evangelical start-up monkey."

"The last thing we wanted was to be trapped in a pitch meeting with some tech desperado while we're a thousand feet in the air," Martha (Diocesan Girls'/Geelong Grammar/Griffith) chimed in.

"The only kind of pitch I know involves cricket. I don't have much of a brain for business."

"How refreshing," Martha said.

Rufus turned to John. "So you work for Martha too?"

"My bank does. Sorry for the subterfuge," John said.

"Believe me, I get it. In London I have to go by another name."

"Why is that?" Martha asked.

"I'm an artist, and I want my work to be judged on its own merit."

"Why wouldn't it be?"

"Because people tend to judge me just based on my name."

Martha was still confused. "What's so special about your name?"

Rufus looked at her a bit awkwardly, and John jumped in. "Martha, in certain circles, Rufus is rather famous. He's got one ninety K followers on Instagram."

"Actually, someone else made that account. I'm not on Instagram," Rufus clarified.

"No wonder there's nothing but shirtless pictures of you on it!" John guffawed.

Martha gave Rufus a curious look. "Wow, I had no idea we were going ballooning with someone famous. John didn't tell me a thing about you except that you were mates at school."

"I'm really not famous," Rufus insisted.

Before John could explain any further, Mehmet the pilot interrupted their chatter. "Okay, everyone, I need your attention. Before we take off, here are a few safety rules," Mehmet said. After giving them a quick rundown, he fired up the flame and the balloon lifted off slowly and steadily into the air. Everyone gazed out at the view in awe.

"I didn't think it'd be so quiet," Martha said, almost in a whisper.

"This is what I love about ballooning . . . the absolute peace," Mehmet said.

The three of them soaked in the glorious sight of the other balloons rising all around them in unison, and the crisp blue sky was invaded by a riot of colors. "Isn't this quite hard to do? To get all these balloons to float at the same level?" John asked the pilot.

"It's actually nearly impossible to be this synchronized. That's why we're up so early—the wind currents are calmest in the morning. And we've got basically most of the top balloonists in the world right here, and this is a fun challenge for all of us," Mehmet replied.

"I take it you're not from Morocco?"

"No, I fly mainly in Cappadocia. This is new terrain for me, but we've been rehearsing all week, and praying for the weather to cooperate. Today has been perfect, although I'm sure quite a few balloons will be blown off course. Thankfully, there's a Jeep assigned to each balloon, following from below. So if we land in Agadir, so be it."

As John continued to converse with the pilot, Martha saw Rufus leaning out the other side of the gondola taking pictures with his phone.

"Hey, don't lean out too far! I'm getting dizzy just watching you," Martha gasped.

"Are you okay?" Rufus turned around in concern, putting his arm around her shoulders.

"Better now, thanks. I just won't look down."

"I just took a picture of my aunt in that balloon over there," Rufus said as he showed off the photo on his phone.

"Is Rosina Leung really your aunt?" Martha asked.

"Of course she is. What else could she be?"

"There was a bet going around our table last night that you were her fuckboy."

Rufus made a face like he was going to retch as Martha giggled.

"May I ask what you are famous for?"

"Absolutely nothing. I was born the Viscount St. Ives, and one day I'll become the Earl of Greshamsbury. But I come into that title only when my father dies. So it's a promotion I'm not exactly looking forward to."

"I see. You're Eurasian, aren't you?"

"I am. My dad's English, and Mum's from Hong Kong."

"That's where I was born! You know, right after my mom gave birth, my father bought a ninety-carat yellow diamond at auction from Christie's and presented it to me at the hospital. It was an extremely rare diamond called the Golden Star, and he renamed it the Golden Martha. It made the front pages of all the newspapers. 'Billionaire Buys Newborn Daughter Forty-Eight-Million-Dollar Diamond.' Ever since then, I've been fodder for the papers, mainly in Asia. So I understand your problem."

"You're rather famous in certain circles too."

"Yes, but thankfully when I went to boarding school in Sydney, it was such a relief because no one knew who I was. The attention only returned when my father died and I got my promotion."

"I'm sorry."

"It's fine, it's just my life. I always knew it would be inevitable."

"That's precisely how I feel," Rufus said with a wry smile.

A majestic white balloon rose up in the center of the circle of balloons, and on board were the bride and groom with the priest. Mehmet handed Rufus, Martha, and John each an iPad that had a live video feed of the bridal balloon along with headphones so they could listen to the ceremony.

The priest began to speak:

"I have known Amanda Joy for several years now, and Christian I've recently come to know. What strikes me most about this beautiful couple is how well matched they are when it comes to their generosity of spirit, how they seem to put their families, friends, and community ahead of themselves. When Amanda and Christian first told me about their idea to get married in a hot-air balloon surrounded by all their loved ones, I thought, to be honest, that they were both a little insane. But after further discussion, I came to realize that Amanda and Christian were doing what they always do—they wanted to do something special for everyone on their wedding day, not just for themselves. They wanted to take you all on a once-in-a-lifetime adventure, as you witness their vows in the most unforgettable way. So here we are together in the clouds, witnessing the miracle of God's creation, this beautiful planet of ours. We are also witnessing the miracle of science, thanks to the Montgolfier brothers, who created the first balloon to take flight in 1783. But perhaps most important, we are witnessing together the miracle of love, when two fine people find each other and decide to dedicate their lives to one another. So, without any further ado, Christian, do you take Amanda to be your lawfully wedded wife?"

"I do," Christian replied.

"And, Amanda, do you take Christian to be your lawfully wedded husband?"

"I do," Amanda could be heard saying.

"Then by the powers vested in me by the state of California, I pronounce you husband and wife."

As the couple kissed, the cheers of a hundred and fifty guests hovering high above the Atlas Mountains filled the air. Mehmet opened a side basket and took out a bottle of chilled Bollinger along with champagne flutes for everyone. "Time for the toast!"

For a moment, the popping of corks high above Marrakech

sounded like a fifty-gun salute. The wedding guests shared a toast as the fleet of balloons drifted east toward the rising sun.

"To Christian and Amanda!" Martha cheered.

"To the high life!" John toasted.

"To the coolest wedding ever!" Rufus declared, clinking glasses with everyone as he thought for the first time about his own wedding and how he could make it even more epic than this one. He gazed at the empyrean sky and the snow-flecked mountains in the distance, wishing he could be sharing this incredible occasion with Eden. He missed her terribly and wondered what she was doing at this very moment . . . it was Saturday, and they were supposed to be spending the day together. He had planned to take her on a drive down the Devon coast, or perhaps even as far as St. Michael's Mount in Cornwall, but here he was, stuck on a balloon in the sky. He snapped another photo of all the balloons in formation and texted it to Eden, only to discover that the photo wasn't sending. Apparently none of his numerous texts to her all weekend had gone through.

"You're looking far too serious for your own good," Martha said to him.

"Am I?"

"Definitely. You seem very far away."

Rufus smiled. "You know, since you told me that story of you being in the papers as a baby, I have one for you. When I was sixteen, this ghastly magazine came to my school one day to cover a charity fashion show we were putting on. It was a mad time getting ready and someone snapped a picture of me when I wasn't looking. Before I knew it, that picture went viral and basically ruined my life."

John laughed. "I remember that. You were standing there in nothing but your boxer briefs, ironing your shirt."

Martha's eyes went big for a moment as she stared at Rufus. "Shut the front door! That was you? Now I know why you look so familiar! You were 'Master Rufus Gresham' in *Tattle* magazine! I tore out that photo and pinned it on my wall! I had a crush on you for about a decade!"

Rufus immediately turned beet red.

III

LE ROYAL MANSOUR

MARRAKECH, MOROCCO • *AFTERNOON TEA*

Steps away from the teeming cacophony of Jemaa el-Fna Square in the heart of the medina was a palace hotel so unparalleled in opulence, its spectacular architecture, bejeweled spaces, and lushly sculpted gardens defied hyperbole. Built by the king of Morocco with no expense spared to showcase the work of the finest artisans that his country had to offer, the Royal Mansour was meant to host royalty and heads of state from around the world with a sense of beauty and a level of service they would never forget.

This legendary service was on full display in Rosina's sumptuous private *riad*, where the regally attired personal butler hovered behind Rufus's shoulder holding a gleaming silver teapot in his white-gloved hand. The butler flicked his wrist expertly and a long, luxuriant stream of mint tea flowed from the spout and hit the glass placed on the low table with immaculate precision.

"Seriously the most impressive thing I've ever seen! Do you ever miss?" Rufus asked, marveling at how the butler managed to pour the tea from such a distance without a single drop spilled.

"*Hiyah,* don't insult my butler!" Rosina scolded as the man shot Rufus a wounded smile, making it clear that he *never missed*. Rosina grabbed one of the *ghoribas dyal 'asal*—cookies with honey and orange zest—and dipped it into her mint tea before devouring it in one bite. She had summoned Rufus to her *riad* to recap the events after the wedding ceremony, since they had been in different balloons.

"Can you believe the coincidence? That of all the pictures in the world, Martha tore *mine* out of a magazine?" Rufus remarked.

"I remember it was such a sensation when that picture of you was published. You have no idea of the impact it made, because you've never lived in Asia. Do you know how unusual it was back then for *Tattle* magazine, the bastion of British elitism, to actually print a photograph of an Asian man who wasn't David Tang? In those days in Hong Kong we used to study the magazine like the gospel, so the minute that photo came out everyone was talking about it. Who was this young Asian Adonis in the party pages of *Tattle*? I could proudly tell everyone it was my nephew!"

Rufus shook his head in disbelief. "I remember being so mortified when that picture came out, all my schoolmates taking the piss. Even after all these years I felt a bit sick when Martha knew the photo!"

"Well, now you can finally use the photo to your advantage!"

"I suppose, but here's the thing . . . I have been mulling it over for the past two days but I just can't come up with a strong pitch for Martha. I mean, what sort of moneymaking venture could I possibly pitch that her team might actually think is viable? Do you suppose Uncle Peter might give me some pointers?" Rosina frowned at her nephew as he went on talking. "I was thinking maybe there's a way to do something with Bella Resorts, like maybe if we packaged some creativity retreats? Would that bring in bigger profits and attract a new sort of customer? I could get Augie and Maxxie involved, they could program healing retreats at all our resorts. I keep thinking that people these days crave connection and meaning, everyone's gotten so stultified by mindless luxury. Maybe if we created an app that went along with it, Martha would be interested . . ."

Rosina shook her head. "Oh my goodness, don't tell me your mother is right. Are you really that stupid? Do you really think I flew you all the way to Morocco to pitch Martha Dung some new app?"

"What else am I here for?"

Rosina flailed her arms up in exasperation. "To seduce her, you moron!"

"Oh come on now, Auntie . . ."

"Listen, Martha's already confessed to being obsessed with you since she was a young woman! Now she's just waiting for you to sweep her off her feet."

"I highly doubt that. She's not looking for romance of any sort and what's more, I'm not in love with her."

"In the immortal words of Madame Tina Turner, what's love got to do with it? I thought you would have come to your senses by now and realized that you have never been in the position to marry for love. You were born to inherit a great title and a heritage estate and all the privileges and burdens that come along with it. Now, before Hawaii, you might have had some wiggle room and could have married someone suitable that you also happened to love, but as of this moment you no longer have that option. *You must marry money!* And Martha's the perfect candidate. She can write one check that will wipe away all the Gresham debts without even noticing a dent in her wallet."

"So why can't Uncle Peter do the same and lend us the money?"

"Are you joking? We don't have that kind of money available! Everything we have is pledged to the Leung Family Foundation! We are very cash poor, and don't forget, we are in the autumn of our lives. You know your poor auntie's fifty-seven, I'm going to qualify for a free Oyster card soon.[*] I've stopped buying French wineries, your uncle's stopped buying Rothkos, we're finished with acquiring! Your uncle is determined to die penniless—he plans for all his billions to go to the foundation.[†] Martha, on the other hand, is still young and has billions to spare. Do you know how much MD Capital generates? Every time she farts she makes a billion! I'm telling

---

[*] *The 60+ Oyster card provides free transport on the tube and buses for all Londoners over the age of sixty. Rosina actually got hers last year.*

[†] *It's worth noting that Rosina never calls her family foundation a "charitable foundation." It's a private foundation that benefits from tax-exempt status, which in turn benefits her family.*

you, Martha is the answer to your problems. There's no easier way to save your family from being thrown into the gutter."

"Come on, my family isn't going to end up in any gutter. Augie and Maxxie have his family's money and Bea's own career is taking off. She'll be fine. One of Father's friends will make him a board member of something, and my mother can always become an interior decorator."

"Bea's entire 'career,' as you so charitably call it, is predicated on being Lady Beatrice Gresham of Greshamsbury Hall. Without that grand house, she is a nothing. Do you honestly think *Vogue* would have any interest in her if she was a penniless aristocrat living in Shepherd's Bush? And your father can only make a few hundred thousand pounds a year being a board member of something, and that isn't even enough to feed his horses. How is he ever going to survive if he can no longer lead the Boxall Hunt? As for your mother, I can't believe you would want to condemn her to a life as an interior decorator, of all things. I can't imagine a worse job in the world—to be at the beck and call of tasteless vulgarians forcing her to recreate rooms with suicidally neutral palettes or bitching about why their de Gournay wallpaper still hasn't arrived. I've known your mother far longer than you have, and believe me, she is a woman who requires significant funding to maintain her very existence. Couture is her oxygen—without her seasonal ration she won't be able to breathe! Do you want to be responsible for killing your own mother? Are you that cruel of a son, to stand there and watch your helpless parents wither away when all you have to do is marry a billionaire?"

"You make it sound like it's so easy. Martha was in love with a picture, she doesn't know the real me."

"So let her know the real you! Show her your travel pictures, take her windsurfing or rock-climbing or whatever it is you do."*

"Martha's surrounded all day long by these brilliant guys who, as

---

* *Just like all his other Asian relatives, Rosina didn't have a fucking clue what Rufus really did.*

you yourself put it, invent entire industries. I'm not marriage material compared to any of them."

"You are severely underestimating yourself. All you have to do is
glance in her general direction and she will wet her knickers."

Rufus snorted. "I can't believe you're saying this!"

"Believe it, it's the truth. It's time you made use of your god-given
talents."

"What does that even mean?"

"Rufus Francis Leung Gresham, do you really need me to spell
it out for you? You are a beautiful man. Use it to your advantage!"

"You're joking, right?"

"I'm dead serious! Aside from the young Aaron Kwok, I cannot
think of a man more beautiful than you."

Rufus could feel his cheeks flushing bright red.

"Now, the most charming thing about you is that you don't seem
to be aware of the effect you have on people, and you don't use your
looks like a weapon. But your looks, however much you choose to
deny it, are the key to your securing your fortune and the welfare
of your entire family for generations to come. How many Gresham
earls over the centuries made marriages for financial gain? Quite a
few, I bet."

"It's hard for me to take this all in," Rufus said with a heavy sigh.

"Well, it's high time you do. Put your big-boy trousers on and do
your duty. Future generations are counting on you. Tonight is the
wedding banquet. By the time the dessert wines are served, I expect
Martha to have fallen head-over-heels in love with you."

"That's a rather tall order . . ."

"No it's not. All you have to do is shut your mouth and look at
her with those freakishly big green eyes of yours. I'll take care of the
rest."

IV

JARDIN MAJORELLE

MARRAKECH • WEDDING BANQUET

christian + amanda
repas de noces

**Sea Scallops with Golden Kaluga Caviar |
Leek fondue, whipped onion and truffle**
Louis Roederer Cristal "Gold Medallion" Orfevres Limited Edition Brut Millesime

Pepper-Crusted Rooibok Carpaccio | Wild sage oil and caper berries
1992 Screaming Eagle "First Flight of Eagles" Cabernet Sauvignon

Smoked Quail | Lardon gastrique and yuzu honey
1972 Domaine Comte Georges de Vogüé Musigny Blanc Grand Cru

Yellow-Backed Bream with Andalusian Pan con Tomate | Sauce vin jaune
2019 Château de Beaucastel Châteauneuf-du-Pape Blanc Roussanne Vieilles Vignes

Kagoshima A5 Wagyu Beef | Smoked apple, pumpkin, and jus de boeuf
Dominio de Pingus 1995

Golden Kelp Panna Cotta with Sea Buckthorn Caramel

Preserved Lemon Cake with Elderflower Drizzle
2018 Nino Franco Vigneto della Riva di San Floriano Superiore

---

menu created by eric de carysforte

To most people on the planet, the wedding banquet of Christian Radford and Amanda Joy Finch would have constituted one of the most unforgettable experiences of their lives. The dinner took place among the rare botanical specimens of one of the most enchanting gardens in the world, the Jardin Majorelle.* One of the world's greatest chefs had created a delectable feast of exorbitant meats and precious seafoods caught that very morning off Mutsu Bay in Japan and flown in by private jet, in the same way that an equally exorbitant and precious pop star had been flown in as a surprise to serenade the wedding guests.

But Rufus was not having much fun. His mind was preoccupied by the quagmire that he found himself in. He was caught between his own desires and his sense of duty to his family. He had been commanded by his aunt to seduce and charm Martha Dung, a woman he barely knew and was inclined to neither seduce nor charm. Yet, he couldn't help but be fascinated by the spectacle that seemed to accompany this woman. She was certainly the center of attention at this wedding—whenever she moved, the swarm of tech bros buzzed in formation around her like giant gnats while her security team kept a watchful eye from the periphery. Over the glacially paced dinner, Rufus witnessed the game of musical chairs around her table as every brogrammer and wantrepreneur took turns getting his fifteen seconds of face time. Even now, it looked as though there was a TED conference orbiting around her on the dance floor. How was he supposed to get her attention?

As Rufus ate dessert and watched the action from behind a giant cactus, Rosina, glittering in a gold and silver sequined cheongsam, stealthily slipped into the seat next to him and whispered in his ear, "What are you doing?"

---

* *The gardens were planted by the painter Jacques Majorelle over four decades and lovingly restored by the legendary designer Yves Saint Laurent and his partner Pierre Bergé in 1980. The villa itself and all the architectural features within the gardens are painted in a distinctive shade of ultramarine called Majorelle blue that has so enchanted visitors over the years that there are now warning signs all over the garden basically stating, "Don't try this at home, folks, it only looks this great under the bright Moroccan sunlight."*

"I'm enjoying this lemon cake and watching a bunch of wankers try to dance."

"Stop stuffing your face—you should be out there stuffing Martha's face!"

"What if she doesn't like lemon cake?"

"With your tongue, silly boy!"

Rufus winced at the image. "Auntie Rosina, times have changed. You can't just go up to a woman anymore and even introduce yourself, much less shove your tongue down her throat. It's all beside the point anyway because I'll never be able to get a moment alone with Martha. She's constantly surrounded by groupies."

Rosina glanced over at the dance floor. "Look at that hairy oaf dripping his sweat all over her. You need to cut in before she drowns."

"I believe that hairy oaf invented the cloud."

"Who cares? You think she wants to be dancing with the Hairy Cloud when she could be dancing with you? Now, I'm going to have a little chat with Christine Lagarde, and by the time I'm done squeezing some intel out of her on the next set of rate hikes I expect to see you at the very least twerking with Martha."

Rosina got up and began jabbing her fingers through Rufus's hair. Then she reached down and unbuttoned two buttons on his shirt, exposing most of his chest. "There. Much better. Now, get on with it!"

She took off, leaving Rufus feeling rather icky. He was suddenly transported back to Greshamsbury Hall, age nine, and perched on a stool in his bathroom as a stylist slathered a big blob of mousse onto his head. Rufus grimaced as the woman pointed the hair dryer right into his face, almost burning his forehead as she mussed up his hair. Arabella entered in a stunning tartan Vivienne Westwood ball gown, ready to be photographed by Nick Knight for *Dazed and Confused* magazine. She assessed her son, who was going to be a prop in one of the fashion shots. "There. Much better."

"It just needed a bit of texture, ma'am."

"He inherited my Chinese hair, it's always been too straight and too black. I wish he had the curly luscious locks of his sisters."

"Are you kidding? I'd kill for hair like his! It's divine," the stylist cooed.

"You think you want straight hair, but I promise you don't. Now, can we put a bit of makeup on him? Maybe blue lipstick and a little glitter eyeshadow? Something to make him look a little cooler next to me."

"Absolutely, ma'am. We'll transform him into a mini Malcolm McLaren."

Rufus sat on his stool, not daring to move an inch but absorbing every word. As long as he could remember, his mother had always fussed over the way he looked. It was as if she disapproved of his appearance—his shock of black hair was never quite right; his eyes, even though they were thankfully not slitty (his mother's words), were spaced too far apart; his chin was too sharp; and his nose was all wrong.

"Where did that nose come from? It's neither Chinese nor English," she would say as she paraded him in front of one plastic surgeon after another, as each one tried to convince her that he was too young for rhinoplasty and if she would simply be patient he would grow into his nose. Not content, she would fixate on his physique, badgering his endocrinologist about the fact that he wasn't growing fast enough. He remembered being asked to leave the examining room on one visit when he was thirteen, and the minute he was outside he could hear his mother whispering loudly through the door:

"*Doctor, I have to tell you . . . I have a cousin back in Hong Kong, Malcolm, who never grew. Malcolm is a midget.*"

"*We don't use that word anymore, Countess. We call them 'little people.' Or 'people of short stature.'*"

"*Whatever. Malcolm is a dwarf of short stature, and I'm sooooo afraid it runs in the family. Don't you think Rufus is too skeletal and short for his age?*"

"*He's a normal boy, well within range.*"

"*Within range? His little sister is almost taller than him now, and have you seen how his rib cage juts out like one of those famine victims'?*"

"He is thin, but many boys are at his age. I'm perfectly certain he will catch up once he begins puberty."

"Can't you give him steroid injections or something? Like what we give our horses?"

"Countess Gresham, your son is not a horse."

Thankfully, his mother did not treat him like a horse, and by the time he turned fifteen, everything began to change. He grew over a foot in one year, his hair became denser and wavier, and his once-awkward features—that angular chin, deep-set eyes, and incongruously long nose—coalesced into what could only be described as an accident of smoldering beauty just as his scrawny physique filled out like a magnificent kouros. When he was sixteen, *Tattle* took its infamous picture, blowing up his world overnight.

Suddenly, it seemed like everyone around him started acting strangely. His father began calling him "Tadzio" and then chuckling to himself for some baffling reason, and Augie and Bea didn't mind him tagging along on their outings and even started setting him up with their friends, while his mother began dragging him to her fashion events as opposed to hiding him away like the pale creature in the attic. He would come home to find his closets bursting with new clothes sent by designers whose names he couldn't pronounce, and Arabella began policing his appearance in an entirely new way.

"Rufus, don't cut your hair, I want it to get longer and then I'll take you to Sam's to get it cut exactly like Takeshi in *Fallen Angels*."

"Rufus, why don't you wear those asymmetric trousers that Yohji sent for the fundraiser at Quaglino's, you'll look so cute in them."

"Rufus, you're coming to the opening at the Tate Modern and I want you to put on that sheer top with the jeans that Gaultier sent over."

"Mum, those jeans are completely ripped at the crotch, I can't wear them."

"Just wear those DSquared2 briefs underneath and it will look fab peeking through!"

"Mum, I don't think you want me to be seen in public in those DSquared2 briefs. They're kind of . . . bulging."

"Silly boy, that's the whole point!"

He couldn't fathom what she meant by that, and he was baffled by all the fuss. On the inside, he felt like the same Rufus, but obviously, he could see that his appearance had changed, and this in turn changed how every single person treated him—except for Eden. She was the only one who didn't treat him any differently. She was the only constant in his life from the time he was that strange-looking boy to this very day, when everybody seemed to demand a piece of him. She was the only one who knew him through and through, who knew him better than he knew himself sometimes. Rufus was still lost in his recollections at the wedding banquet when he felt a tap on his shoulder. He turned to see his old friend John.

"Do you have a moment?" John inquired.

"For you I have all the time in the world."

"Come with me," John said. They walked through a bamboo grove on the south side of the garden and came upon an ornate iron gate. John opened the gate to reveal two black Mercedes SUVs with dark-tinted windows idling in the street. The lead SUV was filled with security guards, and John opened the back door to the second car. Rufus peered in and saw Martha seated within.

"Wanna get out of here?" Martha asked.

Rufus beamed in surprise and got in. John shut the door behind him and took the front passenger seat.

"Where are we going?" Rufus inquired as the cars took off speeding.

"I needed to get away from that wedding dinner before I bought another company. I have a very hard time saying no to persuasive techies and John tells me I'm spending too much money."

John turned around and faced her. "I think you and I both know that last start-up selling fractional jet ownerships in the metaverse was a waste of money."

"If I'm right and it makes a profit, I'm going to force you to fly coach in the metaverse," Martha quipped, before turning back to Rufus. "What a day! I really need to unwind. How do you feel about getting wet and naked?"

Rufus raised an eyebrow. "Why not."

V

LE PALAIS RHOUL

PALMERAIE, MARRAKECH · *MIDNIGHT*

Arriving at the magnificent Greco-Roman–style guest palace that Martha had rented out for herself and her entourage, John announced he was retiring for the night, leaving Martha and Rufus to partake in the sybaritic pleasures of a late-night massage in the palace's private spa. After they had been pounded, pulverized, exfoliated with charcoal gloves, and spritzed with orange water, they lay on opposite ends of the octagonal pool deep within the candlelit hammam. The intoxicating aroma of oud filled the air as the sound of gently trickling water echoed sensually through the decadently marble-clad space.

"How was your massage?" Martha asked through the unfurling steam.

"Funny you should ask. I went into my treatment room, and this huge man with a gigantic belly protruding over his loincloth told me to take off all my clothes and lie on the ground. So I obeyed. Then he pressed my face to the cold, wet marble and proceeded to twist me around like a rag doll and cracked every bone in my body, bones I didn't even know I possessed. I feel like minced meat and I think I'm scarred for life."

Martha laughed heartily. "You're the most intriguing man I've met in a long time, Master Rufus Gresham."

"In England, only little boys are called 'master.' "

"I know. I'm using it for old times' sake. Reminds me of the Enid Blyton books I used to read."

"I loved Enid Blyton! The Barney mysteries were my favorite."

"That explains a lot. You're a lot like Barney—mysterious and intriguing."

"I always thought I was more like Snubby. How am I intriguing?"

Martha paused for a moment, pondering. "Every guy I meet either wants to seduce me, marry me, or sell me something, but you . . . I'm still trying to figure you out."

"How do you know I'm not trying to seduce you?"

"Ha! You would have done it long ago. I can read the room."

"Maybe I'm just waiting for some sensation to return to my limbs."

Martha laughed again. "You're very kind to humor me, but I do have *some* degree of self-awareness."

"What do you mean by that?"

"A guy like you would never normally go for a girl like me."

"That's simply not true—" Rufus began.

"Stop it! What did your last three girlfriends look like? Let me guess . . . they were all tall, blond, and had a more than passing resemblance to Hailey Bieber?"

"My most recent girlfriend *was* blond, and fairly tall, but she wasn't a hot model type, more like a hot art historian type."

"Still, she was *hot*. The only thing that guys find hot about me is my money, and I can always smell that kind of guy from a mile away. You're trying to charm me, I know, but you're not actually interested in my money. You seem like a man who's conflicted. It's like you want something from me, but you don't really quite know what."

Rufus paused for a moment, surprised by her acuity. "My aunt wants me to get to know you. To be honest, *she* wants me to seduce and charm you."

"Why is Rosina Leung so intent on seeing me seduced? Is she wanting to throw me off guard so that her husband or her creepy sons can make a play on one of my companies?"

Rufus chuckled. "They are a rather creepy lot, aren't they? No, it's nothing like that at all. Rosina is trying to help me. My family's in a bit of a bind, and she thinks you're the solution."

"Ah. How much of a bind?"

"Around half a billion pounds, I think."

"That's a lotta dough to spend on one guy, however charming."

"Well, she thought we'd get married, and you wouldn't have a problem spending that kind of dough on your husband. Of course, that's *her* idea, not mine—she entrapped me on her plane and ambushed me with her plan. I would never marry for money."

"I know you wouldn't," Martha said, before letting out a deep sigh. "Why the hell does every Chinese auntie think I need to get married? It's like they are all brainwashed into this reverse sexism. A Chinese man who's wealthy and successful can be single forever or have a hundred girlfriends. But I'm a woman, so that means I'll never be acceptable until I get married and start producing babies. My own mother is obsessed with finding me a man and has never acknowledged a single thing I've accomplished. Every time I talk to her, it's the same. *Are you dating anyone? Stop working so much, it's giving you wrinkles. It's time to get married—you're already an old maid. You're going to die alone, and the servants will steal all your Chanel handbags when you're on your deathbed.*"

"Sounds like she's projecting her own fears onto you."

"Absolutely. I told her, 'Mom, when I'm on my deathbed, I'm not going to be thinking about Chanel handbags. I don't even own one!' "

"My mum tells me that I need to give her grandchildren before my sperm get too old and my kids turn out, in her words, 'not normal.' "

"Do we have the same mother? I've heard similar things about my eggs."

Rufus laughed, slipping into the warm water and floating out to the middle of the pool. He stared up at the dramatically domed ceiling over the pool, the glowing points of light from the antique copper lantern dangling high above filtering through the steam reminding him of a spaceship hovering amid the stars. A vision of Eden standing in his outdoor shower at night suddenly flickered in his mind.

Martha stared openly at his washboard torso skimming the surface of the water. Finally she blurted out, "You are ridiculously hot, Rufus Gresham."

Rufus laughed uncomfortably. "I'm not sure what to say in response to that."

"Just say thank you. I can't be the first person to say it."

"It's always a bit weird when people compliment me on my looks, since I had absolutely nothing to do with it. It makes me feel like a freak, actually."

"A freak? Really?"

"A lot of people who comment on my appearance couch the compliment with questions like, 'So, what *are* you? Are you mixed?' It makes it feel like I'm some sort of exotic specimen. Or worse, I've even had people say to me, 'You're so lucky you're hapa. All hapas look hot.' The subtext being that if I wasn't of mixed heritage, I wouldn't be attractive. It's quite fucked up."

"All the same, I'd be happy to trade bodies with you any day."

"You say that, but do you know what that actually means? The minute I walk out the door, I can feel all eyes on me, automatically judging me. Most people assume I'm dumb, shallow, or arrogant. Or all three. They think I'm going to be unfriendly, so they put up their guard first and treat me coldly. Or it's the opposite reaction, and they get *too* friendly. They chase me around the room like I'm just some fuckboy who will jump into bed with anyone."

Martha sighed. "Now I feel like a shit. I'm doing to you exactly what people do to me. People look at me and all they ever see is dollar signs. It's the same, isn't it? I'm extremely loaded, you're extremely hot, any kind of extreme always has its downsides. I'm sorry, I wish I could take my words back. I'm too blunt most of the time."

"It's fine. Look, it's hard to talk about all this without sounding like some entitled prat. I know I'm bloody lucky, but it's always been difficult for me to make real friends—people who genuinely want to connect with me, rather than with my title or my country house or my family's resorts. I don't usually complain like this, but I'm being completely open with you because I think you'll understand."

"You have no idea how much I do. There are so few people in this world I can actually trust. Everyone assumes my life is a perfect fantasy, or that I don't deserve any of my fortune. No one realizes how much work it is to be responsible for my company. Sure, I was extremely fortunate to inherit it from my father, but I was barely twenty and you can't imagine the pressure I was under not to fuck it up. Suddenly, I was responsible for tens of thousands of employees, and I still am. These are real people with families, with children, with lives, and I don't take any of it lightly. I've had to work a hundred times harder than everyone else just to prove that I'm not some spoiled heiress. My father was a bit of an old-fashioned sexist—he never imagined a girl would be good at business and thought I should just marry some bloke who could manage it all. But I proved him wrong. Bit by bit, I've transformed his legacy into my own. I've taken terrible, polluting factories and turned them into clean energy businesses. I've shut down all companies I didn't agree with ethically and begun investing in new technologies. When my father died, he was worth three billion dollars—I've turned it into fifty."

"That's bloody impressive."

"Personally, I'd still rather be fuckable than rich any day."

"Trust me, it really depends who's doing the fucking."

Martha guffawed. "Rufus Gresham, I like you more than I ever thought I would. You're so much more than just a guy who irons his shirt topless."

"Let me share a secret with you . . . I don't actually know how to iron."

"Haha, neither do I. So . . . I'm guessing you're in love with that cute blond art historian but your family doesn't approve?"

Rufus paused for a moment, wondering whether he felt comfortable enough to confide in Martha fully. "Actually, the girl I'm in love with has gorgeous dark hair just like yours. She's Chinese, and everyone in my family adores her, except my mother."

"Classic. Why doesn't Mummy approve?"

"I don't think she considers her to be posh enough, and she doesn't have the sort of fortune that can help restore the family coffers."

"What does she do?"

"She's a doctor."

"Don't all Asian mothers love doctors?"

"You haven't met mine."

"How long have you two been together?"

"We're not, but we've been the best of friends since childhood, really."

"So even though you're not technically together you'd like to marry her someday?"

Rufus swam nearer to where Martha was lounging and put his chin onto the lip of the pool. "You know, for the longest time I dreaded the thought of marriage. Knowing that duty dictated I should get married and produce an heir to continue the Gresham line, I always resented it. But being here at this wedding, seeing the way Christian talked about Amanda during his toast and watching the two of them on that balloon ride today, it made me realize how much I actually want to marry Eden someday. But I've mucked it all up, so it's never going to happen."

"What did you do?"

"I lunged at her in the middle of the forest like a gorilla in heat."

Martha bellowed with laughter. "No you didn't!"

"I did. It was in the middle of a wedding banquet, with lava flowing around us, and I lost my mind trying to inhale her face."

"Sounds rather romantic."

"It wasn't very romantic for Eden. I shocked the bejesus out of her, and things between us have never been the same since."

"You need to woo a woman slowly, don't you know that?"

"Apparently I don't. I was caught up in a moment and felt the urge to express all of my feelings, which as it turns out is always a mistake for me."

Martha rolled onto her back and inhaled the steam deeply. "Let me see if I understand this . . . if you can fix your family's financial problems, your mother won't care if you marry Eden."

"Uh, not exactly. If I manage to fix the finances, then I'm sure she'll want me to marry a princess."

"A princess?"

"Yes, a French one."

"Ahhh. I see what's happening now . . . Mummy's one of those snobby bitches who wants her kids to marry up at all costs."

"You hit the nail right on the head."

"I think you need to tell your mother to shove it."

"You haven't met her."

"I'd like to. And I'd love to meet Eden." Martha entered the pool, floating up alongside Rufus. "You know, I have the most fabulous idea. Take me to Greshamsbury."

"If I take you home, my mother's going to immediately jump to conclusions."

"That's exactly what I'm hoping for . . ."

VI

LE ROYAL MANSOUR

Rosina sat up in bed with her breakfast tray, eating her perfectly prepared omelet and drinking her black coffee as she scrolled through her phone. She came upon a news item and immediately started to text Arabella.

> **Rosina Leung:** It's working. Check Page Six right now.
> **Arabella Gresham:** For what?
> **RL:** You'll see.
> **AG:** One minute . . .

Arabella clicked on her Page Six app and loaded the home page of breaking gossip. Scrolling down past the usual nonsense about football players and fake housewives she didn't care about, a headline caught her eye:

MARTHA DUNG'S SKY-HIGH ROMANCE

Love is literally in the air for Martha Dung. The Chinese heiress was photographed embracing a mysterious young man in a hot-air balloon high above Marrakech yesterday, the same man spotted leaving the ultra-exclusive Palais Rhoul this morning in a very rumpled tux. Sources have confirmed that the lanky lothario is none other than Rufus Gresham, Viscount St. Ives, the international playboy photographer who was named *Tattle*'s Most Eligible Bachelor three years in a row. Rufus, in addition to possessing the most symmetrical twelve-pack on the planet, is in possession of one of Britain's oldest and biggest fortunes. If this isn't a match made in the heavens, we don't know what is.

Arabella could feel the blood rushing to her head. She started texting back feverishly:

AG: Oh my god oh my god oh my god can this be true?

RL: I've been watching love blossom with my very eyes.

AG: I googled her. She's so dark. Is she Mongolian?

RL: She is Chinese, born in Hong Kong just like you!

AG: How come I don't know the family?

RL: Father was from Fujian and settled in HK after you left.

AG: Mainland new money. And the mother?

RL: Former Hong Kong starlet.

AG: One of those. Does she speak English well?

RL: The mother? Slight Shanghai accent but acceptable. She only wears Chanel and Akris, you'll love her.

AG: I meant Martha. How's her English?

RL: Perfect. She studied in Australia.

AG: God help us. Where did she go to uni?

RL: No idea. Trust me, you're not going to care where she went to uni when she bails out your family and funds ten new hotels for you.

AG: How much is she worth?

RL: Her net worth exceeds that of everyone on the Sunday Times Rich List.*

AG: Sounds too good to be true.

RL: Please stop looking a gift horse in the mouth when I am trying to save your ass.

AG: Ok, ok, I'm jumping up and down!

RL: So is her mother. She's dying for Martha to marry a good title.

---

* *According to the 2022* Sunday Times *Rich List, siblings Sri and Gopi Hinduja top the list as the richest family in the UK with a net worth of £28.472 billion.*

AG: At least we have one thing in common.

RL: Rufus just informed me he's inviting her to Greshamsbury. Turns out she's obsessed with royals and has been in love with Rufus since that infamous photo was published!

AG: Really?

RL: Isn't it meant to be? Once she sets eyes on Greshamsbury Hall it will be a fait accompli.

AG: Parfait!

RL: Time to roll out the red carpet. She needs the Full English.

AG: She'll have cucumber sandwiches and Branston pickle coming out her ears.

RL: Don't Branston pickle her, she needs the royal treatment. You need to throw a ball in her honor and invite every grand Brit you know.

AG: I'll get the Devonshires, the Yorks, the Kents, the Michaels of Kent, the Gloucesters, the Grosvenors, the Cadogans, the Norfolks, the Northumberlands, the Richmonds, the Rothschilds, the Butes, the Bamfords, the Guinnesses, the Goldsmiths, Dame Maggie Smith, the Manners sisters, the Van Cutsem brothers, the Spencer twins, the Spencer-Churchills, the Mittals, the al-Thanis, the Astors, the Dufferin & Avas, the Duffields, the d'Abos, the de Bottons, the de Waldens, who else?

RL: I'd like to meet Prince George.

AG: Sorry, not gettable yet.[*]

RL: Damn. One thing: We need to make sure Rufus is kept away from Eden Tong. We don't want him to relapse.

AG: Leave Eden to me.

---

[*] *His mother won't allow him to go out on school nights.*

VII

CAFFÈ NERO

GRESHAMSBURY, ENGLAND · *SAME MORNING*

Eden was about to leave for her morning run when she received an uncharacteristically early text from Bea, who normally slept in past ten on most days.

> **Beatrice Gresham:** Bonjour! Can you meet for breakfast?
> **Eden Tong:** At your house? I can come by on the way home from my run.
> **BG:** Can we do Nero's instead?
> **ET:** Sure.
> **BG:** Perfection. Stop by after your run and we'll walk down together.
> **ET:** Great!

Following her usual route up the hill behind the garden of the cottage, she ran along the crest, skirting Boxall Park for two miles before looping back around toward Greshamsbury Hall. Cutting through Greshamsbury Hall's upper garden toward the Big House, Eden ran past the North Lodge gatehouse with her AirPods blasting Cocteau Twins and didn't hear the guard stationed inside the guardhouse calling after her.

The guard came running up alongside her. "Miss, miss!"

"What?" Eden stopped but kept jogging in place.

"I'm sorry, you can't jog here."

He was some young bloke she didn't recognize. "I'm Eden. I live at the cottage."

"This is private property. You can't run through these grounds."

"I know, I live at the cottage. It's part of the estate," Eden explained between breaths. "This is my normal route every morning."

"Yes, but there's a new rule. No one allowed past the North Lodge gatehouse."

Eden finally stopped running. "I'm not some random person. I'm Eden Tong, I've lived here all my life."

"*You've* lived here all your life?" the guard said in a tone that implied that someone who looked like her couldn't possibly have grown up in these parts.

"Well, since I was five."

"I'm sorry, I'm under strict orders not to let anyone through these gates. Especially joggers. You're going to have to turn around and leave."

"This is ridiculous. I'm actually on my way to meet Bea at the house!"

"I don't know anyone by that name."

Eden rolled her eyes. "You know what, just call up to the house and ask for Hemsworth. Please."

The guard eyed her suspiciously, entering the gatehouse and picking up the old phone. "Just doing my job, miss."

"I get it," Eden replied.

A few minutes later, Hemsworth could be seen walking up the hill from the house.

"Hemsworth, you really needn't have come up . . . ," Eden said apologetically.

"No worries," Hemsworth said. "Look, we have new security rules that have just been put in place. We're not allowing anyone to jog through the grounds anymore."

"Really? Even me?"

"Sorry. No exceptions, unfortunately," Hemsworth said, looking quite sheepish. "The new rules are that we're not supposed to allow anyone up to the Big House."

Eden had a sudden realization. "Can I assume that these new rules were put in place by the countess and included specific instructions regarding *anyone*?"

Hemsworth cracked a smile. "You can."

"I see . . . Will you let Bea know I tried to come get her as we had planned, but since *anyone* is no longer allowed at the Big House, I'll just meet her at Nero's?"

"Of course. Good seeing you, Eden. I hope the rules will revert soon."

"Same here," Eden said with a smile.

Fifteen minutes later, Eden and Bea were seated at the window table inside Caffè Nero in Greshamsbury village, Eden sipping her morning latte and Bea nursing a warm cup of ginger tea as she apologized profusely. "I'm so sorry. This is all so absurd. Mummy's just in the foulest mood at the moment. I'm sure the ban will pass, give it a little time."

Eden, dunking a chocolate biscotto into her latte angrily, was unable to mask her emotions. "I'm trying to be understanding, but this is getting ridiculous, Bea."

"You know Mum's barely recovered from the wedding, and it doesn't help that *Hello!* won't stop covering the whole debacle. Apparently Joan Collins chipped a nail while escaping from the lava."

"So Joan Collins is the reason I've been banned from entering the grounds of Greshamsbury Park?" Eden scoffed.

"It's not just the wedding. It turns out"—Bea lowered her voice as she scanned the busy café, making sure other customers couldn't hear them—"these financial difficulties are real, Eden. Things haven't been good since everything went tits-up in Hawaii."

"Really? That's hard to believe."

"I can't believe it either, but Mum's telling me I need to find a very rich young prince to marry as soon as possible. She's arranging for me to meet up with one of the handsome Brunei princes in London, and she's even willing to forgo the five-year plan."

"There was a five-year plan?"

"Yes, she was planning for me to be married the summer of my twenty-eighth birthday."

"Why twenty-eight?"

"It's some Chinese astrology thing. That's the most auspicious year for me to get married. Which is why I needed to speak with you, actually. I need your honest opinion as a friend and your advice as a doct— Oh shit, don't look out the window!"

Before she could help herself, Eden reflexively turned and saw Arabella glaring back at them as she walked down the village row with Hugo Anstruther, the Greshamsbury estate manager. Arabella spotted them immediately and barged into the café.

"What are you doing here, Beatrice?"

"Oh, hello, Mummy. I'm just having brekkie with Eden," Bea replied sweetly.

"Good morning, Lady Arabella," Eden said perfunctorily.

"Don't you Lady Arabella me. Why are you here?"

"Uh . . . I come here every morning," Eden replied slowly, afraid of where this conversation was heading.

Lady Arabella turned to the young barista working the milk frother behind the counter. "You! Are you the manager?"

"What, ma'am?" the lad shouted through the noise.

Arabella raised her voice. "Where is the manager?"

"Uh . . . is there a problem with your coffee?"

"Get your manager NOW," Arabella said in a tone so menacing that the barista hightailed it into the back room.

"Hugo, please come in. I want you to witness this," Arabella called out to her estate manager.

"Mummy, what are you doing?!" Beatrice whispered as the other customers began to gawk.

A woman came out of the back office and addressed Arabella. "I'm Svetlana, the shift leader. Can I help you?"

"Do you know who I am?"

"No."

"I'm the Countess of Greshamsbury. This is *my* village, this is *my* building, and I control the lease. From this moment forward, that girl over there is no longer allowed to be a customer at this café, do you hear me?" Arabella pointed at Eden.

Svetlana looked at Eden in bafflement. "I'm sorry, I can't do that.

We don't discriminate at Caffè Nero, ma'am. Every paying customer can enjoy our coffee."*

"We'll see about that. Hugo, put in a call to the corporate offices of Caffè Nero," Arabella commanded, before glowering at Svetlana. "I'd look for another job if I were you."

"Mummy, why are you doing this?" Bea protested.

"This is what happens when you disobey me. I told you specifically that I no longer wanted you to associate with that girl and you didn't listen. So, not only is she no longer welcome at Greshamsbury Hall, she's no longer welcome at Caffè Nero or anywhere in this village."

Eden took a deep breath and tried to remain calm. "Lady Arabella, I am truly sorry if I've let you down—"

"Let me down?" Arabella began to laugh. "You didn't let me down at all. You proved to be exactly what I've always known you to be. You're a tricky slut who slept with my son in Hawaii!"

The customers gasped as Eden shook her head vehemently in protest. Arabella continued to act outraged, clearly relishing her audience. "You're actually trying to deny sleeping with my son when half the island overheard him saying it on the hot mic?"

"You only heard half the story. I slept over at his house, but I didn't sleep *with him* in the way that you're inferring."

"So you're telling me you've never slept with my son?"

Eden paused for a second, fuming that she even had to answer such a question. "Never!"

"If that's the case, does Freddy Farman-Farmihian know he's the father of your baby?"

Eden gazed at Arabella in utter shock. She found that her throat was closing up and she couldn't speak.

"Mummy, please stop!" Bea cried.

"Why should I stop? Do you know what I found in Eden's room at the Four Seasons?"

---

* *As the Caffè Nero website states, "You'll find us to be a bunch of dynamic and diverse people who are respectful and supportive of one another."*

"What?" Bea asked.

"A used pregnancy test! And it was pinker than the loo at Annabel's!"

Eden had recovered enough to find her voice. "Lady Arabella, I don't know what you're talking about. I've never taken a pregnancy test in my entire life!"

"Are you just saying that because I've ruined your secret plan?"

"What secret plan?" Eden glanced at Bea, who looked utterly stunned.

"You deliberately sabotaged Rufus and Solène because you thought you could have him all to yourself, didn't you? You stole *my* brilliant plan to make Rufus jealous with Freddy and turned it around by having Freddy chase you around the island and put you up in a fancy suite, while at the same time you were teasing Rufus with midnight showers and not-so-innocent sleepovers. But this little pregnancy has messed things up quite a bit, hasn't it?"

"This is absolutely crazy! I'm NOT pregnant!" Eden cried.

"Is that what you're planning to tell Freddy? Come now, every baby deserves a chance. Beatrice, let's go."

"No. I'm staying right here," Bea said in a quavering voice.

"Beatrice, if you don't come with me this instant, I'm cutting off your Coutts account."

Bea looked pained, but she remained in her seat as tears streamed down her face.

Arabella turned around in fury, promptly colliding into a man holding an iced latte. The coffee exploded all over Arabella's blouse.

Arabella shrieked in horror as the man apologized and clumsily began blotting Arabella's chest with the tiny square napkin that had been folded around his cup.

"Stop molesting me!" Arabella screamed, before turning back to the girls. "See what you've done!"

"You should go," Eden said quietly to Bea.

Bea got up reluctantly and followed after her mother as she

stormed out of the café without another word. Arabella didn't need to say anything else; her mission was accomplished. Within minutes, the story would spread to every household far and wide, and Eden Tong would never be able to show her face anywhere in Greshamsbury again.

VIII

BOULEVARD OAKS

HOUSTON, TEXAS • *A FEW DAYS PRIOR*

The long branches of live oaks planted along both sides of South Boulevard arched across the sky to create an incredible canopy of foliage that cast geometric sun-dappled patterns onto the pavement, giving the street an almost fairy-tale quality.* Thomas had come here straight off the British Airways flight from London, and he didn't recognize this elegant neighborhood at all—not that he would; in his two years spent in Houston almost three decades ago, he hardly saw anything aside from his apartment and the treatment rooms within the sprawling MD Anderson Cancer Center.

As he walked up the curved driveway of the classic Georgian red-brick house, a hulking man in a black suit with a telltale earpiece opened the front door, his jacket flapping open wide and providing a clear glimpse of the SIG Sauer tucked into his waistband holster. Thomas was wordlessly ushered through the grand foyer with its gracefully curving staircase and into the library, which was now command central for the team of doctors who managed the care of their esteemed patient. The lead physician, Dr. David Biekert (Armand Bayou Elementary/Clear Lake/Cornell/MD Anderson UTHealth), looked up from his laptop and smiled broadly. "Thomas Tong! Man, it's been way too long."

---

* *In 1987,* The New York Times *proclaimed Houston's South Boulevard the "most magnificent residential street in America." Wes Anderson fans will also recognize the street from his film* Rushmore.

"Good to see you, Dave," Thomas said, beaming. "How's our patient?"

"Feisty as ever and not listening to a damn thing we say. Yesterday he demanded to play a round of golf at River Oaks, at high noon in eighty-five-degree weather.* He had Olaf carry him from his golf cart to every hole. He's paying the price today."

"When was his last infusion?" Thomas asked.

"Monday."

"Really? And he was able to stand on a golf course yesterday?"

"What can I tell you, Thomas, the sonofabitch is messing up all our stats. If you told me five months ago when he arrived in a coma that he'd still be here today, I'd have said you were smokin' somethin'."

"It's a testament to the miracles you've been performing on him here."

"Nah, I think he's just sticking around for the pizza. It's pizza day today—you're in for a treat."

"Can I head in?"

"Enter at your own risk," Dave said, grinning.

Thomas went through the double doors into what had once been the formal living room, overlooking a stately Italianate lawn with an infinity pool that seemed incongruously slick compared to the rest of the house. The living room had been converted into a medical suite cum trading floor with a hospital bed set up in front of a bank of huge TV screens, each showing stock market live feeds from around the world. A shrunken man lay in the bed with his fingers on a keyboard and an oxygen tube at his nostrils. He wore a clunky headset over his bald head, an angry keloid scar with the shape of a gasoline cap protruding from the left side of his forehead. Three nurses sat in chairs just behind him, ready to jump at his every command, as he spoke into his headset in a slow, slurred voice, pausing to catch his breath between sentences:

* *Dr. Biekert is lying, of course. It's Houston we're talking about here—it was at least ninety-five degrees with 90 percent humidity.*

"Farhad said, 'Rene, come on . . . you have so many power plants . . . sell me one, pleeeeeeeease?' I said, 'Seven billion . . . you can have it tomorrow' . . . and he said, 'Five point five . . . you can afford to give me this one . . . I saved your ass on the Doha deal.' I said, 'You stingy prick . . . trying to cheat me even now . . . this is not a negotiation . . . At seven billion I'm giving it to you . . . I already gave you . . . my mistress . . . she calls me up every day and whines . . . that you won't buy her . . . a megayacht. If you want her to . . . keep putting her tongue up . . . your sandy asshole . . . while she finishes you off . . . call up Vitelli and order her . . . a two-hundred-and-thirty-footer . . . so she can sail around Sardinia . . . with her head held high.* If you buy her a new yacht . . . spend, say, three hundred mil . . . I'll make it six point two . . . you'll still be saving half a billion . . . Final offer.' That cockroach took the deal . . . Heh."

He finished his call and looked up slowly. "*Um gau cho, ah!* Do my eyes deceive me? Has the great Dr. Tong . . . finally deigned . . . to pay me a visit?"

"You're not supposed to be talking on the phone, Rene," Thomas scolded him.

"I need to make money . . . I'm a dying man."

"You have enough money for a hundred lifetimes. You need to gain some weight. You ought to be eating more."

"How am I supposed to eat . . . when everything tastes like shit? What's this genius new pill I'm on . . . the one that's supposed to extend . . . my life by fourteen days? I asked that *gweilo* . . . 'How do you know it's working? When do we start . . . counting the fourteen days?' Maybe if you let me go . . . back to Manila . . . I can get some decent food."

"I bet you can find great *siew yuk* here."

"I want to go home. I've been in this . . . hellhole long enough."

---

*   > *Ninety-eight feet = superyacht*
      > *Two hundred and thirty feet = megayacht*
      > *Two hundred and ninety feet = gigayacht*

"Being here saved your life, Rene. That's what you begged me to do, if you recall."

"Yes, MD Anderson has kept me alive . . . with all their fuckin' poisons . . . but tell me . . . will I live long enough . . . to see any of my money . . . from Francis Gresham?"

"I would hope so."

"That unlucky fucker . . . I heard about the volcano . . . Doris Hoh told me . . . she twisted her ankle sprinting out of that forest."

"Well, as a matter of fact, Francis could use another line of credit. And I see a way this could be a win for you."

"Don't bullshit me, Thomas. Gresham is finished . . . nothing will save him now."

"*You* can save him. If you assume all the debt and we help him to restructure his entire portfolio of hotels, you could see a sizable profit on your investment. Don't forget, every hotel is situated in the most prime location. Bella Hong Kong is off Star Street in Causeway Bay. Bella Antwerp is right next to Vlaeykensgang. There's pure profit on the real estate even if the hotels never see another guest."

"How much would it take?"

"Half a billion."

"And what can he offer up as collateral?"

"The only thing he has left: Greshamsbury Hall. His own house."

"The jewel in the crown. Didn't he swear . . . he'd never mortgage that?"

"He has no choice. Unless he wants to lose everything."

"And if he does . . . I still get the house."

"You get everything *and* the house."

"How much is the house worth, with everything in it?"

"The modern art is already mortgaged to other banks, but the house itself, the land, and the heirloom art and furniture is probably worth close to a hundred and fifty million."

"You and I both know I'll never . . . live to see this house."

"Rene, you're in all the medical journals. You've defied all the odds so far."

Rene held up his hand and weakly waved off Thomas's comment.

"I had my lawyers here last week. You need to know . . . I've made you the executor . . . of all my trusts."

Thomas looked momentarily stunned. "Really?"

"Pablo Aguilar, my CFO . . . will run day-to-day . . . but I'm giving you oversight . . . of Luis Felipe's trusts . . . until he turns thirty-five."

"Rene, I'm not sure I want to be placed in that kind of role. I'm not Luis Felipe's favorite person as it is . . ."

"That's why I did it. You're the only one . . . I can trust to . . . say fuck you to Luis. Speaking of which . . . I want to get out . . . of this armpit of hell . . . and see my boy."

"Your boy should be here with you. Where is he?"

"He's very busy spending my money. Why don't we surprise him . . . and pay him a visit? If I'm well enough . . . to play golf, I'm well enough . . . to get on a plane."

"Maybe after your next infusion," Thomas said.

"No! Today!"

"Let's talk to Dave about it. But first, I'd like to get a drink."

One of the nurses immediately sprang up. "What can I get you, Dr. Tong?"

"Do you have any juice? Actually, I'll get it myself." He left Rene's room and headed toward the kitchen, thinking it would clear his head.

In the immense, gleaming kitchen, a chef stood at the island carved out of a single block of Breccia Capraia marble kneading pizza dough. Thomas smiled at her. "Sorry to bother you. Might you have any orange juice?"

"Right over there in that fridge on the left," the woman said. "Cups are over in the cabinet behind me."

"Thank you," Thomas said as he poured himself some freshly squeezed juice.

The chef began tossing the dough with the flair of a flamenco dancer.

"You're really good at this," Thomas complimented her.

"Not really, but I fake it well," the chef said with a grin.

"I'm Samin"—(Marie Curie Elementary/Muirlands/La Jolla High/UC Berkeley)—"by the way."

"Thomas."

"You want some pizza? It'll be ready in twenty minutes."

"Definitely. I've heard about your pizza," Thomas said as he gulped down the juice.

"Yeah, the doctors demand it at least three times a week. You like cherry tomatoes and burrata?"

"Love them."

"Where did you come in from?"

"England."

"You just arrived?"

"Straight from the plane."

"Mr. Tan doesn't get many visitors. Those lawyers from the Philippines and you have been pretty much it."

"His son hasn't been here?"

"I didn't even know he had a son."

"Yes, Luis Felipe."

"I dunno . . . maybe he came earlier, before I started."

"You didn't start when they first rented the house?"

"No, I replaced the first chef. Mr. Tan wasn't happy with Yotam, so they got me by promising to make a huge donation to my favorite charity.* It was supposed to be a short gig. They told me he wouldn't live past the month. And now I've been here four months! Not that I'm complaining—it's given me time to work on my book. I'm glad Mr. Tan's still around. He's a nice guy. You know he's endowing the new pediatric cancer wing?"

"I heard about that."

"You know what else he did? Tammy, one of the night nurses, her daughter got into an accident. Some asshole in a Ford F-150 was texting and rammed right into her. Broke her collarbone and totaled her car. Mr. Tan paid all her hospital bills *and* bought her a brand-new car. A Volvo SUV, can you believe it?"

* *NoKidHungry.org.*

"I can."

"So how do you know Mr. Tan?"

Thomas paused before answering. "Just old friends."

He refilled his orange juice and took it back to Rene's room, sitting down by his bedside. The patient's eyes were closed, but he started to speak, startling Thomas a bit.

"Okay . . . I'll extend Francis . . . a hundred-million-dollar line of credit . . . from one of my banks. But I want the title . . . deed to Greshamsbury Hall . . . in my hands."

"Fine. He will be very grateful."

"You know I'm betting . . . he loses everything. I'm betting I get . . . that house."

"I know," Thomas said grimly. He got up, walked outside, and stood by the side of the pool in the sweltering midday sun, watching the water flow over the edges into a hidden drain. He sent a quick text to Francis:

> **Thomas Tong:** Rene said yes. $100 million to tide you over.
>
> **Francis Gresham:** Oh thank god. THANK YOU!!!
>
> **TT:** You're welcome.
>
> **FG:** You're a miracle worker.

Not quite, Thomas thought to himself. He looked back into the house and saw Samin carrying a big wooden platter of pizza toward the dining room. He wished he had answered honestly when she asked him how he knew Rene. Something about the way Samin looked at him made him want to tell her the truth. He wanted to tell her, *I know Rene because of my dead brother.*

But of course he did no such thing. Thomas Tong was a great doctor, and an even greater keeper of secrets.

IX

THE COTTAGE

GRESHAMSBURY, ENGLAND · *LATE MORNING*

Eden left the café and stumbled up the country lane toward her home in a daze. She felt like she had just been pushed off a tube platform and right into an oncoming train. What had just happened? One minute she was having a morning coffee with Bea and the next thing she knew she was literally being banished from the village where she had grown up.

Her first instinct was to reach out to Rufus. She sent him a text, but she could see on her phone that her text wasn't reaching him. Rufus had been off the radar all weekend, and the last she had heard from him was a text last Friday evening, when they were supposed to meet for dinner:

> **RG:** You won't believe this. My plane got diverted and now I'm being waylaid by another of Mum's schemes.
>
> **ET:** Where are you?
>
> **RG:** Paris, but we're taking off again for god knows where.
>
> **ET:** Tahiti?
>
> **RG:** I hope not. Sorry about dinner, I'll make it up to you.
>
> **ET:** Don't worry about it. Safe travels and see you soon.

Eden could see now that her last message to him hadn't gone through either. She didn't know what to make of his text, and she wasn't sure whether or not to reach out to him now. As much as she hated to admit it, everything had changed since that last night on

the island. As furious as she was with Arabella, Eden was forced to
wonder if she had been right in a way. Was it all her fault? Did she
unintentionally make herself an object of temptation and lead Rufus
astray? Did she commit the ultimate act of betrayal to the Greshams
by distracting the future earl, who was always destined to marry
someone of equal social standing?

Since Eden was very young, she'd had an intuitive awareness of
her place in the Gresham hierarchy. She knew that while Arabella
didn't mind her becoming friends with her children, there was an
invisible line that could never be crossed. As a little girl, she could
take tea with the children in the nursery, but she was never to be
seen at the house whenever the grand people came down for the
weekend. In her teens, she was always invited for sleepovers and
camping trips, but she had never holidayed abroad with them at
any of their resorts. She played tennis all summer long with Rufus
and Augie and Bea, but she never once joined them in the Royal
Box at Wimbledon. She wasn't to the manor born—she was the girl
next door, the daughter of the family doctor, nothing more, and she
knew her place well. The minute she was presumed to have stepped
beyond her place, she was smacked down hard. Now her thoughts
wandered to her father, as she worried about how he would react
when he heard about what had transpired with the countess. He
would surely be hurt and offended on her behalf, and it would no
doubt complicate his relationship with the earl, his dear friend, and
Arabella, who was his patient. Perhaps it would be best if he heard
it all from her first, before any of the village gossip trickled down to
him. It was a blessing that he was out of the country at the moment.
It would give her time to prepare exactly how to tell him, and maybe
if she didn't seem too affected by it, maybe if she pretended to laugh
it off as another of Arabella's quirks, he would be less bothered. Perhaps she should send a preemptive text. She knew he was in Asia,
and as she took out her phone, wondering whether it was too late
to call him, another text appeared on the screen. It was from Deepa
Poovadan, her supervising physician at the hospital, and the message read:

Eden, I have spoken to the team. Best you take the week off.

Eden immediately called her back. "Deepa, I just got your text and I'm not sure I understand. I have back-to-back patients starting at ten. Why are you asking me to take the week off?"

"We . . . um . . . we just thought . . . in light of the situation . . . ," Deepa stammered.

"What situation are you referring to exactly?"

Deepa sighed. "This morning, Eden. At Nero's . . ."

"I don't see how that pertains to my ability to perform my duties."

"But . . . are you sure you're feeling okay?"

"Why wouldn't I be?"

"How far along are you?"

"Deepa! I'm not pregnant! And even if I were, I'd probably be able to work right up to the moment my water breaks, just like you did."

"It's just that *all* the patients are talking about the incident. The waiting room is in an absolute tizzy. One of Dr. Thorne's patients actually *requested* to see you."

"First of all, there was no incident, only a private conversation that's obviously been wildly misconstrued."

"I see. Well, we just think it's for the best that you consider taking a leave of absence, until things settle down and a proper investigation can be rendered."

"Investigation?!" Eden exclaimed.

"Please don't raise your voice, Eden. Believe me, I'm on your side. You hurling your cappuccino all over the countess was a boss move, if I might say."

"Whaaaat? I did no such thing."

"So you didn't scald the right side of the countess's face?"

"Oh for fuck's sake, it was an iced latte that some bloke spilled onto her. I had nothing to do with it. This story has gotten completely out of control."

"Which is why we suggest you lie low for the moment. We have to preserve the integrity of the hospital, we can't have things devolve into an episode of *Love Island*."

"I assure you the truth is more like *The Great British Bake Off*."

"Far too much drama for us!"

"Fine," Eden said, relenting. She hung up in frustration and cut through the lavender field in order to get up the hill more quickly. By the time she had reached the gate of the cottage, she realized that tears were streaming down her face uncontrollably. Why the bloody hell was she crying? She was so angry at herself for crying. This was all so ridiculous—she was a grown woman, a doctor, and Arabella Gresham had in barely twenty minutes successfully ruined her reputation all through the county even though she had done absolutely nothing wrong. All she had ever tried to do was to be helpful to the Greshams, to be the most loyal friend to all of them. She hadn't even wanted to go to Hawaii. She'd never asked to be kissed by Rufus. That damn kiss had ruined everything. So why was she the one feeling all the guilt, as if she had committed a cardinal sin?

Eden suddenly felt the same wave of emotions that had come over her that day in Hawaii when that fashion editor lying on her bed at the Four Seasons had barked at her as if she were some kind of lower-status employee. It was as though a veil had been lifted, and she now saw with alarming clarity that she had spent most of her life sublimating herself whenever she was around the Greshams—never appearing at the Big House without looking immaculate, putting on her best manners at all times, always striving to be the perfect child. And yet, she must never be faster or funnier or prettier or smarter than, or in any way outshine, Bea and Augie. When a model scout once approached her in Soho when she was sixteen, she laughed it off and refused to take the woman's business card. When she scored distinctions on five A levels, she didn't tell a soul except her father for a week.

She had told herself a story for so long that she was accepted and safe in her own village, *that she belonged*, but all this time, there was one person who had been lurking in the shadows, always observing and assessing and discriminating against her. The one other woman in all of Greshamsbury who looked like her: Arabella. What she had assumed was self-absorbed indifference from the countess was actually pure disdain, as if she were some sort of second-class interloper who didn't belong in the village, much less anywhere near the manor house. She wondered if she would ever feel at home here again.

Walking up the garden path, she arrived at the front door of the cottage and saw that it was blocked by a giant package wrapped in cellophane and tied with an elaborate silk bow. She unlocked the front door, dragged the package into the hall, and grabbed a pair of scissors from the chest of drawers in the foyer. Underneath the acres of cellophane was a handsome wicker hamper with leather handles. As she began to unfasten the lid, a wisp of smoke wafted out through the cracks of the hamper. She stepped back for a moment in alarm before carefully flipping open the lid. The smoke turned out to be vapors from dry ice, and nestled in the packing hay was a mound of fresh pineapples and coconuts, cans of coconut cream, an exquisite bottle of Appleton Estate rum, a set of Baccarat crystal tumblers, and ube syrup from Hawaii. A handwritten note read:

Here's a good recipe:

2 ounces rum
3 ounces coconut water
1 ounce pineapple juice
¾ ounce coconut cream
1 ounce ube syrup

Now you can make your own ube coladas,
but be sure to save some for me.
Love ya,
Freddy

Eden began to laugh. Wiping away her tears, she dialed Freddy's number. He picked up after several rings.

"You realize it's almost two a.m. here in LA?"

"I'm sorry! I was so surprised, I just got your present. Did I wake you?"

"No, not at all. I'm at the Fleur Room."

"Is that a club?"

"Sure is. I'm here with my sister and some friends. You oughta be here with us."

"I wish I could be. I was having the worst morning, but then your gift arrived and it really cheered me up."

"Amazing! Are you okay? What's wrong?"

"Oh, nothing. Everything's turned upside down here. I think I might have lost my job."

"Really? Well, if you don't have a job anymore, you should come to LA. My sister's engagement party is this weekend and you should be here!"

"I can't go away right now, I just got back in town."

"What does that have to do with anything? Let me send the jet for you—"

"Don't you dare!"

"Why? You just said you don't have to work, and correct me if I'm wrong, but you've never been to LA before?"

"No, just New York . . ."

"Then you really have no excuse. It's gonna be so fun. You've never been to a big Persian engagement party!"

"I can't come to your sister's engagement, I don't even know her."

Suddenly a bright, sharp woman's voice came booming over the line. "Hi, this is Daniela. My brother hasn't stopped talking about you since he got back. I want to meet you, you're coming to my party. We are sending the plane and I expect you to get on it or I will be very offended."

With that, Daniela hung up the phone.

Beverly Hills

*If you stay in Beverly Hills too long,
you become a Mercedes.*

—ROBERT REDFORD

It was because of Debussy. If the volunteer pianist in the lobby of MD Anderson hadn't been playing "Claire de Lune," Dr. Thomas Tong would never have stopped on his way up to his office, and he would have never noticed the woman sitting on the sofa near the piano. She was an Asian woman wearing a cloche hat, sipping tea out of a Starbucks paper cup. He always noticed other Asians when he was here in Texas. He studied the woman for a moment as he stood listening to the music. He could tell in a flash that she was a patient, probably here for a chemo infusion. Her chic little hat was a telltale sign that she had lost her hair. Even though she was painfully thin, she had a pretty face. Something about her looked familiar, but he didn't have time to think much more about it as he rushed up to his office.

The physician's assistant placed a stack of patient files on his desk. "With Dr. McKinley out on maternity leave, Dr. Varshney has reassigned all the patients today."

"Great. So you're telling me I wasted my whole night going through today's patient files?"

"Yep. You could have been watching Felicity,*" the assistant quipped.*

Thomas flipped through the first file, Faye Wang, a patient from Vancouver, Canada, with metastatic breast cancer. The door opened and another clinician showed the patient into the room. Thomas looked up to see the woman in the hat enter. "Ms. Wang. Good morning."

The woman froze in her tracks, her eyes flickering with fear. That was the moment Thomas recognized her fully. She had obviously recognized him immediately, but he had never met her in real life, only seen her in pictures.

"Have a seat, Ms. Wang. Let's look over your CA125 numbers," he said matter-of-factly, as though she were any other patient. But she wasn't just any other patient; she was a ghost. This woman sitting across from him who called herself Faye Wang was actually Mary Gao, his late brother's girlfriend. And Mary Gao was supposed to have died three years ago in Perth, Australia, after a botched abortion.

Things to Do with Eden in LA
by Freddy Farman-Farmihian[*]

MUST DO
Lakers Game
Troubadour (if anyone good is playing)
Spa day at the Peninsula Beverly Hills
Banks's pickleball party
Fly to the Wynn Las Vegas
Drinks at Fleur Room, the Wolves, Death & Co.,
the Roger Room, Sunset Tower, Ace Hotel

MUST EAT
Fred's Pasta at Mauro Cafe
Pastrami and latkes at Nate 'n Al's
Hamburgers at the Apple Pan
Garlic noodles at Crustacean
Best flourless chocolate cake on the planet at E. Baldi
Drive to Laguna Beach for lunch at Nick's
Ice cream at Saffron & Rose
Shabbat dinner at Cousin Jack's

MUST SHOP
Ron Herman, Just One Eye, Bode, The Row

CULTURE STUFF (ONLY IF SHE ASKS)
Academy Museum[**]
Dad's wing at LACMA[**]
Getty Villa[**] (plus lunch at Geoffrey's Malibu)
Huntington Library, Art Museum, and Botanical Gardens[**]
Griffith Observatory[**]

---

[*] *Bad ideas vetoed by Daniela Farman-Farmihian*
[**] *Neither Freddy nor Daniela has ever gone to these places (they have never been east of Chateau Marmont)*

Holmby Hills

LOS ANGELES, CALIFORNIA • *LATE MORNING*

Everything about the place looked so familiar to Eden. The hanging plants in the window across the courtyard, the rice cooker with the flower pattern on the side, the pair of wicker chairs on the balcony. But this was not any home she had ever lived in. As she wandered around the dimly lit space, she realized it looked just like the flat from one of her favorite films, *Norwegian Wood*. Rufus walked into the living room holding a small birthday cake, his face glowing like a Botticelli in the flickering candlelight. He put the cake down on a yellow lap tray with chrome legs. "Why are you wearing that? It's obscenely tight on you," she said with a little laugh, pointing at his graphic patterned polyester shirt. She began undoing the buttons on his shirt until it was completely off, took one of the candles from the cake, and dripped wax down his chest. Rufus flinched for a moment but then held still as the wax trickled down his *linea alba,* the line that ran down the middle of his torso. "Feels ticklish," Rufus murmured softly. She stared into his hazel green eyes for a moment, then she leaned in and began to trace the line of wax with her tongue. It tasted like salted caramel. She felt her face getting warmer as she ran her tongue on his bare skin all the way down, down, down to the waistline of his low-slung jeans. Her face was getting so hot she felt as though the candle wax was burning into her skin.

Eden awoke with a start, opening her eyes and squinting immediately against the beam of sunlight coming through the window and landing directly on her face. She was lying on the edge of the biggest

and plushest bed she had ever slept in. Where in the world was she?
Oh yes, Beverly Hills. It was all coming back to her now, through the
fog of her hangover. After being picked up at Van Nuys by Freddy
and Daniela (Sinai Akiba/El Rodeo/Beverly Hills High/Vassar/
FIDM), Eden was whisked directly to dinner at Nobu Malibu,
where they were joined by Daniela's fiancé, Lior (Collège Français
de Tel-Aviv Marc Chagall/Institut auf dem Rosenberg/Stanford/
INSEAD), and Banks (Maggy Haves/Westlake Elementary/
Crossroads/Pepperdine), Freddy's best friend since sixth grade.
After they devoured too much black cod with miso, yellowtail
sashimi with jalapeño, soft-shell crab rolls, and sake, Banks had
invited everyone for more drinks at the Fleur Room, which Eden
was informed was the hottest nightspot of the moment, after which
a bleary-eyed Eden was taken back to Freddy's house and finally
allowed to go to sleep.

Eden rolled out of bed with a reluctant groan and stumbled into
the bathroom, realizing in the clarity of morning that the space
was five times the size of her bedroom in Greshamsbury. Recessed
lights behind the floating mirrored wall automatically came on, casting a flattering peachy glow on her face, and she couldn't help but
notice the deliciously heated Portoro marble floors on her bare feet.
Beyond the carved marble sink was a claw-footed copper bathtub
and a glassed-in shower big enough to fit a whole rugby team.

Eden sat down for a moment on the curved sofa in front of the
window, trying to imagine the sort of life where she could take
long baths in that gorgeous copper tub, lounge in one of the many
fluffy Frette bathrobes hanging on silver hooks against the wall, and
devour a few of the macarons in the glass candy dish so temptingly
placed right beside the sofa on a little golden stand. She lay back
on the sofa, trying to make sense of the dream she had just awo-
ken from. It was fading fast, but she was perplexed by the snippets
she could remember. Why on earth was she dreaming of licking
candle wax off Rufus's chest? Obviously Rufus was on her mind,
and she reached for her phone. Still no text from him, not a peep
in days. And the Signal app automatically deleted all the previous

texts after twenty-four hours, so it was almost as though their text conversations never existed. Feeling a bit forlorn, Eden reached into the candy dish for one of the macarons, only to discover that it was made of ceramic.

"Bloody hell," Eden cursed to herself as she put the macaron back onto its deceptively tempting dish. She rose from the sofa, splashed some water onto her face, and ran her fingers through her hair. After freshening up, Eden tiptoed down the sweeping staircase that curved below a magnificent domed rotunda, which was dominated by an impressionistic portrait of a beautiful dark-haired woman in a pink ball gown and rococo furniture of the type usually found at Versailles. Although Freddy had warned her last night as they pulled up to the gates of the pseudo-Italianate mansion that the house was "full-on Persian palace" and said, "You'll have to excuse the décor, I had nothing to do with it," Eden found herself quietly impressed by how elegant and intimate the house felt in spite of its ornate furnishings.

No one seemed to be around, and after wandering through a series of reception rooms filled with gilded furniture redolent of the old world, she stumbled upon the huge kitchen, where a woman in her fifties was unfolding sheets of thick paper napkins—the kind found in the washrooms of expensive hotels—from an industrial-size box and placing them in dozens of meticulously neat piles on the marble countertop.*

"Morning, ma'am. I'm Sonia. Freddy and Dani are out on the terrace having breakfast," she said, gesturing to another doorway. "What would you like to drink?"

"Some coffee?"

"You want cappuccino, espresso, macchiato?"

"Can you make a latte?"

"Of course. You want oat milk, almond milk, rice milk, soy milk, hemp milk?"

"Uh . . . do you have milk . . . from a cow?"

---

* *Don't even ask what's happening here. It would violate the NDA signed by a former employee of a certain huge-ass estate.*

"Yes. Whole milk, half-and-half, two percent, skim, or lactose free?"

"Whole milk is fine, thank you," Eden said, leaving the kitchen before Sonia might ask her to select sugar options. Down a hallway, a gracious set of arched doors opened out onto a terrace that over-looked formal gardens straight out of a château in the South of France. Even though she had grown up amid the splendor of Greshams-bury Hall, there was something to Eden about the way the Farman-Farmihians lived that seemed exponentially more decadent—here in Southern California, the fountains seemed fuller, the peonies seemed plumper, the pool sparkled brighter, and the tennis court blinded with its perfect white lines, just like the white Ginori china sparkling on the breakfast table where Freddy and his sister peered intently over an intricate seating chart.

"No, no, you can't seat *Khaleh* at that table. She'll be opposite from Leila, and you know they haven't spoken since Paris,"* Daniela said.

"Didn't that happen before I was born? Those cousins still aren't speaking?"

"Hell no."

Freddy looked up and spotted Eden coming out onto the terrace. "Hey, hey, she's alive!"

"Good morning," Eden said.

"Did you sleep well?" Daniela asked.

"My god, I didn't want to leave the bed. That's the best mattress I've ever slept on," Eden sighed.

Freddy gave his sister a look. "See? See? I told you the mattress was worth it." Turning back to Eden, he said, "That's Drake's mattress."

Eden looked confused. "Drake, the musician? He slept in my bed?"

"Not your bed, but one just like it. It's custom-made in Sweden and we waited eight months for it."

"Call me cheap, but I don't believe in spending more for a mat-

---

* *A most unfortunate incident at the Ritz Paris in the eighties involving a just-delivered Christian Lacroix pouf dress, a pot of hot chocolate, and a Maltese gigolo.*

tress than a Bentley," Daniela shot back. "Anyway, it's your house. I'll be moving out soon."

Freddy made a sad face.

"Where are you moving?" Eden asked.

"Oh, just nearby. I'm redoing a house in Trousdale, that's why I'm squatting here at the moment."

"Oh. Doesn't your father live here as well?"

Freddy and Daniela laughed at the same time.

"No. My dad's latest wife doesn't think this house is up to her standards. She and my dad live in Paris and Monaco these days, where she mixes only with snotty French Persians," Daniela explained.

"I think being around my mom's furniture also freaks her out," Freddy chimed in. Suddenly it all made sense to Eden—this was Freddy's childhood home, and it remained a shrine to his late mother. Eden stared out at the colonnade of Roman sculptures in the rose garden as the putter of a leaf blower revving up could be heard in the distance.

"Fuck, here they come," Daniela groaned.

"Who?" Eden asked, puzzled.

"The bane of my existence! Our neighbor's damn gardeners! Ugh, Tom and Richard promised they weren't supposed to start until eleven."

"It *is* eleven," Freddy answered.

"I'm going to my dermatologist. I'll see you at dinner." Daniela blew Eden a kiss, hightailing it off the terrace.

The housekeeper brought out Eden's latte, and as she attempted to sip her coffee and relax into her chair on the lovely flagstone terrace, the hum of a single leaf blower soon turned into a roar of raging machines.

"Jesus, how many of them are there?" Eden finally asked.

"WHAAT?" Freddy shouted.

"HOW MANY GARDENERS ARE THERE?" Eden shouted back.

"I DUNNO. PROBABLY A DOZEN. THEY COME BY THE TRUCKLOAD."

"IT SOUNDS LIKE THE FALL OF SAIGON!"

"YEAH? I'M SO USED TO IT I DON'T EVEN HEAR THEM. IT'S JUST A FACT OF LIFE HERE. EVERYONE'S GOT GARDENERS, EVERYONE HATES LEAVES."

"CAN WE GO INSIDE?"

"SURE. WHY DON'T YOU GET READY FOR LUNCH? I'M TAKING YOU SOMEPLACE VERY SPECIAL."

Less than an hour later, Freddy was giving Eden a driving tour of Bel Air and Beverly Hills on their way to lunch. Driving down a street flanked by towering palm trees in his British Racing Green G 63, they turned onto Maple Drive. "This is one of my favorite streets in the Flats," Freddy said.

"I don't see any flats," Eden said as she looked at the gracious houses along the curving, sun-dappled street.

"No, this area of Beverly Hills is called 'the Flats' because it's on flat land, as opposed to where I was just driving you up in the hills. It's actually the most desirable part, super-high demand. If any of these houses come onto the market, they're snapped up within hours of the listing going live."

"Aren't these houses very expensive?" Eden asked, staring at a gorgeous Spanish Mediterranean house.

"These are actually the cheaper houses in the neighborhood—twelve to fifteen million on average."

"What a bargain," Eden laughed.

"Yeah, some people I know have ten of them."

"*Ten* . . . of these houses?" Eden tried to clarify.

"Yeah. They're the best investment, because historically the values go up eighteen percent a year. So having a house in the Flats is a better return than most stocks or bonds. I know families who just collect them and leave 'em empty. Half of the houses on these streets are empty."

"Why leave them empty? Why not at least let them out?"

"You don't want renters messing things up. Plus, you get the tax deduction from not renting it. I mean, a house on this street could easily rent for $40,000 a month, so that's a $480,000 loss on each house you can write off every year."

Eden tried to absorb Freddy's words, quietly horrified. "So these massive houses are sitting empty when there are homeless people living on the street?"

"Yeah, but homeless people won't want to live here anyway."

"Why not? Look at that house over there. I bet two dozen people could easily live there."

"Yeah, but they probably wouldn't feel comfortable in there."

"Oh really? Tell me what homeless person wouldn't feel comfortable in that mansion, swimming in the pool during the day and sleeping on Drake's mattress at night?"

Freddy laughed uncomfortably. "No, you're absolutely right. I just don't have a clue how to solve this problem myself."

"I'm not asking you to. I'm just astonished by LA, that's all, and how worlds apart everything is."

"You sound like my mom. She was always embarrassed by our house and said it wasn't right to live in such a huge estate when there were poor people everywhere. If it were up to her, our family would have stayed in Encino."

"So your mum didn't choose the house and design it herself?" Eden asked in surprise.

"Hell no, my dad insisted on buying it and hired decorators from France to do everything. My mom couldn't have cared less. She wasn't interested in all that stuff, she just wanted to be a mother."

"Your mum sounds like a lovely woman."

"She was," Freddy said before he turned to Eden with a funny look. "Do you ever dream about your mother?"

"All the time. Don't you?"

"Yeah. I have this reoccurring dream that we're having tea together at the Peninsula Beverly Hills. She loved taking me there for tea and telling me stories of her youth in Tehran."

"My mother keeps appearing in the strangest places in my dreams, but I can never understand a thing she's saying. I wish we could have a normal conversation as two adults. I'd love to hear her voice again. Sometimes I think I've forgotten what she sounds like. It'd be nice just to be able to call her up and hear a good yarn."

"My buddy Banks gets mad whenever his mom calls him. He has no idea what it's like . . . I would give every cent I have to get the chance to talk to my mom again just once." Freddy took a quick gulp, as if he were swallowing his emotions.

They drove in silence for a few more minutes before the car pulled up outside a distinctively striped marquee tent that extended nearly to the edge of the sidewalk. This was the discreet entrance of La Cienega Villas, which allowed arriving guests maximum protection from being photographed at an unflattering angle by the press.

A valet opened the car door on Eden's side, and she was quickly escorted into the safe confines of the tent. Freddy said to her solemnly, "You're about to enter the most exclusive private club in the country, probably the whole planet. Money alone won't get you in here."

Standing behind the glossy reception counter were three strapping hosts with matching jawlines dressed like Edwardian cricket umpires. "Mr. Farman-Farmihian, we have your table ready," the host sporting cool ponytail dreads said before thrusting a clipboard with a sheet attached in front of Eden. "I need you to sign this."

"What am I signing?"

"Your life away. Just kidding. This is our standard NDA for guests. Nondisclosure agreement," he added unnecessarily as he handed her a pen.

"What am I agreeing not to disclose?" Eden asked in amusement.

"Everything. You saw nothing, heard nothing, spoke nothing, you weren't actually even here."

Eden chuckled as she signed away, murmuring under her breath, "Do I even exist?"

The host stared at her earnestly. "Now, I just need to see your phone."

"My phone?" Eden looked at the host in confusion.

"Yeah, hand him your phone," Freddy confirmed.

Eden took out her cell phone, and the host carefully placed stickers emblazoned with the insignia of the club over the camera lenses on both sides of the device.

"It's to make sure you don't sneak any photos," Freddy said with a wink. "This place is paparazzi-proof. The highest of high-profile people and the A-est of A-list celebrities hang out here, and we all want to feel safe and comfortable."

A model-pretty hostess led them through the door, and suddenly they found themselves in a lush tropical garden with tables placed around frothy fountained pools. The atmosphere felt like a pool party, with Portishead pumped through the speakers and everyone in a celebratory mood. Every head swiveled to check them out as they entered the garden, quickly swiveling away when they saw that they were nobodies. As Eden settled into her wicker chair feeling rather self-conscious, she glanced at the neighboring table and saw a cute West Highland white terrier staring at her intently. It then turned, as if bored, back to the chic blond lady swathed in cashmere huddled in conversation with an Asian guy in a striped sailor tee.

Achilles, Freddy's favorite waiter, sauntered up to the table like he was about to launch his best pickup line. "Mr. Farman-Farmihian, what fabulous sneakers you have on today! Pray tell, are those original Air Jordans?"

Freddy grinned. "You bet! You know what's special about these?"

"Oh I know, they're the Flu Game Air Jordans, the ones Michael wore in the 1997 NBA Finals when he had the flu but still won against the Utah Jazz."

"Yes, but these are the *actual pair* he wore," Freddy said proudly, putting his feet up on the table, removing one of the shoes, and holding it up to Achilles's astonished face. "Look, there's even the snot stain where he sneezed in the shoe. He was changing out of them in the middle of the game when he had a sneezing fit. It was televised, and I have video documentation of that sneeze."

"Holy moly! Look at that beautiful snot! You're a very lucky man, Mr. Farman-Farmihian. Arnold Palmers, zucchini crisps, and pigs in blankets to start?"

"You read my mind! And let's add the fish tacos too. Eden, you're gonna looooove their fish tacos. Achilles, Eden's my friend visiting from England."

"Cheerio." Achilles flashed a smile at Eden as he leaned in close to Freddy's ear and said in a low voice, "You wanna know who else is visiting from England today? A certain British pop star who wants to be an actor having lunch with a certain A-list producer, a certain billionaire film investor kid, and also a legendary supermodel and her influencer daughter, and the daughter's boyfriend, who also wants to act."*

"Where are they sitting?" Freddy asked, looking around.

Achilles tilted his head surreptitiously in the direction of the Cabana Room.

Freddy turned to Eden and whispered loudly, "Don't look now, but when you get a chance, look through that set of French doors and you're gonna see some famous celebs you might recognize."

Eden turned slowly, peering into the glassed-in room.

"Do you see him? One of the biggest pop stars in the world having lunch with an A-list producer, that supermodel from the nineties, and her daughter and—"

"My father," Eden muttered.

"What?"

"That's my father sitting in there!" Eden said in disbelief.

Freddy stood up to see more clearly. Sure enough, seated inside at the far end of the table between the British pop star and the supermodel was Dr. Thomas Tong.

---

* *Out of respect for their privacy, these high-profile individuals will not be identified by their names (or their schools).*

La Cienega Villas

WEST HOLLYWOOD • *LUNCHTIME*

"Aren't you gonna say hi?" Freddy asked excitedly.

"I'm not sure . . . ," Eden demurred, the shock of seeing her father here in Los Angeles suddenly paralyzing her in her seat. "I think he's with his patient, and I reckon he wouldn't want to be disturbed . . ."

"Of course he would!" Freddy said, getting up and striding boldly into the Cabana Room. Eden watched curiously as all the heads swiveled from Freddy to her. Her father stood up, looking in astonishment through the window at her. She knew her father had gone to treat one of his VIP patients who was gravely ill, and she had assumed he was in Asia, where most of his VIP patients tended to be. She never asked where he was off to on his medical trips, as she had too much respect for the oath of doctor-patient confidentiality to pry into his medical affairs.

The pop star got up from his seat and poked his head out the door. "Oi! Eden? Get over here!" He waved excitedly. Eden could not believe that the famous pop star was yelling her name. She walked over and felt as if she were having an out-of-body experience as he gave her a big bear hug. As she entered the room, the hugfest continued; first her father, then the producer, the supermodel, her daughter, and even the daughter's boyfriend got up and hugged her.[*]

---

[*] *In Los Angeles, complete strangers will give you a full-body hug upon meeting you for the first time, especially if you happen to meet them at Soho House Malibu, E. Baldi, Matsuhisa, or Hinoki & the Bird at lunchtime. These strangers may also say "Love ya" as they are leaving and "Let's get together soon." You will never, ever see them again.*

"You didn't know you were both in town at the same time?" the pop star asked, grinning like a Cheshire cat as he glanced from father to daughter.

"No, we didn't," Eden said. "This was a spur-of-the-moment trip for me."

"For . . . for me as well," Thomas stammered, looking completely shocked.

"Thomas Tong, why have you been hiding your stunning daughter from us?" the producer declared.

"Obviously because of you!" the supermodel shot back as everyone laughed.

The only person at the table who hadn't acknowledged Eden was an overly muscular Asian guy in his midtwenties dressed in extra-tight gym clothes and chunky gold-rimmed sunglasses slouching at the end of the banquette. He stared into space disinterestedly before suddenly blurting out: "I was at an auction at Sotheby's in Hong Kong, bidding on a Murakami. And some bastard at the back of the room kept bidding against me. Finally I turned around to check out my competition and saw that it was my dad!"

"You're kidding! And you didn't know he'd be there bidding on the painting?" the producer asked.

"I didn't even know he was in Hong Kong! The fucker never told me where he ever went from day to day."

"Who won the Murakami?" the supermodel asked.

"I did, of course. Dad stopped lifting his paddle and I placed the winning bid! His stupidity cost me an extra two million."

"But wasn't it worth it for the story?" the producer quipped. The group laughed politely as Eden wondered whether he was some famous Asian celebrity whom she didn't recognize.

Freddy, meanwhile, turned to the British pop star. "Hey, I think my dad's company produces all your concert merch."

"Really? Your dad owns F-Star?"

"Yep."

"Then I must thank you—you're making me pots of money! Of

course, you guys must be loads richer if you're the ones making all my T-shirts!"

The muscled young guy, who clearly did not appreciate the attention being drawn away from him, pushed his table out loudly so that he could get up. He stood up with a slight wobble, and Eden realized that he was drunk.

"I'm outta here. John, count me in for twenty million on the film." Putting his veiny bulging arm over the pop star's shoulder, he added, "As long as this fucker's in it, I'm sure it won't lose too much money."

"It'll be a surefire hit!" the producer declared.

"I'm on the first card and I get to play the pimp?"

"Absolutely."

"And we all get cameos?" the supermodel's daughter's boyfriend asked.

"Everyone here gets a cameo!" the producer promised.

Thomas turned to Eden. "I have to join him. Must get back to my patient."

"Yes, of course," Eden said, sensing that her father seemed on edge even though he was clearly pleased to see her. She figured that he was still trying to maintain his patient's confidentiality amid this awkward reunion.

"How long are you here for?" Thomas asked.

"Probably till next Monday. Freddy's sister's engagement party is this weekend."

"Deepa must have been in a charitable mood to let you take all this time off."

Eden's face clouded over. "That's another story. Are you here for a few days?"

"Yes, I think so. My patient insisted on coming to LA to see his son," Thomas said, gesturing toward the Asian Adonis, "but I don't think we can leave."

Eden understood her father implicitly. His patient didn't have long. "Well, if you have a spare moment, perhaps we could have a phone chat while we're both in the same time zone."

"Yes, I'm sure I'll be able to squeeze that in. Maybe tomorrow afternoon? What time will you be free?"

Before Eden could reply, the young guy interrupted Thomas. "Hey, you want a ride or not?"

"Yes, of course," Thomas said.

"Dad, I'll just text you later when I know—"

"Why don't you just come over if you wanna see your dad so bad?" the guy cut in again.

"That won't be necessary," Thomas said, looking momentarily alarmed.

"My father's right. I wouldn't want to intrude . . ." Eden sensed that her father did not want her to visit him.

"You wouldn't be intruding. Dr. T, she's a tourist, I'm sure she'll want to see Cloudline."

"I really don't need to—" Eden began, but Freddy's ears perked up.

"Wait a minute—*you* bought Cloudline? You're Louie—"

"Luis Felipe Tan" (International School Manila/Masters School [expelled]/TASIS [expelled]/UC San Diego [expelled sophomore year]/Florida International University [dropped out after one semester]/Stella Adler Academy of Acting [asked to leave]), the guy said, completing Freddy's sentence.

"Whoa—congratulations, dude! My buddy invited me to a party at your house."

"Which one? I have parties every week," Luis Felipe said.

"I think it was the NFT party."

"Were you there?"

"No, I was being starved to death at Rancho La Puerta."

"The next time someone invites you to a party at my house, you should come."

Freddy grinned excitedly. "Can we come today? Eden, you gotta see Cloudline! It's the sickest house in all of LA!"

"Ahem, we *do* have a very sick patient in the house—" Thomas interjected.

"Yes," Eden agreed, "we really mustn't disturb—"

"Disturb what? Dad's bored out of his fuckin' skull! I'm sure he'd love to meet Thomas Tong's daughter! Come over for drinks later and I'll have my assistant give you a personal tour of the estate," Luis Felipe decreed before stumbling out of the Cabana Room.

Eden turned to her father in concern. "You're not seriously going to let him drive?"

"Don't worry," Thomas said with a little laugh. Eden and Freddy followed Thomas out to the street, where a convoy of SUVs idled just beyond the striped marquee tent. A pair of menacing bodyguards in dark suits shadowed Luis Felipe into a custom matte-silver-wrapped Lamborghini Urus.

"His license got suspended last year, for the second time. If he gets caught driving again, he'll go straight to jail," Thomas explained before getting into the car.

III

Cloudline

BEL AIR · *LATE AFTERNOON*

"And this is Sir Luis Felipe's private car museum . . . ," Tessa, the personal assistant of Luis Felipe, announced as the elevator opened onto the lower level. Freddy stared at the sight before him slack-jawed. His mind couldn't quite process what his eyes were seeing. Before him were forty, maybe fifty, of the world's most exotic sports cars, displayed in perfect symmetry on shiny blackened-steel floors that glowed with recessed up-lights delineating each car. It was like a scene out of a sci-fi movie, the entire south wall of the bunkerlike space opening up to panoramic views of Benedict Canyon, with the late-afternoon sun glinting against the rare metallic finish of each automobile.

"I guess he has a thing for cars," Eden said.

Freddy laughed. "Eden, you don't understand—this is the 1963 Ferrari 250 GTO. It's worth sixty million dollars, at least.* That's the Bugatti La Voiture Noire—that's twenty million. And holy fuck—that's the Rolls-Royce Sweptail. There's only one in the world of these two cars and now I know who they belong to. There's half a billion dollars' worth of cars right here alone!"

"These are just a few of his favorites," Tessa explained as she led Freddy and Eden on the tour of Cloudline.

"How many cars does Luis Felipe have?" Freddy asked.

---

* *Actually, in 2018 a Ferrari 250 GTO sold for $70.2 million.*

"Between Sir Luis Felipe and Sir Rene, three hundred and fifty-one."[*]

"Only?" Eden quipped.

"Most of the cars are kept in Manila, London, and Dubai," Tessa revealed.

"Pity he's not allowed to drive any of them," Freddy whispered to Eden.

"I suppose he can look at them while he swims," Eden noted, pointing up at the ceiling, which was actually the glass bottom of the Olympic-length zero-edge pool.

"Yes, ma'am. Sir Luis Felipe likes to sit at the swim-up bar with his drinks and look down at his cars. We always make sure to position his current favorites right below the skylight," Tessa revealed.

Eden smiled, quietly appalled. She had imagined Cloudline to be some sort of historic Hollywood estate where legendary movie stars might have lived—David Niven, perhaps, or Merle Oberon—but instead she found herself in a hilltop property so humongous and so aggressively modern that it more resembled one of those over-the-top resorts she occasionally saw on Instagram.

All she wanted to do was to see her father, but upon arriving at the gatehouse and going through the security check (this was the first home she had ever visited where she had to go through a full-body scanner), she and Freddy were met by the beautiful petite Filipina personal assistant in a figure-hugging white jumpsuit and five-inch stiletto ankle boots, who immediately ushered them onto a golf cart and took them on this interminable tour. Freddy seemed awed by everything, but Eden wished she could fast-forward through the tour—everything about the place reeked of excess and lacked any modicum of soul.

"The architecture was inspired by the movie *Iron Man*," Tessa

---

[*] *Neither of them was actually knighted by a royal monarch. "Sir" is simply a courtesy title commonly used by Filipinos, so if you need a little ego boost, book a trip to the Philippines.*

began as the golf cart made a sharp turn and they caught sight of the gargantuan curved glass, steel, and concrete structure hugging the mountainside.

"Shit, I really need a new house," Freddy muttered under his breath.

"Why? You have a gorgeous house!" Eden whispered back.

"Sure, but I'm suddenly feeling like I'm only middle-class rich."

"Because you don't live in a house that looks like a Hyatt resort?" Eden rolled her eyes and turned to Tessa. "Luis Felipe and his family live here?"

"Sir Luis Felipe is single, ma'am."

"He lives here *alone*?" Eden asked incredulously.

"No, he has many animals and guests, and there is always an artist-in-residence."

"What does Luis Felipe do?" Freddy prodded.

"Sir Luis Felipe is an entrepreneur and philanthropist."

"Really? What sort of philanthropic causes does he support?" Eden asked.

"Um . . . let me get back to you on that," Tessa said.

As they pulled up to the towering brushed-steel front doors, Freddy whispered to Eden, "It's all Daddy's money."

"I'm shocked," Eden whispered back with a wink.

Tessa proceeded to lead them on a well-rehearsed tour through the main reception rooms, the recording studio, the screening room, the retro eighties video arcade, the casino, the spa and gym, the shisha lounge, the shooting range, the pickleball court, the petting zoo, and the aforementioned car museum. Freddy was left fantasizing about his next house while Eden couldn't quite believe that all this existed for the amusement of a young man who looked like he'd barely started shaving.

Throughout the house were portraits that Luis Felipe had commissioned of himself from different contemporary artists. There were paintings and murals and a life-size nude[*] sculpture of him

---

[*] *Nude except for his Calvins.*

posing just like Michelangelo's *David* and even digital video installations of his likeness everywhere. Just as Eden was about to ask a question about the art, they were shown into a vast studio with paint-splattered floors and a huge retractable skylight.

"This is the Artist's Loft. Sir Luis Felipe hosts a different artist every month, and the hottest rising stars in the art world get the privilege of staying at Cloudline and creating an artwork in collaboration with sir. Our current guest artist is the international sensation Pine Delfern, who created this image," Tessa said, pointing at an eight-by-twelve-foot photograph tacked to the wall depicting Luis Felipe posing as the victim of a robbery gone wrong. His body lay sprawled halfway out the raised door of a Mercedes gullwing onto the slope outside the Chateau Marmont, with a gunshot wound oozing out of his abdomen, staining his crisp white Tom Ford tuxedo jacket, while a beautiful blond girl in a gold-spangled sheath wept over his body, the rivulets of mascara running down her pretty face rivaling Tammy Faye's. Eden wished that Rufus could be here to see all this, if only to witness his reaction to the photograph.

"Pine calls it *They Killed Him for His Royal Oak,*" Tessa noted.

"Oof! Definitely not worth dying over!" Freddy cackled.

Eden studied the photograph for a moment. "You know, I don't think a gunshot to that particular spot would be fatal. The bullet might have grazed his gallbladder or his spleen, but he wouldn't bleed out like that. Now, two inches higher and he'd be dead meat."

"Haha, only you would notice that! Eden's an amazing doctor—I personally witnessed her save the life of a French princess a few weeks ago," Freddy informed Tessa.

"I didn't really," Eden protested.

"How wonderful. The next time Sir Luis Felipe poses for an artwork where he gets murdered, perhaps we could get you to be our medical consultant," Tessa said earnestly.

Eden didn't know what else to do except nod.

"Well, this concludes our tour. I do hope you've enjoyed visiting Cloudline," Tessa said.

"Thank you, Tessa! It's even more impressive than I could have imagined!" Freddy offered solicitously. "Eden, enjoy your time with your dad. Be back to pick you up at seven."

"No need, Freddy, I can take an Uber back to your house."

"Nonsense, I'm just ten minutes away, and plus, we're going to dinner with Dani, remember?"

"Ah, yes. I'll see you at seven p.m."

Eden got into the golf cart again with Tessa and they zoomed over to an outdoor pavilion perched at the highest point of the sprawling estate, where she found her father waiting with a chilled bottle of Sancerre and an elaborate charcuterie platter. Unbeknownst to her, Thomas had deliberately arranged for the tour to take at least an hour and for drinks to be served in this out-of-the way spot. He had also spent the past few hours calling in favors and hastily arranging for Rene to be taken to the hospital for a PET scan, just to be sure his patient and his daughter would not cross paths.

As father and daughter enjoyed their wine and the view of the lights coming on within all the grand houses dotting the canyon, Eden caught Thomas up on the happenings at Greshamsbury. Even though she glossed over much of Arabella's antics, Thomas was utterly horrified.

"Arabella's completely lost the plot," Thomas said, shaking his head in dismay. "Let me call Francis—we'll get this sorted at once."

"No, no, Dad, you've got more important things to worry about right now and poor Francis isn't to blame. There's no need to bring this up with him. Arabella's obviously in post-wedding trauma and not being herself. I was simply in the wrong place at the wrong time, and she conveniently took it out on me."

"She had no right to! As usual, you're being more understanding than Arabella deserves. To banish you from the Big House is one thing, but to sully your professional reputation in the way that she has is unconscionable. I *will* talk with Francis, and I'm sure he'll agree with me that Arabella needs to make proper amends. In the meantime, there's no reason for you not to hold your head high in Greshamsbury. Everyone is well aware of what Arabella can be like."

"That's why I'm telling you to stand down. It will all blow over in a few weeks, and I don't want to make things more awkward for Bea or Rufus," Eden said, taking a sip of her gin and tonic.

Thomas sighed. "You have a big heart, my dear. Always putting the Greshams ahead of yourself . . ."

"Well, as you yourself said, we all know what their mother can be like. We don't have to put up with it on a daily basis like they do," Eden said.

"That is true."

"How have you been, Dad? I still can't believe you're here, of all places."

"I wasn't supposed to be, but my patient insisted on coming to spend time with his son."

"Luis Felipe's father?"

"Yes."

"If his son is any indication, I'd reckon it hasn't been an easy time for you."

"The son's fine, he's not a bother. The father's the one that's been the challenge. I've been treating him for four years now, and it's been a nonstop battle."

"What type of cancer?"

"Adenocarcinoma."

Eden's eyes widened. "Four years! Rather impressive he's lasted this long."

"He's an incredibly complicated man, and he's a fighter, that's for sure, but there's not much fight left in him."

Eden squinted as she noticed the most peculiar sight beyond her father's shoulder. A Fellini-esque procession was moving slowly up the hill toward the pavilion. It consisted of a shrunken man wearing a woolen cap, swathed in an Hermès Avalon blanket, with tubes coming out everywhere—his nose, his arms—being wheeled by a hulking Nordic male nurse, followed by half a dozen or so nurses carting medical devices and machines that were hooked up to the man. Was this her father's mysterious patient?

"Here comes your fighter, I think," Eden said.

Thomas swiveled around in shock. "Good god!"

Before Thomas could intercept them, Rene and his entourage arrived at the pavilion. Thomas looked at the male nurse in dismay. "What happened, Olaf? You were supposed to be going to Cedars-Sinai."

"Dr. Tong, I tried. Mr. Tan got a text and made us turn around," Olaf nervously explained.

"Thomas Tong, you fucking asshole . . . why didn't you tell me . . . your daughter was visiting? I had to . . . find out from Tessa," Rene breathlessly admonished Thomas.

"Rene, I'm sorry, I didn't think you'd mind if my daughter paid a visit while you were out getting your PET scan," Thomas said, all flustered.

"Do I mind? *Nei lyun gong mat yeh?** Why should I take . . . another PET scan . . . to tell me all the fascinating new places . . . my cancer has spread? I want to meet . . . your daughter." Rene craned his neck toward Eden, who was sitting at the far end of the table. "Come over here . . . what's your name?"

Eden got up from the table and crouched down next to Rene's wheelchair. Even with a cursory glance she could tell he was in very bad shape. "Hello, sir, I'm Eden," she said with a smile.

Rene stared at her intently. "Thirty years I've . . . known your father . . . and not once has he . . . even showed me . . . a picture of you. How old are you?"

"I'm twenty-seven," Eden replied, surprised to learn that this man had known her father for so long. She had assumed he was one of her father's newer clients from China.

"And you were . . . born in . . . England?"

"No, Houston."

"Ah yes . . . where your dad was . . . doing his residency."

"Actually, it was where he did his specialization in oncology. But we moved to England when I was three, after my mum died."

---

* *Loosely translates to "What nonsense are you talking about?"*

"Your poor mother . . . she was ABC, an American-born Chinese?"

"Canadian-born Chinese, actually."

"What . . . was her . . . name?"

"Faye."

"Faye what?"

"Faye Wang."

"Faye . . . Wang . . . how interesting."

The blood pressure machine started beeping, and Olaf shot Thomas an anxious look. Rene's blood pressure was suddenly rising faster than a rocket.

"Rene, we need to get you back to your suite now," Thomas cut in urgently.

"Fuck you . . . I'm having . . . a conversation."

Eden glanced at the reading on the blood pressure monitor, marveling that he was even alive, and continued calmly, "Mr. Tan, why don't we continue this back in your room?"

"You won't . . . leave?"

"I'm right here and I'm not going anywhere," Eden replied, taking his hand.

The entire group decamped to the guest wing of the main residence, which had been transformed like the Houston house into a state-of-the-art medical suite. As soon as he was settled onto his bed, Rene resumed his conversation with Eden.

"Tell me . . . your mother . . . what did she do?"

"She worked in public relations, but after I was born she was a full-time mother . . . until she got sick."

"She had cancer too?"

"Yes."

Rene was quiet for a few moments before he spoke up. "We can send . . . robots to Mars . . . but we still can't conquer . . . this silly disease. You know I was . . . supposed . . . to be dead . . . four years ago but . . . your father has kept me . . . alive."

Eden smiled at him encouragingly.

"But what is the . . . point of being alive . . . when everything tastes . . . like horse shit and . . . you can't chase . . . all the pretty girls? I used to love coming to LA . . . so much temptation . . . now . . . what's the point? I am a . . . eunuch in a harem."

"You've managed to have more time with your son . . . ," Thomas remarked.

"Yes . . . Luis Felipe . . . and where is he? I've seen him . . . twice since we got here. He's too busy . . . meeting with . . . those Hollywood grifters. He should be here meeting you."

Just then, Tessa poked her head into the room. "Miss Eden, Mr. Freddy has arrived to fetch you."

"Thank you, Tessa."

"Tessa . . . where the hell is my son?" Rene barked, straining himself.

"Sir, I believe he is hosting a sneaker release party at the Ron Herman boutique."

Eden couldn't believe her ears. If this were her father, she would not be hosting a party right now. She wasn't even sure he would make it through the weekend. Turning back to Rene, she said, "Mr. Tan, I'm afraid I have to run to dinner."

"Eat some . . . good food for me."

"It's been a pleasure."

"You'll come . . . and visit me again?"

Eden glanced at her father before answering. "Yes, of course."

"I'll tell you stories . . . about your father . . . that will make your hair . . . stand on end."

"You better! Now, rest up, and I'll see you soon!" Eden gave Rene's hand a squeeze, hugged her father, and left the suite with Tessa.

A few moments later, Rene summoned Thomas to his bedside and asked weakly, "Your girl . . . still lives . . . with you?"

"She does."

"Lucky bastard."

"I am. Now, you should really stop talking and get some rest," Thomas suggested.

Rene ignored him. "I can tell she's . . . a good doctor."

Thomas nodded. It took everything in him to discuss his daughter with Rene. He had tried so hard over the decades to build an impenetrable boundary between his patients and his private life.

"I've fucked things up . . . with my son . . . haven't I?"

"You just need to rein him in."

"I gave him . . . the world . . . and he hates me for it."

"It's not too late for you to change your relationship with him, Rene."

"Yes it is," Rene said with a deep sigh.

IV

Daddy Mustang

HOLLYWOOD, CALIFORNIA · *EVENING*

As they sped down Sunset Boulevard, Freddy eagerly gave Eden the lowdown on the treat that awaited them. "Michelle Obama just ate here with her daughter. Harry Styles slept on the banquette after winning his Grammys. And Leo's a regular. Daddy Mustang is—"

"The most exclusive restaurant in the world?" Eden cut in.

"How did you know?"

"Because that's what you've said about every place we've been to since I arrived in LA!" Eden said with a laugh. "Tell me, do you ever go anywhere that *isn't* exclusive?"

Freddy appeared momentarily flummoxed. "Sure . . . I go to plenty of normal places, like, uh . . . South Beverly Grill."*

"I'm so relieved to hear that."

"But why would I take you to any normal places—I'm showing you the very best my hometown has to offer! Wouldn't you do the same for me if I came to visit you?"

"I'd take you to our local Caffè Nero, but I'm afraid I've been banned from it."

"Caffè Nero? Sounds super cool. Why did they ban you?"

Eden laughed. "It's a long story."

They pulled up outside a one-story strip center, in the middle of

---

* *Some people call South Beverly Grill the "Chili's of Beverly Hills," because it's the kind of joint where you'd see groups of local teenagers scarfing down $27 French dip sandwiches and $15 hot-fudge sundaes.*

which was a single wooden door painted glossy black. A tall, spindly man with floppy blond hair stood outside at a metal podium, the kind used by high school band conductors, his face aglow from the iPad in his hand.

"This is it?" Eden asked, a little surprised by how nondescript the entrance looked.

"Yup, this is Daddy Mustang. It's so cool you'd never know it was here. We gotta thank Dani—you have no idea what it took for her to score a table tonight!"

"Did she have to book this a few weeks ahead?"

"A few weeks? Ha! First of all, they don't have a phone number, so the only way you can get a reservation is through their website. Tables only open up the week before, at twelve oh one a.m. on Sunday night, but by the time you click on it at twelve oh one and one second, all the tables for the week are booked up!"

"How is that even possible?"

"I know, right? The website is a total scam, because tables are never available online. It's worse than scoring tickets to a Taylor Swift concert, because at least those tickets actually exist somewhere. This place just has to pretend that they're open to the public and ordinary people can dream of eating here when it's literally impossible. The only way to get in is to hire a top publicist, put them on retainer for eight thousand dollars a month, and once they've generated enough media hits for you and your Wikipedia page is at least six paragraphs long and your social media accounts are all fully verified with throbbing blue check marks and there are enough googleable pictures of you at the Met Ball or the Vanity Fair Oscar party, your publicist may then dare to call the reservation number that's a more closely guarded secret than the president's phone line with all the nuclear codes, and if they actually pick up, which is rare, there's a fierce woman on the line who sounds just like Jamie Lee Curtis who mans 'the Daddy List,' because apparently every month they update this list of everyone on the planet who's cool enough to dine here, and your publicist simply has to say 'I represent Eden Tong' and there will be a pause while pseudo Jamie Lee checks the Daddy List and if your name isn't already on it, you can forget it, you're fucked and never getting in, but once you make the list you're allowed the privilege of booking a table like eight months from now."

"So your sister is on the Daddy List?"

"Yep, she finally made it on the list this year," Freddy said as they approached the host stand by the door and he eagerly announced, "We're with the Farman-Farmihian party."

"Terribly sorry, but we don't have a booking with that name," the host said in a British accent that was so over-the-top, Eden figured it must surely be put on.

"Er . . . can you check your reservation list again?" Freddy asked, noting that he hadn't even glanced at the iPad on the podium.

"I know everyone who's coming tonight, and there's no Farman-Farmihian," the host replied curtly.

"How about 'Daniela'?" Eden offered.

The man stared at Eden in surprise, clocking her accent, which was many tiers posher than his. "Daniela what?"

"I suppose it would be Farman-Farmihian," Eden replied.

"Sorry, nobody by that name."

"How about Abe Froman?" Eden quipped.

"No Abe Froman," the host replied grimly, not getting her joke.

"Wait. How about Princess Soraya?" Freddy suddenly blurted out.

The host's demeanor immediately transformed. "Of course. The princess is inside."

"Thank god!" Freddy exhaled in relief as the host tapped on his iPad and pointed it toward the glossy black door. The telltale click of the door unlocking was the sweetest sound Freddy had ever heard, and they soon found themselves entering a handsome wood-paneled mock tavern with black and white titled floors, forest-green velvet banquettes, and vintage Scandinavian bronze lamps on each table. Everything glowed that beautiful McNallyesque golden glow, and the place was packed with raucous diners reveling in the fact that they were being seen at the hottest restaurant in town. Eden spotted Daniela waving to them from the long bar at the back of the room.

"I'll meet you in a sec, gotta pee like a Russian racehorse!" Freddy said.

Eden waded through the crowd and made it up to the cramped bar, where Daniela greeted her with a big hug. "Isn't this place fabulous? I don't even want to tell you how many publicists had to die for us to get a table here."

"I'm not going to ask!" Eden laughed, scanning the room and noticing yet again that all the women were dressed to the nines, while most of the men—especially the older ones—looked like they had come straight from the gym in their sweatpants, sneakers, and baseball caps. Eden leaned in to Daniela's ear. "So I'm noticing something about L A. Why is it that every guy is dressed like—"

"An overgrown man-child?"

"I wasn't going to put it like that, but yes! The rich kids all dress like old men, and the old men dress like kids."

"That's because everyone's obsessed with youth in this town. The women all get so many fillers they look like ventriloquist dummies, while the men dress like they're sixteen and get hair transplants. That's why you see so many baseball caps, they're all hiding their scars until their hair fully grows back. It's also a power thing. The sloppier you look, the more important you are. See the guy over there who looks like a football coach from a small Texas town who should have retired two decades ago? He's the head of a major film studio. And the geezer over there in the Hawaiian shirt who looks like he woke up hungover from a Jimmy Buffett concert? He's a gazillionaire who's sold three of the world's biggest media companies."

"Fascinating . . . ," Eden said, staring at the ruddy-faced man and noticing the bread crumbs all over the front of his Hawaiian shirt.

"They're all competing to look like teenage hobos, because it means they are too important to give a shit. So every climber tries to ape this look. Most of them are just agents or talent managers. You can tell because they're the ones wearing the expensive hoodies with their Nautiluses. The Nautilus is a dead giveaway."

"What's a Nautilus?"

"It's a watch."

"Oh, like the one the man next to us is wearing?"

Daniela glanced down at the man's wrist and shook her head contemptuously. "No, that's an Oyster. Oysters are for real estate brokers hawking overpriced houses in the Bird Streets.* Nautiluses are for midlevel entertainment execs. Look at that guy in cargo shorts and flip-flops over there—he's not even wearing a watch. *That's true power.*"

The hostess came up to them. "Your Highness? I have good news. The party at your table was just served their desserts, so that means you'll be seated within thirty, forty-five minutes, tops."

"Fabulous," Daniela said.

After the hostess had left, Eden said, "So I had no idea you were a princess."

Daniela burst out laughing. "I might have taken some liberties . . . that's my future mother-in-law's name. Yeah, Lior's mom is descended from Afghan royalty, even though he grew up in Rome and Tel Aviv."

"How cool. I've always wanted to visit Tel Aviv."

"Well, you're coming to my wedding—it's going to be there!"

"Twist my arm! When's the big day?" Eden asked.

"We're doing it in November when it cools down."

"Sounds perfect." Eden hesitated for a moment before she ventured to ask, "Tell me, how did you know that Lior was 'the one'?"

"You know, this is going to sound crazy, but my mother told me."

"Your mother? I thought . . ."

"Yep, she's been dead for years. I was in Tel Aviv a few summers ago, at the Hotel Montefiore celebrating a girlfriend's birthday, and Lior was at the bar with his buddies and the second we locked eyes on each other, it was as if I could feel this energy wave sweep over

---

* *An exclusive neighborhood where the streets are all named after birds, this celebrity enclave is also, in the words of a noted property guru, "filled with the type of houses where one guy who gets rich on crypto will buy the place, four of his buddies will move in, and they'll party five nights a week and spend a hundred K a month and within two years the guy will go bankrupt and be forced to sell the house at a loss."*

me and I heard a voice that said, *Joonam, this is the man for you.* Only my mother called me Joonam."

"So what happened? Did you approach him?"

"Of course not. I proceeded to ignore him all night, he never once approached me, and then he disappeared, so I figured, oh well, maybe I was wrong. Later that evening when I got back to my apartment, who should be standing there in the lobby waiting for the elevator but Lior! That's when we started chatting, and it turns out his family had a vacation home in the building too, just like us, but our paths had never crossed because we were only there during American school holidays, while he was only there during European school holidays."

"It was meant to be!" Eden said excitedly.

"Wait, there's more! Weeks later, after we had begun dating, his mother comes to visit, and guess what? Turns out she knew my mother, and my mom actually met Lior as a little boy, before I was born! So I really feel like she's somewhere up there watching out for me, making all this happen."

"How wonderful!" Eden said, suddenly feeling a pang of sadness as she quietly wondered whether her own mother was somewhere watching out for her as well.

"How about you? Have you met 'the one'?" Daniela asked.

"Well . . . I'm not sure . . ."

"Oh come on, spill it! Freddy said there was someone back in England? Some boy-next-door duke that's in love with you?"

Eden giggled. "He's a viscount, not a duke. And he's my best friend."

"He's your best friend and he's in love with you but you're not into him?"

Eden shook her head vehemently, her cheeks flushing.

"Something's wrong with this picture here. I can clearly see he inspires feelings in you. Look at you—you're red as that Negroni on the counter."

"It's complicated. Rufus is destined to marry a woman of similar background, who can be his countess."

"Didn't you grow up next door to him? If that's not a similar background I don't know what is," Daniela said, shifting in her bar stool as her neighbor kept brushing up against her.

"No, no, Rufus was born into the aristocracy. I was born in Texas, I'm a nobody to his mother. And besides, I have no interest in being the lady of the manor. That's not the life I want."

Daniela raised an eyebrow dubiously. "Tell me, when was your last relationship?"

"A couple of years ago during my medical residency. He was Scottish and we were both on the night shift in the critical care unit. We bonded over the long hours and the absolute insanity of our work situation, but the minute the residency was over, things fizzled out."

"That's a pity. I bet he looked hot in his scrubs," Daniela remarked, glancing around in annoyance.

"He did look quite fit in his . . . are you all right?" Eden asked, noticing Daniela's mouth was suddenly agape.

Daniela leaned into Eden's ear. "Don't look now, but the guy behind me is . . ."

"Let me guess . . . Shawn Mendes?"

"No, Shawn left earlier. Do you see what the guy's doing?"

Eden peered over her shoulder, where a man with his back to Daniela seemed to be chatting up a woman perched on a bar stool. "Uh . . . he's talking to his date?"

"Look closer. *At the girl.*"

Eden looked at the woman's face and noticed that she was furrowing her brow in a strange, rhythmic manner. Was she having some sort of seizure? A transient ischemic stroke? Eden looked down and noticed that the man's right arm was halfway up the woman's skirt, jabbing away.

Eden couldn't believe her eyes. "My god . . . is he . . . ?"

"He's fingering her!" Daniela mouthed.

Eden's jaw dropped.

"Does he not notice he's in a restaurant surrounded by two hundred people?" Daniela said purposely loud, but the man paid no attention and was now thrusting his arm frantically, elbowing Daniela in the waist.

"Oww!!" Daniela yelled out.

The woman suddenly blurted out, "Baby, I'm squirting!"

"And I've just lost my appetite!" Eden said.

"You and me both. Let's get some air," Daniela said as the two of them made a beeline for the door. When they were both finally outside, they looked at each other and burst out in laughter.

"I don't know why I'm laughing," Daniela said, doubled over. "That was SO GROSS."

Eden was laughing so hard she had tears in her eyes.

A woman in her sixties with overly plumped lips stepped out of a Bentley and walked toward the girls. She glanced at Eden, who was leaning against the host stand, and said, "I want my usual table in the garden."

"I'm sorry, I don't work here," Eden said, still laughing.

The woman turned to Daniela and said coldly, "You! I want to be seated in the garden tonight under the big heater."

"Can't help you, I'm not the hostess," Daniela said.

"What are you, then?" the woman asked, trying to frown, but her forehead was too frozen.

"I'm Princess Soraya," Daniela shot back as Eden kept giggling.

The woman scowled at the both of them and tried to open the door herself. "Eh! Why won't it open?" She whined for a moment, tapping against the doors weakly before some diners suddenly emerged and she pushed her way in past them.

"Rich, entitled, and clueless—it's a lethal combination. I hope they send her to the bar," Daniela said as they both cracked up again.

A few minutes later, the blond Englishman emerged from inside, glaring at them imperiously. "You can't stand there. You're going to have to leave."

"We're waiting for our table," Daniela said.

"You've just lost it."

"What? Why?"

"We've had a complaint about you two."

"A complaint?" Daniela tried to clarify.

"You were extremely rude to Nancy Doheny. Have you any idea who she is?"

"I don't care who she is. She was the one being rude to us."

"Yes, she was clearly confused and annoyed that she couldn't get inside," Eden added.

"Look, I don't know what happened, but we don't tolerate offensive behavior here."

Daniela's face went red with anger. "Excuse me? There's some guy literally finger-banging a girl at the bar, and you're calling *my* behavior offensive?"

"You are clearly being offensive to me now."

Just then Freddy peeked his head out the door. "There you are! I was wondering where you two disappeared to!"

"You all need to leave," the host said.

"Why?" Freddy was very confused. "What happened?"

Eden sighed. "Come on, let's just go."

"No! I am not leaving. We have done nothing wrong and we want our table!" Daniela seethed. "I want to speak to your manager."

"I *am* the manager."

"No you're not. Get your manager now!"

A familiar voice piped up behind them. "Yo! What's the holdup?"

Eden turned around and saw Luis Felipe, dressed like a caricature of a nineties rapper in a white tank top, oversized white jeans, shiny new gold sneakers, and ropes of gold and diamond chains around his abnormally thick neck. He was flanked by two women in barely there cocktail dresses along with a pair of his ubiquitous bodyguards bringing up the rear.

"Oh, hi," Eden said. "Apparently we're being thrown out."

"Fuckin' hell, what did you do?" Luis Felipe chortled, clearly more intoxicated than he had been earlier.

"Absolutely nothing," Eden replied.

"Lemme fix this. Hey, dude, there's been a mistake . . . ," Luis Felipe yelled out.

"Stay out of this," the host said, pointing a finger at Luis Felipe, before turning to Freddy and Daniela. "You can leave freely, or we can escalate this—"

"Yo, Edward Cullen! These are my guests. Take the big fat pickle out of your ass and let them in," Luis Felipe shouted.

"Okay, you're not coming in tonight either!" the host decreed.

"Wait, are you talking to me?" Luis Felipe's eyes went big with genuine shock.

"Yes, you. All of you, get off my sidewalk now!" the host hissed.

"Actually, it's *my* sidewalk. Get the fuck away or else," Luis Felipe said, menacing.

"Not a chance. You're plastered. Leave now or I'm calling the police!"

Luis Felipe turned to the bodyguard to his left. "Fuck him up."

Before anyone could register what was happening, the bodyguard performed a blindingly swift maneuver and the host was suddenly on the ground, doubled over and moaning in agony.

"Right in the nuts!" Freddy gasped as the other bodyguard kicked him again.

"Stop that!" Eden yelled.

The host vomited on the pavement. Eden rushed to his side and held him by the shoulders, glaring up at Luis Felipe angrily. "Why did you do that?"

Luis Felipe stood there grinning maniacally.

The manager came rushing out of the restaurant with two waiters. "Whoa, whoa, whoa, what the fuck? What the fuck?"

"Hey, Nico," Luis Felipe said.

The manager froze. He held his arms out to stop the other two waiters from making any further moves. "Heyyyyyy! Mr. Tan. Dining with us tonight?" he said in an overly convivial tone.

"Yes, and I've been waiting out here way too fucking long."

The manager's eyes darted for a split second to his fallen colleague on the ground. "I'm sooooo sorry, Mr. Tan. Er . . . weren't you going to be three?"

"We're six now. I want the Chef's Table in the VIP room."

"Of course, of course . . ."

As the two waiters helped the host to his feet and rushed him through the door, the manager held the door wide and the two women accompanying Luis Felipe barged inside eagerly.

Luis Felipe turned to Eden, Freddy, and Daniela. "Coming?"

The three of them hesitated, unsure what to do.

"You're missing out on a great dinner . . . ," Luis Felipe said as he disappeared through the door.

"What the hell," Freddy said as he followed after Luis Felipe.

"Freddy!" Eden called out after him in dismay, before turning to Daniela. "I'm not having dinner with that sadist! Can you believe what he did to the poor man?"

Daniela sighed. "Hate to say it, but this is nothing. I went to Beverly High. You have no idea what kind of vicious shit I saw. Personally, I'd like to see what this crazy 'roid monster gets up to at the Chef's Table, wouldn't you?"

"Not really. At this point, I'm happy never to see him again."

"Come on. Freddy's trapped with them, we can't ditch him now. Plus, you can check on the guy who got his balls kicked in."

"Yes, I suppose."

Daniela grinned. "One thing's for certain—we're not going to have to wait at the bar anymore."

V

The Chef's Table

PRIVATE DINING ROOM AT DADDY MUSTANG · *EVENING*

Conversation between Daniela Farman-Farmihian, Jenna, and Lexi . . .

"That's the most incredible ring I've ever seen. Is it a sapphire?"

"No, it's a Paraíba."

"A para-yee-what?"

"A Paraíba. They're found in Brazil. Here, try it on . . ."

"OMG . . . it feels amazing. I can feel it throbbing!"

"Jenna, don't hog the ring!"

"Wait your turn, Lexi. I'm still feeling the stone."

"It's my engagement ring."

"You didn't want a diamond?"

"This is much rarer than any diamond. They don't exist anymore, they've been completely mined out."

"I'm not even going to ask what it costs. It'll probably cover our rent."

"Yeah, Jenna, like for a whole year!"

"You two live together?"

"Yeah. Lexi and I have a cute place on Harper, off Fountain, you know, in one of those old Spanish courtyard buildings?"

"It's totally like Melrose Place. Everyone's fucking everyone and our landlord runs it like it's his private club. He only rents to actors, and they have to be super hot to qualify. Julia Roberts once lived there, when she was just starting out, and that Aussie dude who's always shirtless in *True Blood*."

"We totally lucked out. My friend Selena booked a series that shoots in Vancouver, so she sublets to us."

"Daniela, where do you live?"

"Trousdale."*

"Is that in the Valley?"

"No. So both of you act?"

"Yeah. Did you see *The White Lotus*?"

"Yes! I loved it! You were in that?"

"I was up for the role of the bitchy daughter's best friend."

"And I'm doing an indie horror film in Croatia this summer."

"And I've starred in a few things for streamers that almost got series orders."

"What about you?"

"I'm in the garment business."

"What's that?"

"I design and manufacture athleisure."

"OMG, you're in fashion?"

"I wouldn't call it that. I basically make joggers and yoga pants for the mass-market retailers, like Ross and Target."

"Did you go to fashion school?"

"For a couple of years, but I left the program. I was running my company while going to design school, but I realized that everything I was learning was actually tanking my business. Every time I tried to release something chic, it wouldn't sell. But the uglier I made the clothes, the more they would sell like crazy."

"People just want ugly clothes. I walk down the street and I just see everyone dressed like sluts or slobs."

"All the girls have their butts hanging out, and the guys are in gray sweatpants jiggling their junk for the whole world to see."

"No one cares about glamour anymore. I mean, except us, of course. Your dress is amazing. Gucci, right?"

"Simone Rocha."

---

* *Most young people who live in Beverly Hills don't usually say that they live there. They may say they live "in Trousdale" or "off Coldwater" but will never say "Beverly Hills." (The inverse is true of people who live in the neighborhood of the Beverly Hills Post Office, who will tell every single person they meet.)*

"Don't know him. I thought it was Gucci or maybe Louie Vetton."
"Speaking of Louie, how do you both know our host?"
"Who?"
"The guy across from us. Psycho killer."
"Hahahaha, Luis Felipe. He's actually super sweet."
"We met him at Burning Man."
"He had the most unnnn-believable camp! There was a weed sommelier and a sushi bar. This Japanese dude with one of those *Karate Kid* headbands was making unagi rolls for everyone in the middle of the desert!"
"It was, like, a hundred fifty degrees, so everyone wanted to eat Luis Felipe's sushi."
". . . And go skiing."
"Skiing? At Burning Man?"
"Yeah, Luis Felipe had the best snow"—she makes a snorting gesture—"like mountains of it on huge silver platters."
"And the best shrooms. OMG, I lost a whole week of my life on a quarter of a mushroom but it was uhh-mazing."
"Are you coming to the house later? He's having a huge party. It's gonna be EPIC."
"Excuse me, but isn't his dad very sick at the house?"
"Really? I had no idea his dad was even in town."

Conversation between Eden Tong and the manager . . .
"And what can I get you tonight, miss?"
"May I ask how the host is doing?"
"The host?"
"The man that was hurt outside?"
(Glances at Luis Felipe warily before answering.) "Oh, Milo. He's fine, we sent him home."
"He really ought to go to the hospital for an MRI."
"He'll be okay."
"He was coughing up blood. There's a possibility he could be bleeding internally."
"Thank you for your concern." (Glances at Luis Felipe again.)

"Now, the chef recommends the Caesar salad chiffonade to start and the white truffle agnolotti. We just received the most divine truffles from Alba . . ."

Conversation between Freddy Farman-Farmihian and Luis Felipe Tan . . .

"This Tomahawk rib eye is absurd. It's like melt-in-your-mouth ridiculously good."

"What did I tell you? The food here is tops."

"Yeah, thanks for convincing us to stay. And thanks for setting up the tour of Cloudline. Molto impressivo, dude."

"Yeah? What was your favorite room?"

"Definitely the secret taco stand in your screening room."

"Me too! I hired this guy that has the only Michelin-starred taco truck in Austin to set it up for me. Then I stole all his cooks, hahaha."

"Boss move. I also loved the artist loft. It's cool that you let artists work in your home."

"When I went to Miami last December, I noticed that every billionaire art collector had an artist staying at their house. The artists were all sucking up like crazy, following them around everywhere, and I thought, *They're like cute little pets, art pets. So I'm gonna have a different one every month.* I feed them and give them a place to stay, and in return I get a free artwork from a hot artist. The last one who stayed with me, I hated her painting, but I flipped it for half a mil."

"Another boss move. I'm guessing you must also be an investor in Daddy Mustang?"

"No, but I'm backing the new Baby Mustangs in Las Vegas, Dubai, and Macau."

"So that's how you get to sit at the Chef's Table. I thought only LeBron got to sit in here."

"LeBron and me. It also doesn't hurt that I own this strip center."

"Haha, so you really do own the sidewalk!"

"I think I own the sidewalks all the way to Highland."

"Cool. I'm in commercial real estate too."

"Course you are. What Persian isn't?"

"Haha. So you ever interested in investing out in Malibu? I'm setting up a new consortium that—"

"You can stop with the real estate talk, it bores the shit out of me."

"Sorry. So . . . what excites you?"

"Movies. I finance movies."

"Oh yeah? Any movies I know?"

"None of them are out yet. But by this time next year I'll have three films in the can."

"Cool. What are the titles? I'll keep an eye out."

"They are all top secret, but one of them is with the biggest pop star in the world. You'll definitely be hearing all about it when it's time."

"Cool. Are those actresses going to be in your movies?"

"They wish! Hey, is your friend trying to be an actress?"

"Who, Eden? No, Eden's a doctor."

"No shit? I thought she was just another desperate actress in town for pilot season."

"Not at all. She's here for my sister's engagement party tomorrow. That's my sister Daniela talking with your friends."

"Haha, I thought you were doggin' both of them."

"Gross. No, Eden's strictly a friend."

"So you won't mind if I take her home and Eiffel Tower her with Jenna and Lexi?"

"Uh . . . I guess you're welcome to try."

Conversation between Luis Felipe Tan and Eden Tong . . .

"What do you think?"

"Of what?"

"Of the food."

"It's rather good."

"That's it? This is the hottest restaurant in America right now and you think it's 'rather good'?" (Puts on a very affected British accent.)

"Well, to be honest, the pasta's overcooked and the sauce is a bit heavy for my taste."

"Want me to have the chef's kneecaps broken?"

"That's not funny."

"Jeez, lighten up, I was just kidding."

"It might have been funnier if I hadn't witnessed your bodyguard beat up that host."

"That ass face needed to be taught a lesson. He disrespected us."

"I think you and I might have different ideas about respect."

"You know he treated us the way he did because we're both Asian. If we had been white, he wouldn't have dared treat us that way."

"What are you talking about? He was rude to everyone. He was rude to Daniela first."

"My point exactly. She's Persian, and he treated her like a carpet he could piss all over. You live in England, right?"

"I do."

"Most racist fucking country I've ever been to. And all the Brits at my boarding school in Switzerland thought they farted sunshine."

"I'm guessing it was a very posh school. Things are different these days. We've got our problems, but for the most part it's easier nowadays to be accepted."

"Accepted is different from respected. I spend time in England myself—I own a penthouse in Knightsbridge and a golf club I've never even been to. I can tell you the Brits have *zero* respect for Asians. If you're not white and Anglo, you'll always be a foreigner to them. Remember, for four hundred years they were our colonizers and we were their slaves. So it's time we taught them a lesson."

"By having some poor chap roughed up by your bodyguards?"

"Nah. Most of the time I just whack 'em with my big fat wad of cash."

"I wonder what your father might think of that."

"My father was the one who taught me all this! You think he's some saint just because he's got cancer now? Ha! Did you know he grew up in Hong Kong, where he was shit on daily by the Brits? Then he moved to the Philippines and built one of the biggest fortunes in the world. Only Filipinos treated him decently. He taught me the most important lesson of all: *everyone has a price.*"

"That's the most important lesson he taught you?"

"Yes. Anyone can be bought, sold, and controlled."

"I see . . ."

"What are you doing after dinner?"

"Going home."

"No you're not. I'm having a huge party tonight, and it's going to be epic. You're coming back to my house."

"I don't think so."

"I'll give you a million dollars to come back to my house tonight." (Eden rolls her eyes.)

"Two million."

"I'm not playing your game."

"It's not a game."

"The booze and whatever else you're on are clearly impairing your judgment."

"Hey, I'm baked as a banana bread, but I'm not drunk. Can't you tell the difference, Dr. No? I'm dead serious, I will write you a check right now for two million dollars if you come home with me tonight."

"I'm not a Murakami painting."

"Three million dollars."

"Good night." (Eden folds her napkin, places it on the table, and gets up, as everyone stares at her.)

"Think you're too good for my money? Give it all to charity if you're Mother fucking Teresa."

"You could just do that yourself. Try Doctors Without Borders."

"Are you really going to deprive Doctors Without Borders of three million dollars in order to satisfy your ego and prove me wrong? Think how much you could do for them just by coming to my party."

"You know, instead of throwing a party or throwing your money around, maybe you ought to think about being with your father. All he wants to do is spend time with you. He really doesn't have much longer, and I guarantee you all the money in the world will never bring him back."

(Eden exits.)

VI

Cloudline

Thomas paced the terrace outside the guest wing, wondering what was taking so long. His medical team had been asked to leave the room after Rene suddenly summoned his lawyers, and Thomas hadn't been allowed access to his patient for almost two hours. A hummingbird buzzed by his head, and he watched as it chased away the other hummingbirds trying to feed off the gooseberry bushes in the garden.

It was like watching fighter pilots engaging in an aerial dogfight, and he couldn't help but marvel at the energy these tiny creatures possessed, the unfathomable energy that allowed them to flap their wings eighty times a second and fly nearly four thousand miles from Mexico to Canada year after year. No wonder the scarlet-breasted hummingbird was guarding its nectar so unrelentingly. It wasn't even the biggest one, but what it lacked in size it made up for in ferocity.

Thomas reflected on his patient lying barely ten feet away on the other side of the travertine wall. For decades, Rene had been one of the most feared corporate raiders in Asia, mercilessly gobbling up companies, firing thousands at a time, and ruining his competition without any hesitation. Thomas had been terribly conflicted for years, wondering why he expended so much of himself treating a patient who was so reviled, whose empire did so much harm to others and to the planet. And now here he was, the mighty Rene Tan, lying on a hospital bed in Los Angeles, the final bit of life force ebbing out of him.

The doors finally opened and the cabal of suited men and women emerged, a few nodding at Thomas in recognition but saying nothing. Thomas rushed back into the room with his medical team, not happy with his patient's condition. "That meeting took much too long, Rene. You really strained yourself."

"I had . . . shit to deal with," Rene said. "The coyotes . . . are already . . . smelling the blood."

"What does that mean?"

"Pablo Aguilar . . . is getting greedy. I need . . . my succession plan . . . to be ironclad." Rene grimaced as pain shot through his body like lightning.

"What's your pain level, one to ten?" Thomas asked.

"Eleven thousand. Thomas . . . you need to keep . . . Luis Felipe . . . away from Pablo," Rene muttered weakly before closing his eyes.

"Dr. Tong, I think it's time we increased his oxycodone and maybe even consider Dilaudid," the palliative care specialist suggested.

"I'm not sure . . . ," Thomas said cautiously.

"Give me . . . the fucking . . . good stuff," Rene demanded.

"The good stuff will kill you faster, Rene."

"Give it!" Rene groaned, his eyes clamped shut in pain.

The door opened and Eden entered, dressed in a saffron Jenny Packham cocktail dress with an exquisitely pleated organdy skirt that seemed to float around her.

Thomas looked at her in surprise. "What are you doing here?"

"Tessa texted me this morning and asked me to come over before my party. I thought you knew," Eden said with a little frown as she gave her father a quick peck on the cheek. She walked over to Rene's bed, and even before she got close to him she could tell how much his condition had deteriorated overnight. "Mr. Tan . . . Mr. Tan . . . ," she said softly.

Rene's eyes flashed open and he stared at Eden standing there in her goddesslike gown. Tears suddenly began streaming down his cheeks, and catching his breath, he blurted out in Cantonese, *"Mary ah . . . nei heui jo bin dou ah?"**

Eden looked at her father, puzzled. Thomas sprang up from his chair. "This was a bad idea. You'd better leave . . ."

"No . . . no . . . ," Rene protested as he grabbed Eden's arm forcefully. *"Mary . . ."*

"Rene, this isn't Mary," Thomas said. "Let her go."

"Mary, ngo hei mong nei ho ji jun leung ngo."† Rene held on to Eden, his body convulsing with sobs.

"We upped the oxycodone," Thomas explained to Eden. "He's hallucinating."

Eden nodded, leaning in closer and saying soothingly, "Mr. Tan, it's me, *Eden Tong.* Thomas Tong's daughter."

"Eden," Rene exhaled, finally calming down and coming out of his fugue state. "You look like . . . a beauty queen."

"Thank you, Mr. Tan. I'm dressed for an engagement party."

"You're . . . getting engaged?"

"No, my friend Daniela is."

"When's your turn?"

Eden giggled. "I'm not sure."

"Are you in love?"

Eden giggled again. "I'm not sure."

"You'll know it . . . when you are."

"Yes, Mr. Tan."

"Eden . . . do me . . . a favor."

"Yes?"

"Stop calling me . . . Mr. Tan."

"What should I call you?"

"Call me . . . Uncle Rene."

"Yes, Uncle Rene."

"Do me . . . one more favor?"

"Yes?"

---

* *"Mary, where have you been?"* in Cantonese.

† *"I hope you will forgive me"* in Cantonese.

"I want you . . . to get to know Luis Felipe . . . better."

"I'll try."

"Be nice to my son."

Eden hesitated for a split second before answering, "Of course."

.

Daniela Farman-Farmihian looked positively angelic in a vintage gold lamé Galanos gown as she mingled with her engagement party guests over cocktails in the magnificent rose gardens of the Huntington museum. At the appointed time, the doors flanking the terrace opened and the guests were invited into the historic mansion that was home to one of the world's leading art museums.

Entering the opulent brocade-walled dining room where the feast was being held, Eden was astonished to find herself face-to-face with Gainsborough's painting *The Blue Boy.* She'd had no idea that one of the most famous British works of art resided here, and as she sat eating her dinner amid the regal portraits and priceless furnishings, she couldn't help but feel strangely wistful for Greshamsbury Hall. Would she ever be allowed to roam freely through the grounds again, or enter the house that had always been so much a part of her life?

Suddenly she became aware that Banks, Freddy's friend seated to her right, was speaking to her. "I'm sorry?" she said, smiling apologetically.

"I said, I'm not sure this Screaming Eagle cab 1995 that everyone's raving about goes with the turbot."

"Tastes okay to me, but I'm not an oenophile."

"Are you okay?"

"Oh! Yes, I'm fine."

"You were staring off into space. I thought you must be transfixed by the Kehinde."

"What's that?"

"The Kehinde Wiley painting, *A Portrait of a Young Gentleman.*" Banks gestured to the arresting portrait of a young Black man in a psychedelic orange T-shirt in an ornate black gilt frame that was hanging on the wall facing them.

"Ah, yes, rather curious that it's here amid all these stuffy Victorian portraits, isn't it?" Eden remarked.

"That's precisely the point. Kehinde painted it to shake things up. To see this Black kid in streetwear, fused into that William Morris wallpaper pattern and striking the exact same pose as *The Blue Boy*, it's having a dialogue across the centuries with an iconic portrait of Victorian privilege. It totally transforms this room, makes everything relevant again. Whoever put it here is fucking brilliant."

Eden nodded. "You're right, it does change the energy of this room. How do you know so much about art?"

"I collect a bit," Banks replied modestly.

"I wish you could be having this conversation with my friend Rufus—he's an artist and he'd be much better qualified to speak to you."

"You don't need to be another artist to appreciate great art. What does the painting say to you?"

Eden stared up at the painting. The man's defiant stance and insouciant stare reminded her of Luis Felipe, and a wave of guilt swept over her as she recalled running into him in another grand mansion just a couple of hours ago . . .

He was dressed in a shiny blue tracksuit and festooned with gold chains, and she could smell the freshly sprayed cologne on his skin as he came down the stairs. Staring at her dress, he said with a smirk, "Look who's here—the girl who cannot be bought. Where are you off to this time?"

"I'm going to Daniela's engagement party."

"Who's that?"

"You met her at dinner."

"Oh, the Persian princess. Need a ride?"

"It's in Pasadena."

*"Shit, that's practically another time zone."**

---

* *Pasadena is barely forty minutes away from Luis Felipe in Bel Air, but most people on the Westside think of Pasadena as another country. Also, the Huntington is actually in San Marino.*

"Where are you off to?"

"A screening."

"Um . . . you might want to be with your father tonight."

"I'll see him later."

"You may wish to reconsider, especially if it's some movie you can always see another time."

"I'm not going for the movie. I'm going to mingle."

"Let me be direct with you, Luis Felipe. I think you should stay home. I don't think your father's going to make it through the night . . ."

"Please don't tell me how to deal with my dad."

"I just don't want you to have any regrets—"

"Mind your own fucking business! You have no clue how much my dad's tormented me my whole life! I don't need my last memory of him to be fucking tormenting me from his deathbed, okay?" Luis Felipe suddenly shouted, his face flushed as he turned and bolted out the door.

"The painting's that powerful, huh?" Banks said, startling Eden back to the present.

Eden suddenly felt light-headed. The whole room felt like it was closing in on her. She rose from the table and headed out a side door onto a serene columned portico. She took a few deep breaths in the cool night air, hoping to center herself. Try as she might, her mind kept fixating on what was happening back at Cloudline. She wondered why she felt so saddened by the imminent passing of a man whom she had only met two days ago. She couldn't shake off the look on his face, the way he wept when he held on to her hand, the plaintive cries in Cantonese that she couldn't comprehend. There was something so familiar in the sounds of the dialect that her mother used to speak to her as a child. It was a language that seemed so intimate to her, and yet so unfathomably far away. She suddenly recalled the lullaby her mother used to sing to her every night. Her mom would hum the tune over and over again as she fell asleep in her arms. She could remember her voice blending with the hypnotic whirring of the ceiling fan and the scent of her mother's body; she always smelled faintly of lavender, from the body lotion she would smear on her skin. She felt that familiar ache, the grief that came in waves and never went away completely even after all these decades. Eden had a sense that she should really be at her father's side right now, though she didn't wish to be intrusive. She took a photo of the beautiful columns lit up at night and texted it to him, followed by a quick message:

Eden Tong: Just checking in.

A few moments later, her father responded:

Thomas Tong: Great shot. How's the party?

ET: Wonderful. How's the patient?

TT: In and out of consciousness.

ET: Dinner's almost finished. Want me to head back?

TT: Really no need.

ET: Sure you'll be okay?

TT: Don't worry about me. Enjoy your party.

ET: Okay.

TT: Love you.

ET: Love you too.

•

Thomas kept vigil in Rene's suite that evening. He texted Luis Felipe fourteen times, urging him to come home and see his father before it was too late, but Luis Felipe never responded. It was as if he could sense what was happening and wanted to stay as far away as he could. At midnight, Thomas finally crashed on the sofa in the suite. Around four in the morning, he was suddenly shaken awake by Bianca, the night nurse. "He's asking for you, Dr. Tong."

Thomas got up from the sofa and padded toward Rene, who suddenly looked more alert than he had in days. His eyes were wide open and he had a strange smile on his face.

"Mary was here," Rene muttered.

"Mary?"

"My sister . . . did you see her?"

A chill went down Thomas's spine. He knew that Mary had died many years ago and didn't quite know what to say. "She was in . . . in the room?" Thomas whispered, his voice cracking.

"Right beside me. Singing that song. That scene where she's dancing . . . Mary would watch it over and over."

"Yes, she would," Thomas chuckled, knowing instantly what Rene was referring to.

"Play it for me . . ."

Thomas got his phone out and quickly found a YouTube video of Faye Wong in the film *Chungking Express*, dancing with abandon around a little flat in Kowloon as the iconic tune from the Mamas and the Papas blasted on the soundtrack. He held the screen up to Rene's eyes, and before the song had even ended, Rene was gone.

California dreamin'
On such a winter's day

VII

Greshamsbury Hall

ALEC FREUND • STRINGER FOR GETTY IMAGES

They call us "paps," but I prefer "photojournalist." I covered the Bosnian war, I was in Tunisia during the Arab Spring—not to brag but my work has won loads of awards. Sometimes you just need a break from the hard stuff, so when my agency emailed me to cover this assignment, I thought, why not? I know a great pub in Greshamsbury that serves a terrific chicken tikka masala, I'd stop in there after the job. By the time I get to the gates of Greshamsbury Hall, it's already a zoo and there's a dozen other paps staking out the best positions. Turns out this lady, Martha Dung, is more famous than I'd realized, and there's a big bounty for a good shot of her with her new beau. Before I know what's happening several Range Rovers come zooming past, and everyone runs, surrounding the lead car so it can't bloody move. They're thrusting their cameras against the tinted windows; some tosser jumps on the hood and screams, "Martha! Smile, Martha!" I go into a trance when I'm taking pics, it's like I'm having an out-of-body experience. I remember I couldn't get anywhere near the damn car, so I climbed up the front of the tall iron gate and pointed my lens right onto the sunroof of the car and fired away. And that's how I got the money shot of the two of them, the viscount glaring up at me and Martha huddled beside him, grabbing his arm in terror. That's the shot the *Mirror* used the next day, with the headline 'It Must Be Love.' "

CHARLIE HOUGHTON • FOOTMAN

Two days before the viscount returns from Morocco, this poncy fellow shows up. Baron Nicolai Cabernet Chode or whatshisname starts ordering us around like we'd never done our jobs before. He's obsessed over the arrival of the new future countess and wants to make sure the moment of her arrival has more pageantry than the bloody changing of the guard at Buckingham Palace. Six footmen per car, and apparently every piece of luggage must be lifted precisely three feet off the ground, no higher, no lower, and all doors to the arriving car must be opened simultaneously and synchronized like it's *Swan* fuckin' *Lake*. And speaking of ballet, we got togged up in red, white, and gold livery straight out of some low-rent ITV production of *Pride & Prejudice*, with britches so tight I didn't know where to shove my todger. The baron wanted us to wear powdered wigs too, but thank god Hemsworth drew the line at that. He clearly wasn't happy to be dressed in anything but his usual designer denims, but he went along with the baron. So the big moment arrives and we're all standing there in V-shaped formation as the cars approach up the long driveway. It's a windy day, and out of nowhere this paper serviette from Nando's lands on the gravel right by the front steps. Baron von Wanker, swanning around in a cape, is peeking from the window and starts shouting, "What's that on the gravel? Someone pick that up now!" Hemsworth is stationed at the front door, so he quickly runs down the steps, bends over to grab the Nando's paper serviette, and we all hear this *bzzzzzt*. His tights split apart, right up the crotch, and he's wearing bright red Calvins underneath, so he looks like he's bleeding out the arse. Hemsworth turns to me and says, "You're me now," and bolts out of sight. The first car pulls up and we rush to open the doors at the same time, it's perfection. Since I'm Hemsworth now, I stand at the front door and bow ceremoniously as the lady comes up the stairs. She's got tattoos up her arms and is dressed in white overalls and Birkenstocks and looks like she's on her way to the Glastonbury Festival. This is the richest girl in the world? Much cooler than I expected, but of course Rufus only brings home cool ones. I liked the vegan girlfriend from three years ago, personally, she shared some of her hash with me and boy, was it premium stuff. As Rufus approaches I bow deeply but haven't a clue what I'm supposed to say, so I blurt out, "Welcome home, Master Rufus." And then I think, *You twat, greeting him like he's six years old!* Rufus grins at me and says, "Charlie, you look like you're about to sink the fleet at Waterloo." And I respond, "Aye, aye, Cap'n!"

BARON NICOLAI CHALAMET-CHAUDE • ART ADVISOR

First and foremost, I felt that it was essential for Ms. Dung to be properly edified about the family she is potentially marrying into, so I strategically positioned myself and the dowager marchioness at the left corner of the Great Hall just as the viscount and Miss Dung were entering the house. People fail to realize that the Great Hall functions rather like a whispering gallery. It's an acoustically perfect space, so as the couple walked through the front doors they could already overhear me enlightening the dowager marchioness on the painting we were standing in front of: "This is the Lord Robert. Now, see the fabric draped behind his chair? Gainsborough cleverly painted this fabric as an homage to the *Bayeux Tapestry,* because as you may recall the famous tapestry includes a *possible* depiction of Eustace II, the Count of Boulogne, and Lord Robert is his direct descendant." And the dowager marchioness, bless her heart, said right on cue, "Eustace II? Didn't he reign in the eleventh century? My goodness, next to the Greshams, we're practically fishmongers!" Rufus came right up, black as thunder, but he didn't forget to bow to the dowager marchioness before asking me, "Why the bloody hell are there paps outside? Our car almost ran over one of them." I duly informed him it was because of the great ball that was to take place that evening, taking care to drop a few of the important names attending that Ms. Dung might recognize—you know, all the minor Rothschilds and the Getty-adjacents. "Where's everyone now?" Rufus asked, and I informed him that everyone except myself and the marchioness was at the morning hunt. Right on cue, Arabella comes galloping up the back garden, dismounts from her dapple gray mare, and enters through the conservatory doors, exquisitely backlit all the way down the corridor until she arrives in the Great Hall looking absolutely drop dead in her Huntsman breeches and riding boots, crisp white shirt à la Doña Carolina Herrera, and sublime Codognato serpent bracelet. "Ah, Rufus, you're home. And who do we have here?" she says coolly, breathless from her morning ride. I'm telling you, it was the most glorious entrance ever, and I could see that Ms. Dung was suitably intimidated and impressed. No one would have suspected we had rehearsed this five times after carefully studying Kristin Scott Thomas's fabulous entrance in *Gosford Park* over and over again.

ROSINA LEUNG • HOUSEWIFE

I took Arabella and Nicolai Chalamet-Chaude (whom I've known since he was Nicky who answered the phones at Robert Kime) aside and told them what bloody fools they were. In one fell swoop they ruined all the groundwork I'd laid for the past week! Trying to be snotty and intimidate Martha Dung? How very stupid. This girl couldn't care less about all your royal nonsense, she's already been a guest at Highgrove and could buy up Greshamsbury and your resorts and still have enough left over to buy Scotland. So why are you doing your best impersonation of Madame Chiang Kai-Shek? Do you really want to give the girl second thoughts about having you as her dear mother-in-law? Charm offensive, my dears, charm offensive. You need to woo her like she's the empress of all China. So Arabella starts rushing around like a chicken with her head cut off. *Oh no oh no oh no, Nicolai, it's all your damn fault—you and Julian Fellowes!* And then she summons Hemsworth in a panic. *Has Miss Dung been shown to her room yet? We need to switch rooms, she's our honored guest, we need to give her the King Edward Suite.* And I said, wait a minute, that's *my* suite. Give up your damn bed if you want to but don't you dare move me!

ANYA JOVANOVIC • JUNIOR HOUSEMAID

I was refreshing the logs in the fireplace of the viscount's bedroom when the viscount entered, carrying his own duffel bags. I knew immediately that the countess would get so mad if she saw him doing that, but the viscount always does things his way. He greeted me by my name—he's the only one that remembers my name in this damn house—and asked me if I knew where Lady Beatrice was. I told him Lady Beatrice was up in London getting her hair done and would be back just in time for tonight's ball. He thanked me and then as I left the room, I told him I was on #TeamEden and he gave me a look and asked what I meant by that and I realized oh fuck why did I say anything? I panicked and ran off. I maybe shouldn't have done that but I really need this job even though the pay is shit, but my girlfriend is the shift manager at Caffè Nero in the village and it's so convenient to see her this way and I don't want my visa canceled by the countess.

HEMSWORTH • BUTLER

The viscount came up to me, looking worried. He said he had just walked over to the cottage and it appeared as if everyone was away. Where was Ms. Tong? he wondered. I told him that to my knowledge both she and the doctor were away. Why? he asked. I said I couldn't tell him. *Couldn't* because I didn't know, or because I *could not*, he asked. I told him bluntly I didn't know where Dr. Tong or Ms. Tong was, but I believed they were overseas. Did something happen? Sorry, mate, that I *could not* say. I was under the strictest orders. But then I said, you know, Margaret made treacle pudding for you. She knew you were coming home, and that you always love your pudding with tea.

MARGARET ASHBY • CHEF DE CUISINE

I've known Rufus since he was in diapers, I would never mince words with him. Now, the countess did pass along orders not to discuss the recent goings-on in the village with Rufus, so I was in a bit of a pickle when he came after me asking where Eden was and why everyone was being so evasive. I sat him down at the kitchen table with his treacle sponge, poured warm custard all over it, and told him to eat. He sat there politely picking away at his pudding, but he wouldn't eat. Now, I have never known Rufus to lose his appetite, it bloody broke me heart. So I thought to myself, *He's the next earl, my duty is to this family, not to the countess.* We Ashbys have worked for the Greshams for four generations. So I told him everything I knew.

JACKIE ZIVENCHY • EVENTS DIRECTOR

My clients are like a basket of fruit. Some are nice as peaches, some are rotten bananas, some are sour lemons, and some are acquired tastes, like durians. Arabella's a total durian. Some people love her, some people hate her, and if you touch her the wrong way she might prick you with her spikes and draw blood. She's not nasty per se, she's never once raised her voice at me, and she's always grateful for the work I do. The peculiar thing about her is that whenever she's entertaining at Greshamsbury Hall, she likes to pretend that she's done everything herself. Not that she arranged each centerpiece or basted the pheasants with her own hands—everyone knows she has an army of staff—but she wants to be perceived as the creative genius behind everything. So my assistant Kirsten and I were in the scullery, putting the finishing touches on all the swag bags, when I get a warning on my headset. *CM heading toward you.* "CM" stands for "Countess Monster," and that meant that Kirsten and I had to immediately be out of sight. Arabella never likes to see me on the event days, I suppose so that she won't have to confront the reality that it was *my* idea to have one long table lit by hundreds of lamps with different-colored vintage lampshades, inspired by Rune Guneriussen's site-specific installations, or it was *my* idea that every course served tonight should be an aphrodisiac. I mean, she really wants this Martha gal to seal the deal with Rufus, doesn't she? Arabella likes to pretend I don't exist so she can fully soak up all the compliments that come her way from all her guests—that she's such a visionary, that she throws the most original parties, that she's the reincarnation of Mona von Bismarck, yada. Anyway, we get the signal to hide, but there's absolutely nowhere to hide in the scullery, so guess what? Kirsten and I end up jumping into the huge metal garbage cans in the corner. So here we are hiding like Oscar the Grouch, imagining how he must have put up with life in a garbage can,* when I overhear two people enter the room talking. Turns out it's *not* Arabella, it's Martha Dung and Rufus, and this is what I overheard:

"So it turns out my mother has literally run Eden out of the village, and there are rumors going around that Eden may or may not be pregnant, and that she may or may not have attacked my mum and ruined her Gabriela Hearst peasant blouse with cappuccino. Eden's not responding to my texts, but I've managed to find out where she is after texting with Freddy Farman-Farmihian."

"Where is she?"

"She's in Los Angeles, and I have this feeling she really needs me right now."

"That's bullshit, and you know it. *You* are the one who needs *her*. You've been acting like a lost puppy from the moment we arrived."

"I have, haven't I?"

"Take my plane, I'll text my pilot right now."

"But the ball . . . I can't leave you alone at the ball tonight . . ."

"I'm a grown woman, Rufus. Believe it or not, I can handle your ball."

LADY BEATRICE GRESHAM • MODEL AND ENTREPRENEUR

I was just back from London and on my way up to Mummy's rooms to show her my chignon festooned with hundreds of white butterflies—a reinterpretation of Elizabeth Taylor's updo for the Ca' Rezzonico ball—when I heard Mummy screeching, "What do you mean the viscount has left? Left for where? Left for how long?"

---

* *Everyone knows that Oscar the Grouch didn't actually live in the silver garbage pail visible on* Sesame Street. *The pail is purely an entrance to a sprawling subterranean complex that tunnels far beneath the boxes, garbage, and various ephemera. Over the decades, we've been given glimpses of his cushy abode, and if memory serves, there was even an episode where Oscar was sitting in his Jacuzzi wearing a shower cap.*

I paused, wondering whether I should turn around, when Hemsworth came running out saying, "Call a doctor, your mother says she's having a heart attack." Since Dr. Tong was out of the country and Mummy would have refused to see him anyway, Dr. Fillgrave was summoned from Barchester. As I suspected, she was not having a heart attack, but her blood pressure was rather elevated and the doctor decided a sedative was the best course of treatment and administered it before anyone could stop him. But then poor Mummy missed her own ball! When she came to the next day, she was inconsolable, but Martha Dung did something magnificent—she had Maggie prepare chicken soup in a double boiler for Mummy, took it up on a tray herself, and announced that she had such a good time at the ball and she was so impressed with meeting all of Mummy's distinguished friends, like Captain Ross Poldark, that she was going to let out Boxall Park next door and throw a return ball in honor of Mummy. Floods of tears from Mummy, who kept sighing gratefully, "Now, this is daughter-in-law material! She even knows how to *bou tong* for me!"* "How did you know how to fix Mummy?" I asked Martha. "You forget, I also have a Chinese mother," Martha said with a wink.

* *Cantonese for "boil soup," the phrase refers to the ritual of preparing a healing medicinal brew (usually for one's elders who one hopes will remember them fondly in their will).*

VIII

The Screening Room

"Didn't your father fly you to Thailand to get you devirginated at some fancy brothel the minute you got hair on your balls?" the middle-aged guy wearing the Lakers cap said.

"It was Macau. He flew me to this super-VIP brothel in the penthouse of a casino, and he insisted on watching," Luis Felipe replied. "So here I am, going at it on top of this whore, and my father suddenly says, 'Stop! Get off her! She's much too loose. Let's find one that's a better fit for you!'"

"Cheers to Daddy!" the guy said, lifting his beer up high.

Eden glanced at her father in horror and whispered, "Who *are* these people?"

"I believe that's Luis Felipe's entertainment lawyer," Thomas whispered back.

The film producer from lunch at La Cienega Villas spoke next. "The story I love about your dad is when he got so mad because he couldn't find the right plane with the maximum range to fly him from Manila to LA without having to stop over somewhere. His G4 couldn't do it, so he bought a G5, and when the G5 couldn't do it, he got the G550. Didn't he end up buying three different jets?"

"Five. I got the hand-me-downs, and I still fuckin' can't fly to Manila without having to refuel in Tokyo," Luis Felipe grunted.

A guy wearing a white puffer vest said in a thick Spanish accent, "Luis, remember the time your dad made you fly commercial from

Geneva to Manila? To punish you after you got kicked out of TASIS? You got so depressed being on that plane you said you almost wanted to pull the handle on the exit row door and jump out, hahaha."

"I seriously thought about killing myself on that flight. I had never ever flown an *airline* in my life, and the bastard fuckin' put me in Swiss Air Lines *business class*. Have you any idea what hell that was? How is anyone supposed to fly for fourteen hours straight without a proper bedroom? I can't even go six hours without sashimi," Luis Felipe moaned.

"You were obviously suffering from PTWD," the supermodel who was at La Cienega Villas chimed in.

"What's that?" the lawyer wearing the Lakers cap asked.

"Post-traumatic wealth disorder. It's a real thing. My children had it when we had to move into a temporary house in Brentwood after the Malibu fire destroyed our compound. They just could not cope with the shame of being in Brentwood. And everything about that house depressed them—the pool, the tennis court, the giant outdoor trampoline. That's when my daughter tried to get a face tattoo and my son started cutting himself."

"Would you like a Kobe beef slider?" Eden heard a voice beside her say. She turned to see a woman holding up a platter of over-stuffed mini-hamburgers that were still oozing blood.

"No thank you," Eden replied, not having the slightest bit of appetite. She had come to Cloudline to pay her respects at Rene's wake, but this surreal event held in the massive screening room of Luis Felipe's house with its bizarre cast of characters wasn't like any other wake she'd ever attended—it felt more like the VIP area at Coachella. She wondered how soon she could get out of here without seeming rude, even though she didn't think Luis Felipe would even notice or care. She had approached him to offer her condolences when she had first arrived at the house.

"I'm so sorry," Eden said simply.

"It's okay."

"And I must apologize for how I spoke to you last night."

"Why? You were right. He did die," Luis Felipe replied, looking her straight in the eye.

Eden pursed her lips, not sure what else to say. Their awkward exchange was mercifully interrupted by Jenna, the actress who had been at Daddy Mustang, who rushed in with a hug. "Louie baby, I'm sooooooo sorry!"

"Hey, babe," Luis Felipe mumbled.

"Lexi had to do a self-tape, she'll be here soon. Here, I brought you this book. You gotta read it. It'll, like, change your life," she said, thrusting a copy of Joan Didion's *The Year of Magical Thinking* into his hands.

Not sure about that, Eden thought to herself, wondering if Jenna had actually read the book.

As more guests arrived and the supermodel continued to drone on about post-traumatic wealth disorder and its terrible effects on her children, Eden leaned in to her father's ear again to ask, "Where's Luis Felipe's mother?"

"She lives in Beijing these days, I believe."

"Is she coming to LA?"

"I'd be surprised if she came."

"Really? But her son's father just died . . ."

"Yes, but they don't have a relationship at all."

"Really? Didn't she raise him?"

"No. Luis Felipe was raised by a series of Filipino nannies and she had no involvement."

"That's rather odd, don't you think?"

"She was never really a mother . . . more a surrogate. You see, Rene specifically chose her for her genes. He wanted to engineer the perfect son, and she was a tall, stunning lady from Northern China. She gave him a child, but then she went on to marry a top politician in China and has a whole other family with the man."

Eden said nothing, but she suddenly felt more sorry than ever for Luis Felipe.

"I told you, Rene was a very . . . *complicated* man. You were lucky to have met him when you did—in his final days he was much more . . . subdued."

"Now that he's gone, when do you think you'll be coming home?"

"Probably at the end of the week. I need to stay a couple more days to meet with Rene's lawyers and get a few things squared away with Luis Felipe."

"You might try getting him to cut back on his drinking. I don't think I've ever seen him sober."

"He hasn't been sober since he was sixteen," Thomas said, shrugging wearily. "His father tasked me with helping him deal with his addiction issues long ago, and as you can see I've been failing."

Eden shook her head sadly as Luis Felipe grabbed a mic, hopped onstage, and announced, "You know what time it is? Do you know what time it is?"

The back wall of the screening room lifted up like the door of a freight elevator to reveal a Mexican-style cantina with three chefs manning sizzling taco stations as a mariachi band entered along with an army of waiters bearing trays of tequila shots and mysterious-looking covered baskets.

"It's time for tacos, tequila, and toads!" Luis Felipe yelled into his mic.

The waiters opened the baskets to reveal that they were full of live Sonoran Desert toads.

"Everybody gets to lick a toad!" Luis Felipe yelled again as the crowd cheered.*

Eden turned to her father with a look of incredulity. "Tell me this isn't really happening."

---

* *Even though hallucinogenic toad licking has replaced mushroom parties as the hottest thing in Hollywood, the National Park Service has issued a serious warning against the activity: "These toads have prominent parotid glands that secrete a potent toxin. It can make you sick if you handle the frog or get the poison in your mouth. As we say with most things you come across in a national park, whether it be a banana slug, an unfamiliar mushroom, or a large toad with glowing eyes in the dead of night, please refrain from licking."*

"I'm afraid it is."

"I think this might be my moment to slip out."

"Of course. Thank you for coming, dear. I know it would have meant a lot to Rene."

"I don't think this psychedelic toad-licking fiesta is going to turn out well. I hope you won't have to resuscitate anyone tonight."

"Oh no, I'm leaving right after you," Thomas replied. Eden gave her father a hug and left the screening room quietly. As she emerged through the front doors, the fresh air hit her face and she felt as though she could breathe again. Her shoulder muscles began to ease as she realized how tense she had been inside that mausoleum-like screening room. A uniformed attendant standing by a line of waiting golf carts waved at her with a friendly smile. "Ride to the parking lot, ma'am?"

"Thank you. I think I'll walk," Eden replied. She strolled down the long driveway, still feeling chilly despite the sun shining down on her. Arriving at the guest parking lot, which resembled a luxury car dealership, she reached into her handbag for the key fob to unlock the car Freddy had lent her. She had selected the least flashy car from the Farman-Farmihian garage—a Porsche Macan that Freddy said was the one their housekeeper used.

Eden got into the driver's seat and turned on the engine, and the radio came on automatically, playing Fleetwood Mac's "Songbird." It was one of her favorite songs, one that was hardly ever played on the radio, so she rolled down the windows and turned up the volume, letting Christine McVie's voice echo through the canyon.

And I love you, I love you, I love you,
Like never before . . .

As the song was ending, Eden burst into tears uncontrollably. She didn't want the song to end. It was so lovely; it reminded her of England, of home. She missed the cottage, she missed her bedroom with its view through the trees of Greshamsbury Hall in the distance. She missed lying on the bed and staring out at the great house, seeing the dimly lit window under the tallest gable and knowing Rufus was in his bedroom as well, probably listening to Brian Eno or reading one of his Cormac McCarthy novels. She felt sad for Rene and a life interrupted in its prime; she felt sad for his son, so scarred by growing up with everything in the world; she felt sad for her father, who had fought for so long to find a cure for his patient.

This whole city, she realized, was tinged with sadness. Everything about the place seemed desperately out of balance. Even as she drove down Benedict Canyon Drive with all the pristinely trimmed hedges giving occasional glimpses of the magnificent estates that lay beyond, estates that most people could never ever dream of living in, she could feel the sadness emanating from behind every façade. She thought of Maria Wyeth, the heroine of another book by Joan Didion, who would spend days on end driving the highways of Los Angeles in aimless desperation. She thought of Luis Felipe curled up and seething in his business-class pod thirty-five thousand feet in the sky. She thought of the children of the former supermodel, jumping up and down on a big outdoor trampoline listlessly dissatisfied.

She arrived at last at Freddy's mansion and waited as the ornate iron gates opened slowly. As she pulled into the immaculately tiled driveway, she saw a man standing under the ivy-clad porte cochere and thought she must be hallucinating. She slammed on her brakes, rushed out of the car, and ran up the steps, right into Rufus's arms.

IX

1801 Century Park West

Diego San Antonio y Viscaya had come straight from the airport after a fourteen-hour flight on Philippine Airlines, and he was downing a double espresso to steel himself for the morning's meeting when the receptionist showed Thomas Tong into the sleek conference room at Carlisle, Caffey, Wiedlin, Schock & Valentine.

"Thomas! Good to see you," Diego said, putting down his coffee cup.

"No, no, don't get up," Thomas said as he headed over to Diego's chair by the window to shake his hand. "Did you just get in?"

"Came straight from the airport."

"What a view!" Thomas said, looking out the floor-to-ceiling window at the Century City skyline.

"This area feels a bit like Bonifacio Global City to me," Diego said.

"Yes it does. It's a metropolis within a metropolis. Less green than Manila, though."

"I don't think I've seen you in Manila since that memorable shabu-shabu dinner at Doris Hoh's. When all the power went out and we couldn't use any of our hot pots?"

"Haha, yes, that was a fun dinner. No, haven't had a chance to come over since then. How's Marion?"

"Doing very well. And your daughter . . . Eden?"

"Yes, she's very well. She was actually just in Los Angeles."

"Rene told me."

"He did?" Thomas was a bit surprised.

"Yes. You know we talked several times a day. He was quite taken with your daughter, very impressed," Diego said.

Before Thomas could respond, half a dozen other lawyers entered the room, all legal representatives of Rene's from the far-flung corners of his empire. Jane Carlisle, the lead lawyer hosting today's meeting, scanned the room. "Is our esteemed guest still not here?"

Thomas shook his head. "He was up very late last night, hosting yet another party at Cloudline. This time the LAPD paid a visit to have it shut down."

Jane rolled her eyes. "Most of our billable hours on Luis Felipe involve dealing with the LAPD or Interpol. Now, I told his assistant Tessa the meeting was at ten o'clock sharp, just to give him an additional hour to be late, and he's still not here!"

A few moments later, the door opened and Luis Felipe waltzed in with an extremely wild-looking cat on a studded leather leash.

"Is that a very small cheetah?" Emile Schaffhausen, the lawyer from Zurich, gasped, staring in fascination at the black-spotted feline with its unusually elongated neck and large pointy ears.

"Everyone meet my latest little kitty cat, Special K. She's an African serval," Luis Felipe said, sliding into a chair at the head of the table as the creature climbed onto his shoulder.

Jane gave the cat a weary once-over and cleared her throat. "Mr. Tan, on behalf of everyone at Carlisle, Caffey, Wiedlin, Schock and Valentine, I'd like to extend our heartfelt sympathies on the passing of your father. He was a great man who—"

Luis Felipe waved his hand dismissively. "Janie, we already had a wake, I don't need to hear any more of this crap. I know you guys all bill by the hour, and unlike my dad, I don't like to waste time or money, especially when it's mine, so let's just get on with it."

Jane pursed her lips for a moment. "Very well. Since Mr. San Antonio y Viscaya is the lawyer overseeing Rene Tan's personal affairs in the Philippines, I will cede the floor to him."

"Thank you, Jane. I'll make this very quick and easy—"

"Good. I think Special K's getting hungry. Hey, could we get Special K some Greek yogurt? Like a Chobani, maybe? It's the only thing that doesn't give her the runs," Luis Felipe said, placing the cat onto the glass conference table as several of the lawyers recoiled preemptively in anticipation of the creature's explosive diarrhea.

Ignoring his antics, Diego continued, "Now, your father established an umbrella trust to administer his estate and preserve all his personal and business holdings throughout the world. It is called the R. S. Tan Trust, and as you are the primary beneficiary of the trust—"

"What do you mean *beneficiary*? Am I not the president of this trust?"

"There is no president, only a trust protector, and that is—"

"Diego, let me make this easy on you. Just tell me where to sign to take control of all my dad's companies."

Diego paused and looked Luis Felipe in the eye. "Pablo Aguilar, your father's longtime lieutenant, will be assuming day-to-day control of your father's companies, on behalf of the trust—"

"But I control the trust, right?" Luis Felipe shot back.

"You do not. The trust will be overseen by a board of trustees, of which Dr. Thomas Tong is the trust protector."

Luis Felipe pivoted to Thomas in annoyance. "Who the fuck died and made you Jay-Z?"

"Your father did, actually," Thomas said.

Diego continued, "Yes, your father appointed him to be the lead. Your father wanted to ensure that your health and livelihood are maintained in the style to which you are accustomed. All the residences shall remain at your disposal—this includes Bel Air, Forbes Park, Coron, Knightsbridge, Central Park South, Emirates Hills, Point Piper, Cap Ferrat, and St. Jean Bay.* The trust will handle the upkeep and expenses of all these properties. You will also have all the automobiles, the Gulfstream 550, and the yacht at your disposal—"

---

* *Diego's referring to Rene Tan's residences in ultra-exclusive neighborhoods of Los Angeles, Manila, Palawan, London, Manhattan, Dubai, Sydney, the French Riviera, and St. Barths.*

"Damn right I will. It's called the *Luis Felipe*, for fuck's sake!"

"—but all these assets are to remain the property of the trust and cannot be divested. Your father also empowered the trust to make decisions on your monthly disbursement—"

"Disbursement? The fuck is that?"

"It's similar to an allowance, to be determined by the board of trustees. After consulting with the board members, most of whom are in this room right now, we've determined that starting this month, you'll be provided with a disbursement of two hundred fifty thousand dollars, in US currency."

"Two hundred fifty thousand dollars a day?"

"Per month."

Luis Felipe almost leapt out of his chair, startling his serval. "You must be fuckin' kidding me! I could spend that in an hour! That's not even one decent watch, or one night's bottle service at—"

Diego continued in a calm tone, "Your disbursement will be revisited on a biannual basis, or quarterly if economic circumstances change, until you attain the age of thirty-five."

"What happens when I'm thirty-five?"

"The trust will be dissolved and you will be in full control of all the trust's assets."

"Thirty-five is a friggin' lifetime away—"

"There is one important clause of the trust that you need to understand. Everything—the continued use of all the properties, automobiles, yacht, and plane, and your monthly disbursement—will be contingent on your entering a twelve-step program at one of the approved facilities on this list."

Jane slid a sheet of paper with a list of all the five-star rehabs in the world across the table toward Luis Felipe.

"The Hills, Kusnacht Practice, Promises, Paracelsus, is this some kind of joke?" Luis Felipe looked around the room and laughed contemptuously. "Fucking hell, I'm being punk'd right now, aren't I? Is there a camera hidden somewhere, behind that chalkboard maybe?"

"There are no cameras in this room and that's not a chalkboard—it's a Cy Twombly! We are being one hundred percent serious. You're only twenty-three and you've already had acute pancreatitis twice and almost overdosed numerous times. Your father has been so concerned for your welfare—" Jane began.

"Really? Where the fuck's he been my whole life?"

Emile chimed in, trying to defuse the tension. "Look here, your papa wants to ensure you live to a ripe old age to enjoy all the fruits of his labor."

Luis Felipe glared at the men and women around him. He balled up the paper in his fist and threw it at his serval, which caught it in its mouth and started to chew on it. "This is such bullshit! There's no way in hell I'm going to rehab again, especially not Paracelsus. Did you know their sushi chef is fuckin' Albanian? I demand to see the will!"

"There's no will, Luis Felipe. The trust circumvents the need for any will. This way things remain completely sealed and private, as your father wanted it," Diego replied firmly.

"Liar! My dad told me years ago that he had a will and I was getting everything! I'm his only son, for fuck's sake."

Jane jumped in, backing up Diego. "Billionaires don't have wills—they have trusts, foundations, flow-through corporations, and other generational-wealth-sheltering tools at their disposal. Your father was constantly tinkering with his estate planning. His most recent amendments took place on the day he passed."

"Wait a minute. He changed the trust *the day he died*? Isn't that illegal? He was a fuckin' Froot Loop by then!"

"He was very much compos mentis, I can assure you. I saw him myself on the day he passed," Jane insisted.

"I see what's happening here. You're a bunch of fuckin' thieves! You're trying to cheat me out of what's rightfully mine."

Luis Felipe yanked hard on the leash of the cat, and it began to pee all over the conference table. "Good job, Special K!" Everyone backed away from the table as Luis Felipe got up. "I'm the sole heir to the estate of Rene Tan! This trust thing is a sham, and I demand full control of my father's company! It's my birthright!"

Emile tried to calm the situation. "Your papa is only looking out for your best interests. He spent his life building up all his various businesses and did not wish to see it all going down the toilet. He felt that you were not yet ready to assume the position—"

"Stop calling him my 'papa,' you creepy Nazi fuck! Do you know what position you can assume? You can go choke on your own balls upside down!" Luis Felipe raged, the veins bulging on his unnaturally thick neck. "I'm gonna hire the best fucking lawyers on the planet to sue each and every one of you until you have no assholes left and are shitting out of mold-infested colostomy bags! Fuck you all!"

Luis Felipe scooped Special K into his arms and stormed out of the room.

Jane exhaled audibly, looking around the table. "That went well . . ."

"Better than I was expecting, actually," Thomas said.

"At least that mini-cheetah did not have very much urine to dispense," Emile remarked.

Diego had the last word. "What the poor boy fails to realize is that his father already hired the best lawyers on the planet."

Thomas said nothing, but secretly, he was already dreading what was about to come.

X

US Route 90

JEFF DAVIS COUNTY, TEXAS · *TWO DAYS LATER*

They had been driving all morning, not stopping since they'd grabbed breakfast tacos from a diner on the outskirts of El Paso. For long stretches they would listen to music or chat every now and then. It had been like this for two days now, Rufus telling her about his time in Morocco, Eden filling in the blanks on Los Angeles. Mostly they just stared at the endless highway, enjoying the comfortable silence of each other's company.

Shortly after they were reunited at Freddy's house in Beverly Hills and cleared up all the absurd rumors, Rufus turned to Eden and suggested, half-jokingly, "Since you're not pregnant with Freddy's baby, and since Interpol isn't after you for scalding my mum's face with a flat white from Caffè Nero, shall we rent a convertible and drive to New York?"

"Aren't you marrying Martha Dung at Westminster Abbey?"

"Uh, that's not till next Tuesday. We have time."

"Let's do it."

"Really?" Rufus looked at her in amazement, not having expected her to say yes.

"Why not? I've always wanted to drive across America."

"Guys! You know what you should do?" Freddy said excitedly. "Take one of the 'Raris. Seriously, just pick your favorite color, drive to Vegas, and check in to a suite at the Wynn. I'll book you a table at Nobu Vegas!"

"No, no, you should have dinner at é by José Andrés, that's the best restaurant in Vegas, and I can call José for you," Daniela chimed in. "And then from there you should drive to the Amangiri resort in Utah, it's heaven on earth, just don't look at the bill when you check out."

Eden and Rufus nodded politely at all their suggestions.

Two days later, after renting a Jeep Wrangler convertible and assiduously avoiding Las Vegas but making stops at Joshua Tree National Park, Cathedral Rock in Sedona, and Through the Flower art space in Belen, New Mexico, they found themselves speeding down a lonely highway in West Texas. Rufus had taken this long detour in search of something he said was going to be a special surprise.

"What is it?" Eden asked curiously.

"It wouldn't be a surprise if I told you, would it? Just keep a look-out."

"What am I supposed to be looking out for?"

"Oh, you'll know it when you see it," Rufus said mysteriously.

It was the wildest, most desolate road either of them had ever been on, just black tar and flat gray scrub on both sides of the highway as far as the eye could see. Far off on the horizon, a tiny speck morphed slowly into something bigger and bigger, and as they drew nearer Eden suddenly caught sight of it:

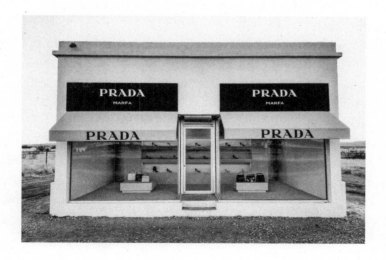

A Prada boutique in the middle of nowhere.

"What the——?" Eden blurted out as Rufus hit the brakes and rolled up beside the small white stucco building along the side of the empty highway.

"I've always wanted to see this," Rufus said gleefully as they got out of the car.

"God in heaven!" Eden exclaimed. Here on US Route 90, 1.4 miles northwest of Valentine, Texas (population 109), was an actual replica of a Prada boutique that looked like it had been teleported directly from Madison Avenue. The black and white sign along the front of the small, sleek white stucco building read *Prada Marfa,* and beyond the plate-glass windows the space was painted in the brand's signature pistachio green, with three sleek shelves displaying rows of shoes and two platforms arrayed with handbags. Eden tried to open the door but found it disappointingly locked.

"It's not a real shop. It's a site-specific land art installation by Elmgreen and Dragset. To me, it's a statement about urbanization and materialism. You know, how everything's become a luxury brand these days. Brilliant, isn't it?" Rufus ruminated.

Eden walked a few steps backward to study the shop from the edge of the highway. "Wicked! It perfectly sums up my entire experience in LA."

"That city really did a number on you," Rufus remarked.

"More than I realized."

They walked around the back of the Prada Marfa store and stared out onto the vast expanse of desert as a dry breeze caught their faces.

"Look at all this empty space out here. Miles and miles of it," Rufus said.

In the distance, a big white blimp suddenly floated into view. "Is that another art project?" Eden wondered.

"No. I read about this——it's a US border patrol surveillance blimp," Rufus answered. "We're only a few miles from the Mexican border."

Eden gazed up at the blimp now pivoting ominously toward them. "So . . . how are these blimps going to stop people from crossing the border?"

"They're basically giant drones with cameras. They're just watching us, recording everything. I reckon if they see something they don't like they send the border patrol agents out."

Eden shook her head sadly. "Think of all the men, women, and children risking their lives right this second trying to cross this desert just to get the chance at a better life here. And if they survive they still have to deal with this welcome party from the border patrol. It really puts things in perspective, doesn't it?"

"We are so bloody lucky," Rufus said.

"You know, when I think of what I saw in LA, it just makes my blood boil. All the giant houses sitting empty, the pointless private clubs and restaurants, the way Luis Felipe lived—one man-child occupying a soulless mini-city on a mountaintop with fifty cars in the garage—it was an orgy of excess. But all these houses are run by armies of immigrants. You see them up and down all those streets—they're the gardeners, the housekeepers, the construction workers, they're doing all the work nobody else wants to do. So why make it so hard for them to come here and do it? It's such a tragic farce."

They got back into the car and kept driving along the highway for another thirty minutes until they arrived in Marfa. As they drove through town, Eden looked out her window and was surprised to see art galleries dotting the main drag, intriguing little shops next to old gas stations, and Airstream trailers transformed into food trucks. Young hipsters wandered around the dusty streets looking like they had just stepped off planes from Stockholm, Tokyo, and Reykjavík. "I feel like we've somehow been transported to Camden," Eden commented.

Rufus laughed. "I've been wanting to come here for years. The artist Donald Judd came out here in the 1970s. Not much was happening, so he was able to buy up abandoned office buildings, the old supermarket, big chunks of land for cheap. He used all the spaces to make and display his art, and he invited his friends to create art installations here as well, to create artworks that they could make only out here with all this space. Artists like John Chamberlain, Dan Flavin, Yun Hyong-keun. So now this remote little town six hours

from the nearest city has become a mecca for artists and art aficionados. Marvelous, isn't it?"

They crossed railroad tracks and went down a dirt road leading
to an old military base that Donald Judd had transformed into his
perfect vision of a museum—the Chinati Foundation. After buying
tickets from the young Swedish intern who couldn't seem to figure
out how to use the Square app, Rufus excitedly made a beeline for a
pair of gigantic artillery sheds. They entered the first shed and found
themselves coming face-to-face with Donald Judd's minimalist
masterpiece *100 Untitled Works in Mill Aluminum.*

Across two vast hangarlike buildings with poured-concrete floors
and glass walls along each side, Judd had sculpted one hundred large
rectangular aluminum boxes and spaced them in three equidistant
rows. Rufus stood in the middle of the monastic space, utterly transfixed by the majesty of the monumental art installation. The rows
of boxes shimmered in the sunlight, casting geometries of shadows
across the space as the light shifted. He didn't say a word, but Eden
could tell how moved he was. This was his Fallingwater, his Notre
Dame, his Santiago de Compostela. Eden left him and wandered
through the space, realizing as she studied the boxes more closely
that no two were alike. Even though they were of the exact same
dimensions, each box was configured differently—some missing a
side, some missing a top, some bisected like Mondrianesque puzzles.
Each box seemed to emanate a mysterious power, and Eden found
herself being quietly mesmerized by the installation and the Zenlike
tranquility of the space.

Eden glanced back at Rufus leaning against the window perfectly
still, staring intently at the artwork as the afternoon sun cast a halo
around him, and she almost gasped in astonishment. He looked just
like a fierce archangel that had descended from the heavens. Only
he wasn't an angel—he was very much a human made of flesh
and blood. He was so different from any other man she knew—
so unafraid of his emotions, so gentle and brimming with heart. How
was it that a man born into such extreme privilege could have managed to be filled with so much humility, to be so utterly lacking in

pretension and ego and any interest in material trappings? In a flash, she realized how incredibly attractive he had become to her, how deeply she loved him, like never before. She found herself blushing at the intensity of her own thoughts and forced herself to look away.

After a while, they left the room of boxes to explore other artworks around the property. They discovered barracks filled with ethereal Dan Flavin light installations, a haunting re-creation of an abandoned Soviet classroom by Ilya Kabakov, and monumental sculptures by Claes Oldenburg and Richard Long. Rufus walked around each art installation in sheer delight, taking picture after picture. At the far end of the base, they came upon a wooden bench in the shaded porch of an old fort. They sat down on the bench side by side, staring out at the town glimmering in the distance, not saying anything for a long while.

"I'm so flooded with ideas, I feel like my head's about to explode," Rufus said.

"I bet. I can't wait to see what comes out of all this," Eden said encouragingly.

"I just want to go back to my studio and make work."

"What was your favorite installation? The one hundred aluminum boxes?"

"I loved it, but you know, it's less about the individual art pieces and more the sum of what Judd's created here that's most impressive to me. He came here and saw Marfa as this blank slate that he could reinvent, building by building, and mold an entire town to his vision. I want to do something like this in Greshamsbury."

"What a great idea. You've never set any of your art projects at Greshamsbury!" Eden said excitedly.

"Actually, I wasn't thinking of myself but of other artists. We have so much land, so many derelict buildings on the estate that could be revived and reimagined by artists. There are so many brilliant people I know who are struggling to get noticed and who can't seem to break through. Artists of color, especially, who are totally sidelined because their work is too experimental or uncomfortable or just not fashionable enough for the art mafia. Like my friend Kiana, who you met in Hawaii. Her sculptures are so original and fresh but she's obviously not sleeping with the right art dealers—she can't get a solo show to save her life. I want to provide her with a stipend she can actually live on, and give her a place to create and showcase her art in all its glory. And this idea extends beyond Greshamsbury. We could showcase amazing art installations at all the Bella resorts around the world—Antwerp, Hong Kong, Hawaii. The resorts could all become art destinations. Think of the amazing things that could be created in all these places, and how great it would be for the local communities. I think that's the way to save all the resorts, to save everything."

Eden loved seeing the way Rufus's eyes lit up as he spoke. "I think you're really onto something here!"

"You don't think I've gone stark raving mad?"

"Not at all," Eden said, her mind flashing back to Luis Felipe and how different his motives were from Rufus's. Rufus cared so ardently about nurturing other artists, while Luis Felipe only used them for his own amusement and profit. "It's the most exciting plan I've heard for Greshamsbury in years. Much better than putting in that giant Tesco by the roundabout."

Rufus smiled at her, feeling relieved. "You're the only person that's always believed in me, in my art and all my wild schemes and ideas. Why do you do it? Why do you put up with me?"

Because I love you. The words came straight to Eden's head but she found herself unable to say them. What if he'd come to his senses and realized that they were better off as friends? Did she want to destroy the most important relationship in her life? "Habit, I suppose," she finally answered.

"I hope it's a habit you'll never be able to quit," Rufus replied, before immediately thinking, *Fuck me, what a bloody idiotic thing to say, so cliché and juvenile.* He shook off his embarrassment and leaned against the cool concrete wall.

Eden gazed at him, and he flashed her a quick smile, that same gorgeous, conspiratorial smile she saw whenever she poked her head into his bedroom and he looked up from his desk, or when he first caught sight of her on their morning runs, or the times his mother said something outrageous at the dinner table, or the millions of other times that smile had made her heart skip a beat. Now she could feel her heart pounding in her ears, pounding out of her chest. *Carpe diem,* she thought.

Before he had time to process what was occurring, Rufus felt soft lips brush against his. Eden's lips. Was this really happening? Was he hallucinating from the heat? Eden was kissing him, fondling the hair on the back of his neck, pressing into him. He reached around to stroke the small of her back and felt her tremble.

Martha's words suddenly came into his head. *You need to woo a woman slowly.* He pulled back for a moment. "I don't want to make the same mistake that I did in the forest. I don't want to rush things—"

Eden cut him off. "You're not rushing. I'm in love with you, silly rabbit."

"You are?" Rufus could hardly believe his ears. He was about to respond when Eden kissed him even more forcefully, quickly getting up and straddling him. As she wrapped her legs around him, he could feel his jeans tighten in agony. He slid his hand under her blouse and just as he began to tease the tip of her—

"Er . . . excuse me, might one of you happen to be Rufus?" said a voice out of nowhere.

Rufus and Eden froze, turning to see the Swedish lad from the museum office standing at the corner bashfully.

"Yah, that's me," Rufus said, mortified, as he let go of Eden's breast.

"There is a telephone call for you at the office. I believe it is an emergency," the Swede said.

Rufus got up from the bench, wondering how anyone could have possibly found him here, when it dawned on him—*Bloody Instagram.* He had been live streaming video and posting pictures when they first arrived and there was still a spot of decent Wi-Fi.

They made their way back to the office and Rufus grabbed the cordless phone anxiously. "Hello?"

"Rufus? Is that you?" It was his mother.

"Yes," Rufus replied gruffly.

"Oh thank god I found you! The worst thing has happened, the worst. Your poor sister," Arabella sobbed hysterically.

"What happened to Bea?" Rufus asked in a panic.

"No, it's Augie. Poor Augie!" his mother cried.

XI

Greshamsbury Hall

GRESHAMSBURY, ENGLAND • *THE NEXT DAY*

(IN THE GREAT HALL . . .)

Rufus had just arrived home from Marfa and was rushing up the stairs when Hemsworth intercepted him. "Hey, Rufus! Bea wanted me to tell you that she's in the boathouse."

"The boathouse? Okay. I was going to look in on Augie."

Hemsworth gave Rufus an apprehensive look. "I think you might want to see to Bea first . . ."

"Ah, Roger that."

(IN THE BOATHOUSE . . .)

Bea was curled up on the sycamore Jean-Michel Frank daybed with cucumber slices over her eyes and a pot of ginger tea at her side when Rufus came in. Liam and Noel, the Irish setters, jumped up eagerly to greet Rufus.

"How's tricks?" Rufus asked, sitting down at the foot of the daybed and petting the dogs.

"Throbbing migraine."

"Sorry to hear that. Why aren't you in bed?"

"Much more peaceful here than in the house," Bea replied. "Thank heaven you're back! It's been a shit show around here, and I've been on the receiving end."

"From Augie?"

"Mummy and Augie both."

"Why?"

"Apparently it's all my fault, because I didn't tell them what happened at the Big Kahuna."

"The Big Kahuna? I'm not following . . ."

"The day of the *Town & Country* photo shoot on that nude beach . . ."

"You mean *Kehena* Beach?"

"Yes, Kahuna Beach. There were these Japanese hipsters, this young couple doing *shibari*—you know, decorative rope bondage—right in front of everyone in the middle of the beach. They had the prime spot, and the photographer wanted them to move but Gopal Das said it was a public beach and they had every right to be there."

"Okay . . ."

"Anyway, the fellow was very slowly and methodically tying his naked girlfriend against a large piece of driftwood, trussing her up like some pheasant. His rather thick-waisted girlfriend had the ugliest tattoo I've ever seen on her belly. It was some sort of fish creature, terribly naff—"

"I don't understand what this has to do with Augie's—"

"Be patient. So while Augie was getting her hair done in the makeup trailer, Maxxie started talking to the Japanese couple. He was inordinately curious about the bondage and was being rather friendly with them. You know how he is. Next thing I know, there he is, trying out a few knots on the girl."

"So?" Rufus asked.

"Well, I witnessed all this, because they were shooting me just a few feet away from the couple and I had my back to the sea, so I could see everything that was happening. And I didn't think to mention it to Augie until yesterday. So now everyone's blaming me for Maxxie running off with some Chinese girl at Machu Picchu."

Rufus gasped. "Maxxie ran off with another woman?"

"Yes!"

"In the midst of his honeymoon with Augie?"

"Yes! Apparently Augie got altitude sickness when she arrived in Cuzco, and by the time they got to Machu Picchu she was flat on her back. And meanwhile Maxxie was getting some other slapper flat on her back."

"My god . . . poor Augie," Rufus sighed, truly heartbroken for his sister.

"Poor Augie is right, but it's not my fault she got altitude sickness and couldn't defend her own turf."

"Who's saying it's your fault?"

"Mummy, of course!" Bea groaned, so agitated that the cucumber slices slid off her eyes. She patted around till she found them and placed them back on her eyes before continuing, "Mummy said that Maxxie's behavior on the nude beach was a warning sign that he had a roving eye, and I should have told them about it. I mean, it was the day before the wedding, we were rushing around from photo shoot to photo shoot and I'm trying to strike glamorous poses in my Molly Goddard dress while there were todgers flopping everywhere around me! I was bloody distracted! How was I supposed to know that Maxxie doing bondage with the Japanese hipsters would lead to him running off with some Chinese girl after the ayahuasca ceremony? I mean, Maxxie's always had a thing for Asians. He's even hit on me numerous times. He's half Viking, don't they try to shag everyone?"

Rufus sighed. "Okay, I'm going to Augie now."

"I believe Gopal Das is with her, trying to stage an intervention. She hasn't eaten in days and she's in a very delicate state."

"Duly noted."

"Don't tell them where I'm hiding."

"I won't."

(IN LADY AUGUSTA'S SUITE . . .)

"Breathe through your feet," Gopal Das instructed.

Augie lay on her yoga mat on the floor with a lavender sachet eye pillow strapped to her face, taking deep, heaving gasps.

"That's it. Let the oxygen ground you to the earth. Connect with Gaia. Now repeat after me . . . *My soul is safe.*"

"My soul is safe . . . ," Augie chanted through her breaths.

"My soul is beautiful and strong . . . " Gopal Das lit some dried sage and began waving the smoke over Augie's body.

"My soul is beau-ti-ful and"—she sobbed—"strong."

"I will not be defined by who loves me . . . "

"I will not"—*sob*—"be defined by"—*sob*—"who . . . boo hoo hoo hoo." Augie was overcome with tears. Rufus entered the room and she opened her eyes, looking at him like a pitiable tortoise stuck on its back. "Rufus!" she wailed.

Rufus got down on the floor and hugged his sister. "I'm so sorry, Augie," he said softly as she continued to sob in his arms.

"You are most welcome to lie down and breathe with her," Gopal Das said.

"Oh, okay. What do I do?"

"It's a three-stage breath. The first breath fills your lower belly, and the second breath fills your upper chest, then you exhale it all out."

Rufus nodded. "Just like pranayama yogic breathwork."

"Exactly!" Gopal Das said, impressed that Rufus knew.

Brother and sister began to breathe on the floor in unison, holding hands. Suddenly Augie cried out, "It's all my fault it's all my fault it's all my fault."

"Shall we examine that thought? Why do you think this is your fault?" Gopal Das asked in a neutral tone.

"I allowed it to happen. I was generous and open, I wasn't possessive. When she was vomiting into the bucket after her first dose of the ayahuasca, I told Maxxie to go help her. I mean, there was such an immense amount of honk coming out of her, someone had to hold her hair back. Maxxie loves women in distress, that's his biggest turn-on."

"What I'm hearing is that you are generous and open. What I'm hearing is that you are confident and self-actualized and Maxxie doesn't feel like he deserves you. Repeat after me: *I deserve to be loved by someone who deserves me.* You say it too, Rufus."

"I deserve to be loved by someone who deserves me," Rufus and Augie chanted together as Rufus thought, *I don't deserve to be loved by Eden but she loves me anyway.*

"Gopal Das, something else is coming to me in the breathwork. I don't know if it's a positive thought or a negative one," Augie said.

"Just let the thought out. Let it exist in the universe," Gopal Das said.

"Do you really think Mummy's right? That Maxxie had an Asian fetish and I wasn't quite Asian enough for him after all because I'm only half?"

"I believe Maxxie is in conflict with his body. What his heart desires is at war with what his loins desire," Gopal Das ruminated.

"I can tell you Maxxie's loins desire everyone. Asian, half Asian, it didn't make a difference. He even came on to me," Rufus said.

"HE DID?" Gopal Das and Augie said in unison.

"Loads of times. I think Maxxie is just an equal-opportunity horn-dog."

There was a knock on the door, and Anya the housemaid peeked her head in.

"Sorry. Viscount St. Ives, her ladyship would like to see you in her boudoir at once."

"Tell her I'll be there soon," Rufus said at first, but the look of terror on Anya's face made him change his mind. "Actually, why don't I come with you now."

(IN THE COUNTESS'S BOUDOIR . . .)

Rufus walked into his mother's boudoir to find her lying on her Carlo Bugatti chaise longue, the Korean beauty mask draped over her face making her resemble an Egyptian mummy. What was with all these Gresham women and their propensity for putting things over their faces, Rufus wondered.

"Rufus, is that you?"

"Yes, Mother."

"Why didn't you come to see me at once?"

"I went to check on Augie first."

"Don't lie to me. You went to talk to Bea first, and then you proceeded to Augie. I know everything that happens in this house."

"Not lying, Mum. I didn't realize you needed to see me so urgently," Rufus said patiently.

"Of course I need you urgently! Look what you've done!"

"What have I done?"

"Your poor sister and her disaster of a honeymoon! All this is your doing!"

Rufus took a deep breath and sank into an armchair. "So now it's my turn. First it was Bea's fault, and now it's mine. I'd love to know how I was responsible . . ."

"If you would have gotten engaged to Solène de Courcy like a good boy, none of this would have happened! We could have merged our hotels with the de Courcys' and all our money problems would have been solved!"

"First of all, I was never in love with Solène de Courcy, so nothing would have ever happened. Second, merging Bella Resorts with the De Courcy Group—if the de Courcys would even allow such a thing to happen—would not have solved a thing. But I fail to see what any of it has to do with Augie's problems."

Arabella let out a sigh that sounded a bit like a gurgle through her gooey face mask. "My stupid boy, you are sooo naïve! Maxxie found out that we're going broke and that's the real reason he left Augie."

"Not what I heard. Maxxie apparently fell for some girl who had a vomiting fit."

"That's just what Augie wants to believe, that he married her for love. Maxxie married her for her money!"

"Wait a minute, I thought Augie married Maxxie for *his* money?"

"*Hiyah*, they both married each other for their money, except there is no money left! Maxxie's father is down to his last Bacon and the mama only has a ranch full of useless llamas.* Do you know who that vomiting girl is that Maxxie ran off with? She's not just some random Chinese girl, you know. Rosina told me she was married to several of the richest men in Asia and just won a huge divorce settlement from an Arab sheikh! She's a billionairess who can fund Maxxie's princely lifestyle and his eco-tech dreams."

"Then good riddance to Maxxie! Augie's much better off without him," Rufus said.

"The press hasn't gotten wind of the situation yet, so we need to go into full damage-control mode . . ."

"I think you're overreacting, Mum. Why would the press even care?"

"*Hiyah!* The press will be all over this! Prince Maximillian of Liechtenburg runs off with a cougar billionairess, Kitty something-or-other, in the middle of his honeymoon with Lady Augusta Gresham? I can already see the headlines. We need to preempt this with a bigger headline. You need to announce your engagement to Martha Dung at once!"

Rufus let out a guffaw. "That's not going to happen, Mother."

"Why not? She loves it here. I took her riding around the estate. She loves our cheese farm."

"Martha loves cheese, it doesn't mean she wants to marry me."

"She rented out Boxall Park next door and she's throwing a ball in my honor there! How many more signs do you need that the girl is ready for you to get down on bended knee? You need to go to her at once! Go, go, open the center drawer of my bureau and you will find a ring in there. A magnificent cabochon emerald engagement ring from Faraone Mennella."

---

* *Arabella is wrong on two counts: First, Princess Hanne Marit owns alpacas. Second, llamas are actually tremendously useful. In the Andean cultures, they have for centuries been used as pack animals and as meat. These days, in addition to being livestock guards, their coarse outer hair can be used to make great rugs and wall hangings, making them the perfect hipster pet.*

Throwing up his hands in frustration and summoning his courage, Rufus continued, "It's time you realized something, Mother. The only woman I will ever marry is Eden Tong."

Arabella dismissed his statement with a contemptuous scoff. "No you're not!"

"Tell me, what is it about Eden that you so object to?"

"She's a lying little rat."

"Eden is the most truthful person I know and you owe her an apology for all your deluded accusations."

Even beneath her stiffening beauty mask, Arabella was rolling her eyes. "She's also Chinese."

"Oh, and Martha isn't?"

"*Hiyah,* there is the right kind and the wrong kind of Chinese!"

"Please enlighten me, what is the *right kind of Chinese?*"

"Martha Dung is the right kind. She has an aristocratic bearing, she's not too dark, she's not too short, and she is well educated."

"Eden Tong is beautiful, she's fairer *and* taller than Martha, and she graduated from Cambridge with honors—not that any of that matters a whit to me."

"Martha Dung has the ability to save our lives—"

"That's a funny one! If you had a heart attack this minute, who would you rather have trying to save your life—Dr. Eden Tong, practicing NHS physician, or Martha Dung, cheese lover?"

"Don't be cheeky with me! You know very well what I mean—Eden may know CPR, but Martha can save our resorts, our home, and your future with her billions!"

"There! I wanted to hear you say it. Martha's the right kind of Chinese to you only because of her money!"

"What's wrong with that? Do you not require money to live and breathe?"

"I do, but I'm perfectly content to live off what I make for myself. You know I'd happily live in my surf shack forever!"

"That surf shack cost me five million dollars! Do you have any idea how much it takes to afford your hippie artist life? Do you know what we spend on property taxes for Puako Beach Road? Putting in that new septic system? And you won't even let me Airbnb it when you're not there! When was the last time you sold one of your damn pictures? All you Gresham men are good for nothing. Everyone thinks I won the jackpot the day I married your father. Ha! If only they knew the truth. I've spent decades working myself to the bone trying to restore the family coffers, only to have my own son mock me and accuse me of being money hungry when all I am trying to do is ensure that he has a future!"

Rufus sighed, softening a bit. "Has it ever occurred to you that it's maybe not a future I want? Do you really want to know why I spend so much time in Hawaii? Whenever I'm here, I feel this tremendous guilt for everything that's been given to me. I'm in line to inherit this vast piece of land from ancestors who spilled oceans of blood to possess it, I'm part of this patriarchy that keeps the power in the hands of the very few. And I've done fuck all to deserve any of it!"

"*Hiyah*, listen to you! You don't appreciate your privilege because you've never had to struggle a single day in your life. You have no idea what I've been through, the things I had to do to survive— sharing a rat hole in Paris with twelve other models, being harassed every day by pervert photographers, how much I had to fight as a Chinese woman to gain a single grain of respect in a world that you stride through so comfortably. You don't see any of it precisely because I set it all up for you! If you weren't born the half-British Viscount St. Ives with that jawline of yours, you would understand my pain. You would experience the racism I encounter every single day when I step out the door, and you would have some gratitude for the life I've fought so hard to give you. I don't regret a single thing I've done and I'm not going to apologize to anyone."

"Mother, I know how hard you work, and I am grateful for all you have done. Truly I am. But you didn't raise me to take advantage of anyone under false pretenses, especially when there's another woman I want to marry."

"Obstinate child! I would have thought all that Eden nonsense would be over by now. I mean, you had plenty of time to sleep with her and get her out of your system during your *Thelma & Louise* road trip."

Rufus stared at his mother, not quite believing his ears. "I don't know what you think happened on my road trip, but no one got shot or drove off a cliff,* and Eden's not someone I can just 'get out of my system.' I'm in love with her. I've loved her since the day I first met her."

"Don't be ridiculous, you were six."

"I think I knew even then that she was going to become the most special woman in my life."

Arabella gave him a look of horror, before bursting into tears. "How dare you say that! Your mother is supposed to be the most special woman in your life! *Hiyah,* see what you've done? You've ruined my face mask!"

Rufus shook his head in frustration and left the room.

---

* *No one slept with Brad Pitt either.*

XII

The Cottage

It had been a long day at the clinic catching up on a backlog of patients, and Thomas had just arrived home and was settling into his favorite armchair with a tumbler of scotch and Earth, Wind and Fire on the record player when Diego de San Antonio y Viscaya called from the Philippines.

"Houston, we have a problem," Diego said.

"What's up?"

"I just received a call from our boy Luis's new lawyers. He's hired the biggest ambulance-chasing bastards in Los Angeles."

"What does it matter? Rene's trust is ironclad."

"Yes, but they are waving their dicks and trying to justify their hourly rate to Luis Felipe by challenging the trust. Apparently, Luis Felipe is refusing to go to rehab, so they've decided to sue the trust and jam things up for as long as they can in an effort to postpone the inevitable."

"I was afraid he'd do that. That boy will do anything not to have to confront his own demons. Doesn't he realize we're only trying to help him? Before he requires a liver transplant?"

"I'm sure his liver will be grateful, but the rest of him sure isn't. Those bottom-feeders have been digging around with their forensic accountants and they wanted to know about the promissory notes from the Earl of Greshamsbury."

"What about them?"

"They want to call in those loans."

"They can't without our approval."

"Well, actually, it seems they can. Those loans aren't in the trust."

Thomas bolted up in alarm. "What do you mean?"

Diego sighed. "Apparently, because Francis needed the loans to be secret, Rene made those loans out through an entity in the Channel Islands that exists outside the trust. The entity holds the loans, and until Francis is able to pay it back, it basically owns all of Greshamsbury."

"Can't we put this entity in the trust?"

"Not retroactively. And since the entity holds the only assets that exist outside of the trust's protection, those bastards have pounced on them like a pack of rabid coyotes. Luis Felipe is desperate for funds. It seems he went on a bender in Vegas last weekend and he's racked up quite a few bills."

"I'll bet he has. He has a huge gambling problem."

"Oh, the bills are just for the legal fees after he tried to accost Katy Perry. Apparently he jumped onstage and insisted on doing a duet of 'Roar' with her during her live show."

"Well, she clearly didn't want to hear him roar, did she?"

Diego chuckled. "No, she didn't. On top of having to bail him out of that mess, his lovely lawyers are threatening to launch a lawsuit against *you*."

"Me? For what?"

"Gross negligence, improper conduct, you name it. They claim you had undue influence over Rene, that you were looking after your own interests and forced him to issue those loans to your friend Lord Francis."

Thomas sighed wearily. "Rene lent the money on his own accord and you know that."

"I know that and you know that, but I have to warn you, it may not look good to a jury since you yourself reside on Greshamsbury lands."

"No, I suppose not."

"We need to placate Luis Felipe. Can't Francis pay back part of the loan? A hundred million perhaps? That should tide him over for a year at least."

"Not at his burn-through rate."

"Well, we need to throw him a bone, or he'll go after the whole carcass."

"It would do Luis Felipe absolutely no good to go after the Greshams and render them insolvent. He'd come away with far less money if he did that."

"You try reasoning with the kid."

Thomas deliberated for a moment. "Look, Francis and I are working out a plan to divest some of the resorts and raise cash where we can, but that will take a bit of time."

"Unfortunately, we don't have time. I believe Luis Felipe and his low-rent vampires are threatening to come to Greshamsbury. You know, to kick the tires a bit. They can smell the money, and they're out for blood."

"What other good news do you have for me today?" Thomas said with a grim laugh.

"Sorry to be the bearer of bad tidings. Just wanted to give you fair warning."

"Thank you, Diego. I'll see what I can do." Thomas ended the call, downed his scotch, and got up from his armchair with a small groan. Now, where did he put his Barbour? He needed to go to the Big House and see Francis at once. He walked into the kitchen and found his waxed cotton jacket draped over a chair. He put it on as he walked out the back door and took the shortcut through the box-wood maze up the hill toward Greshamsbury Hall.

When he was almost up the hill, he could hear the rumble of a car coming down the lane. The car seemed to be moving faster than usual for a country lane, and Thomas nearly didn't have time to get out of the way before an old mud-covered Land Rover came speeding up. It was Francis behind the wheel.

"Ah, just the man I was looking for!" Francis said jovially.

"I was on my way up to see you."

"Hop in, I'll drive you back down!" Francis said as Thomas got into the passenger seat. "I just had a call from a fellow named Louis Philippe. Rather amusing chap."

"Amusing? That's not a word I'd ever use to describe him."

"He was jolly and chattering a mile a minute."

"Must be the cocaine talking."

"Har har, very funny. Anyway, the cocaine wanted to know all about Greshamsbury Hall."

Thomas felt a chill go down his spine. "I hope you didn't tell him anything . . ."

"Well, he was mainly interested in knowing whether we had a wine cellar, and how many bottles we had put down, that sort of thing, so I didn't see much harm in telling him."

"He isn't supposed to call you directly."

"Oh, I don't see the harm now that his father's gone. He was very charming, and he's got quite a thing for tawny port, it seems, so I invited him to dinner tomorrow."

Thomas closed his eyes for a moment in utter dismay. "Tell me you didn't."

"Of course I did. He's in London, staying at his flat in Knights-bridge, so I told him to pop over. Did I do something wrong? You've gone white as a sheet."

"Francis, he's coming to case the joint. See how much Greshams-bury Hall might be worth to him if he were to liquidate everything tomorrow."

"Aw, he's not going to do that! Why would he want to call in the loans now when he's got billions at his fingertips? The boy's just inherited everything lock, stock, and barrel!"

"No he hasn't. He's being forced to abide by the rules of a very restrictive trust."

"Don't I know how that feels! We can swap stories."

"Francis, you don't know the boy like I do."

"Well then, I'd like to. Look, we'll put on a charm offensive. I'll bring out a fine bottle of Taylor Fladgate, Margaret will cook up a storm, and Arabella will wow him with her—"

"Fuck! Arabella. The thought of Luis Felipe at her table . . . it's not going to go well, Francis," Thomas said grimly.

"Course it will! She'll be thrilled to entertain him and eager for the strapping young heir to meet Beatrice."

"Not a good idea. You don't want Bea anywhere near him, trust me. He's an alcoholic, for starters."

"Come on, you know alcoholics only exist in America."

"You don't understand. Luis Felipe is almost certain to arrive hammered, high, tripping on toads, or all three. We must prepare Arabella; she'll need to exercise the utmost restraint. I should prescribe her some Xanax before the dinner . . ."

"Oh, she's got plenty of that."

"All the same, I'll come up to the house with you to give Arabella the lay of the land."

"Don't worry so much, Tom. Leave it to us. We've had Fran Lebowitz to dinner, don't you remember? If we can charm her, we can bloody well charm anyone."

XIII

Greshamsbury Hall

GRESHAMSBURY, ENGLAND • *THE NEXT EVENING*

The earl, as usual, was wrong. Arabella was not the least bit thrilled by the idea of receiving Luis Felipe Tan at Greshamsbury Hall, and she was outraged that her husband had so recklessly extended the invitation without first consulting her.

"This is a mistake," she said.

"Mistake or not, we must do this, Arabella. We must charm the young man, and you're so good at that sort of thing."

"I will not be available tomorrow evening. There's a Pick Your Own Offers promotion at Waitrose."

"He's worth a hundred billion dollars, Arabella. Maybe more. Don't you think Bea would like to meet him?"

"My goodness! You're going to pimp out your own daughter just because he's a billionaire? What kind of father are you? Bea is going to marry a gorgeous Greek prince that I've picked out just for her."

By the next day, Arabella had softened a bit and grudgingly accepted that she needed to offer the barest hint of civility to the man who had such outsized control over her present fate. She peeked out the window to see his matte black Sikorsky S-76D helicopter land on the Great Lawn, and she noted that it took two of his bodyguards three minutes to cajole the visibly inebriated young man out of the aircraft. *Let him sober up a bit,* Arabella thought. After making him wait in the drawing room with Francis, Rufus, Thomas Tong, and Gopal Das for thirty minutes, Arabella finally deigned to come downstairs, making an entrance in an oddly casual Catherine Walker pantsuit flanked by Bea and Augie.

Francis beamed in relief at the sight of them. "Ah, here they are! Luis Felipe, may I present my wife, Arabella, and my daughters, Augie and Bea."

"*Countess* Arabella, the Princess Maximillian, and the Lady Beatrice," Arabella icily corrected her husband, before giving Luis Felipe the once-over. *What a ghastly common face. And look at the cut of his dinner jacket—must have been made by Italians.*

I'm gonna fuck with this snotty bitch, Luis Felipe thought as he bowed ceremoniously at the ladies. "*Cuntess* Arabella, which part of China are you from?"

Arabella gave Luis Felipe a withering look. "I'm from Hong Kong."

"Really? My dad was born in Hong Kong."

"I thought he was Filipino."

"Nope. Moved to the Philippines in his twenties, but he grew up in Wan Chai. Isn't that where you're from?" *Like all the prostitutes.*

"No, I grew up in Kowloon Tong. Was your mother from Wan Chai?" Arabella shot back.

"She was from Shenyang, but she met my dad in the Philippines. I was born in Forbes Park." *In a house much bigger than this old dump and with three times the servants.*

"I don't know the Philippines. I believe some of the maids we had growing up came from Cebu."

Thomas, not wanting the exchange to degrade any further, quickly cut in. "Lady Arabella, Luis Felipe and I were just discussing the superb artwork over the mantel. The Judy Chicago."

"Yeah, is that thing spinning? I swear to god it's spinning," Luis Felipe said.

Arabella rolled her eyes. *It's spinning because you're drunk as a skunk.* "That lithograph is not spinning."

"Perhaps you could give Luis Felipe a tour of the art collection? He's quite the collector," Francis merrily suggested.

"Oh, he won't be impressed by our collection," Arabella said. *Not enough big-dick art for you, I'm sure.*

"Here, let me show you some of my favorite artworks . . . ," Rufus politely offered.

"Hold your horses, Sad Keanu, I'd rather your daddy show me his famous wine cellar," said Luis Felipe.

"Yes, show him the wine cellar, Francis," Arabella said. *And drown him in one of the barrels while you're at it.*

As soon as he was out of earshot, Thomas turned to Arabella with an imploring look. "I realize he's a handful, but for your own sake, will you *please* try to be gracious to him?"

"Oh, am I not being gracious enough? Should I do a little lap dance like one of those nice ladies in Wan Chai? Do a trick with Ping-Pong balls?" Arabella said mockingly.

"Arabella—"

"Don't Arabella me—he was being an offensive little prick and he bloody knew it!"

Rufus stepped in. "For once I have to agree with Mum. If he wasn't too pissed to feel it, I'd smack him in the face."

Thomas sighed in resignation.

Francis and Luis Felipe returned from the wine cellar and everyone adjourned to the dining room, where footmen awaited behind each chair around the banquet table. With a subtle nod from Hemsworth, the footmen began to fill every guest's wine goblet simultaneously. "Fill it to the brim," Luis Felipe said to his footman as he glanced around the table. "Wait a minute, someone's missing. Where's your daughter?"

"Both my daughters are right here," Francis said.

"No, I meant Tong's girl. Where's the disapproving Eden?"

Everyone at the table remained silent, so it fell on Thomas to respond, "Eden could not be here tonight."

"She had better plans?"

"Working late, I believe," Rufus said.

"I just saw her walking up the hill," Gopal Das said, unaware of the fatwa against Eden at Greshamsbury Hall.

"So she's home!" Luis Felipe said.

"I would think so," Gopal Das continued, puzzled as to why Augie kept pinching his thigh.

"Don't you guys live next door?" Luis Felipe asked.

"We do," Thomas replied.

A mischievous look came over Luis Felipe's face. "She's avoiding me, isn't she?"

"Not at all."

"Then tell her to come join us now."

Thomas looked beseechingly to Francis. "Oh yes, of course. Hemsworth, could you get someone to run over to the cottage and ask Eden to join us?" Francis said, deliberately avoiding his wife's furious stare.

"Yes, my lord," Hemsworth replied.

Fifteen minutes later, just as the asparagus bisque was being served out of the Puiforcat tureens, a rather mystified-looking Eden entered the dining room in the same flowing black floral dress she had worn to Augie's wedding ceremony, her just-showered hair hastily slicked back and bold red lipstick quickly applied. Sensing the awkwardness in the room, she quickly greeted everyone as if nothing had ever happened.

Luis Felipe whistled as he looked Eden up and down. "Wowza! You clean up gooooood! Where was this girl in LA?"

Eden smiled wanly, taking a seat that had been hurriedly added at the far end of the table.

"Wait, come sit next to me. Cuntess Arabella, why don't you switch with her?"

Arabella took a sharp breath, too incensed to speak.

"That is the countess's seat. The countess always sits across from the earl, to the right of the honored male guest," Thomas explained.

"Turban dude, switch with me. You're the honored male guest now." Luis Felipe got up and moved to take Gopal Das's seat between Augie and Eden. "Can't escape me now!" Luis Felipe said, jabbing Eden on her bare shoulder. "So, tell me why you're avoiding me."

"I had other plans. You came on such short notice," Eden said diplomatically.

"I can always come on short notice." Luis Felipe snorted at his own joke. "So . . . hot date? Matched with someone on Hinge?"

"Nah, I much prefer meeting random strangers at pubs."

"Aha! You *are* avoiding me! You'd rather be at the pub hooking up with strangers than at a dinner in my honor," Luis Felipe continued to tease.

"For fuck's sake, Eden's not avoiding you! She wasn't invited to dinner!" Augie suddenly blurted out.

"Oh. Why? Eden, did you do something naughty?" Luis Felipe teased.

"She's persona non grata because Mummy has a ridiculous grudge against her," Augie said.

Francis cleared his throat loudly. "Augusta, are you feeling out of sorts?"

"I am not out of sorts. In fact, I'm feeling better than I have in days."

"You've been sick?" Luis Felipe asked.

"No, just sad. You see, my husband left me for another woman who's much richer and sexier." Arabella and Bea gasped audibly, but Augie ignored them. "I've had enough of this bloody farce, and I'm sick of never saying what's on my mind. It's exhausting and soul depleting, isn't that right, Gopal Das?"

"It is if it makes you feel that way," Gopal Das replied.

"Cuntess Arabella, why the ridiculous grudge against Eden?" Luis Felipe asked.

"I do not have a ridiculous grudge," Arabella responded dismissively.

"Then explain to our honored guest why Eden's been banished from this house and for all intents and purposes the village," Augie said.

"I'm just not a fan of deceit in my house or my village," Arabella said lightly.

Eden was about to respond when Rufus spoke up in her defense. "How has Eden deceived you? She hasn't done a thing!"

"Eden tried to deceive me and failed pathetically, but she succeeded in deceiving you. You're just too much of a simpleton to see it."

Thomas Tong stood up and looked across the table at his daughter. "Eden, let's go."

Rufus glanced at his mother angrily. "Look, you've offended Dr. Tong with your delusions!"

"I have no delusions. You're the one that still won't accept that Eden seduced Freddy Farman-Farmihian just to make you jealous."

Luis Felipe winked at Eden in amusement. "You've been boning the little Persian?"

Eden shook her head wearily.

Arabella doubled down on her accusations. "Not only did she bone the little Persian, but she slipped up and got herself preggers! And yet my gullible son has fallen for her tawdry little scheme."

Luis Felipe's jaw dropped. "Wait, wait, I can't keep up. Eden's knocked up with the Persian's spawn and Pretty Boy Hapa's in love with her too?"

"Precisely," Arabella said.

Eden threw down her napkin in a fury. "For fuck's sake! I'm going to say this one last time: I've never slept with Freddy, and I've never been pregnant, not that anything I do is any business of yours!"

"What you do becomes my business when you lure my son into your little web! How do you explain the pregnancy test I found in your hotel suite?"

"Where is this test? Where did you find it? I never once saw a pregnancy test while I was in Hawaii!"

"IT WAS MY PREGNANCY TEST!" Bea shrieked from across the table.

Every head swiveled to Bea in shock as she continued. "Yes! I threw it away in Eden's bathroom! I'm the one who's pregnant!"

Francis and Arabella were too shocked to speak, but Rufus blurted the question on everyone's mind: "So . . . who's the father?"

"It was that hula hunk at my wedding, wasn't it? Josh. You two were all over each other," Augie said.

"I am the father," Gopal Das declared.

"Not funny," Augie snorted.

"I'm being serious," Gopal Das said as he walked over to Beatrice and placed his arms around her shoulders affectionately. "Augusta, your sister and I are twin flames. We discovered this about each other the very first time we met."

"I've found my soul mate," Bea declared, looking up at him adoringly.

"No. No . . . this can't be. *Sei gwai! Sei gwai!*"* Arabella muttered, trembling in shock.

Augie promptly burst into tears. "Why is every man I know leaving me?!"

"I'm not leaving you, Augie. Don't you see that more than ever we are family now?" Gopal Das said soothingly.

"No you're not. You're not ever going to be part of this family. I want you to leave this house at once!" Francis commanded, gripping his chair arm in white-knuckled fury.

Gopal Das said, "As you wish, Lord Greshamsbury," and turned to leave the room without further dissent.

"No, Papa, nooo!" Bea cried. "Rufus, stop him!"

Rufus scowled at Bea. "Why didn't you come to Eden's defense when Mum was spreading all these lies about her?"

Bea started to sob. "Oh, Rufus, you have no idea what I've been through! I've been so scared and panicked and I've had to hide this so long so I wouldn't upset Mummy! Eden, I'm so sorry!"

Eden glanced over at Bea, unable to mask her hurt.

Luis Felipe began to laugh maniacally. "Eden, you're way too good for these fuckers. I thought this dinner was going to be tedious as shit but this is the most fun I've had all week! You people treat me

---

* *"Dead ghost! Dead ghost!" in Cantonese, an insult directed toward Gopal Das that would be the equivalent of "Monster!"*

like I'm not good enough to set foot in this house, but it turns out you're just a bunch of lying hypocrites!"

"What are you talking about? We've done nothing but roll out the red carpet for you!" Arabella shot back.

"Oh yeah? You've been so fucking condescending, insulting me at every opportunity and thinking I'm too wasted to notice."

"You *are* wasted!"

"I'm wasted because I have to look at your putrid face! You're nothing but a sad broke bitch married to a pathetic loser with a mediocre wine collection. Well, guess what? Your pee is still gonna stink of asparagus just like mine, and your daughters may call themselves ladies but they're really nothing but whores."

Before he could help himself, Rufus bolted out of his seat and decked Luis Felipe right across the face, sending him tumbling backward in his chair and onto the ground. His bodyguards stationed by the door of the dining room didn't even have time to react.

"You fucker! You broke my nose!" Luis Felipe raged as he got up, holding his hand to his bloody nose.

"You can insult me all you want, but I draw the line at insulting my family!" Rufus yelled back.

"Yeah? You can go rot in hell with your fucking family! I want all my loans repaid within thirty days. Every single penny! Otherwise, I get this house, and the first thing I'm going to do is throw all of you out on your bony royal asses!"

XIV

The Enterprise

WALTON STREET, LONDON · *ONE WEEK LATER*

"There she is!" Rufus said to Eden as he spotted Martha entering the restaurant. He waved to her from their corner banquette at the back of the room. As Martha wove through the lunchtime crowd, looking like a Chinese Georgia O'Keeffe in her starched white blouse, camel prairie skirt, black fedora, and vintage silver squash blossom necklace, Eden got up and greeted her with a big hug. "So lovely to meet you at last!"

"You're real! I'm so relieved! I was half suspecting that Rufus had made you up so that he wouldn't have to marry me!" Martha said.

"Go for it—he's all yours!" Eden replied as both of them laughed heartily.

"What a charming place—the food smells amazing! Sorry I'm late, I couldn't resist a bit of shopping," Martha said as she tried to find space to stow her heaps of shopping bags.

"Ooh, you went to Egg!" Eden said.

"You know it? I thought I was the only one who knew about Egg!"

"It's one of my favorite shops!" Eden replied.

"See, I knew I was going to like you!" Martha said with a wink as the waiter approached their table to take her drink order. "I'll have a dirty martini." Martha glanced at her lunch companions questioningly. "Too early?"

"Not at all. Make that two dirty martinis," Eden said.

The waiter nodded and looked at Rufus. "Refill on your beer?"

"I'll switch to a martini as well," Rufus said.

"Wait, Rufus, will you please do me a favor?" Martha jumped in. "Will you please say 'I'll have a vodka martini . . . shaken, not stirred.' "

Rufus stared up at the ceiling in embarrassment. "Okay, here goes: I'll have a vodka martini . . . shaken, not stirred."

The waiter chuckled as Martha clapped. "Perfection, I think I just jizzed in my pants. Don't you love his accent, Eden?"

"Rufus has a great voice, but you know how it is, the grass is always greener on the other side. Personally, listening to a Southern gentleman gets me weak in the knees. You know, like Sam Shepard. Or Matthew McConaughey."

"Oh no, not me. He sounds overly medicated to me. Speaking of which, dare I ask . . . is the countess still barricaded in her room?" Martha asked.

"Day seven now," Rufus replied. "She went upstairs the moment Luis Felipe left the house and has refused to talk to any of us since."

"Classic move. My mom does it all the time, except she checks herself into her favorite Buddhist monastery and throws away her phone. It's her way of letting me know she's mad at me."

"That's not very Buddhist of her," Eden commented.

"Exactly what I tell her!" Martha said. "How's everyone else holding up?"

"Not so good. The house is a complete war zone at the moment—Bea and Augie are holed up in opposite wings, not talking to each other, and my father's huddled day and night with his bankers and solicitors in the library. It's quite a relief to be in London!" Rufus reported.

Martha gave Rufus a wry smile. "Well, I wish I had better news for you on my end. My lawyers have informed me that Luis Felipe wouldn't even deign to respond to our offer. It's all or nothing for him."

"Thought that might be the case," Rufus said lightly, although it was apparent to both women that he was quite let down by the news. He had called Martha earlier in the week, desperately seeking her

advice, and she had surprised him by offering to buy over the entire
debt to Luis Felipe if he was willing to accept it in installments over
the next twelve months.

"I'm really sorry, Rufus. If I didn't have to answer to my board
and the shareholders, I'd maybe have more wiggle room. But there's
just no way we can raise all the funds by the end of the month. Damn
corporate governance rules!"

"No need to apologize. It was incredibly kind of you to offer your
help in the first place. I knew raising all that money would be an
impossible task," Rufus said.

"To be honest, I don't believe the money will help at this point. I
think Luis Felipe is hell-bent on punishing your family. He doesn't
want the money—he wants you all kicked out of the house."

Rufus put his face in his hands in despair. "It's all my fault. I
shouldn't have hit him. I don't know what came over me."

Eden placed a hand on Rufus's back. "Don't beat yourself up over
this. He bloody had it coming to him—he was being off-the-charts
offensive to everyone."

"Mum was being off-the-charts offensive to you but you didn't get
up and smack her."

"That's different."

"Hmm, not sure about that. You're just a saint, that's all. You've
been putting up with us Greshams for far too long."

"The world has been putting up with Luis Felipe for far too
long!" Martha chimed in. "He's notorious, that boy, I used to read
about him on the gossip sites all the time. He was always trashing
hotels, nightclubs, casinos, you name it. I believe he's banned from
Switzerland—apparently, he tried to import plutonium from Russia
while he was at boarding school there. He was fourteen and trying
to build his own nuclear device! I think the only way he could get his
father's attention was by behaving badly."

"And with his father gone, I suppose he's got nowhere to channel
all his grief and rage except on us," Rufus said with a sigh.

"You know, I think maybe I should try talking with him. As offensive as he was the other night, I was mostly spared from his wrath. Maybe I can make an appeal to him," Eden suggested.

"Don't waste your time," Rufus scoffed.

"I think it's worth a try. There's a glimmer of humanity somewhere within those reptilian eyes, I've seen it."

"I understand why Rufus adores you now—you always look for the best in everyone. I'm the opposite—I'm a paranoid, jealous little rat," Martha said.

"I find that hard to believe," Eden said with a laugh.

"Look, you're doing it again. Jeez, Rufus, she's a keeper. You guys can come live with me if you really have no place to live. Where would you prefer to be . . . Sydney, Venice, Hong Kong, or San Francisco?"

"You have houses in all those places?" Eden asked, wide-eyed.

"Those are the city houses. I might also have a few country houses," Martha whispered, suddenly looking bashful.

The waiter returned with a tray of dirty martinis. "Just in time. Let's order some lunch while we discuss where we should live. I'm famished," Rufus said.

XV

Rutland Gate

After having been given the grand tour of Cloudline in Los Angeles, it didn't faze Eden the slightest bit to discover that Luis Felipe's London abode consisted of four town houses joined together to create one sixty-two-thousand-square-foot monstrosity overlooking Hyde Park. She was let into the embassy-sized foyer by one of his ubiquitous bodyguards, escorted up the grand staircase by another, and ushered by a third into the vast living room flanked by huge Basquiat paintings on each end.

There she found Luis Felipe slouched on the capacious curved sofa, staring blankly as *The Sound of Music* played on mute against the projection screen hanging from the ceiling. Scattered around him was the detritus of his addictions—empty glasses, wine bottles, and a smorgasbord of illegal substances along with a bowl of half-eaten ramen.

"I had a nanny who would play this movie over and over for me. Every time that horny nun sang 'Edelweiss,' she would just cry and cry," Luis Felipe said as Eden entered the room.

"That's very sweet."

"I had her fired. I told my dad she was touching me in my swimsuit area when she wasn't. He had her deported."

Eden didn't react to his story. She simply sat down on one of the club chairs across from him.

"She was the nanny before the one in middle school I paid to ride me reverse cowgirl."

Eden gave him a chiding look. "That nanny didn't really exist, did she?"

Luis Felipe smirked. "No, she didn't. How did you guess?"

"I had the unfortunate pleasure of hearing your lawyer tell that story about you being taken to Macau to lose your virginity . . ."

"Oh yeah, the brothel story. That didn't really happen the way he told it. My dad did send me to a brothel, but he didn't bother to come watch."

"You know, I've observed you over the past few weeks, and it's clear to me that you're much smarter and more sensitive than you let on. Why do you find it necessary to make up these stories?" Eden asked.

"I'm just trying to have a little fun."

"You have a strange concept of fun."

"Yeah? Ever had any fun? Like, have you ever really let go of all your inhibitions and gone wild?"

"I don't need to go wild to have fun."

"Ever done shrooms?"

Eden rolled her eyes.

"How about MDMA? LSD? Dmitri? Georgia Home Boy? Aunt Nora? Or just some good ol'-fashioned smack?"

"No thank you. I've treated my fair share of heroin addicts, and I've seen how it's utterly destroyed their lives."

"That's because it was shit heroin. I'm going to a party this weekend in Nevada that's going to be epic. They always have the *finest* heroin, like Château Lafite–level stuff. You should come. You'll experience what real fun is for once in your life."

"I don't actually think you're having much fun, Luis Felipe. I think you're trying to numb your pain . . ."

"Oh thank you, Dr. Freud, or is it Missus Jung? Can you tell I'm grieving over my dead daddy? Is it that obvious that I'm in pain? Let me tell you something, Eden Tong. The day my father died was the first day I felt truly free. It was the happiest. Fucking. Day. Of. My. Life."

"You don't really mean that."

"Fuck you. You sit here judging me, but you don't have a single clue about my life. You haven't walked in my shoes for one second. Do you know what it's like to be the son of Rene Tan? Do you know how many lives he ruined? The thousands of people who died working on his construction projects around the world? Any clue how many cover-ups there were? You only knew him during the last week of his life, when he was eighty percent butternut squash and twenty percent lusting after your snatch."

Eden sighed, recalling her promise to Rene. *Be nice to my son.* "I'm sorry, you're right. I didn't really know your dad, and I haven't the faintest clue what your relationship with him was really like."

"So you want me to tell all? I don't need a pity party from you," Luis Felipe said bitterly as he faced away from her, looking out the window.

"That's the last thing I wish to do. I'm just here to listen, that's all."

"My dad was one cruel skullfucker. He wouldn't let my mom see me—he called her a bad influence and tried to show me a sex tape that he'd secretly recorded of her. Can you fucking believe that? He slept with my first girlfriend and then he told me she was only after my money and he was trying to teach me a lesson. Everything with him was a lesson, it was about toughening me up and preparing me to manage his great and glorious fortune after he was gone. And now look what he's done. I put up with his torture for twenty-three years of my life, and now he's trying to fuck me from the grave with this whole trust bullshit!"

Eden looked him in the face while he ranted. All she saw was a hurt, lonely boy behind all that rage. "If you feel that he was so cruel, why would you want to perpetuate that? You don't really want to throw the Greshams out of their house, do you?"

"Are you kidding? I can't wait to evict those self-satisfied fuckers."

"You do realize that by evicting them, I'm going to be homeless too. The cottage is part of the estate."

"I'm not going to evict you or your father, don't worry. In fact, I think you should move into the Big House. That'll teach that snotty Hong Kong *tai tai* a lesson!"

"I have no interest in living at Greshamsbury Hall."

"That's bullshit. You've secretly fantasized about being the lady of the manor your whole life."

"I really haven't."

"So you're not trying to ensnare the cuntess's precious son?"

"I think you know the answer to that."

"Fräulein Eden's not going to marry Count Rufus von Trapp in a grand cathedral?"

"He's a viscount, and nope, no plans for a cathedral wedding."

"Great. Then why don't you marry me?"

"You don't really want to marry me." Eden laughed.

"I do."

"Look, I'm not marrying you. You're clearly blitzed and you're not being serious."

Luis Felipe got up from the sofa and bent down before her. "Look, I'm getting on my hands and knees. What else do you want? A ring from motherfuckin' Tiffany? Marry me and come live with me at Greshamsbury Hall. Can you just see the looks on their faces when we pull up in a friggin' carriage?"

"You're just doing this to piss off Rufus."

"I could give two fucks about Count Chocula. You know what my dad told me the last time we talked? He said, 'That Eden Tong is a class act. You should get to know her.' "

"Getting to know me doesn't require a marriage proposal."

"Yeah, but I think I'm ready to settle down, have a bunch of kids. Fill up this house. You know there are twenty bedrooms in this house? We could have nineteen kids and not even notice them."

"No thanks. My uterus wouldn't survive."

"I was joking, I only want one kid to terrorize and ruin. Tell you what—if you marry me, I *won't* force the Greshams out of their house."

"I'm not going to play this game with you again. Not when there are real lives at stake. You're about to uproot a family from a house that they've lived in for eleven generations. I know it's not a house you even want to live in—it'll be a massive downgrade."

"You're right about that—it's a sad country shit shack."

"Then do the decent thing. I know you're a decent person, even though you pretend otherwise. Let the Greshams keep their house and take Martha's generous offer."

"Lemme ask you something. Why are you so loyal to that family, when they treat you like dirt?"

"They don't! Look, Arabella might be impossible at the moment, but she's acting under duress. She's in shock over losing her resort, she's dealing with an avalanche of family and business issues, and I'm the convenient release valve for her at the moment. I know she'll come to her senses."

"Yeah, when hell freezes in my asshole. Arabella will never accept you as her daughter-in-law as long as she lives. You think you're just the whipping post this week? You'll always be the whipping post. I see the way she looks at you, I know she thinks you're trash, just the way she thinks I'm trash. I know her type—she's one of those Asian bitches who hates other Asians. That's why she married the Earl of friggin' Sandwich. She only wanted half-white babies, and now she only wants even whiter grandbabies. But you know what? You can't see any of that because you're blinded by love for her son. Admit it, you're tragically, pathetically in love with that half-breed." Luis Felipe crawled slowly on his knees toward Eden's armchair as he said this.

"I love Rufus, and there's nothing pathetic about that."

"You've never kissed an Asian man in your life, have you?"

"Rufus is Asian."

"The hell he is." Luis Felipe sprang up suddenly and kissed her sloppily on the lips.

Eden jerked her head back, wincing. She could smell a week's worth of booze on his breath.

"What, think you're too good to kiss me? Think you're too damn classy?"

Eden rose from the armchair and marched toward the door. "Class has nothing to do with it. You need to get help, Luis Felipe. Before it's too late."

"Blah blah blah!" Luis Felipe said, sinking back on the floor against the armchair. From where she stood, Eden couldn't help but notice that the sad, angry face in one of the Basquiat paintings exactly mirrored his.

XVI

Greshamsbury Hall

GRESHAMSBURY, ENGLAND • *THE NEXT AFTERNOON*

Rufus woke up to a text from his dad summoning him home. It was something his father had rarely done (he didn't think his dad even knew how to text), so Rufus made a point of driving direct from London.[*] Upon arriving at Greshamsbury Hall, he went straight to the ballroom as instructed. The vast room, rarely used by the family, today resembled a war room, with folding tables lining the space and piles of financial and legal documents covering every available surface. Seated on the neoclassical marquetry floor was Thomas Tong, surrounded by knee-high stacks of documents.

"Dr. Tong! Didn't expect to find you in here," Rufus greeted him.

Thomas barely looked up. "Hello, Rufus."

"I just dropped Eden off at the cottage."

"Ah, she came back with you? I thought she was going to stay in London all week."

"She changed her mind," Rufus said. "You've been here long?"

"Since breakfast. I'm helping your father sort things out."

"You've been helping Father sort things out for as long as I can remember now."

---

[*] *Just like airline website terminology, "direct" doesn't mean "nonstop." Rufus made a slight detour for lunch at Le Manoir aux Quat'Saisons on the way to Greshamsbury, because who in their right mind would ever pass up the opportunity to wander along their lavender-scented footpaths and partake in Le Café Crème—Raymond Blanc's signature dessert of coffee parfait and kirsch sabayon, coffee caramel, chocolate ganache, and chocolate sauce all served in a chocolate cup with a handle?*

"I have, haven't I?" Thomas said distractedly.

"Why do you do it? Why do you put up with the whole lot of us when you don't have to?"

Thomas put down the file he was reading and looked up at Rufus thoughtfully. "I've known your father since we were thirteen, and we'd been through a fair bit before you came along. I can't tell you how many times he came to my rescue on the cricket pitch, not to mention at our social.* Radley in my time was quite different than in yours."

"I'm guessing it wasn't easy for you back in those days . . ."

"I was five feet two until about fifteen, and my hair stood out like porcupine quills. What do you think? Everyone called me 'Chang'—you know, from *Tintin*. But having your dad on my side meant I never had to worry about getting my head shoved into the latrine. You recall he also captained the rugby team."

"He'll never let me forget that. Well, thanks anyway for always being on Dad's side. Where is he, by the way?"

"Upstairs with your mum, I believe. He's been gone for ages."

"I guess this means she's speaking to him again."

"Apparently so. I hear there's some new twist in the plot with Beatrice that necessitated the détente."

"If they're hashing things out with Bea, I think I'll leave them be."

"Oh, Bea's long gone."

"Where did Bea go?"

"Not sure, but she and Gopal Das slipped away two days ago without telling a soul."

"Ah. I'm guessing that's why I was summoned. I should go up."

"Don't sound so excited about it."

Rufus grinned.

"Do try to get your father to come back down, will you? I can't make heads or tails out of this mess," Thomas grumbled.

"I'll try my best," Rufus said as he trudged up to his mother's bedroom, dreading whatever disaster awaited him there. He found his

---

* *"Socials" are Radley-speak for the boardinghouses on campus that students live in.*

mother seated at her Montigny-stamped *bureau plat* while his father slumped on the Koloman Moser settee facing her, looking like a dog that had just been punished.

"Good afternoon!" Rufus said with forced cheeriness.

"Ah, good, good. You're back. Pack your bags. You're going to Venice today," Arabella commanded.

"Venice? You'll need to catch me up," Rufus said.

"Bea's eloped to Venice with Gopal Das," Francis said simply, handing a note to Rufus. Written on Bea's stationery in her florid handwriting was the following:

Dear Mummy and Papa,

Martha Dung has graciously invited Gopal Das and me to her palazzo in Venice, where she will host an intimate wedding ceremony for us. Afterward, we have been offered the use of a marvelous seaside house in Byron Bay where Gopal Das will teach a series of workshops under Martha's patronage. Gopal Das has also revealed to me that he is the beneficiary of a small trust fund from his family in America, so you see we shall not be a financial burden to you in any way. I will have my baby in Australia and will be a respectable married woman if and when I ever return to England with my child. You will no longer have to worry about or be ashamed of me bringing disgrace onto the Gresham name. I hope you in time find the grace to forgive me. I am, for the first time in my life, leading with my heart.

Love always,
Bea

"Well, that's sorted. Are we all going to the wedding?" Rufus asked.

"Going to the wedding? Are you a complete moron? I want you to go to Venice to *stop* the damn wedding!" Arabella shrieked.

"Bea's in love with Gopal Das, and he's always been a decent chap as far as I'm concerned. Why disrupt their plans?"

"Precisely what I told your mother," Francis chipped in as Rufus continued trying to reason with his mother.

"Bea's obviously doing all this to please you, don't you see? She thinks you're ashamed of her, so she's run off to get married without any fuss. Instead of making her feel even more guilty, we should be supporting her, especially at this moment. She's pregnant with your first grandchild!"

"YOU were supposed to give me my first grandchild! Not my youngest daughter, who is still a baby herself. Everything is out of order!" Arabella cried.

"Bea's the same age as you were when you had Augie. Maybe having this baby will be the best thing to happen to her—it will give her some purpose beyond going to parties and attending perfume launches," Rufus reasoned.

"Do you know how important going to perfume launches is? I've spent years carefully crafting Bea's brand, and we were so close to getting an endorsement deal!"

"She can still do all that if she wants to, can't she?"

"Not if she marries the Hindu!"

"If Gopal Das was the maharaja of Jaipur, would you still be objecting that he was Hindu?"

Arabella paused for a moment, clearly caught. "But he's not the maharaja! He's a *haam sap lou** who preyed on my baby! What's wrong with you? Why aren't you defending your own flesh and blood? Maxxie humiliated your big sister—you should be hunting him down and whipping him till he has permanent scars! You know what the problem is? All this British breeding has bred the balls out of you, along with that silly woke school of yours! I should have sent you to Gordonstoun.† Why do I always have to do everything for

---

* *"Horny old man" in Cantonese (and it even sounds pervy when you say the words).*

† *The legendary boarding school in Scotland much beloved by Prince Philip and much detested by his son King Charles III, who was made to go on shirtless runs (no matter the weather) and take ice-cold showers every morning, and where his classmates eagerly boasted of kicking him in the testicles at every opportunity during rugby practice.*

this cursed family? If neither of you will go to Venice to stop this travesty, I'll just have to do it myself. I will not let Bea throw her life away. Anya! Tatiana! Luggage, now!" Arabella screamed into the intercom on her desk.

Francis gave his son a weary look. "There's no reasoning with her when she's like this. Come, let's talk in my room."

They left Arabella's boudoir just as the housemaids were arriving with Arabella's monogrammed Globe-Trotter luggage and headed down the hallway into Francis's dressing room. Shutting the door behind them, Francis immediately poured two tumblers full of Dalmore single-malt scotch and handed one to Rufus as he sat down.

"To your health," Francis said, sinking into his favorite wingback chair with a little groan and taking a big gulp. "I appreciate your coming home on such short notice . . . I needed to discuss something with you in private. I had the most peculiar conversation with Luis Felipe Tan's solicitor early this morning. Perhaps you might have already heard?"

Rufus looked at him, confused. "How would I have heard?"

"Well . . . uh . . . Luis Felipe's solicitor informed me that he'd be willing to accept the loan repayment scheme proposed by Martha Dung and drop all claims over Greshamsbury Hall—"

"Oh thank god! He finally came to his senses!" Rufus cheered, taking a swig of his scotch.

Francis gave his son an uneasy look. "Um . . . he does have one condition: Eden must agree to marry him."

Rufus almost choked on his drink.

"I'm guessing Eden hasn't discussed this with you?"

Rufus sighed. "Eden tried making an appeal on our behalf to Luis Felipe last night and yes, he did propose marriage, but she didn't think he was serious. He was high as a kite, apparently. That man's a sadist . . . he's doing this to torture me, to torture all of us!"

Francis sighed. "Obviously, I don't expect Eden to give a moment's thought to such an outrageous proposition."

Suddenly Arabella burst into the room, her eyes ablaze. "What are you talking about? Of course Eden must marry him!" Rufus glared at his eavesdropping mother as Arabella gleefully continued, "For once in her life that girl can do something useful for us, and I know she will do it! She's a good girl!"

"Oh, so now she's a good girl?" Rufus snorted contemptuously.

"Silly boy, don't you see? Let her marry Luis Felipe, and in a few years when we're able to retain control of everything again she can divorce him if she wants. But she'd be stupid to if she thinks she'll ever do better than him."

Rufus took a deep breath, struggling to contain his anger. "I'm going to try to forget you ever said that."

"No, you must convince her to marry that man!"

"In case you've forgotten, Mother, I intend to *marry* Eden, not talk her into marrying someone else!"

"You will marry Eden Tong over my dead body! It's time to let go of your childish fantasies and fulfill your duty to this family. We are days away from living in the gutter and it's all your fault!"

Rufus let out a mordant laugh. "You're not going to pin this on me. If you hadn't run Eden out of Greshamsbury, she would never have gone to LA and met Luis Felipe in the first place! None of this would have ever occurred! Don't you see that all roads lead back to *you*?"

Arabella groaned in frustration. "Francis! Stop sitting there like a damn dummy! Talk some sense into this useless boy!"

Francis rose from his armchair and—one of the few times he had ever done so—shouted at his wife. "Don't call our son useless! He's the kindest, loveliest, most wildly talented man I've ever known! There's only one person to blame for this whole mess and that's *me*. I was too much of a coward to tell you the truth about our finances! I let you spend like there was no tomorrow! I'm responsible for every penny we owe and now we just have to pay the piper, that's all. Rufus, my darling boy, I hope you can forgive your damned fool of a father for losing everything you were meant to inherit under my watch."

"There's nothing to forgive," Rufus said softly. "I've watched you shoulder the burdens of being the Earl of Greshamsbury all my life, and quite honestly, it's not something I'm cut out for. I see how hard you've fought to restore the house and keep up the Boxall Hunt, the way you try to improve the estate and worry over the lives of every single family in the county. I know how much you love this land, but I've never felt the same connection to it as you have. Maybe it's because I'm part Chinese or maybe it's because I've spent so much time in Asia, but I feel so much more at home in Hawaii. I could live in a shack in Waimea for the rest of my life and be happy with my surfboard and my Leica."

"Son, you'll do better than that. Eden's a brilliant doctor, and if you're lucky enough to marry her, I know you'll always be taken care of," Francis said.

The men hugged tightly as Arabella sat there seething.

"Come, Rufus, let's go to Venice. I want to be at Bea's wedding. She needs her father there to walk her down the aisle!"

"Super! I think Eden will want to come," Rufus said with a grin.

"Of course she must come!"

"How dare the two of you . . . ooh! Ooooh! I think I'm having a stroke . . . ," Arabella whimpered as she began giving little slaps to the side of her face.

"You always think you're having a stroke, but unfortunately you never actually do!" Francis roared, storming out of the room.

XVII

Mount Nicholson Road

THE PEAK, HONG KONG • *LATER THAT DAY*

The elegant verandah of the art deco–style bungalow situated on what was arguably the most expensive residential street on the planet boasted three-hundred-and-sixty-degree views all the way from Victoria Peak to Deep Water Bay and the outlying islands of the South China Sea. Rosina was enjoying the glorious view with her morning *yu juk** and reading the gossip column in *The Post* when she came across this item:

> Martha Dung will unveil her newly restored Venetian palace for the wedding of Lady Beatrice Gresham and Whitney Payne Cabot V, a descendant of the illustrious Boston clan. Lady Beatrice is the Eurasian daughter of Count Rufus Gresham† and Hong Kong–born Countess Arabella Gresham. The countess is the sister of Peter Leung. Lady Beatrice's sister, Lady Augusta, recently married Prince Maximillian of Liechtenburg, and her brother, Viscount St. Abs, is rumored to be engaged to none other than Martha herself. No doubt many highborn families from Asia, Europe, and North America will be in attendance.

---

* *"Fish congee" in Cantonese. Rosina's chef prepared her rice congee with dried scallops, fresh pomfret, abalone slices, delicate slivers of ginger, and a sprinkling of golden fried shallots.*

† *It should be Lord Francis Gresham, of course, not Rufus.* The Post *needs to hire better fact-checkers.*

Rosina immediately picked up her phone and dialed Arabella's number. The call went straight to voicemail, so she left a message:

"Arabella! My goodness, I go on safari for two weeks and look what happens!* Bea's getting married! And Rufus engaged to Martha! You must be on cloud nine!"

Twenty seconds later, her phone rang—it was Arabella on the line, sounding like she had a stuffy nose. "I'm screening my calls."

"I figured. Where's our invitation to the wedding in Venice? Peter will be very hurt if he doesn't get an invitation even though he is far too busy to attend."

"There are no invitations—at least, not from me. I'm not going to any wedding."

"And why not?"

"My daughter is dead to me. My useless husband, my useless son, my other useless daughter, they are all rotting corpses as far as I'm concerned."

Rosina rolled her eyes. "*Hiyah!* What happened? Isn't Rufus getting engaged to Martha? That's what *The Post* is reporting."

"For once I wish the gossip in *The Post* were true. No, the boy that was once my son is too stupid to get engaged to Martha. He has been ensorcelled by that witch Eden Tong."

"Eden Tong! There's something about that girl that has always bothered me. I've never quite put my finger on it . . ."

"She's a scheming little *ghat jat*.† She is the architect of our destruction. Twelve generations of Greshams have lived at Greshamsbury Hall, and all of it is to be lost now because of this cursed girl. *Sum toong, ah!*"

"At least Bea's going to be marrying into American royalty . . ."

"What are you talking about? Bea's marrying a ghastly charlatan ten times her age only because she's pregnant with his child!"

"My god!" Rosina gasped.

"My god is right! I tried to convince Rufus and Francis to defend

---

* *Rosina wasn't actually on safari. She was in Seoul getting a very subtle brow lift.*

† *"Cockroach" in Cantonese.*

her honor, but they ignored me and took off for Venice to celebrate this tragic union. Francis has treated me terribly; you won't believe the horrid things he said to me. You know what I've realized? I am the victim of racism within my own family! I don't have a drop of British blood, but the rest of them all do, which is why they've ganged up on me like this," Arabella cried.

"You poor thing," Rosina sighed supportively as she googled "Whitney Payne Cabot V" on her phone. Some pictures from a family wedding in Nantucket immediately popped up. "Oh wait, she's marrying that long-winded shaman from Augie's wedding? The one with the iridescent turbans and the beard?"

"That's the one. I think he must have lice in that beard."

"He may have lice, but at least he *is* a Cabot!"

"What's that?"

"*Hiyah,* don't you know? The Cabots are an old-guard family from Boston! Haven't you heard the saying 'Where Lowells speak only to Cabots, and the Cabots speak only to God'? The Kennedys, Vanderbilts, Rockefellers—they're all peasants compared to the Cabots."

"Are you sure? Is the family so old that they've lost all their money? He behaves like he's penniless."

"Arabella, he's a WASP. They all behave like they're penniless. They're exactly like all the frightfully grand Brits that you know."

"Grand or not, Bea's about to disgrace herself. She's going to be bulging obscenely in whatever wedding gown she wears, and that ginger guru will be dressed up like a Bollywood clown. I can't be there to witness it, I just can't, I will never stop vomiting with shame. *Hiyah,* kids today have no shame. In our day, who could have imagined being visibly pregnant when you got married? It was unheard of! It's still considered shameful in Asia, am I right, or am I old-fashioned?"

"Of course it is. My boys might have gotten a few of their girlfriends and mistresses pregnant here and there, but those are mistresses, *never* the wives. I remember when my dear friend Mary Gao got pregnant, it was so unfortunate. She desperately wanted to keep the baby and we all had to gang up on her and convince her that it would ruin her life! Imagine trying to be an unwed mother in Hong Kong! She would have been finished, no one good would have married her. And she had to marry money! Her family was respectable but not very rich, and her only asset was her beauty. She was a former Miss Hong Kong, you know?"

"A Miss Hong Kong pregnant out of wedlock? What a scandal! What happened to her?"

Rosina sighed sadly. "*Gam seui, ah!*[*] She flew secretly to Perth to have an abortion, but shortly afterward we heard she died of sepsis. She was one of my closest friends, and I never got to say goodbye. It happened so suddenly, and you know what, the strangest thing of all is how——" Rosina suddenly let out a gasp before going very quiet.

"Rosina? Are you there?"

"*Hiyah,* how am I so stupid! It's been staring me right in the face this whole time . . . ," Rosina muttered to herself.

"What's staring you in the face?" Arabella asked, confused.

"Arabella . . . where's Thomas Tong now?"

"I have no idea. He's no longer my doctor," Arabella said coldly.

"I mean, is he in England, Asia, America?"

"I would assume he's right down the road in his tiny sad cottage."

"Sit tight. I'll call you back. I may have unearthed something . . . to your benefit. Trust me, this is going to change everything!"

"What? Tell me!" Arabella demanded.

Rosina hung up without another word.

---

* *"So cursed!" in Cantonese.*

VI

VENICE

Connie looked at Venice far off, low and rose-coloured upon the water. Built of money, blossomed of money, and dead with money.

—D. H. LAWRENCE

Coron, 2013

They were speeding past tiny atolls in the most crystalline blue waters Thomas had ever seen. With the spray of salt water on his face and the sun on his back, he felt invigorated after his twenty-plus-hour journey from England to this remote island chain in the Sulu Sea. This trip had been six months in the making, and after the most delicate of negotiations, under the cloak of intense secrecy, he was finally going to meet Rene Tan, the mysterious financier who had agreed to lend Francis Gresham a hundred million dollars, off the books.

Thomas glanced at the silent man sitting at the back of the boat, a semiautomatic rifle lodged between his feet. The speedboat pulled up to the jetty of an island, and as Thomas disembarked he could see in the distance a magnificent sleek glass house peeking out through the dense tropical foliage. Soon, he was ensconced within the compound of this private estate, seated on an antique wooden chair with incongruously long arms, drinking ice-cold kalamansi juice and gazing out at a beautiful lagoon.

Behind him came the gravelly laugh of a man's voice. "Do you know what the chair is for?"

Thomas turned around and saw a man in his fifties, thick around the middle but robust in stature, dressed in a nylon jogging suit and baseball cap. "I don't," Thomas said, rising from the chair to shake his hand.

The man did not extend his hand. Instead, he said, "That's a nineteenth-century birthing chair. The woman puts her legs up on those wide arms, and it helps position her when she goes into labor."

"Of course," Thomas said. "You must be Mr. Tan?"

"Indeed I am."

"You've got quite a place here. It's the most beautiful private island I've ever been to."

"You go to many private islands?"

"This is my first, actually."

"Mine too. No one invites me anywhere. I'm not fit for polite society, you know. All the Filipino grandees, they'll do business with me, but I'm never invited over to their country estates in Calatagan or their resort villas in Punta Fuego. Which is why I created this paradise for myself. Now of course they are all begging to be invited, but I don't have many people over. Truth be told, I hate rich people. Most of them are motherfucking bores. The older the money, the more intolerable to me. You know, I credit two people in the whole world for making me who I am. The first is Enrique Tan—"

"The industrialist who built much of the modern Philippines," Thomas remarked.

"Yes, you've heard of him. I was his partner on most of those projects. I did all the dirty work, and when he died, childless—well, he had a few bastards here and there but no official kids—he left me the business. And I expanded into construction in South America, Central Asia, and Africa. I'm the one who made this business big-time."

"I see. And who was the other person who helped you?"

"Your father. Dr. George Tong."

Thomas stared at him in surprise.

"You don't have a fucking clue who I am, do you?"

Thomas shook his head.

Rene let out a conspiratorial laugh. *"Let me give you a clue."*

He led Thomas into the next room, a vast, elegant drawing room filled with contemporary tropical wooden furniture. By the fireplace that was large enough to roast a whole cow was a Bösendorfer concert grand piano. With the flick of a button, the piano began playing by itself. Debussy's *"Clair de Lune."* A chill went up Thomas's spine as he approached the piano. Sitting on the ledge of the piano was a single silver-framed photo of Thomas's wife.

Eden's mother.

THE EARL OF GRESHAMSBURY
REQUESTS THE PLEASURE OF
YOUR COMPANY AT THE SOUL UNION
OF HIS DAUGHTER

BEATRICE *with* GOPAL DAS

AT PALAZZO GATTOPARDO
VENICE, ITALY
SATURDAY AT 6 P.M.

FORMAL OR CULTURALLY
SENSITIVE ATTIRE

I

HOTEL BAUER

Wearing Jacques Marie Mage sunglasses, a Pucci headscarf, and a vintage loden-green Ungaro swing coat, Arabella emerged from the elevator and approached the gleaming black marble reception desk.

"I believe there's a package waiting for me," she said to the man in the navy suit with the face of a Bronzino youth.

"*Buongiorno, signora.* What is the name?"

"Tina Chow," Arabella answered.

"Ah yes, Signora Chow," the young man replied, rifling through a stack and handing over a large DHL envelope. Arabella took the envelope and walked over to one of the art deco club chairs in a quiet corner of the lobby. With trembling hands, she tore open the envelope and slid out a slim burgundy leather folder. As she paged through the materials couriered to her by Rosina in Hong Kong, she could feel her heart thumping excitedly. Rosina was right—what she had managed to unearth over the past forty-eight hours with her team of private investigators not only benefited her, it was a game-changer.

Arabella discreetly placed the precious folder into her Camille Fournet tote bag and walked out the door onto Campo San Moisè. She strolled down Calle Larga XXII Marzo past all the glitzy boutiques, thinking how sad it was that Venice had succumbed to the curse of every city and was now filled with the same brands selling their imitation of luxury to the masses. Halfway down the block, she turned down a tiny narrow lane that led to the Hotel Flora. Passing the quaint wood-paneled bar, she emerged into a secret courtyard garden charmingly overgrown with ivy and saw the person she was there to meet seated at a table in the back corner, punctual as always.

"You came," Arabella said, sitting down on a white wrought iron chair across from her.

"Yes, Lady Arabella," Eden replied civilly, even though she was still furious with her.

"Are you staying at the Aman?"

"No. Why does everyone I bump into keep asking me that?"

"You wouldn't understand. You're sure you weren't followed?" Arabella asked as she glanced around the garden. The only other guests were an elderly couple enjoying their tea next to the burbling stone fountain.

"I don't believe so."

"Where did you tell Rufus you were going after you got my text?"

"No one asked me anything. Everyone's busy preparing for the wedding. Why all this cloak-and-dagger business?"

"I don't want anyone to know I'm here."

Eden rolled her eyes. "You haven't decided whether to attend the wedding, have you?"

"No, I haven't."

"You know the wedding's postponed until next weekend so that more of Gopal Das's family have time to get here? I'm sure Bea would be happy if you came."

"So you've forgiven my daughter?"

"There wasn't much to forgive. I was very upset at first, but I understood why she did what she did. She wasn't trying to hurt me intentionally—she was much more afraid of hurting you."

Arabella took off her sunglasses and gave Eden an assessing look. After a few moments, she continued, "You know, when Francis first asked my permission to let your father and you come live next door to us in Greshamsbury, I have to be honest, I was hesitant. I wondered whether it would be a good idea for my children to live so close to a little girl from Texas who had just lost her mother. Over the years, I've come to see how genuinely devoted you are to my children."

"I love them," Eden said simply.

"So how can you just sit here and watch our lives get destroyed? Within a fortnight, we will all be thrown out of Greshamsbury Hall forever!"

"Lady Arabella, you do realize that my father and I will be losing our house as well. I have no memory of another home besides the cottage."

Arabella paused for a moment. She had clearly not thought of that at all, but it occurred to her that she could use that to her advantage. "All the more reason for me to ask you why you are doing this to yourself. Why are you so intent on destroying your own life, as well as ours? Are you that heartless?"

"You know perfectly well I am not. I'm absolutely gutted about everything that's happened to your family, ever since the first volcanic fissure at your resort. I know how devastating it must be for you to see all your beautiful work destroyed, to see Augie's marriage fall apart so soon, to—"

Arabella swatted away her words of support. "You say all this, and yet you could solve all our problems by simply marrying Luis Felipe Tan."

"Lady Arabella, Luis Felipe doesn't actually want to marry me. He's trying to pull an outrageous stunt and push us all to our limits. Money is meaningless to him. Do you know when I was in LA, he offered me three million dollars just to attend a party at his house?"

"Did you take the offer?"

"Of course not."

"That was stupid of you."

"This is just an escalation of the game he's playing. He knows I would never marry him, that I have no intention of getting married in the first place."

Arabella snorted. "But you dream of marrying Rufus!"

Eden shook her head calmly. "No, that's always been your assumption."

"So now you're denying that you love Rufus?"

"I'm not denying that at all. I do love him. I'm simply saying that it was never a dream of mine to marry him, or anyone for that matter. I don't sit around having Cinderella fantasies like you seem to think that I do. Look, in my regular life I work seventy hours a week and I'm allotted six minutes per patient. Do you know how overburdened the NHS is? I don't usually have the time to attend balls in palaces made out of ice."

"You say you love my Rufus, so how can you bear to watch him lose his birthright? To lose Greshamsbury Hall and everything we've been preparing him for his entire life?"

You don't know your son at all! Eden wanted to shout it in Arabella's face, but she restrained herself. "Rufus has told me about a thousand times since the absurd offer came in that he would much rather lose everything than see me married to a psychopath with addiction issues."

"Send him to a shrink! Send him to a rehab! People can change. You and Rufus have your head in the clouds! Rufus has no idea what he's about to lose. He's just like Luis Felipe—he has no clue what it's really like not to have money, not to be in possession of his lands. And tell me, when will you ever have an opportunity like this again? You complain about your workload. If you marry Luis Felipe you will never have to work another minute of your life. You will want for nothing. Every couture house will be clamoring to seat you in the front row of their shows. I'll even introduce you to my vendeuse at Chanel. You can sit beside me at the shows."

"Lady Arabella, I love what I do, and I have absolutely no desire to sit in the front row of a Chanel show. If I'm ever fortunate enough to afford couture, I'd much rather spend that money on charitable pursuits."

Arabella laughed derisively. "You know what your problem is? You are so self-righteous, you think you're better than the rest of us just because you're Florence Nightingale."

"Florence Nightingale was a nurse. I am a doctor."

"See what I mean? One little degree from Cambridge and you think you're god's gift."

"I was simply stating a fact."

"Yes, but you say it with such conceit. You don't know your place. You never have. Well, let me enlighten you on something. You are not who you think you are. Your entire existence has been one big lie."

"What do you mean?"

"Your father's been lying to you for your entire life. You are not really his daughter."

Eden wondered if Arabella had gone temporarily insane. "What are you talking about?"

Arabella removed the burgundy folder from her tote bag and slid it across the table slowly. "This is your real birth certificate. You were born in Vancouver, Canada, not Houston, Texas. Your mother's real name was Mary Gao. She was a beauty queen . . . She won Miss Hong Kong in the early nineties. Rosina knew her. When Mary found herself pregnant, she ran off to Canada and secretly had you. At some point your father came into the picture, adopted you, and got you a new birth certificate. All these secret documents unearthed by Rosina's investigators prove it."

"Rosina hired private investigators for this?" Eden paged through the folder, not believing her eyes.

"The best in the world, the best that her money can buy. Your father has deceived you your whole life. He's actually your uncle, and your biological father is his brother, Henry—a gambler, a reprobate, an addict. So you see, I wouldn't judge Luis Felipe Tan so harshly if I were you."

"Where . . . where is Henry now?" Eden stammered.

"He was killed by Mary's brother during a bar fight at the Peninsula Hotel in Hong Kong. Here's the headline to prove it."

Eden glanced at the article clipped from the *South China Morning Post* in the 1990s, feeling her body go numb. "So you unearthed all this . . . for what? What does it matter to you who my biological father was? How does this change anything? Whether my mother was a beauty queen or the queen of Sheba, I'm still never going to be good enough to marry your son."

"I am just doing you a favor, I thought you'd want to know the truth. I know you've always yearned to know more about your mother. Now, we can keep this information just between the both of us. No one need ever know, not even my son . . . provided you agree to marry Luis Felipe."

Eden stared at Arabella incredulously. "So let me try to understand what's happening . . . you were given this information by Rosina and you say you're doing me a favor, but what you're really attempting to do is blackmail me. You got your hands on these secrets and you've made a decision to weaponize them. You want me to sacrifice myself to Luis Felipe so that you can continue living in your picture-perfect manor house."

"I don't think it's too much to ask, is it?" Arabella said coolly.

Eden could feel her whole body on fire. "All my life I've tried to look up to you as a mother figure, but somehow I always knew that you could never play that role. You are around my mother's age, you are Cantonese, but even as a very young girl I could sense that you had closed yourself off to me. I have never once been impolite to you, I've always taken great care to be on my best behavior around you, but no matter what I do, I always sense your disapproval. You resented it when I became close to your children, you were always trying to put me in my place as some sort of foundling you had done a tremendous favor. For so many years I would rack my brains thinking, *Why doesn't she like me? What did I do wrong?* It's taken me until now to realize why. It's not what I've done, or what my lineage might be—it's who I am. I'm Chinese. I can't ever change that about me, and I wouldn't want to. But you hate that about me, because for some reason you hate that about yourself. And you may try to find every excuse in the world to deny it to everyone—you may unearth secret documents from halfway around the world claiming that I'm illegitimate, that I'm trying to deceive Rufus, but really, you're only deceiving yourself. You've succeeded in destroying your own life, and now you're trying to destroy your children's lives, but let me promise you one thing: you will never destroy mine!"

Eden rose from the table trembling under the force of her own words and chucked the folder right in Arabella's face. The countess gasped in pain as the edge of the folder cut into her skin, but for the first time ever, Eden resisted her natural impulse as a healer. She turned around, marched across the garden, cut through the dimly lit hotel parlor, and emerged onto the startlingly crowded street. A tour guide holding a stick with a yellow rubber duck at its end led a large group of tourists around the street. *"Die Straße hat ihren Namen von dem historischen Tag des 22 März 1848, als die Venezianer die Habsburg vertrieben und erneut die Republik ausriefen. Hier finden sie die exklusivsten Geschäfte der Stadt wie Giorgio Armani, Gucci, und Dolce and Gabbana. J.Lo und Ben Affleck waren gestern hier einkaufen."* Eden felt her body turn to putty as she was pulled along with the crowd; she felt as though she couldn't breathe. She looked down at the intricate patchwork of cobblestones as they began to spin and spin and she collapsed to the ground.

II

PALAZZO GATTOPARDO

SAN MARCO, VENICE, ITALY • *SAME DAY*

She was drifting under, deep within the lagoon. The water was dark and murky with glimmerings of deep green and gold. She felt herself sinking deeper and deeper, enveloped in the warm ancient waters, lontar leaves and kelp brushing against her skin as tiny translucent fish darted past. She looked down and saw a light glowing in the distance, and as she swam toward it, she saw a woman suspended vertically in the water, her body absolutely still, draped in a diaphanous white goddess gown, its gossamer fabric undulating around her like jellyfish tentacles. As she got closer, she recognized the porcelain-white face of her mother. Her eyes were closed; her long eyelashes had tiny water bubbles at their ends. Her face emanated serenity and calmness. Suddenly her eyes opened, and they gazed at her, filling her with so much love. Her mother's mouth opened, huge water bubbles emerging as she spoke. Even through the cloak of water she could understand every word: *He's keeping you safe.*

She came closer and her mother enfolded her in her arms. Then suddenly behind her came a flurry of motion, the water churning furiously as gigantic white wings unfurled from her back, opening majestically, moving slowly with the current, then in an instant, with one big flap, they began to rise, their bodies ascending through the water and surfacing into the air. Eden gasped, taking in her first gulp of air as she bolted up in the bed and saw a figure silhouetted in the darkness.

"Mama?"

"It's me, Rufus," Rufus said as he moved onto the bed. Eden looked at him for a moment and then started sobbing uncontrollably. Rufus held her in his arms and stroked her back as she cried.

"Shhhh . . . it's okay . . . you're okay," Rufus said soothingly. "It was just a bad dream. You're safe. You're here in Martha's palazzo."

"How did I get here?"

"Gopal Das was passing by as you fainted on the street. He picked you up and took you back here. Don't you remember?"

"I remember now," Eden rasped, her voice hoarse from crying. They lay there together and after a while, they got out of bed and moved onto the loggia, where there was a little bistro table with two chairs facing the Canal Grande below.

"I'm going to get you a drink," Rufus offered. He left the loggia and came back a minute later with a tall glass of iced tea.

Eden took a few gulps of the refreshing drink, her mind coming back into focus. "I didn't have a bad dream. I had a beautiful one. I saw my mother . . . she was right there in front of me. She embraced me and spoke to me."

"Could you understand her this time?"

"Yes. Very clearly this time. She said, 'He's keeping you safe.' Whatever did she mean by that?"

Rufus smiled. "Don't you see? You fainted and Gopal Das was right there to help you. He kept you safe."

"I don't think that's what she meant. Maybe she meant you. Or maybe it means nothing," Eden moaned, and cradled her head in her hands. "My brain's so bloody scrambled after seeing your mother."

"My mother's in Venice?" Rufus looked surprised.

Eden nodded as she began to tell him everything that had transpired that morning. She told him of the secret meeting at the Hotel Flora, the shocking documents that Rosina had purportedly unearthed, and how it all ended.

"I may have scarred your mother for life," Eden said matter-of-factly.

"Fucking hell, she deserved it!" Rufus stood at the stone balustrade shaking his head. "I can't believe this. I can't believe this," he kept repeating.

"Doesn't it all sound so crazy? I kept looking at the papers, thinking they had to be fake . . ."

"Actually, I'm not referring to what Rosina's investigators dug up, I'm referring to my mother. Why would she want to hurt you like this? It's beyond vicious . . . it's unforgivable!"

"So you think it's all true?"

Rufus pondered it for a moment. "I have no idea—I didn't see any of what you saw. I'm only sorry it had to come from my mum. Why on earth would she think she could blackmail you like this?"

"She thought I'd want to hide it from you."

"Why would it matter to me who your parents were? They could both be ax murderers and I'd still love you!" Rufus scoffed. "Actually, I already know your parents—I know your mother through the memories you've shared with me, all the visions and dreams you've had of her over the years. And I know your father, the good doctor who's raised you. I love him for molding you into the beautiful, amazing woman that you are today."

Eden gazed tenderly into his eyes. "Oh, Rufus, I wish you could have been there with me! You could have properly examined everything in that folder. You'd make better sense of it all than me. I was so shocked, I didn't know what to think. Has my father been lying to me my entire life, or could your mum have had those documents faked?"

"I wouldn't put it past her. She's so desperate right now, she'd do practically anything. I bet you Rosina helped her cook up this story. Your real mother was Miss Hong Kong, and your real father was Thomas's brother . . . who was murdered by your uncle? It's all so far-fetched!"

"And yet . . . it's as though I've found a few pieces of a very large puzzle that I've been trying to construct my whole life, and some of these pieces actually fit. My mother . . . in every dream I've ever had of her she's appeared in some fantastical ball gown. I always thought it was just my childish fantasies, but I suddenly have these flashes of memories . . . seeing footage from beauty pageants. I think my mother used to watch videos of her pageants when I was very young. Was she really Miss Hong Kong? Why would Dad hide this from me all these years?"

"Why don't you just ask him?" Rufus suggested.

Eden looked at him hesitantly. "I suppose we could . . ."

"Call him right now. You've always had such a marvelously open relationship with your father; nothing's changed about that. So ask him point-blank. Pull the bandage off right now."

"Pull the bandage off," Eden repeated as she took a deep breath and grabbed her phone. Her father's line rang for a few minutes and then went to voicemail.

"I guess he's with a patient," Eden said, slightly relieved he hadn't picked up.

"Text him," Rufus suggested.

"I have no clue where to begin . . . what should I ask?" Eden fretted.

"Just ask him what's on your mind."

Eden tapped on the text icon and noticed that there was already a text waiting for her from her father. Scanning it, she gasped out loud.

"What happened?" Rufus asked in concern. Eden handed him her phone, and on the screen was a text from her father:

Thomas Tong: Flying to LA again. Luis Felipe overdosed at a music festival. He's in a coma. Please keep confidential.

III

CEDARS-SINAI MEDICAL CENTER

LOS ANGELES, CALIFORNIA • *THE NEXT DAY*

"After I stopped tripping, I got up from the bearskin rug and noticed that his face had turned blue. I shook him but couldn't get him to wake up, so I called his bodyguard, who was just outside our tent."—*Rae Anne [last name redacted], beauty influencer*

"I gave him Narcan and we did multiple rounds of resuscitation while we waited for the heli-evac. After nine or ten minutes of CPR, we managed to get his pulse back."—*Zvi, head of security for Rene Tan Enterprises, former Mossad agent*

"We were midflight when his oxygen saturation began trending downward, leading us to intubate. He went into pulseless ventricular tachycardia (V-tach), so we shocked him to regain a pulse."—*Walter, paramedic from Ultra Concierge Emergency Heli-evac Services*

"Upon the patient's arrival, his CT head scan was negative for any signs of bleeding, but it was clear to us that he had a catastrophic anoxic brain injury due to oxygen deprivation."—*Kevin, attending physician at Cedars-Sinai Medical Center, Los Angeles*

"It's the same sad story. We found fentanyl in his system, no doubt mixed into the cocaine. Every few weeks we get one of these rich kids OD'ing on coke laced with fentanyl. They think just because they're paying top dollar it's going to be safe, but these days with all the shit coming through Mexico and China, it's like playing Russian roulette."—*Gina, Toxicology Unit, LAPD*

"We were having so much fun. Machine Gun Kelly had just performed. We all went back to Luis Felipe's amazing tent, which was decorated like a chalet in St. Moritz, and laid out on these giant white onyx trays was, like, an all-you-can-eat buffet of drugs. Like mounds of cocaine, crazy-expensive gummies, and pills and inhalants and injectables I never even knew existed. I actually only took a few edibles. I was fascinated by the packaging."—*Petra, graphic designer*

Thomas hadn't been able to sleep a wink throughout the twelve-hour flight to Los Angeles. He spent all his time ruminating on what more he could have done to help Luis Felipe and which top specialists he could call on now to help save his life. But all his hopes evaporated when he was shown into the Intensive Care Unit and set eyes on the patient in the bed, a breathing tube in his mouth and a tangled nest of other tubes and lines protruding from every limb, connecting him to the machines that were keeping him artificially alive. He knew at that moment that there wasn't much that could be done for Luis Felipe Tan.

The lawyers Diego San Antonio y Viscaya and Jane Carlisle were already in the room, sitting somberly on metal chairs as they all gazed at the strangely sunken boy almost lost beneath machines.

The attending physician quickly brought Thomas up to speed. "Dr. Tong, we had two physicians do a brain stem reflex test. His reflexes have been nonresponsive and his brain function has been absent for almost twenty-four hours now. We have kept him on the ventilator as instructed, but we really could have pronounced him dead on arrival."

"He's really not here anymore. It's interesting, isn't it? You can tell the soul has left the body," Diego said, almost in a whisper.

Jane dabbed her eyes with a wadded-up Kleenex. "I watched this kid grow up. He was a sweet child, a bit ADHD maybe, but I couldn't help but think that he just needed his mother and father. Those nannies Rene kept in every city were never a good substitute for real parenting. Sure, he kept all of them on staff for years, but there was never any consistency with the nonstop jet-setting. Luis Felipe would be handed off from Alice in LA to Mons in Hong Kong to Berna in Manila, and Rene would just trot him out like a show pony whenever he wanted to win over a new girlfriend. None of those women wanted to be a mother to Luis Felipe. Nanette, maybe, was the only one who really cared for him. I was sorry when she fell for that guy from Intel and broke up with Rene. After that, the kid never had a chance."

Thomas sank onto a chair, grasping his head in despair. "I feel like I've failed him. I've failed his father."

"You did everything you could, Thomas. I've watched you try to help the boy for almost a decade now. Remember the first time he overdosed when he was fourteen at Amanpulo? When all the doctors back in Manila wanted to keep medicating him and pumping him full of drugs and you said, 'Stop, stop all of it and just let everything clear his system!' You saved his life then, as you did many times after. Lugano, Jesus, remember that one? There were only so many times you could save his life," Diego said.

The attending physician looked at Thomas intently. "Dr. Tong, given the circumstances, we are ready to pronounce him brain-dead. Because he has a well-documented history of substance abuse, he's not a candidate for organ donation. As his medical proxy, do you give us permission to remove him from the ventilator?"

"Can we please send in Father Jose first?" Thomas suggested.

"Of course," the doctor said.

The Catholic bishop who had flown in from Manila with Diego came into the room, and Thomas and the two lawyers bowed their heads as the bishop made the sign of the cross and began incanting: "I commend you, my dear brother Luis Felipe, to Almighty God, and entrust you to your Creator. May you return to him who formed you from the dust of the earth. May holy Mary, the angels, and all the saints come to meet you as you go forth from this life. May Christ who was crucified for you bring you freedom and peace."

Thomas nodded after the last rites were said, and the doctors turned off the ventilator and removed all the lines and tubes from his body. Then everyone left the room and headed into a private lounge that was reserved for ICU guests.

"I need a moment," Thomas said before ducking into the nearest toilet. Locking the door, he turned on the tap full blast, leaned against the sink, and began to sob silently.

After a few minutes, he blew his nose and splashed water on his face. His phone vibrated in his pocket, signaling an incoming voicemail, and Thomas went to check it. It was from Eden.

"Hi, Dad. How is Luis Felipe? I hope he's going to pull through. Listen, I know this is the worst possible time, but I need to speak with you urgently. Arabella came to Venice and showed me some astonishing documents. Who is Henry Tong? Please call me the moment you can."

It was as though the ground had suddenly fallen away from Thomas's feet. He felt his stomach clench into a tight ball. He had known this moment might someday come, but he was wholly unprepared for it now. At the same time, he knew Eden so well, and it pained him to hear the distress in her voice. He quickly returned to the lounge, where he found both lawyers answering emails on their phones. Diego looked up when Thomas reentered. "There's a café called Lady M down the street. Perhaps we could head over there to deal with some legal formalities?"

"Actually, that will have to wait. I need to leave right now," Thomas said with an unmistakable sense of urgency. "I must get back on a plane. My daughter needs me."

IV

THE GRITTI PALACE

CAMPO SANTA MARIA DEL GIGLIO, VENICE • *THE NEXT DAY*

The water reflecting off the Grand Canal sparkled on the handsome teak deck of the Riva Lounge, where Rufus was seated watching the glamorous lady in the sleek wooden speedboat arriving at the dock of the Gritti Palace hotel. She wore red sunglasses, a black and white polka-dot dress that flapped elegantly in the breeze, and a matching hat the size of a flying saucer. As she stepped off the boat, every head seated in the terrace restaurant swiveled to register this chic eyeful.

For as long as Rufus could remember, his mother had reveled in making entrances. She was always the last to arrive at any party and even showed up at weddings late, fully conscious that she was upstaging the bride. No wonder she had been a model—she thrived on perpetually having all eyes on her, while he couldn't imagine anything worse. Even though Rufus was furious at her, the decorum that had been ingrained in him since birth compelled him to stand up and greet his mother with a double-cheeked kiss as she approached the table. "You look like Sophia Loren," he said.

"Thank you," Arabella said cordially. "You need to trim your sideburns before the wedding. They're beginning to look like pubes."

Rufus rolled his eyes. "I would assume from your outfit that you're no longer trying to be incognito in Venice?"

"I ran into Peter Marino at the Ca' Pesaro, so everyone knows I'm here now. Have you seen the show there? Raqib Shaw. It's simply astonishing, the most breathtaking enameled cloisonné paintings that will break your heart. You know, Rufus, if you insist on keeping up this art thing you really should switch to painting. Make them very big, like the Anselm Kiefers in the Doge's Palace. Big paintings sell for so much more than those tiny photographs of yours."

Rufus clenched his jaw. "As much as I'd like to chat about my artistic process with you, that's not why I'm here today."

"No, you're here to scold me, I know. *Cameriere, vorrei un Bellini.* Do you want one too? *Due Bellini, per favore.* You know I haven't had a single Bellini yet? I tried stopping by Harry's yesterday but I walked in and it was filled with Japanese tourists, so I immediately turned around. Every one of those women was wearing a sun visor and a fanny pack. Can you believe they are allowing people with fanny packs into Harry's? I don't care if it's a Chanel fanny pack, it's still the end of the world, I tell you."

Rufus slumped in his chair, exasperated. "I don't know how you do it, Mum. You sit there judging everyone in the world except yourself."

"That's not true. I judge myself all the time. I judge myself every morning before I walk out of the house and see my public."

"I wonder if you realize the harm you cause with your words. I somehow developed an immunity to your gibes long ago, but you've managed to give both your daughters eating disorders."

"It's impossible for a woman to be beautiful without an eating disorder."

"That's what I mean—that's the kind of talk that's just batshit bollocks! Do you realize that every single conversation we have, whether it's on the phone or in person, consists of your endless litany of criticisms?"

"Chinese mothers show love through criticism."

"You always say that, but that just doesn't excuse your behavior. I've learned over the years not to internalize everything you say, but you need to know the damage you're inflicting. You've tortured poor Bea to the point where she felt she needed to hide her pregnancy from you, and Augie—I don't even know where to begin. She dreads every call from you. All her meditation and mushrooms—she does all of it to cope with you. But all of this pales in comparison to the way you've treated Eden—"

"There we go! I knew this was going to be all about that girl. What, did she run crying to you? Look what she did to me!" Arabella lowered her sunglasses for a moment, revealing a small gash on her left cheek.

"I'm sorry, but I don't have much sympathy for you today. That little cut will heal, but you might have damaged Eden irretrievably."

Arabella snorted. "I did her a favor! I provided her with the truth!"

"Is any of it true? Or is it all just lies that you and Rosina cooked up?"

"The only person who has been lying to Eden is her father," Arabella shot back.

"But you couldn't resist being the one to break the news to Eden, could you? And then you had the audacity to try to blackmail her with it. Have you not a single ounce of compassion left in your heart?"

Arabella said nothing for a moment. She looked out to the dome of Le Zitelle, the iconic church on Giudecca island, looming in the near distance.* If she squinted and looked past the motorboats to the gondolas bobbing along the waterway, it almost seemed as if a Canaletto painting had come to life. There was only one Canaletto at Greshamsbury Hall, purchased by the earl who liked to dress up in butterfly costumes in the early nineteenth century, and she had moved it from the dining room to her bedroom. The more she thought of that precious painting ever becoming the property of Luis Felipe Tan, the madder she got. "What do you know about compassion? You have no compassion for what I'm going through. Here you are, having a jolly holiday in Venice when I'm desperately trying to save us from being thrown out on the streets by that druggie bastard!"

---

* *Officially known as the Church of Santa Maria della Presentazione, but commonly known as Le Zitelle, the church was created to assist poor girls, those of marriageable age but too poor to have a dowry.*

"Luis Felipe is dead."

"I only wish."

Rufus looked at her in surprise. "You haven't heard? The poor bugger overdosed two days ago in the California desert. They just unplugged him from life support."

Arabella went silent for a moment, processing the enormity of the news with a renewed sense of dread. "So what happens now? Who are Luis Felipe's heirs? Who's next in line to throw us out?"

"I haven't the faintest clue. Luis Felipe didn't have any children, as far as I know. Just a bunch of animals. Maybe we're going to be evicted by a Chihuahua."

Arabella groaned audibly. "You really don't give a damn, do you? You've been released from the inconvenience of having to live up to the responsibilities of your birthright, and now you can just run wild on a nude beach in Hawaii."

"Of course I give a damn. You know I'd do anything in the world for our family. But I didn't cause this mess, and I've tried everything possible to help, but I just can't fix it. I wish you'd stop trying to make me feel guilty about it. Greshamsbury was lost to us long before that volcano erupted. Stop making all our lives hell by trying to change things you can't. Stop trying to change me. I'm never going to live up to the fantasy of what you want me to be, and neither will Bea nor Augie."

"I don't have fantasies, I only have hopes for my children. Until you become a parent, you will never understand what I go through, worrying myself to death about what's to become of all of you in the future! But obviously I've wasted my whole life worrying about you ungrateful children!"

"We are not ungrateful. I'm not, anyway. But I do know that if you can't find it in your heart to be happy for us and to love us for who we are right now, the next few decades are going to be bloody lonely for you!"

Rufus rose from his chair and paused before departing. "I'm going to a family lunch now to welcome Gopal Das's parents to Venice. If you care to join us, we're going to be at Osteria Enoteca Ai Artisti."

Arabella remained at the table as Rufus stormed off. A water taxi pulled up at the dock, and she noticed a short queue of people waiting at the side of the terrace for their rides. The hotel attendant helped a middle-aged Asian couple board the boat, and it sped off while another family of Americans waited for the next one to arrive. Arabella's mind suddenly wandered back decades to Hong Kong in the early seventies, to the taxi line outside of the old Mandarin Hotel on Chater Road . . .

It was pouring rain, and she was ten years old, shivering under an umbrella that was much too small with her mother and brother, waiting patiently in a long taxi line. Taxi after taxi came, and they inched along with the crowd until it was finally their turn. Just as their red taxicab pulled up to the sidewalk, a British woman darted out of the building with two children and cut in front of her mother, absentmindedly knocking her to the ground. Her mother, dressed in an elegant silk frock from Joyce, was soaked from head to toe in a puddle, but the British woman ignored her as she guided her own children into the waiting taxi. As her brother, Peter, rushed to help her mother, Arabella stood in rage, not believing her eyes. She glared at the messy blond children in their garish T-shirts staring at her from inside the taxi. She turned to all the other Hong Kongers standing in the line, incredulous that no one was sticking up for them. It was their turn for the taxi, but no one said anything. They all knew the unspoken rule of life in Her Majesty's Crown Colony of Hong Kong. British first. *At that moment, Arabella realized that she hated the locals standing in silence more than she hated that British woman, and she swore that one day she would make all of them bow down to her.*

Emerging from the memory, Arabella wondered what that ten-year-old would make of herself now. She wondered whatever happened to that common British mother and her children in the taxi line. She had succeeded beyond her wildest dreams. She had become the Countess of Greshamsbury. Look at her now, just look at her now. She sat alone on the terrace of the Gritti Palace on this glorious summer day, for the first time in a very long while sobbing real tears behind her chic red sunglasses.

PAOLIN DAL 1760

"Is it just me, or are all the dogs prettier in Venice?" Rufus remarked as he watched an elderly Italian man in a houndstooth jacket walking through the square with a pair of long-haired dachshunds.

"Everything's prettier in Venice," Eden said as they sat at Paolin, a café that had quickly become their morning haunt.

"Do you think you could ever live here?" Rufus asked as he took another sip of his superb cappuccino.*

"I'm sorry, what did you say?"

"No worries, not important," Rufus replied. He could tell how distracted Eden was. She had been a nervous wreck ever since her father had texted that he was on his way to Venice. Rufus reached out and squeezed her hand affectionately. "It's going to be okay."

Eden gazed at a smartly dressed little boy skipping over a puddle, saying nothing for a few moments. "I don't know. My imagination's running wild. Maybe my mother's still alive? Maybe Dad committed some crime himself? I just don't know what to think anymore!"

"So stop thinking. Be in the moment with me. Have you tried this delicious cornetto over here? It's filled with the most decadent chocolate. It's like an Italian *pain au chocolat*," Rufus said, holding up a

---

* *When in Italy, it is never, ever appropriate to order a cappuccino after eleven a.m. Cappuccinos are only for breakfast; with any other meal it's like ordering milk and cereal after dinner. (Of course, I sometimes enjoy Frosted Flakes for dinner, but don't tell that to an Italian.)*

pastry and waving it in her face playfully. "Come on, submit to the chocolate . . ."

"All right." Eden cracked a smile as she took a bite of the flaky cornetto.

Eden and Rufus returned from breakfast to find Thomas Tong lounging in the piano nobile[*] of Martha's sumptuous palazzo, enjoying a café latte and staring out the window at the postcard views over the rooftops of Venice.

"You're early!" Eden exclaimed as she rushed to hug her father tentatively.

"My flight landed early, and your friend Martha so kindly sent her gorgeous motorboat to pick me up," Thomas said.

"You should have texted us! I would have brought back some freshly baked cornettos."

"It's fine, I'm still full from breakfast on the plane. This is quite the place."

"It's from the sixteenth century. There's even a Tiepolo on Martha's bedroom ceiling!" Eden said excitedly.

"Is there really?" Thomas said distractedly as he glanced over at Rufus, who sensed immediately that the doctor was eager to speak privately with his daughter.

"I'm going to pop out for a bit," Rufus announced.

"Where are you going?" Eden asked, suddenly nervous to be left alone with her father. She hadn't steeled herself mentally yet for their big powwow.

"I thought I might catch that Raqib Shaw show that everyone's raving about," Rufus replied, giving her a kiss before he left the room.

Thomas sat down in a Gio Ponti armchair across from his daughter, not sure how to begin.

---

[*] *No, it's not a musical instrument of noble birth. Italian for "noble level," the piano nobile is the main reception room of a palazzo, and particularly in Venice these rooms would be on the second floor, as being above the ground floor would provide better views and be safely elevated from the* acqua alta, *or high water.*

Eden broke the silence. "How are you?"

"I've been better. It's been an intense few days."

"I can't even imagine. How was the wake for Luis Felipe?"

"Not many people came. A few lawyers, a couple of actresses, some art advisors. His Ferrari dealer was the only one who cried. We shipped his body back to Manila, where he'll be buried in his father's private mausoleum."

"Even though he was so nasty to me the last time I saw him, I can't help but feel enormously sad. He was far too young . . ."

"I know." Thomas looked at his daughter, thinking how young and vulnerable she suddenly appeared. He could see the distress written all over her face, and as hard as it was going to be for him, he knew he needed to put a stop to it at once. "Eden, I'm sorry I've been unreachable until now, and that I've been so cryptic in my texts. I felt that it was important for us to talk about this in person. I don't know what kind of documents Arabella showed you, but it must have all been rather confusing."

Eden simply nodded. She was bursting with questions, but she wanted to give her father the chance to speak first.

"There's so much I wish I could have told you sooner, but I was bound by promises that I made to your mother and to others. Funnily enough, I've now been freed from my burden of having to stay silent. So, yes, you asked me who Henry Tong was. Henry was my brother. He was younger by four years, and we looked nothing alike—Henry was a beautiful child who took after your grandmother's side, and I was always the more studious one, while he was the rambunctious little rascal. I adored him, everyone did, and my parents spoiled him rotten. No one could say no to Henry—he was just one of those kids who had that ability to charm everyone. Henry grew up to be quite the ladies' man. Actually, that's an understatement. He had girls clamoring over him since he was in his early teens, and by sixteen he was sneaking around with much older women, the type that hung out at bars in Lan Kwai Fong. He had a different girlfriend in every district—in the Mid-Levels, there was Elaine; in North Point, there was Dora—you get the idea. As you know, my parents sent me to school in England, while Henry stayed in Hong Kong, so I only saw him on holidays, and I noticed year after year how much he was getting away with."

"The same way Augie feels about Bea," Eden remarked with a smirk.

"Not quite the same, I think. Henry and I were never very close; I was always rather vexed by how he treated my parents. He was always getting into trouble, and he ran laps around them with his antics. My father, being a cardiologist, did well, but his modest fortune was nothing compared to the truly rich in Hong Kong. Henry, who went to Diocesan, the top local private school, was palling around with the children of tycoons, and he needed to keep up. One year I returned to discover that they had bought him a Fiat sports car, but that wasn't good enough for Henry. He totaled the Fiat on purpose and somehow managed to convince my mother to buy him a Porsche. My parents, meanwhile, drove a Honda, to give you an idea of how indulged he was. Of course eventually the chickens had to come back to roost . . . Henry developed a severe gambling problem. He and his high-roller pals had a private poker game every week. Sometimes he did well, other times he was losing by the thousands. My father would pay off his debts every time, so there was never any real consequence for Henry. Then he started going to Macau to gamble at the big casinos, and that's when the real problems began. On one binge, he lost over a million dollars playing baccarat, and he had made the mistake of borrowing money from a triad leader. The interest payments ballooned to an ungodly sum as Henry kept dodging them until finally the triad got him one day, when he tried to slip into Macau again. They held him captive and threatened to cut out his tongue, so my father had no choice, he had to pay off the debt. But it was a big strain on his finances—I was about to start at Cambridge but my father could no longer afford to help me. Guess who stepped in? Lord Peregrine Gresham."

"Lord Francis's father?" Eden gasped in surprise.

"Yes, Francis of course knew of my troubles, and he told his father, who so kindly offered to help pay for my university."

"How incredible. How did I never know this?"

"I never told anyone. And the old earl didn't either. But you see now how indebted I was to the Greshams, and why I felt compelled to open my practice in Greshamsbury and help Francis when he in turn was in a bind. Anyway, Henry felt terrible about everything and swore he was done with gambling. For a while things settled down. He graduated from uni, got a job at Goldman Sachs, and rose through the ranks quickly. Of course once he had a taste of making real money, he fell back into his addiction. He was still running with the posh party crowd, but now he wanted to buy his own flat and impress all his girlfriends, so he began making secret trips to Macau again. From what I understand, one fateful day in 1995, luck blew his way and he won several million dollars over one weekend. He called his friends together to celebrate his good fortune at the bar atop the Peninsula. The drinks were flowing, everyone had too much. Henry, out of nowhere, decided to propose to Gabriella Soong, this beautiful heiress. What no one realized was that he had been having a secret affair for months with another girl in their circle—Mary Gao—and he had gotten her pregnant."

At the mention of these names that Eden remembered from the press clippings in Arabella's blue folder, her eyes began to brim with tears. *So it was all true.* Thomas paused, looking at her in concern. "Shall we take a break? I know this is a lot for you all at once . . ."

"No, please go on," Eden insisted.

"Roger Gao, Mary's older brother, knew that his sister was pregnant. She had told Roger that Henry was going to marry her, so you can imagine his shock when Henry suddenly got down on his knee and proposed to Gabby Soong. We later found out that Henry had no clue that Mary was pregnant. She had actually been planning to tell him after he returned from that trip to Macau, but she never got the chance. It was all very bad timing. Roger felt that his sister had been dishonored and went after Henry in a fit of rage fueled by alcohol. And the unthinkable happened, a freak accident. Roger lunged at Henry at a precise angle that sent Henry tipping over the balcony, and he landed on a dining table below, impaled on a glass candelabra.

If that candelabra hadn't been there, my brother would surely have survived."

"How terrible. So Henry . . . was my biological father?"

"He was. I'm sorry I never told you about him, but your mother swore me to secrecy."

"Do you think—" Eden broke off. "Do you think your brother would have married her had he known she was pregnant?"

Thomas paused for a moment to ponder the question. "I like to think he would have. My brother, rascal that he was, was never a mean person. And Hong Kong society was much more conservative at the time; he would have felt obligated to do right by her. But unfortunately he didn't survive, and now there was tremendous pressure from her family not to disgrace their good name. They demanded that she not keep the baby." Thomas's voice suddenly cracked and he began to weep. "I'm so sorry . . . ," he said, trying to keep going, "I just can't imagine . . . if she had listened to them."

Eden began to cry as well. She got up from her chair and hugged her father tight. "Daddy! I'm sorry you've had to keep these secrets all to yourself for so long. I can't begin to imagine the burden it's been on you all these years . . ."

"It's fine, I simply buried it all away somewhere."

"You're the only father I've ever known, and you'll always be my one and only darling father!"

"I know . . . I know," Thomas said, feeling an indescribable sense of relief. He had always known in his heart his daughter would understand, that she would never hold it against him that he'd kept these terrible secrets for so long.

After they had recovered themselves, Thomas continued his story. "Your poor mother, now shunned by her own family and deserted by her posh friends, felt like she had no good options left in Hong Kong, so she decided to tell her parents that she was going to Australia to have an abortion. In reality, she went to Vancouver, where her friend from her school days, Pia, took her in."

"Auntie Pia!" Eden exclaimed.

"Yes, your godmother."

"So Mum faked her own death?"

"It didn't happen quite that way. She didn't have any intention of faking anything, but after she went to Vancouver and you were born, she realized how much she loved her new life there. She was making new friends, people who were so supportive of her and her baby, and she realized that she never wanted to return to her old life in Hong Kong. She wanted a fresh start, unburdened by her fame. So she had her old friend Nury Vittachi, who was a columnist for the *South China Morning Post* at the time, plant a little story that she'd had complications from the abortion and had disappeared. The story spread and took on a life of its own, the wildest version being that she had died. No one in her family confirmed or denied it, and your mother's intention was always to return to Hong Kong in a few years when her life was more settled and she could say, 'Look, I have a beautiful child and a beautiful life, so sod off!' "

"But then she got sick . . . ," Eden said, putting together the pieces now, as her face clouded over again.

"Yes. She got sick. Now, after my brother's death, I took up my oncology fellowship in Houston. One day, who should walk into my clinic but your mother?"

"Did she come to find you?"

"Heavens, no. Remember, we had never met before and I was probably the last person on earth she wanted to run into, but she had no choice. She was at the best cancer center in the world, and I was randomly assigned to her. It was a complete coincidence. Serendipity, actually."

"She must have been so afraid . . ."

"Not in the least. She was so very brave, your mother. I pretended not to know who she was—I sensed this was what she wanted—but after a few weeks she suddenly announced that she needed to go back to Vancouver and couldn't finish her course of chemo and radiation. I pressed her to stay, seeing that the treatments were working, and that's when she broke down and confessed to me that she needed to return because she had been away far too long from her child. My brother's child. And that's when I told her I had known all along who she was and would keep her secret safe. I convinced her to remain in Houston and to send for you."

"So you didn't actually meet me until I was two years old?"

"That's correct. You were so cute and so knowing even at that age; I adored you immediately. I could see that your mother was in desperate need of the help. She had metastatic breast cancer, she was a single mother, and she was running out of funds, so I told her to move in with me. This is how we became a family. I married your mother so she could stay in the country and receive the treatment she needed. I was completely honest with her from the very start—her cancer had progressed to a point where we both knew she couldn't be cured, but I promised her I'd do everything I could to buy her more time. She wanted to have as long as she could with you, and we managed to give her three extra years."

"If she had died when I was two, I would have no memories of her."

"Probably not. But she got to have three mostly wonderful years with you."

"And I have my memories. I have these snippets, these flashes of moments with her. I remember a small park with a giant oak tree where we used to picnic, and I'm not sure if this is from another of my dreams, but I always see her sitting in the middle of this room with huge dark paintings, very peaceful."

"That would be the Rothko Chapel in Houston. She loved going there with you. She would meditate while you napped in the quiet of the space." Thomas took out his phone and did a quick Google search for pictures.

Eden smiled in recognition as soon as she saw the unique chapel.

"And so I adopted you as my daughter, but your mother made me promise her two things: First, she never wanted you to know about Henry. She wanted you to grow up knowing me as your father, not some playboy who died so tragically. Then she wanted to make sure her parents and her brother, Roger, never found out about you. She felt so abandoned by her parents when she got pregnant, and she could never forgive Roger for his action—his temper and his drinking had in one fateful night ruined her life."

"It makes me sad to think that she felt so angry toward her family that she didn't ever want me to know them," Eden said.

"Your mother loved you more than anything in the world. She wanted to ensure you would be able to grow up untouched by any of that history. All she ever wanted to do was keep you safe."

The words of her mother in the underwater dream echoed in Eden's mind. *He's keeping you safe.* She let that vision sit with her for a few moments, finally understanding her mother's words, before reaching over to clutch her father's hand. "You kept me safe. It was always you, protecting Mum, protecting me."

Thomas smiled at his daughter, his heart too full to speak.

VI

ORIENTAL BAR

HOTEL METROPOLE, VENICE · *THE NEXT DAY*

Thomas Tong entered the dark, atmospheric bar of the Hotel Metropole,* his eyes taking a minute to adjust after his long walk over in the blazing sun. He soon spotted Diego San Antonio y Viscaya and Jane Carlisle huddled in conversation on one of the deep red velvet sofas in the corner.

"Did you both just fly in from LA? I could hardly believe your text when I got it!" Thomas exclaimed as he approached them.

"You rushed off yesterday like a bat out of hell," Jane scolded.

"The mountain had to come to Muhammad," Diego chimed in as he took a sip of his gin and tonic.

"I do apologize for bolting. I had received an urgent text from my daughter," Thomas explained as he sank into a soft velvet chair.

Jane looked alarmed. "Is she okay?"

"She's fine. Much better now that I've had the chance to see her."

"Glad to hear it. We have some unfinished business to discuss regarding Rene's estate," Diego said ominously.

Thomas sighed. "I suppose there must be a whole new nightmare to deal with as members of the executive board wrestle for control of Rene Tan Enterprises? I assume Pablo Aguilar's the front-runner?"

---

* *Harry's Bar may be more well-known, but the bar of the Metropole is where illustrious guests such as Sigmund Freud, Marcel Proust, and Thomas Mann preferred to nurse their Negronis, the latter purportedly even writing parts of his masterpiece* Death in Venice *there.*

Diego didn't answer him. Instead, his voice suddenly took on a formal legal tone. "As I'm sure you are aware, Rene made us work overtime in the days and hours before his passing. Another contingency trust was created, a trust that existed primarily in the event that Luis Felipe did not survive to the age of thirty-five, when he was supposed to gain full control of the R. S. Tan Trust. Numerous clauses were created in this new trust to allow for every contingency," Diego said.

"I'm relieved to hear that," Thomas remarked.

Jane leaned in closer. "I personally witnessed this new trust being signed and executed the morning before Rene passed. Now, your role as the trustee of the R. S. Tan Trust has lapsed due to the beneficiary's passing, and going forward you have been relieved of any responsibilities or obligations to the estate or the trust."

"Thank god. I don't wish to involve myself with any power struggles in the Philippines; I have too much on my plate over here as it is," Thomas said a bit wearily.

"Yes, I'm sure you do. As a matter of courtesy, we wanted you to be made fully aware of the beneficiaries of the new trust, which has been named the MET Trust." Diego took out a thick leather binder from his briefcase and handed it over ceremoniously. Thomas opened the binder and scanned the first page halfheartedly. He only really cared who was next in line to inherit the Tan billions and whether they would show more mercy toward the Greshams than Luis Felipe had. His eyes wandered down a few paragraphs before locking on to a single name. He stared up at Diego and Jane with his mouth agape. "Noooo. This can't be real . . ."

Diego and Julie nodded their heads solemnly.

Thomas turned white as a sheet.

"He needs some water—I think he's about to pass out," Jane said.

VII

PALAZZO GATTOPARDO

Eden was sitting on the balcony of the palazzo, enjoying the sight of all the boats and gondolas passing along the Grand Canal below. She heard footsteps behind her and saw her father emerge onto the balcony.

"Back so soon? Was the Guggenheim too crowded for you?" Eden asked.

"I didn't go to the Guggenheim," Thomas confessed. "I had a business meeting."

"A secret meeting in Venice?" Eden was surprised. "Please don't tell me that you're MI6."

Thomas chuckled. "I wish it were that, but no. Remember how I told you that your mother never wanted her brother, Roger, to know about you?"

Eden's heart sank for a moment. "Oh no. Has he suddenly surfaced?"

"No, not quite. But I feel I must tell you what happened to him."

"I didn't want to pry, but I did wonder whatever became of him . . ."

"After Roger Gao's arrest, my father actually helped to hire the best solicitors for him, and they managed to get him a far more lenient sentence. Roger was sent to Stanley Prison for three years, where he had the tremendous luck of being put in a cell with Enrique Tan, a tycoon from the Philippines who was serving a light sentence for securities fraud. They became fast friends, and after Roger was released he went straight to the Philippines, where he became Enrique's right-hand man and enormously wealthy himself."

Eden's eyes widened. "Wait a minute, is Roger . . ."

"Roger Gao is Rene Tan. He changed his name when he moved there. Rene, from the Latin *renatus,* which means 'reborn,' and Tan, in honor of the man who gave him a new lease on life."

"Rene Tan was my uncle!" Eden said, shaking her head in astonishment. "Did he know who I was?"

"He figured it out when he met you. You told him that Mum's name was Faye Wang. And Rene knew that his sister's favorite actress was Faye *Wong,* from *Chungking Express.* She used to sing that song from the film around him too."

" 'California Dreamin','" Eden murmured with a smile, remembering the tune her mother used to sing her to sleep.

"Yes. He put it all together rather quickly, but he never let on that he knew."

"I'm so glad I got to meet him before he passed."

"Yes, my worst fear turned out to be quite a blessing, strangely enough. And this leads me to the strangest development of all, which came out of today's meeting. I have been tasked with informing you that you are the beneficiary of a trust that Rene established before he died. The MET Trust, which stands for 'Mary and Eden Tong Trust.' "

"So Rene left me a little money?"

"A little. A hundred million dollars."

Eden laughed. "Gosh, let's go shopping!"

"I'm dead serious."

"Stop pulling my leg."

"I've never been more serious. This trust that Rene established for you was meant to come to you on your thirtieth birthday. It seems that after your uncle discovered who you were, he wanted you to have a small legacy from him. Well, small for him. I think he never forgave himself for what happened that night at Felix, and he felt that he had inadvertently destroyed three lives that evening—not just Henry's and your mother's, but your life. I feel this was his way of atoning for that."

"That's quite an atonement. Come on, there's no way he would leave me a hundred million dollars! I barely knew the man." Eden shook her head in disbelief.

"Well . . . to be honest, he didn't leave you that. As it turns out, there was another contingency clause to his original trust. The clause stipulated that if his only son, Luis Felipe, did not survive to his thirty-fifth birthday, everything in the original trust—the R. S. Tan Trust—would flow into MET Trust."

"I'm confused. What does this mean?"

"Well . . . my darling, it means that as his nearest surviving next of kin, you are now fully in control of his entire conglomerate of companies—Rene Tan Enterprises."

"What?!" Eden's eyes widened.

"You are the sole heiress of his business empire, his properties, his chattel—worth, as of market close yesterday, in excess of ninety billion American dollars," Thomas said, his voice quavering.

Eden made a little squeak.

"And perhaps most significantly to you, you've also inherited all the debts owed to Rene, which include the promissory notes from Lord Francis Gresham."

Thomas handed the trust document to Eden. As she began reading it, she put a hand to her mouth and started to tremble uncontrollably. Thomas found himself tearing up as he witnessed his daughter's astonishment and confusion. He let tears flow down his cheeks unabashedly as he cleared his throat and continued, "Now, you have a big decision to make. If you choose to call in those promissory notes, you shall become the sole owner of Greshamsbury Hall. However, you may choose to extend the loan and allow the Greshams to continue living at the manor."

Eden sank to the floor, her body shaking with sobs. Thomas went over and hugged her as both of them cried in relief and joy. After their emotions had subsided, father and daughter stood leaning on the stone balustrade in silence, staring out at the endless mosaic of tiled rooftops and the tourists climbing up and down the Rialto Bridge in the distance.

"I think I'm in shock," Eden finally said.

"Of course you are. I've been in a state of shock myself ever since my meeting with Diego and Jane. I think we need some drinks. Can I make you an Aperol spritz?" Thomas suggested.

"I'd kill for one right now."

Thomas went inside to the bar and began to mix the cocktails as Rufus could be heard coming back into the apartment. He walked through the piano nobile and peered out onto the balcony. "Hi there."

"How was the wedding rehearsal?" Eden asked, trying to sound collected.

"A bit odd. Gopal Das has decided to serenade his bride during the ceremony."

"That sounds romantic," Eden said with a weak smile.

"Not really. He's singing REM's 'Losing My Religion,' and he doesn't exactly have the voice of Michael Stipe. Are you okay?" Rufus asked, sensing that something was off with her. Very off.

"Come with me, I have something to tell you," Eden said, getting up and stepping down into the piano nobile. "Dad, will you make a spritz for Rufus? He's going to need it."

"Why? What's wrong?" Rufus looked at her suspiciously.

She took Rufus by the hand, walked him into the guest bedroom off the mirrored-glass hallway, and shut the door. A few moments later, Thomas could hear loud shrieks coming from behind the door. It sounded like two kids jumping on the bed.

VIII

PALAZZO GATTOPARDO

SAN MARCO, VENICE • *THE NEXT MORNING*

"The first breath fills your lower abdomen, the second breath fills your upper chest. Just like that, good," Gopal Das said as he tapped lightly on Martha Dung's sternum. Gopal Das was leading a sound bath and breathwork session—"We all could use a good detox"— and lying on yoga mats together with Martha underneath the enormous nineteenth-century pagoda chandelier in the *portego* were Bea, Eden, and Rufus.

Gopal Das gently struck one of the many large circular gongs arranged around the perimeter of the space. "This astrological gong is tuned to the frequency of Pluto. Pluto is the planet of transformation and renewal. Let its vibration flow through your body, let it flow deep into every cell of your body. As you breathe in, I want you to think about change. Change is part of life. Small change, spare change, change is a perpetual state of being. We are all transforming in a multitude of ways every single day, with every heartbeat. Do not fear it, do not resist it. Let the change in you begin to manifest love and joy."

Bea lay on her mat, trembling as she drew sharp staccato breaths. "Joy . . . joy . . . joy . . . joy," she chanted tearfully. Unbeknownst to her, Augie had just entered, a little surprised to be seeing all of them lying there on the ornately patterned terrazzo floor. Gopal Das embraced Augie, and as he looked into her eyes, he knew that all was forgiven between them.

Augie took a mat and placed it right next to Bea's, and as she lay down and began to breathe along with the vibration of the singing crystal bowl that Gopal Das was now playing, she placed a hand over her sister's heart. "I'm so sorry. I'm sorry I became jealous of you and Gopal Das," Augie whispered in her sister's ear.

"You were jealous of me?"

"I was jealous you were having his baby, but now I am so happy for you both," Augie said beatifically. "I can't wait to be an auntie and spoil your child rotten with lots of organic toys."

"Oh, Augie, you're going to be the best auntie!" Bea sniffed as the sisters began to breathe in unison. On the other side of the room, Rufus and Eden lay together holding hands as they breathed. Eden could feel herself drifting into a meditative state as the oxygen coursed through her veins. She could feel with every exhale the tension leaving her body, all the stress of the past few days, which had been filled with so much astonishing change. As she continued to breathe, she found herself sinking deeper and deeper into a state of bliss, when suddenly there was a deafening CLANGGGGGG!!!!! followed by another explosive crash.

"Oh bugger! Sorry!"

Everyone bolted up from their mats to see Lord Francis Gresham lying in a heap of gongs. He had been attempting to tiptoe in discreetly, only to end up causing a royal ruckus. "Carry on! Don't mind me," Francis apologized again as Gopal Das gave him a hand getting up.

"Pa! I was so close to reaching *samadhi*," Augie groaned.

"I'm dreadfully sorry. I got Rufus's text to come over when I checked my email down at the internet café—you did mean today, didn't you?" Francis asked.[*]

"I did, knowing you'd probably get it in a month," Rufus said. "Since we've all been shaken awake, shall we proceed with the family meeting that I called?"

---

[*] *Francis does not yet realize that he no longer has to retrieve his text messages from his Hotmail account. He also does not realize that there's such a thing as Wi-Fi at the hotel where he's staying—the Aman, of course.*

"Yes, let's get this over with," Augie said grumpily.

"Why don't I get us all some refreshments," Martha said diplomatically, leaving the ballroom to give the Greshams and Tongs their privacy.

"Rufus, why on earth did you tell Pa to come over and spoil our sound bath?" Bea prodded.

"I thought it best for all of us to talk before your wedding this weekend, since we haven't been able to have a proper discussion about the future of Greshamsbury."

Augie cut in. "I'm glad you're bringing this up now, because I've found a brilliant solution for us. I was having lunch with my friend the Contessa Vivi Chupi, who told me that it's possible to rent a palazzo here. Apparently the little secret of all the jet-setters showing off their exquisitely decorated palazzos is that they don't actually own them. The old Venetian families tend to hold on to their palazzos forever, but they do lease them out to all those wishing to live out their *Brideshead Revisited* fantasies. And it's shockingly affordable—an entire palazzo costs less to rent than some flats in SW3! I think we should find a smart one to rent. It will be a step down from the manor, for sure, but I think living in a chic palazzo would allow Mummy to still hold her head high."

"It's a marvelous idea, Augie, but I don't think you understand fully what it means to be insolvent," Francis interjected.

"How insolvent are we? Don't we have enough to rent a little palazzo?"

"Augie, we're flat broke. As of next week we won't even have a pot to piss in."

"No one's going to be pissing in pots, because we're not going to lose Greshamsbury Hall," Rufus announced.

"Really? Have the new heirs of Rene Tan decided to show us mercy?" Francis asked.

"Why don't you ask the new heiress yourself? She's standing right here," Rufus said, turning proudly to Eden.

Everyone aside from Rufus and Thomas stared at Eden in stunned disbelief.

"It's true. Eden is actually the niece of Rene Tan. Her mother, Mary, was his sister, and this makes her his sole surviving relation. She has inherited everything," Thomas confirmed.

"Good god! I can't believe it. I just can't believe it," Francis said. "Rene came through for us after all, didn't he?"

"He did," Thomas said.

"My dear Eden, you won't force me to give up Greshamsbury just yet?" Francis asked humbly.

"Lord Francis, as far as I'm concerned, Greshamsbury has always been yours and shall remain yours forever!" Eden proclaimed.

"You're an angel. An absolute angel sent from heaven!" Francis said as his eyes became misty. Bea and Augie were still gawking at Eden with jaws to the ground. Now they rushed to her like excited teenagers.

"You're really not going to throw us out?" Bea asked.

Eden gave her friend a shocked look. "Why would I ever do such a thing?"

"I thought you coveted my bedroom!" Augie said.

"Nah, too drafty for me. I've always loved my own room at the cottage."

"Imagine you living at the cottage now! You could buy your own island!" Bea squealed with laughter.

"Speaking of islands, Martha, Eden, and I have been talking, and we've come up with a wonderful idea for Bella Resorts that will help rejuvenate the brand," Rufus said to his father.

"It's *your* wonderful idea, Rufus," Eden corrected him.

"Yes, it's a terrific idea and I want to be the lead investor in it," Martha said, returning with her butler in tow bearing a tray full of champagne for everyone. "I believe this calls for a celebration?"

"Indeed it does!" Francis cheered.

Suddenly, the telltale clop of Aquazzura stilettos against Venetian terrazzo could be heard as Arabella entered the *portego*.

"Mother! When did you get here?" Bea gasped.

"I'm not really here. I'm only here because Rufus said he had urgent news to share," Arabella said as she glared coldly at Bea and

Gopal Das. She turned to see Martha and Rufus standing next to each other holding champagne flutes, and her heart began to flutter excitedly. "Does this mean what I think it means? Rufus, have you finally come to your senses and asked this lovely lady to be your wife?" Arabella inquired, smiling at Martha.

The room went dead silent as everyone looked awkwardly at Eden.

Francis walked over to his wife with a big grin on his face. "You don't have to worry anymore about anything, my love. We shan't be evicted from Greshamsbury Hall, ever."

"How can you be so sure of that?" Arabella shot back.

"I heard it from our new landlady, darling. She's standing right here," Francis said as he raised his glass to Eden.

"Have you gone mad?" Arabella scoffed.

"Yes. Mad with joy!" Francis said.

Augie walked gingerly to her mother and thrust her phone in her face. On the screen was a photo of Eden accompanying a headline from the *Daily Mail:* GRESHAMSBURY DOCTOR INHERITS RENE TAN'S GAZILLIONS.

Arabella stared at the screen, her eyes bulging out before suddenly rolling back in her head as she fainted to the floor with a thud.

"Mary mother of god!" Francis exclaimed.

"She's cracked her skull!" Bea cried.

Without thinking, Eden rushed to Arabella's side and examined her head. "All good, she's fine. Thank god for yoga mats!"

Thomas turned to Martha. "Might you have an ice pack? Or some frozen peas?"

Arabella regained consciousness as Eden crouched over her. "Arabella, can you hear me? Do you know where you are?"

"Yes. You must . . . ," Arabella groaned, murmuring indistinctly.

"I'm sorry, what's that you said?" Eden said, leaning closer.

"I said . . . you must marry my son!"

The Earl and Countess of Greshamsbury

Request the Pleasure of

Your Company at the Marriage

of Their Daughter

LADY BEATRICE

to

GOPAL DAS

(WHITNEY PAYNE CABOT V)

son of Whitney Cabot IV

and Penelope Phipps Cabot

at Palazzo Gattopardo

Venice, Italy

Saturday at 6 p.m.

White tie & tiaras

R.S.V.P.: Giberto or Bianca at the Aman Venice

IX

PONTE VOTIVO

IL REDENTORE, VENICE • *A FEW DAYS LATER*

Once a year, the city of Venice would hold the Festa del Redentore, a feast to give thanks to the end of the plague of 1576. A wooden bridge of barges would be erected across the lagoon from the Zattere to the Chiesa del Santissimo Redentore on the island of Giudecca so that the faithful could make the pilgrimage by foot across the lagoon. Except this evening, Martha had graciously made a hefty donation to the city, allowing the bridge to be temporarily erected for the wedding celebration she was so generously hosting.

As the sun set over the city of water, Lady Beatrice Gresham, with ropes of pearls threaded through her hair, enrobed in an otherworldly oyster-pink Iris van Herpen gown of botanical-inspired pleats that made her appear like a hothouse orchid just beginning to bloom, glided along the bridge on the arm of her father, the Earl of Greshamsbury, who looked especially dapper in his Henry Poole midnight-teal velvet dinner jacket. The Orchestra Filarmonica della Fenice, assembled on a nearby barge, began to play the *adagietto* from Mahler's Symphony No. 5 while Gopal Das, looking especially dapper in white tie and tails and a silvery white turban upon which was affixed a ruby-and-diamond brooch left to him by a doting Cabot great-aunt, walked from the other end of the bridge to meet his bride at the center of the lagoon.

As the wedding guests watched from a flotilla of motorboats and gondolas bobbing up and down on the gentle tide, the bride and groom exchanged their vows in a simple ceremony presided over by the long-suffering rector of Greshamsbury, Reverend Caleb Oriel.* Eden, standing on the prow of Martha's motorboat with Rufus by her side, thought it was the most exquisite sight she had ever witnessed. Bea and Gopal Das looked as though they were deities floating on the horizon line against the backdrop of the Doge's Palace and a sky that was fading from sapphire blue to the palest tangerine.

Immediately following the ceremony, the fleet of boats headed to the Palazzo Gattopardo, where its majestic canal-front bronze doors were opened to receive the guests arriving for the wedding ball. Tall flickering torches surrounded the boat dock just as they had in the time of Marco Polo, and perhaps in homage to the great Venetian explorer, Rosina Leung, clad in a figure-hugging cheongsam of imperial-violet embroidered silk, stood at the threshold of the ballroom just as the wedding guests began to flood in.

"*Hiyah*, Rosina, you made it! You missed such a beautiful ceremony!" Arabella said as she glided over to her.

"It's fine, I hate gondolas—they remind me of floating coffins, and I get seasick. Look at you, sexy mother of the bride! That JAR diamond-and-ruby sautoir perfectly matches your classic Valentino red!" Rosina appraised Arabella's dramatic plunging off-the-shoulder ball gown, which showed off her *belle poitrine* to full advantage.

"From his final couture collection. I literally had to claw it out of Nati Abascal's hands. Now, is this one of your cheongsams made from the fabric of Empress Dowager Cixi's court robes?"

Rosina nodded.

"Incredible! But I do wish you'd stop wearing those fake giant pearls."

Rosina leaned in and whispered, "Let me tell you a secret, Arabella. I don't wear fake jewels. *Ever.*"

---

* *Long-suffering because, truth be told, Caleb had always been rather besotted by Bea and in a different time and novel might actually have succeeded in marrying her.*

Arabella raised an eyebrow in surprise, before she was suddenly caught off guard by yet another surprise at the other end of the room. "I can't believe my eyes. Is that my brother talking to Nicolai Chalamet-Chaude?"

"He insisted on coming along with my boys. They all want to meet Eden."

"Whatever for?" Arabella asked, half worried that one of the Leung boys was going to attempt to make a play for the new mega heiress.

"And speaking of angels, there she is!" Rosina gushed, rushing over to hug an astonished Eden as she entered the ballroom with Rufus. "Eden, my dear Eden! How ravishing you look! Let me guess . . . Erdem?" Rosina eyed Eden's elegantly minimalist lilac column dress, which she'd embellished with a vintage Fortuny shawl that shimmered with shades of violet and turquoise.

"Actually, I rushed out and found this at the Mango boutique this morning," Eden laughed.

"Such practicality! From the first time I set eyes on you I knew there was something special about you! And now I know what it is," Rosina gushed.

"Her ability to eat five hot dogs in under a minute?" Rufus offered.

"*Sei gwai!*" Rosina smacked her nephew's arm playfully.

"So you knew my mother quite well?" Eden asked.

"Mary was one of my . . . my dearest friends," Rosina said, choking up a bit. "It must feel so good for you to know the truth about her life."

"I'm still trying to process it all, but it has been very healing for me."

"Good, good. You know what, let me take you to tea the next time I'm in London. We can go wherever you want, my treat. Claridge's, the Connaught, the Goring, the Savoy. Although the Muffin Man off High Street Ken has just as yummy scones at a fraction of the price. I have so much more to tell you about your mother."

"I would love nothing more than that," Eden said, beaming.

"Perfect! We'll make a date for the Muffin Man, then. I'll have my assistant Kit arrange it with your assistant. Here, are you on WhatsApp? Let me scan your QR code," Rosina said as she whipped out her phone.

Just when Eden thought she'd never be able to get away from Rosina, a knight in shining armor appeared at her side in the form of a Persian prince from Beverly Hills. "Eden Tong, may I have this dance?" Freddy Farman-Farmihian asked with a courtly bow as his beautiful sister stood alongside him in a gold-sequined and black-feathered Elie Saab dress and a showstopping pair of High Radiant diamond earrings from Fernando Jorge.

"Freddy! Daniela! I didn't know you were coming!" Eden squealed in delight as she rushed to hug them both.

"Of course! Bea invited me," Freddy said.

"And I'm just crashing," Daniela said with a wink.

"Well, why don't we move to the dance floor?" Rufus said, gallantly offering Daniela his hand. The four of them descended the steps onto the dance floor, taking in the full spectacle of the ornate frescoed ceiling, three breathtakingly immense Murano chandeliers, and matching wall sconces lit up with thousands of flickering candles that made the glorious space glimmer like gold.

"This palazzo is insane! I'll take this over an ice palace any day," Freddy marveled as he glided across the dance floor with Eden.

"Me too. Speaking of insane, wanna buy a house in Bel Air? I'll let you have it at a bargain price and I'll even throw in all the cars in the Bat Cave."

"It's a deal!" Freddy said excitedly before frowning. "But does that mean you're not going to live in LA? Are we not going to be neighbors and meet up at Beverly Glen Deli for breakfast every Sunday?"

"Rufus and I want to try out the Big Island for a while. Rufus was so inspired by Raqib Shaw's art that he wants to start a new series of big paintings. And I'd like to do volunteer medicine around the islands. Since we'll be in Hawaii, I'm sure we'll be passing through LA quite a bit."

"You better! Now, tell me, why does Augie look so sad?"

Eden looked to where he was staring. "Maxxie ran off with some rich cougar. She's nursing a broken heart at the moment."

"Maybe I can help her heal it."

"You'll have to learn yoga."

"For her, I'd learn to put my legs behind my neck."

"Well then, let's not waste a moment," Eden said, waltzing Freddy right over to Augie. No sooner had she connected the two of them than she felt a tap on her shoulder. It was Peter Leung, Lady Arabella's brother.

"Eden Tong. I must congratulate you on your windfall."

"Thank you, sir," Eden replied as it occurred to her that the imperious tycoon had in all these years never acknowledged her existence until this very moment.

"Call me Peter. Tell me, what do you intend to do with your fortune? If this splendid city could serve as a parable, it's that all fortunes, no matter how immense, require a great deal of care to last generations. Venice used to be the richest city known to humankind; now it is nothing but a sinking theme park run by dissolute aristocrats living off their dusty titles."

"I'm not interested in perpetuating a fortune that lasts for generations. I've seen firsthand how having too much money isn't good for anyone, and I think wealth inequality is one of our planet's greatest problems."

"Very true. You should set up a family foundation like I have that will support your philanthropic goals in perpetuity."

"Oh, I don't think I need all that. I think I'd rather roll up my sleeves and help fund medical research and relief programs where I see fit and give every last cent away in my lifetime. I feel that's what my mother and uncle would have wanted me to do."

Peter grimaced slightly. "Look, it must be overwhelming to suddenly be burdened with such a complex conglomerate, since you're just a doctor. If I can ever be of help, just say the word. You'll find that there will be many fortuitous opportunities for us to partner up, especially since we're going to be family now."

"Oh. But are we?"

"Aren't you going to marry my nephew?"

"Hmm. Why does everyone keep assuming that?"

Peter appeared stunned. "Aren't you two secretly engaged? Hasn't Rufus proposed to you?"

"Once, when he was fourteen. And I said no."

"Well, I shall put in a word with the damned fool. I hear that you and Martha Dung are devising a new concept for Bella Resorts. I hope you know you can count me in for the Series A round."

Eden couldn't help but burst out laughing. "Let me get this straight—your own sister came to you begging for your help when she was about to lose everything, and you said no, but now you want to invest in her resorts?"

Peter looked taken aback. "The situation's changed. With you in charge my sister's not going to be running things into the ground anymore."

"Rufus is going to be in charge. What did you call him again? The damned fool. Yes, talk to the damned fool about it. I'm just a doctor," Eden said as she turned away.

Meanwhile, the other doctor in the room, Thomas Tong, was cutting up the dance floor with Martha Dung, who wore a long ivory cashmere sweater dress with gold sneakers.

"I love that you're the only one here not wearing a ball gown," Thomas said as he whirled her around the room.

"This is my palazzo, I get to wear what I want. I'm wearing Brunello because it's comfortable, and I can actually dance in these shoes. Especially when I have to keep up with the likes of you, Mr. Astaire!"

"Can I share a secret?"

"Please do."

"If life had turned out differently, I might have become a competitive ballroom dancer."

"No kidding? I guess it's true what they say . . . still waters run deep."

"I hear you're going to be embarking on a new venture with Rufus and Eden?"

"I hope so."

Thomas hesitated for a moment before asking, "I do hope that means you'll be frequenting Greshamsbury more?"

"Only if you promise to take me dancing," Martha said, smiling coquettishly.

Standing by the buffet in the immense reception hall next to the ballroom was a stiff-looking couple in their seventies. The white-haired husband in the frayed navy corduroy jacket bore a slight resemblance to Robert Redford, while his perfectly coiffed wife surveyed the chafing dishes in dismay.

"I see where your eyes are. Don't you dare touch that fettucine, Putter. It will clog your arteries in an instant and you shall drop dead in a country that doesn't accept Medicare Part B," his wife, Penelope, said.

"But don't you love that film *Death in Venice*?" Putter popped a prosciutto-wrapped bocconcini quickly in his mouth when she wasn't looking.

"It has nothing to do with being made a widow in Venice. It's about an old man who's obsessed with a beautiful small boy. Now, you are allowed one white asparagus tip."

Putter quickly scooped three stalks onto his plate as he hovered over the truffle risotto longingly. His wife looked across the crowded room, shaking her head. "Who *are* these people? Wid said he was marrying a proper English girl, and all these people look so . . . *international*. Look at that lady with those terribly vulgar mothball-sized pearls. There's no way those are real."

"Pen, I think they are all from China. Wid said his bride was half Chinese."

"Oh look, here comes one of them. *Ni hao*," Pen said with a tight smile.

Arabella smiled back at the Giacometti-thin lady. "I'm terribly sorry, but I don't speak a word of Mandarin," she said in a tone so posh it would have made Princess Anne blush. "You must be the parents of Gopal Das. I am Arabella Gresham, Beatrice's mother."

"Ah, you're the countess! I'm Penelope Phipps Cabot, and this is my husband, Putter. We call our son Wid."

"Wid! That's what I shall call him too from now on. I thought Wid looked positively dashing tonight," Arabella said, noticing that his mother didn't look half-bad in her Carolina Herrera black polka-dot silk button-front gown and double-strand pearl choker.

Penelope rolled her eyes. "If only he had dropped that damn turban into the lagoon. You realize we brought him up as a Methodist?"

"It would have been nice for once to see his hair," Arabella said diplomatically.

"The red hair comes from Pen's side," Putter said, mouth full of fettucine. "We think someone screwed one of the Irish maids a few generations back."

Penelope clamped her eyes shut for a moment, too mortified for words.

Arabella leaned in conspiratorially. "You know, my husband is just like yours. Says whatever is on his mind, and loves his sweets."

Pen spun around in horror to see her husband stuffing his face with rum-soaked chocolate cake. "Putter! You'll fall into a diabetic coma!" Putter immediately spat the cake onto his plate, and Pen continued without missing a beat. "Now, your Beatrice is lovely. I never in my life dreamed that Wid would marry someone as beautiful and well brought up as her. I always feared he was going to disgrace ten generations of Cabots and Phippses and end up with some vegan who didn't shave her armpits!"

Arabella laughed heartily for the first time in a long while. "Mrs. Cabot, may I introduce you to my dear friend the Countess of Carnarvon?"

"I'd be delighted. I had the pleasure of visiting Highclere many years ago, when the dowager countess was still alive," Penelope said as the two women walked off together.

After the flurry of reunions, Rufus and Eden at last found a moment to themselves on the dance floor. "This is nice, isn't it?" Eden said, closing her eyes as Rufus rocked her slowly in his arms.

"It's one of the only weddings I've ever enjoyed, mainly because of this moment," Rufus said as he pulled her even closer.

"Most weddings aren't any fun. Most people go through so much fuss and spend so much money and almost kill themselves just for one day."

"Let's never get married," Rufus said.

"Don't talk nonsense!" Arabella interrupted as she danced alongside them with Francis. "Rufus, have you done the deed yet?"

"Mum, we're trying to dance. Leave us alone."

"I'll leave you alone once you get down on your knees and propose to Eden. Come, there's no time like the present. Do it while the Comtesse de Ribes is still with us, she's about to head back to the Aman."

"I might propose to Eden . . . provided you apologize to her properly."

"Apologize?" Arabella looked at her son in horror.

"Yes, a full apology, Mum, with lots of bowing and scraping. Come, there's no time like the present."

"*Hiyah*, what is there to apologize for? Eden already knows how much I appreciate her and that I was just looking out for you. I'm a Chinese mother, I can't help it, I will always sacrifice myself so that my children will have the best of everything. She understands, she's Chinese like me."

"Yes, yes," Eden quickly agreed, dreading any more fuss.

"I suppose that will have to do," Rufus sighed. "Well, Mother, I'll propose to the woman I love when I feel like it's the perfect moment—and this is not it."

Arabella groaned. "Useless boy! You just want to torture me, don't you? I hope you know my eyes will not close until you make an honest woman out of Eden. Think of what you've put her through! Imagine what a beautiful bride she will make. I just thought of the perfect designer for her wedding dress. Dries Van Noten. If I asked him personally, he would do it. Something that hints of the East, but not overtly, since Eden was born in Canada. And of course my friend Michelle at Carnet must design all the wedding jewelry. And you know I've always wanted to stage a wedding at Temple Church in London, where all the Knights Templar are buried. I love the way they have the boys' choir stand in a circle under the nave and sing, and the sound just fills the whole space. Instead of having flowers, we could hire that set designer, what's her name, that Italian girl who did that spectacular installation out in the middle of the Moroccan desert for Saint Laurent, and . . ."

Rufus looked at Eden in frustration. "She'll never leave us alone, will she?"

"Never," Eden said with a laugh.

Rufus suddenly scooped Eden off her feet, carrying her across the ballroom as the wedding guests cooed in approval at the sheer romance of his gesture. He bore her up the marble stairway and out onto the terrace dock, into the cool Venetian night. A fleet of motorboats was lined up outside by the flickering torches. Still carrying Eden, Rufus called out to the boatmen, "Can one of you take us to the airport?"

"*Si, signore,*" came the reply.

Rufus hopped aboard with his beloved, and fifteen minutes later, they had crossed the lagoon and were running through Venice international airport, still laughing. Arriving at the nearest airline counter, Rufus said breathlessly, "Two tickets, please."

The ticket agent gave him a disapproving look. "Where to?"

"Anywhere. As long as it's with her, and as long as my mother can't ever find us."

Acknowledgments

These marvelous people helped to make this book possible in their own special ways. I am especially grateful to:

Allison Bennett

Laurel Braitman

Ryan Chan

Vivian Chu

Todd Doughty

David Elliott

John Fontana

Simone Gers

Kirsten Haspe

Jenny Jackson

Dr. Kevin Kwan, M.D.

Martha Leonard

Clare Lockhart

Alexandra Machinist

Joshua Maricich

Gillian Longworth McGuire

Christina Nielsen

Samin Nosrat

Daniella Penhaskashi

David Sangalli

Bill Thomas

Su Ann Ward

Jimmy O. Yang

Jacqueline Zirkman

KEVIN KWAN is the author of the international bestsellers *Crazy Rich Asians, China Rich Girlfriend, Rich People Problems,* and *Sex and Vanity. Crazy Rich Asians* was a number one *New York Times* bestseller and major motion picture and has been translated into forty languages. In 2018, Kevin was named by *Time* magazine as one of the one hundred most influential people in the world.